"[Walker] de_____with sexual tension and a spine-tingling mystery. *The Departed* will keep readers turning pages faster than they think trying to put the pieces of the puzzle together." —*Fresh Fiction*

"Walker fans will be captivated by this fast-paced story with passionate characters and a suspenseful plot that will leave their emotions bare. A well-crafted combination of paranormal, romance, and suspense, this book has everything." —*RT Book Reviews*

"An entertaining romantic urban fantasy police procedural." —*Genre Go Round Reviews*

"Chilling [and] heart-wrenching . . . A richly emotional and wildly imaginative story that grips the reader with genuine, vivacious characters and a sinuous, flowing plot." —*Fallen Angel Reviews*

THE MISSING

"Suspense that can rip your heart open and leave you raw . . . The characters are absolutely fantastic, from the leads to the side characters." —*Errant Dreams Reviews*

"Walker pulls it off brilliantly . . . [She] certainly has a future in paranormal and/or romantic suspense." —*The Romance Reader*

"Great romantic suspense that grips the audience." —*Midwest Book Review*

CHAINS

"This book is a double page-turner. The story is thrilling, and the sex just makes it better—two great reasons not to put it down until the end!" —*RT Book Reviews*

continued . . .

"Breathtakingly wonderful . . . Smoothly erotic . . . Utterly amazing . . . Will definitely keep your pulse racing!"
—*Errant Dreams Reviews*

"Exciting erotic romantic suspense."
—*Midwest Book Review*

FRAGILE

"[A] flawlessly sexy suspense novel . . . Exhilarating."
—*RT Book Reviews*

"An excellently crafted mystery and romance!"
—*Errant Dreams Reviews*

"Suspense, romance, and an ending that I can't say anything about—because that would be a spoiler . . . I recommend reading this one."
—*The Best Reviews*

"Intense, sexy . . . Ms. Walker has created another unforgettable . . . fast-paced, edgy tale."
—*Fallen Angel Reviews*

HUNTER'S FALL

"Shiloh's books are sinfully good, wickedly sexy, and wildly imaginative!"
—Larissa Ione, *New York Times* bestselling author

HUNTER'S NEED

"A perfect ten! . . . [A] riveting tale that I couldn't put down and wanted to read again as soon as I finished."
—*Romance Reviews Today*

HUNTER'S SALVATION

"One of the best tales in a series that always achieves high marks . . . An excellent thriller."   —*Midwest Book Review*

HUNTERS: HEART AND SOUL

"Some of the best erotic romantic fantasies on the market. Walker's world is vibrantly alive with this pair."
—*The Best Review*

HUNTING THE HUNTER

"Action, sex, savvy writing, and characters with larger-than-life personalities that you will not soon forget are where Ms. Walker's talents lie, and she delivered all that and more."   —*A Romance Review*

"An exhilarating romantic fantasy filled with suspense and . . . star-crossed love . . . Action-packed."
—*Midwest Book Review*

"Fast-paced and very readable . . . Titillating."
—*The Romance Reader*

"Action-packed, with intriguing characters and a very erotic punch, *Hunting the Hunter* had me from page one. Thoroughly enjoyable with a great hero and a story line you can sink your teeth into, this book is a winner."
—*Fresh Fiction*

"Another promising voice is joining the paranormal genre by bringing her own take on the ever-evolving vampire myth. Walker has set up the bones of an interesting world and populated it with some intriguing characters."
—*RT Book Reviews*

WRECKED

Shiloh Walker

BERKLEY SENSATION, NEW YORK

THE BERKLEY PUBLISHING GROUP
Published by the Penguin Group
Penguin Group (USA) Inc.
375 Hudson Street, New York, New York 10014, USA

USA / Canada / UK / Ireland / Australia / New Zealand / India / South Africa / China

Penguin Books Ltd., Registered Offices: 80 Strand, London WC2R 0RL, England
For more information about the Penguin Group, visit penguin.com.

WRECKED

A Berkley Sensation Book / published by arrangement with Shiloh Walker, Inc.

Berkley Sensation Books are published by The Berkley Publishing Group.
BERKLEY SENSATION® is a registered trademark of Penguin Group (USA) Inc.
The "B" design is a trademark of Penguin Group (USA) Inc.

For information, address: The Berkley Publishing Group,
a division of Penguin Group (USA) Inc.,
375 Hudson Street, New York, New York 10014.

ISBN: 978-0-425-26445-4

PUBLISHING HISTORY
Berkley Sensation mass-market paperback edition / April 2013

PRINTED IN THE UNITED STATES OF AMERICA

10 9 8 7 6 5 4 3 2 1

Cover art by Diego Cervo/Shutterstock.
Cover design by S. Miroque.
Interior text design by Kristin del Rosario.

ALWAYS LEARNING   PEARSON

Dedicated to my excellent agent, Irene, who keeps me sane. HelenKay Dimon, who loves to lend an ear, and a couple of awesome readers who spent a wonderful weekend in Tucson with my husband and me . . . that was where I discovered the idea for this book. Thanks, E, Minn, and Shimmy!

And always for my family . . . I love you!

Inspired by the wonderfully fun
Wreck This Journal
by Keri Smith.

My Life by Thirty

1. Own my own catering business (goal met age 26)

2. Buy my own house—no fucking condos, damn it (goal met age 28)

3. Get a boyfriend—a serious one (goal met age 28)

4. Get married (June 4!!!!)

5. Sever all ties with female parental unit and never go back (goal met age 18)

Chapter One

Standing in front of the neat little writing desk, Abigale Applegate stared at the journal. Back when she'd made out the list, she hadn't had much of an idea of what a business plan was. Oh, she'd heard the term. Her agent had tossed it around during brainstorming sessions with her mother. Her mother would then loftily discuss it with people in whatever social circle she'd decided to torment with her presence.

After *all*, a *business plan*, a *life* plan . . . some sort of *plan* was necessary for a child star. Because a *child* star wasn't going to be a *real* star once she grew up without having some sort of plan, her mother had liked to point out.

Yeah, she'd heard the phrase before. Over and over, *ad nauseum*.

But Abigale hadn't understood it.

There had been times when she'd heard the damn phrase so much, she'd just wanted to scream. But then she'd come to realize, it wasn't the *planning* that bothered her.

It was the fact that somebody else was doing the planning.

Somebody else was in control.

Right up until she turned seventeen and seized control herself. Wrested it away from her mother in an ugly court battle and made her life her own. She'd left the house only hours after her father's funeral, but it had taken months to finalize everything in court, and her mother had fought it every step of the way. Of *course* she'd fought it; if Abigale was on her own, then her dearest mother couldn't spend all the money Abigale had made. It was during those long, endless months of fighting everything out in court that Abigale had come up with her *own* plan. She would plan out her own life. Get away from her mother, the life her mother had mapped out, and all those manipulative plans to control her life and force her back into a world where she no longer belonged.

Abigale Applegate had grown up and at seventeen she was no longer cute little Kate from a show that had once made millions of people laugh.

Back when she was a kid, she'd been "discovered," landing a starring role in a sitcom, *Kate + Nate*, but those two cute kids no longer existed. Kate had grown up. Nate had joined the army and died a heroic death.

Her co-star Zach Barnes had done some bit acting for a while and then decided to call it quits and go to school.

Abigale had called it quits and run as far away from Hollywood as she could get. She didn't want to be an actress.

She just wanted a normal life. A normal job. A home. A husband. Kids.

And up until two hours ago, she'd thought it was all within her reach. That final goal, only two months away: get married. A knot the size of the Grand Canyon seemed to have settled in her throat and she couldn't breathe around it.

Her fiancé had just dumped her, the son of a bitch. That egotistical, stupid, *blind* son of a bitch.

I'm sorry, Abigale, but you're not being true to yourself. How can I marry a woman who won't be true to herself? How can I trust you to be true to me? Roger had watched her with sad, compassionate eyes and the entire time she'd wanted to hit him.

She'd kept the wild impulse under control, just like she kept all her wild impulses under control. She didn't give in to crazy urges and she didn't dance in the rain; she'd never had a torrid affair and she hated chaos. That didn't mean she wasn't being true to herself.

Abigale knew what she wanted, damn it.

Tears burned her eyes and she blinked them away.

You are an actress . . . a star. Why do you pretend otherwise?

"Conceited ass." She dashed the back of one hand across her eyes. A *star*? She tried not to think about how often he'd thrown in lines like *Abigale is an actress* and the little jokes he'd liked to make about how they wouldn't always be in Arizona—*bigger and better things ahead for Abigale!*

She'd told him more than once that she was done with that life. And how many times had he patted her hand, running off at the mouth about how she just needed to think of the *right way back*. She'd tried to tell herself he was just being supportive in case she *wanted* to go back, to let her know he'd be there for her.

Feeling nauseated, and *so* damned angry, she had to acknowledge the truth now. He wasn't being *supportive*. He'd wanted her back in that life. It was his way of catching the limelight; she'd met too many users not to realize it, but how could it have taken her so *long*? Had he loved her *at all*, or had he just been with her because of the life she used to live?

The son of a bitch had no idea what being a *star* meant. It had been hard back then and it would be even harder now.

Anger burned inside her even now. He was *wrong*. She didn't miss anything about that life. She didn't miss the early morning calls, the invasion of her privacy—and *hello*, that still happened. And although it hadn't been as much of an issue during her career, she knew she'd never be able to deal with the current physical standards being impressed on women in the entertainment industry.

Abigale kept in shape because she enjoyed it, but she

was a size ten and by Hollywood's standards, that was bor-
derline grotesque. She'd seen some of the gossip rags when
they caught pictures of her. They only bothered when there
was nothing else going on because she was old news and
she only showed up in California when she was visiting
friends. Their main bitch was her weight.

Her favorite headline was THE SAD STATE OF CUTIE
KATE'S CURRENT LIFE . . . HER WEIGHT HAS GONE OUT OF
CONTROL!

And Roger thought she missed that life?

Clenching her jaw, she reached for the pen on her desk
and carefully drew a line through goal number four. Then
she focused on the list itself. It was worn and faded, the
paper thin from how often she'd handled it. It had been
years since she'd all but run screaming from the home her
mother had purchased. Ran away, just hours after her father's funeral, and she didn't regret leaving. Not once.

The writing blurred before her eyes but she blinked until it became clear and then she reached out, touching the
faded ink. This list had been her guiding light, the driving
force behind her entire life.

"Now what?" Abigale whispered.

Because she had absolutely no idea what to do next, she
turned away and walked across the pale green carpet and
sank down on the bed. She curled up on her side and pulled
a pillow to her chest, closing her eyes.

She wasn't going to cry about this, damn it.

She wasn't.

Zach Barnes read the note. Then he dropped it,
pressed his fingers to his eyes, and rubbed. He'd been up
late last night, working on some designs. He was tired. That
was all. He'd read it again and the message would be different.

He knew it.

But when he picked it back up, the message remained
the same.

Abby called. Wedding is off.

The wedding. The day he'd been dreading for the past year. He had it circled in black marker on his calendar and although nobody else knew, he'd taken to calling it "Black Saturday." The bleakest fucking day of his entire life . . . the day the woman he loved was going to marry somebody else.

It was two months away and he'd been wishing like *hell* he could be anywhere else, do anything else, even if it involved hot coals, torture, and fire ants. But when your best friend was getting married, you had to be there. Especially when she'd asked you to give her away.

He was going to have to walk her down the aisle. He was going to have to lift her damn veil . . . So what if it was viscerally painful for him? It didn't matter that he'd been in love with her his entire life. She'd found the man she wanted to marry and it wasn't him. He had to deal with it, right?

Except this message said the wedding was off. It wasn't adding up in his head. He'd wanted this, but hadn't dared to hope. He wanted Abby to be happy, but happy meant not being with him, apparently. Talk about a conundrum, because for him to have what *he* wanted, it involved Abby not getting what *she* wanted. And now, he felt half sick with guilt, even though he'd never done or said anything to get in her way.

"Damn it," he muttered, scrubbing a hand over his face.

Carefully, he folded the note into a neat little square, slid it into his back pocket, and then looked up. He'd gotten into work early. He usually did, even when he couldn't sleep, because he still got a thrill when he walked through Steel Ink.

His own place. Yeah, it was a little tattoo shop tucked off 4th Avenue in Tucson near the university. It was one of probably close to a dozen and in the first few years, he hadn't been sure if he'd make it or not. But he was doing fine.

Not a lot of people had taken him seriously when he'd decided this was what he wanted to do with his life. Well,

his folks had. Even if his mother had been mildly horrified at first. She loved him dearly and he adored her, but she
still couldn't quite comprehend this part of him.

It didn't matter, though. This place made him happy and
that was all that mattered to her.

In the back, he saw a black-and-white striped head of
hair. Keelie was the only other person who'd get in this
early. They didn't unlock the doors until one on Sundays,
but she was like him, and just loved being here. She was his
partner. She *should* love being here.

Zach's boots thudded on the floor as he crossed over
to where she was setting up for the day. She glanced up
at him, her mismatched eyes glinting. One blue eye, one
brown, and there was a sly smile in those eyes. "You look
intense there, superstar."

"You talked to Abby?"

"Nobody else here to talk to her." She shrugged. "Called
about twenty minutes ago."

"What exactly did she say?"

Keelie rolled her eyes. "She called and asked for you. I
told her that you weren't in, to try your cell. She said she'd
already tried that—you forgot to charge it again, didn't
you?"

Zach glared at her. Hell, he didn't know if he'd forgotten to charge it. He'd left the damn thing in his office again.
"Not the point, Keelie," he said edgily.

"You're grouchy. You didn't sleep again?" As he continued to glare, she sighed and lifted her hands. Her black
bangs fell into her face and she impatiently shoved them
back as she met his gaze. "Lighten up. Man. Anyway, she
said she just wanted to let you know that the wedding was
off—and seriously off, so if you wanted to go ahead and
make plans for June, you could."

"And?"

"That's it." Keelie leaned a hip against the counter, pinning him with a steady look. "You going to stop pining
after her and make a fucking move now?"

Instead of answering her, he turned around and headed

for the door. "I'm going to call Javier, see if he can help out for a while this afternoon. I need to go see her."

"You think you might want to wait a while?" she called out after him.

"She just called off her wedding." He stopped in the door and looked back at her. Their gazes locked and he said softly, "She's my best friend, Keelie. Where do you think I should be?"

It was a bit of a drive from his shop to her place on Swan. He'd quietly relocated to Tucson within six months of her setting up her catering business. It hadn't been entirely easy convincing her that it had been pure luck that he'd found the ideal spot for the business he wanted to open right in the exact city where she'd chosen to call home . . . but he thought maybe she'd been relieved to see him.

Happy to have him around again.

They'd spent most of their childhood around each other, and nearly all of their teenaged years. They were best friends, and time, distance, and her impending marriage hadn't changed that. Neither had the gut-wrenching need he had for her.

Hopefully she'd be glad to have him there now, and she wasn't going to pack up and disappear again now that the wedding was off. He'd have a hard time convincing her that he'd *accidentally* ended up in the same city as her again, he figured.

Of course, it wouldn't stop him from doing it. Wherever Abby went, that was where he'd go.

Her car, a restored '69 Mustang, sat in the driveway. It was the one thing that didn't fit the practical life she'd laid out for herself—he got why she needed the routine and structure. He really did.

Even when her mom had been planning her entire life down to the nth degree, Abby's life had been sheer chaos. Early morning calls, the insane hours, not to mention her mother herself. It only made sense that Abby wanted to settle down and just have something . . . normal.

But sometimes he thought she'd gone a little too crazy with it. She was so focused on her plan, she never let herself live.

Abby hadn't ever really had a chance to live. That batshit crazy mother of hers had seen to that. Back when they'd been doing the show, they'd worked their asses off, that was a fact, but he'd still gotten to have a life. His mom and dad had been damned determined about that. Hell, he suspected most of Abby's *good* memories came from the times she'd spent with him and his folks. And there hadn't been enough of those times, he knew.

The van for the catering business was in the drive as well. As he jogged up the steps, he debated about letting himself in. He'd had a key pretty much since the day he'd arrived in town, but that didn't mean he went walking in whenever. Was now a good time to use it?

Muttering under his breath, he rubbed the back of his neck and stared at the door. "Okay. Knock first," he told himself. That was what he'd do. If he knocked first, and she didn't open, he'd let himself in.

As the third knock echoed through her empty house, Abigale pressed her face into the pillow. She didn't need to look to know who it was, and she didn't need to ask.

There was only one person who'd be there just then.

Zach.

She loved Zach dearly but she just couldn't handle him right now. She couldn't handle *anything* right now. She could barely handle the silence of the house. Thinking. Breathing.

Just *existing* hurt right now.

"Damn it, Abs, if you don't open the fucking door, I'm going to let myself in," he shouted. If she hadn't left her window open a little, she never would have heard him.

She closed her eyes. "Just go away, Zach."

"You've got thirty seconds, sugar!"

Groaning, she hugged the pillow tight and she huddled in on herself. He wasn't going to go away, she knew that. But if she got up and tried to go down there to let him in, she'd just shatter. Or explode. She was barely staying in one piece as it was.

He had a damn key. He could use it. Assuming he remembered it. The bum barely even remembered to keep his phone charged. He didn't like to check his e-mail. The ache in her chest spread and the sobs she'd been fighting crept further up her throat as she heard the beep from her alarm.

"Time's up, Abs," Zach called from downstairs.

He reset the alarm and locked the door. The quiet of the house gutted him. Abby didn't do quiet. She loved music . . . it didn't have to be loud or anything, but she loved music and if she was home, it was almost always playing.

Silence greeted him. Cold, brittle silence.

His first stop was the kitchen. When she was sad, happy, pissed, whatever, Abby cooked. That was just her thing. Like he went to his sketchbook and worked on new designs. But the kitchen was empty, silent.

The ache inside him spread just a little more. He paused by the hook just inside the door and touched the apron hanging there. Simple and efficient. Just like her. Sexy as hell. He had it bad. Groaning, he curled his hand into a fist and left the kitchen before she found him pawing the damned apron.

He'd managed to hide how he felt for more than seventeen years. Granted, it had started out as a bad crush that he'd kept hidden and it had just grown and grown. Still, it was what it was and he wasn't going to let any clues slip now, of all days. Maybe later—

Stop, Barnes. Find her. Help fix it. Then worry about your own shit.

Being there for Abby had been all he'd ever wanted to do with his life. It wasn't going to change now.

Since he was there, he checked out back, but the pretty little space she'd designed for herself was empty as well. She wasn't in the library and as he moved through the painfully quiet house, dread curled through him, tightening his gut and sending goose bumps crawling across his skin.

That feeling increased as he mounted the stairs and then he looked inside her room.

For a hard, awful second, everything in the world stopped. Color drained, his heart ceased to beat, and everything just ended.

She lay on the bed, the bright banner of her hair spread around her like a cape. Her eyes were closed and her skin was unbelievably pale.

"Abby?"

She opened her eyes and looked at him. The soft, dark brown eyes were dull. Lost.

Broken . . .

Then she closed her eyes. Not a single word was said.

Crossing the floor, he kicked off his boots and then settled on the bed behind her. He didn't touch her, although everything inside him screamed for it. He wanted to wrap himself around her and rock her, hold her, stroke away the misery he knew was inside her. The raging beast of want that lived inside him wanted to strip her naked and fuck her, but that was something he'd lived with for a long while and he could deal with it.

Her pain was harder to handle and he didn't know how to fix it and make it go away.

The misery he sensed inside her made him want to howl and break things but at the same time, he needed to comfort her and just find a way to make it all better.

But he didn't touch her.

He could wait until she was ready.

The soft, sad little sniffles started about a minute after he lay down. Two minutes after that, she rolled toward him and squirmed closer until she could settle her head on his chest. Once she'd done that, he let himself wrap his arm around her and the soft, sweet warmth of her body against his was both agony and ecstasy, the best kind of pleasure and pain known to man.

He kept his other hand on his belly and a minute later, Abby reached out and started to trace the tip of one shell pink nail over the barbed wire design he had entwining his wrist. Now, if she'd just keep that up . . . he had tats going up his entire arm and she could stroke him all damn day—

"Roger left me," she whispered.

Don't say anything, he told himself.

Abby sniffled again and shifted her finger to the next tattoo, an eastern dragon that wrapped around most of his forearm. "He says he can't marry me because I'm not being true to myself," she said.

Zach closed his eyes. He never thought there would be a day when he actually agreed with that tightwad. Why in the hell did they have to agree on the one thing that would cause Abby pain? Turning his head, he rubbed his cheek against her soft, crazy curls. "Roger is an asshole," he said.

"Yes. And he's fucking *wrong*," she said, heated fury slipping into her voice.

He didn't say anything. There wasn't any point. It wasn't up to him to tell Abby how to live her life. Even if she was stifling herself. Even if she was miserable half the time. Even if—

"He started rambling on about how I'm *supposed* to be an actress. I belong in that world and I'm denying myself and if I can't be true to who I am, then he can't expect me to be true to him," she said.

Zach opened his eyes. "He what?"

She sat up and shoved her hair back from her face. The red curls tumbled right back into place and her dark brown eyes sparked with fury. "You heard me." She pulled away from him and slipped off the bed. "That dipshit honestly thinks I *miss* that life."

She started to pace, the slim-fitting skirt she wore clinging to a world-class ass. Mentally slapping himself, he drew one knee up to hide his hard-on. "Lots of idiots in this world can't get the idea that we don't miss that life." He shrugged, not too worked up about the *idea* of that. What pissed him off was that Roger had hurt her. "That's their problem. He actually called the wedding off over this?"

"*Yes!*" she wailed. Then she started to cry.

It was another punch to the heart. He went to her and she tried to push him away. "Damn it, I'm fine," she said even as she tried to catch a breath. "I just . . . just need to . . ."

"You just need to get this out," he said, swinging her up into his arms.

"Zach! Put me down. I'm too heavy . . ."

"No, you're not. And hey, I've always had this fantasy . . . sweeping a damsel into my arms and all that shit," he teased, trying to make her smile. And he wasn't even lying, really. He did dream of doing things like this . . . with her. Only her. Always her. As he settled on her bed, his back against the painted doors she'd used as her headboard, he stroked a hand down her curls. "You go on and cry, sugar. You need to do it."

"Crying doesn't solve anything," she whispered. And tears continued to run down her cheeks.

She wasn't a pretty crier. Her nose was red, her eyes were puffy. And all he wanted to do was wipe away every damn tear. Kiss her. Then go strangle Roger, beat some sense into him, whatever it took to make her happy. Hell, if he had to, he'd drag the fucker to the church for the damned wedding. Except Roger couldn't make Abby happy. Not the way she deserved. That was the real bitch of it all.

"Not everything has to be solved. Not everything needs to be a solution or an answer." Guiding her head to his chest, he hugged her. "Cry. Scream. Talk to me. Whatever you need to do, sugar."

Chapter Two

The woman who shall not be named was calling
again.

Abigale eyed the phone with acute dislike as she finished working on her list. She'd already contacted just
about everybody regarding the now-cancelled wedding.
The only thing she hadn't done was cancel the honeymoon.

A trip to Alaska.

Roger had balked. He'd wanted to go on some world
tour, but she'd wanted to go to Alaska. It had been a dream
she'd had for several years, but the timing hadn't ever been
right. Until now. Why not for a honeymoon?

In the end, they'd compromised. She'd promised him a
longer trip for their one-year anniversary if he'd do an
Alaskan trip for their honeymoon. Now she wondered why
he'd even bothered.

You're not being true to yourself—

Groaning, she dropped her pen and pushed back from
her desk.

Those words kept echoing through her head, over and
over.

Even after nearly a week, she was still hearing those words. It was weird that she heard *them* more often than everything else. Those words chased her in her sleep. She'd been in the middle of putting together a dinner menu for a client and all of a sudden, nothing else in the world would matter, because she'd find herself remembering those words.

Those words.

The hell she wasn't being true to herself. She'd gotten away from a life she'd hated. How much more *true* could she be? She'd been living her life exactly as she'd wanted and had been walking right down the path to the happy goal she'd set.

Until he derailed it.

And yet, here it was nearly ten o'clock on Friday, five days after the dismal, depressing end to her engagement, and she was *still* thinking about those words. Those words actually seemed to bother her *more* than the fact that he'd ended things, the bastard.

"What I need to do is make another plan," she mumbled.

Her life, once more, had been thrown into chaos.

She left her office and headed upstairs to her bedroom. She hadn't looked at her business plan since she'd marked the wedding off the list but it was time, she decided.

Grabbing her journal, she went back down to the office and settled on the couch. There was a pen tucked in a little loop and as she started to think, she pulled the pen out and tapped it against her lips.She didn't start to make any notes. Not yet. Her thoughts needed to settle. Needed to focus.

Did she need a man? That was the question. She wasn't one of those women who believed a man was necessary to fulfill or complete a life but Abby *wanted* a man. She *wanted* marriage. Her throat tightened a little as she thought about the other things she wanted . . . kids, at some point. Not just to have that happy, stable life she'd never had for herself, but she wanted a family. She saw a mom at a baby shower and her heart ached with envy.

Some women didn't want to be mothers and she completely respected that; she understood. Hell, some women should never *be* moms. Her mother sure as hell didn't need to procreate but she'd done it and made Abigale's life hell.

Abigale would love whatever child she had.

"Maybe I should just think about doing it on my own." But that thought left her cold. She wanted a *family.* With all that entailed. A father for her kids . . . a partner. Somebody who would make her laugh. Make her think. Keep her company when she wanted it and if she was in a bad mood, leave her alone. Somebody who could blow her mind away in bed and still be a friend.

"You want a fairy tale."

Roger had been okay in bed, but he hadn't exactly been a friend, something she could acknowledge . . . *now.* The only guy who had ever really made her laugh, made her think, kept her company when she needed it, and left her alone when she wanted . . . hell. That was Zach. But he was her best friend.

When the alarm sounded sometime later, she yelped in surprise. Panic surged through her, until she realized it was the regular alert.

The annoying little computerized voice announced, "Disarmed."

There was only one person it could be. She'd deactivated Roger's code and even if she hadn't, he wouldn't come by this late without calling.

Zach, on the other hand . . .

He appeared at the door, gold-streaked brown hair falling into his eyes, five o'clock shadow darkening his jaw. The faded black t-shirt he wore left much of his arms bare, leaving his tattoos visible.

She'd never, ever tell anybody that she absolutely adored the way those tattoos looked.

Not in a million years.

"Hey," she said, smiling. He was one of the very few people she didn't mind seeing right now. Maybe even the *only* person.

The phone started to ring again.

Without saying anything, he ambled over to it and

glanced at the display. A sneer curled his lip and he glanced at her. "She who shall not be named is calling." A wicked smile danced across his face and he asked, "Can I talk to her? Pretty please?"

A laugh bubbled out of her and she grinned at him. "I don't care. As long as *I* don't have to." She wondered just how in the world her mother had gotten her number. Again.

Zach grabbed the phone halfway through the second ring. "Heya, Blanche!"

Abigale propped her arm on the back of the couch and watched as he leaned against her desk, one arm folded over his chest. It had his bicep bulging and the scrolled design there caught her eye. Something warmed inside her. Shifted. Frowning, she looked away from his arms and watched his face.

"Yes. She's here . . . Nah, I can't put her on the phone. Why? Oh. She doesn't want to talk to you. As in . . . ever. Remember that deal about how you kind of, sort of tried to keep her away from all the money she'd earned? How you tried to whore her out for any and every damn part that you could get? Expected her to go weeks living on nothing but water and salads because she was getting too *female*?" He didn't look so happy now. Fire snapped in his blue eyes and a growl had edged into his voice.

Okay. Maybe she should—

"Then there was that shit about how I caught one of your fucking boyfriends trying to paw her. Remember that? Oh, you fucking bitch, don't you tell me I don't know what I saw—yeah, you do that. Crazy piece of work." He slammed the phone down and then looked over at her.

"Your mom doesn't remember me," he said soberly.

Abigale lifted an eyebrow at him. "Really? I can't imagine how she could ever forget you."

He grinned as he came to flop down on the couch. He settled down and stretched out long, jean-clad legs in front of him, crossing them at the ankle as he rolled his head over to look at her.

He had something in his hand. A book, she noted. He

glanced at her journal and then up at her face. Some of the heated anger had faded from his eyes. Some. Not all.

Abruptly, she reached out and touched his cheek. The rough stubble abraded her palm as she said quietly, "Always my knight in shining armor, Zach. Thank you."

A dull red flush crept up his cheeks. "I'm no knight, Abs."

"You've always been mine." She shrugged and pulled her hand back. Tucking the pen back into her journal, she closed it and tossed it onto the table in front of them. "You and I both know what that boyfriend of hers was trying to do when you showed up at the house that day."

It had been nearly seventeen years since that day. An awful day. Every once in a blue moon, she'd find herself waking from a nightmare where Zach hadn't arrived in time and—

Stop it.

It hadn't happened.

Once her mother had started making merry with her money, she'd started making merry with lots of other things. Like drugs, booze, and her wedding vows. Oh, she'd probably been sleeping around before, but as Abigale got older, it was more obvious just how screwed up her mother was.

While her dad was out, still working a job because her mother insisted it provided *a sense of normalcy*, her mother had used those hours to bring countless men into the home that had been built with money Abigale had earned.

When she was fourteen, one of those men had crept into the study where Abigale had been working on a school assignment. He'd been drunk, his hands big and hard and cruel.

Her mother had been passed out on the couch and the housekeeper was out shopping.

Trapped and scared, Abigale had screamed for help.

Help had come in the form of a pissed off fifteen-year-old Zach Barnes who'd had his mom drop him off. He had his skateboard and he'd used it like a club, bringing it down on the bastard's head.

It wasn't the first time Zach had saved her.

It hadn't been the last. He'd been saving her from herself, saving her from a variety of things, throughout their entire friendship. Maybe he didn't see himself as her knight, but she sure as hell did.

He leaned forward and touched a hand to the stamped leather journal. "Writing bad poetry and sonnets about your unending love for Roger the Rat?" he asked.

"No. I gave up on the bad poetry when you threatened to show my journal to Luke Perry so he could see what I had written about him." She snorted and drew her legs up, shifting to look at him. "I'm trying to think up the plan for my life now that it's been thrown off track."

He groaned and dropped his head back on the seat. Eyes closed, he dragged a hand over his face. "Sugar, you can't *plan* life." He looked back over at her and said softly, "Life is supposed to just happen."

"Hey, I planned quite a bit of *my* life," she said, sticking her tongue out at him.

His gaze dropped to her mouth.

Her heart stuttered to a stop for one brief second and then it started to race. Hard and fast, like it did on the rare occasions when she let herself take the Mustang out to the desert and just open her up. The moment shattered as he looked away and she wanted to smack herself.

This was *Zach*, damn it.

Yeah, she was no longer engaged to a guy who'd been . . . well . . . uninspiring in bed and maybe she needed to live a little bit. But this was Zach. Her best friend. Her oldest friend.

"But you tried to plan your personal life . . . who you'd fall in love with. It doesn't work that way," he pointed out. "You practically chose him out of a catalog, Abs, and that's not how it works. Look at *The Bachelor* and see what a fucking joke *that* is."

She rolled her eyes. "Hey, are they still calling you about that celebrity thing they want you to do?"

"Not after I told them I wasn't a good fit since I had the

bodies of two dead girlfriends stored in my freezer." He shrugged and started to tap the book in his hand against his leg.

Her jaw dropped. "You didn't!"

With a sly grin on his lips, he glanced at her. "Now, Abs, sugar. You know me better than anybody else in the world. Would I really say something like that?"

"Oh, shit." She cringed and covered her face with her hands.

He started to laugh.

"You are insane!" She kicked him in the thigh. Her foot bounced off the muscled length and he just laughed harder. "One of these days, you'll say something like that and the cops will show up at your door, Zach."

"Hey, wouldn't be the first time." He shrugged.

Glaring at him, she kicked him again. "That's not funny." He *had* had cops show up at his door; the first time had been after he'd hit that bastard in the head with his skateboard. The son of a bitch had tried to press assault charges. She'd been hiding out over at the Barnes' place— a normal thing for her, really—and when the police showed up, she'd almost fallen apart.

He caught her ankle in his hand and turned around to face her. Dropping the book in his lap, he kept one hand wrapped around her ankle and used the other to rub her foot. She jumped as he ran his thumb down the arch, too firmly to tickle, but there was something about the touch that managed to send shivers up her spine. What the hell? He'd touched her plenty and it hadn't ever hit her like this; she knew it hadn't.

"So tell me about this new life plan of yours," he said.

"I can't." She closed her eyes. Seemed to be a wise move, she thought. If she wasn't looking at him, she might stop having these weird, hot little pangs hitting her square in the belly. Except the pangs just kept getting worse.

"Why?" He tickled her.

She yelped and jerked on her foot. "Stop that!" Opening her eyes, she glared at him.

"You used to tell me everything," he said, smiling at her.

"Yeah, well, I can't tell you a plan that I haven't come up with," she pointed out, still squirming.

"Be still." He went back to work and despite herself, she all but whimpered as he hit a spot on her arch with his thumb. "So you don't know what you're going to do next. That's got to have you all twisted up."

Yes. "I'm fine."

"Liar." He smiled as he said it. "You don't know how to not do plans. What do you *want* to do?"

You—

Blood rushed to her face and she dipped her head, letting her hair fall down to shield her expression while she tried to figure out just what in the *hell* was wrong with her.

Had she lost her *mind*?

Swallowing, she said, "I don't know what I want right now, Zach."

The embarrassment faded as those words hit her square in the chest. It was the absolute truth. She had absolutely no idea what she wanted in life. Well, other than this bizarre urge to jump Zach, and she was positive that stemmed from the fact that she was just suffering from some sort of post-breakup stress.

Panic slammed into her and she started to shake.

"Zach . . . I don't know what I want." She tried to pull her foot away. She needed to get up and move. *I have to think. Got to get this planned out. Have to know—*

"Abby."

She jerked on her foot again. "Let me go," she snapped.

"Not happening. All you want to do is get up and start having a meltdown, sugar." He tugged on her foot and said, "Come here."

She blinked at him. "What?"

Heaving out a sigh, he reached for her and hauled her into his lap.

She stiffened and shoved against his chest. "Zach, would you—"

"Calm down," he said easily. He settled her on his lap. She'd spent more than a few nights like this when she'd been falling apart. Either on his lap while she cried after her dad died, or curled up against him after a marathon movie session. It shouldn't be a big deal. Why it suddenly felt so different, she didn't know. Unless it was just post-breakup stress. Yeah. Had to be that.

"You're too wound up about this," Zach said quietly. He stroked a hand down her back and eased her against his chest.

Wound up. Yes, she was definitely that and there was no denying that she was certainly freaked out about the current chaos of her life, but that wasn't the *only* problem. That was what really had her sitting there so rigid and unyielding, despite the fact that she wanted to wilt against him and just . . . be. Just like that.

Except if she didn't relax, he was going to figure out, fast, that something was up. Then she'd have to lie or something because she couldn't very well tell him that she was having these crazy thoughts. And great, *now* she was rambling inside her own head.

Get a grip. She took a slow, deep breath and blew it out. Focusing on the dragon that wrapped around his left bicep, she stared at the scales. Wound up. Yes. She was. But it was hard to say what she was more worked up over, the screwed-up wreck that was her life, or the hot mess that was her body.

But she couldn't exactly relay that last bit. He'd *get* the first bit. And it was definitely not helping that she didn't have a plan. Slowly, she said, "You know how I am, Zach. I just work better with a plan. I'll figure this out and get my head together and make a plan."

She lapsed into silence, still staring at the dragon on his arm. The scales were green, done with such incredible detail that it had left her speechless when she saw it for the first time. It hadn't helped much when she realized he'd been the one who had come up with the original design.

"So this plan. You just need to figure out what you want," he said, toying with a lock of her hair.

"How am I supposed to figure it out?" she said quietly, forcing herself to focus on what he was saying.

"I dunno. Although if it's that hard to understand, you could always try just going with the flow for a while. Just live a little."

"Yeah. Like that's going to happen." The heat inside her veins started to spread as she shifted around and her hip bumped against something long, thick, and hard— wonderfully hard, branding itself against her hip. *Oh . . . hell.* Her heart sped up and she thought that maybe, just maybe, she was going to lose her damned mind, but then he shifted and moved her back onto the couch. So casually. So easily.

Like he just adjusted his shirt collar or something.

But instead of adjusting a collar, he leaned forward and grabbed the book from the coffee table.

"Here. I bought you something."

Her heart thudded, slow and heavy, and her tongue seemed to glue itself to the roof of her mouth and her fingers were all shaky. Not to mention her belly was tight and hot and the butterflies dancing inside her gut were going haywire.

A little dazed, she looked down at the book. It took a minute for the title to make sense. Then it took another minute for her to really get what she was reading. Once she finally did, she looked up at him. "Ah . . . is this a joke?"

"Nope."

Frowning, she stroked a hand down it and murmured, "*Wreck This Journal*?"

"You're always writing your plans, making your notes in nice, neat, pretty little journals. Maybe you need to take a different approach. Granted, I didn't realize you were having business plan hang-ups when I saw this, but . . ." He finished with a shrug and reached out, caught a lock of her hair again.

She swallowed and pretended not to notice. "So you bought me a journal that I'm supposed to . . . what?"

"Open it up."

She frowned and opened it up, scowling when she saw a warning on the second page. "What the . . ."

"Keep reading."

Two seconds later, she put it down.

He laughed and took it away.

She cringed as he opened it wide and cracked the spine on the book. "There," he said, putting it into her lap. "I took care of that one. I know how you are about breaking spines."

"That isn't a journal," she said, shaking her head. "A journal is where I can write my thoughts. My plan."

"You can still do that." He leaned in and flipped through the pages. "Look, there's room. But there's also other stuff. You need to quit focusing so much on how you *think* your life is supposed to go and just let your life *go*. Live it, sugar. Stop trying to control it."

Live it.

An hour after Zach had left, Abigale found herself laying on her belly, staring at the very odd journal with its badly cracked spine.

Wreck This Journal.

"What do I want?"

An image of Zach flashed through her mind and she pushed the idea out. Maybe it wasn't *Zach* she wanted. Just . . . something. Maybe he was right. Maybe she'd been controlling herself for too long. Stifling herself. It could just be some innate urge to *live*.

Although damn it, her body . . . and more . . . kept trying to flash images of Zach at her. Zach with his lazy smile and the way he'd wrap her hair around his finger, the way he'd understood the thing with the journal.

"Stop it," she muttered. "Zach is a friend. Your friend. Your best friend. Think about the plan, okay?"

Her hand shook a little as she reached for the pen tucked inside her pretty, neat leather journal.

Wreck This Journal.

It had some *insane* things inside it. Things like *spill cof-*

fee on the pages. Mail it to herself. Take it in the frigging shower, for crying out loud. She didn't know if she'd be able to do *all* of those things, but she was going to try.

And she had a plan in mind now.

Two pages after the spine-cracking instructions, she found a blank page and there, she wrote up at the top:

Wreck this life: My new plan

Her hand started to shake and she had to stop, suck in a deep breath. "Wreck my life. What in the hell . . ."

She almost sat up and closed the silly thing, almost put it away. This was *nuts*.

But even as she thought about it, she made herself remember what Zach had said.

Stop trying to plan her life so much. Start trying to just live.

For her, that was practically anathema. But that was what she needed to do. What she needed to focus on.

"Just write it down, damn it." Gripping the pen, she wrote a neat little *1*.

1. Stop worrying so much about the future

Okay. The first step. The next idea was easy.

2. Call Roger and tell him off

Once she had that down, the next few things came in an outright rush.

3. Flip off the next photographer you see

4. Get a tattoo

5. Have a torrid affair with a hot guy

Staring at it, she rubbed her fingers over her lips, reading it through again. And again. Stop worrying. Call Roger. Flip off photographer . . . get a tattoo?

Have an affair . . . !

Her belly was in knots now, just looking at the list. Completely knotted and twisted and she thought she just might be sick. And when she thought about number five, images of Zach kept dancing through her mind. Part of her was gleefully shrieking, *Yeah, try to convince yourself that you don't want him . . .*

But it was *Zach*. How could she want him?

Another little voice whispered, *how can you not?*

He was hot, hot as lightning-hot, and in theory, she *knew* that. It was a little different with somebody you'd known all your life. Hell, the two of them had sat around snickering together when they'd discovered how to find bad porn on the Web back when they were still kids. Zach had *really* gotten in trouble over that one and he'd never once told his mom that Abby was the one who'd showed it to him.

But it wasn't *just* that he was hot. She was a child of Hollywood and she'd grown up around beautiful people. Maybe she didn't live that life anymore, but she knew how superficial beauty could be. Zach was anything *but* superficial. He was real. He was kind. He was funny. And under the kindness and the humor, there was an edge to him that had emerged . . . somehow. She didn't really know when, but sometimes just standing near him, even knowing him as well as she did, it sucked the breath out of her.

Yeah, why *shouldn't* she think about it?

But thinking about it and *doing* something about it were two different things. She couldn't go chasing after her best friend. She'd barely managed to seduce the guy she was engaged to.

With a weak laugh, she rolled over onto her back and stared up at the ceiling. Zach was no Roger. Even she could admit that . . . Zach was a hell of a lot more, and she couldn't even keep *Roger* interested in her.

Zach was a friend. A sexy friend. Her *best* friend, but it was going to stay on a friendly level and she just needed to get this whatever-it-was out of her head. Grabbing the journal again, she opened and read the list through. Nerves pulsed inside her. Could she *do* this? she wondered.

Panic gripped her, hard and tight and she was almost certain that she couldn't. Didn't know how and the longer she stared at the list, the harder it got. No. That was it. She couldn't do this. Reaching for the page, she went to rip it out.

Before she could crumple it in her fist to do so, though, she stopped. Stopped and sat up, staring down at the page while her heart started to race. "What's so damned hard about any of this?" she whispered.

Zach had a gazillion tattoos and it wasn't like he'd mind giving her one.

She could handle that.

Telling Roger off? She *wanted* to do that and hey, what a way to prove him wrong. He thought she wasn't being true to herself? Here was just one more way to show him how very wrong he was.

Flipping off a photographer was a bit more than she'd ever thought about doing, but if she started to get hesitant about it, she'd just remember how they *always* seemed to grab the worst pictures imaginable and then turned around and sold them to the worst gossip rags . . . hey, flipping them off was taking the *high* road, really.

Stop worrying would be hard, but she needed to do it.

The last one was the one that made her belly cramp and twist with fear.

She'd never had a fling. Yeah, maybe she'd thought about it a time or two, maybe there had been some really hot guys who had caught her eye, but memories of all those guys her mom had brought home? The thought of just casual sex left a bad taste in her mouth. In all of her life, she had two lovers. That was it.

But if she was going to reach out and grab life . . . why not?

She'd needed a plan.

Now she had one.

"I'm going to do it." She stroked a finger down the list and stopped by number four. It was going to be the easiest, she figured. Get that done, because once she committed herself to the plan, she would be a lot less likely to back out of it.

Tomorrow, she'd take the first step in checking things off her list. It wasn't going to be the cohesive life plan her last one had been, but maybe that wasn't a bad thing.

After all, look at where her last plan had landed her.

Chapter Three

"You got company."

Keelie stood in the doorway, watching him with a disgruntled look on her face.

"Why don't you handle it?" he said, looking back at the bills spread out before him. They might be partners, but she couldn't do numbers. The one time he'd made her handle the bills for the month, she'd paid two vendors twice and hadn't paid the water or the electric bill. Since then, he'd handled the paperwork. But he made *her* do more of the housekeeping shit. He figured it was fair.

"Because Abby doesn't want to talk to me," she said with a smirk.

He stood so fast, he knocked over the lukewarm coffee that he'd meant to dump earlier.

"Son of a *bitch*!" he snarled, rescuing the bills from the spreading puddle.

"Suave, man. You're so suave," she said with a smile. She came over and tugged out the towel she kept tucked in a back pocket, using it to sop up the coffee. "Good thing you already drank most of it."

"Thanks." After they'd dealt with the mess, he shot a look at the clock. It was creeping up on nine—almost closing time. This time of year they didn't get too busy during the week, so he didn't keep very late hours on weekdays.

He didn't know why Abby was here, but maybe they could get a bite to eat or something.

"Are you ever going to tell her?"

He glanced up at Keelie. "What?"

A grin twisted her lips and the piercing just above the right corner of her mouth winked in the bright lights of the office. "Don't act like you don't know what I'm talking about. I know the symptoms of the lovesick." She shrugged and turned away. "Just wondering if you're ever going to do anything about it."

"Ah . . . it's complicated," he said softly. Of all the people to see it so clearly, why did it have to be Keelie? She was the one most likely to tell all the wrong people. As in . . . *Abby*. "I can't just go and blurt it out, Keelie. It's too . . . complicated."

"So is life, but you're out here living, aren't you?"

It's not that easy. He could tell her that. *It's none of your business.* Yeah. That would work, too. But in the end, he didn't say anything. Didn't see the point. He knew what he was doing. As much as he'd like to tell Abby how he felt, considering she only saw him as a friend and wasn't interested in anything else, well, he'd rather at least have her as friend. There was no way he was going to risk losing *that* much of her.

This way, he could still take care of her, as much as she'd let him.

It sucked and didn't do anything to fill the hole in his heart, but not having *anything* would leave a bigger hole.

He headed out to the main area of Steel Ink and found Abby standing in front of the main design wall. Her back was turned and for a second, he let himself just stand there, staring. She'd straightened her hair, that incredible curly mass of hair, and it hung down her back in a smooth, straight banner of deep, dark auburn.

Back when they'd been entertaining the world as Kate and Nate, her hair had been a brighter shade of red. She'd been around fourteen when it had started to darken and the studio hotshots hadn't liked it. Since *they* hadn't liked it, her bitch of a mother hadn't, either.

Which meant she'd been forced to deal with having her hair dyed, keeping it that carroty shade for the next two years. Then they'd gotten the word that the show was being cancelled.

It had been one of the worst days of his life—at the time.

But he knew it had been one of the best days of hers. Right up until she realized what it meant to her mother.

Because he couldn't think about Blanche without wanting to spit nails, he made himself cut that line of thought off. "Hey, sugar," he drawled, watching as she spun around.

The flippy little skirt she had on sent his blood pressure soaring somewhere into the stratosphere and he could feel the oxygen in his brain dwindling away. The nervous smile on her face caught his attention and even as he found himself thinking, *Fuck, she's beautiful*, he narrowed his eyes and speculated just what in the hell she was up to.

Abby didn't *show* nerves.

She felt them. He knew that.

But she didn't *show* them.

"Hey, Zach."

She glanced down and he followed her gaze, saw that she had the journal he'd picked up for her. "Did you bring that here to beat me up with it or something?"

She laughed. "Well, there is something about an unexpected action . . ." Then she shrugged. "Nah. I actually figured out a plan. It's a weird one, but I'm here to ask you to help me do one of the things on the list."

"Okay . . ." He hooked his thumbs in his pockets and waited.

"I want a tattoo."

Zach closed his eyes. Reaching up, he rubbed his right ear and then said, "You want what?"

"A tattoo." She wiggled the book . "I wrote it down and

everything. I did it last night and I've thought about it all day and I'm sure I want to do it, so stop looking at me like I've lost my mind, okay?"

"You wrote a plan that includes getting a tattoo," he said slowly. His mind was churning at the very idea of it and his blood was boiling. Putting his hands on her . . . *focus on the issue at hand, Barnes!* "And you want me to do it."

"Well . . ." She grinned at him and the dimple in her chin winked at him. "The tattoo part is in the plan. And who else would I ask? You're my best friend, right?"

He pressed the heel of his hand to his eye. "You sure about this, sugar?"

"Yes." She tapped the book against her leg, looking around. "Ah . . . does that mean you'll do it?"

"Like I'd let anybody else," he muttered. "Do you know what you want?"

She shrugged. "I hadn't really thought it through *that* far. I was kind of thinking you could help me figure it out."

He shoved a hand through his hair and glanced around. The parlor was empty. "When did you want to do this?" He could take some time to think up some designs for her. Take some time to get a grip and—

"Now."

So much for taking time to get a grip.

"Okay."

Bent over the table, she watched as he sketched out another image. Keelie had left, locking up the front door and lowering the blinds. Zach seemed completely focused on the task at hand. "You got any idea where you want to put this?" he asked.

"Ah . . . well, I was thinking that I'd rather have one that doesn't really show. It's for me, not anybody else." She scooted back from the desk and went over to the design wall, studying some of the pictures. The back of her shoulder seemed innocuous enough, but this was something she was doing for herself. Not to show off and she wanted it personal. Completely personal. She saw one woman's picture—the woman was pretty damn clearly showing off—she was sexy as hell, Abigale had to admit, but did she really have to have her jeans open like that?

Although one thing was clear. She wasn't about to have him doing it on her hip like *that*. She'd have to all but pull up her skirt. Considering the way she was having trouble thinking clearly around him just now . . . ? Yeah. Not happening. "I guess my lower back."

Glancing down at her skirt, she frowned and turned around to find Zach staring at her. His gaze dropped back down to the sketchbook in front of him. "Will this skirt work okay for this?"

"Yeah. You're fine. You wanna take a look at any of these?"

She crossed the floor to study the designs and frowned. They all looked so . . . simple.

"What's wrong?"

"Well . . . they're pretty, but . . ." She glanced at the vivid color on his arms, the intricate detail, and then back at the sketches. "Aren't they kind of plain?"

"Sugar, you've never had a tattoo before. Trust me. You want simple. They hurt. And the more intricate it gets, the longer it takes."

"Oh." Well, technically she *realized* it wasn't going to feel good. But having it pointed out to her made some of the nerves inside her flare to life.

A warm hand brushed down her arm and she turned her head, found Zach watching her closely. "You know, this isn't anything you have to do," he said quietly.

"Yes, it is. I want to." Tearing her gaze away from his, she looked at the designs. One in particular had caught her eye the second he'd drawn it. Simple or not, it was lovely. The stylized dragonfly made her smile. It was pretty, fantastical, and silly.

"I think that one is just about perfect," she said, tapping it with her finger.

"Okay." He checked the clock. "I need some time to get this ready. Don't suppose you feel like ordering us in some pizza or something, do you? You can put a movie in while I do this."

"Sure." She tugged her phone out and then glanced at him as he pushed back from the desk. "I . . . ah, well, I didn't know it was any more complicated than you just doing it."

A grin tugged at his lips. "Well, if you had the design in mind already or brought one with you, we could move a little quicker. But yeah, it takes a little while." He gestured down the hall. "The number for the best local pizza place is hanging on the fridge in the break room if you want to use them, or we can use Rosatti's."

Once she left the room, Zach dropped his head down on his desk and groaned. He had to do this. He knew he did. And he wasn't going to deny a very huge part of him *wanted* to do this—wanted it so bad, his hands were shaking from it, but how in the hell was he supposed to handle this without losing his damn mind?

"By doing your damn job." She came here because she wanted some ink. So that was what he was going to do.

As he pushed back from the desk, he kicked the chair she'd dragged over and her purse fell. The journal slid out as he scooped up the purse. He went to dump them both back on the chair, but found himself flipping through the journal. She hadn't done much of anything.

But then he stopped.

One page held her neat writing.

She'd titled it. That was typical Abby, although it made him a little nervous. *Wreck this life*. What the hell . . .

But the first few goals had him smiling. Tell off Roger. Cool. Flip off the photographers? He'd been telling her to do that for years. Stop worrying so much. Wonderful.

The tattoo . . . yes. She was serious.

But the last one had the blood draining out of his head. *Fffffuuuuuccckkkkk* . . .

Snapping it closed, he dumped the book on top of her purse and shot upright. Have a fucking affair? *What the hell?*

Thunder crashed inside his head. At least it felt that way, although more than likely, he was having a stroke or something. His feet seemed to get in the way as he turned around and started for the door. They needed to talk.

Abby had just broken things off with that prick she'd been engaged to. She was upset and feeling a little lost, needed to do something crazy. He could understand that, he thought. And while he was completely on board with her learning to live a little, the idea of her having a fucking affair with some guy who wouldn't give a damn about her made him want to chew glass and break things. Lots of things.

Still, that journal was her personal property and he hadn't had any right to go rooting through it. He hadn't expected to find anything like *that* and how could he explain that he'd read it? He couldn't lie to her. But did he tell her that she needed to think this through?

Damn it.

Following the sound of her voice, he stopped in the doorway and made himself close his eyes while she finished placing the order.

Breathe, man. Gotta breathe. Gotta think. Gotta be calm.

First he had to explain just how he'd managed to see it in the journal. He hadn't exactly been prying . . . well, he had, but he was her best friend and he was nosy, and she knew that, and . . .

Feeling the weight of her gaze, he lifted his lashes, not looking directly at her. Not yet.

But Abby wasn't looking at his face.

She was eyeing his arms. Catching her lower lip between her teeth, she tugged on the soft curve and he almost went to his knees at the sight. A second later, she glanced away, but then she looked back.

The thunder that had been crashing inside his head grew louder and louder.

Have a torrid affair.

Damn it, if she was dead set on *that* idea, she could have an affair with *him*, he decided.

Even as the idea slammed into him, he tried to brush it aside. He'd kept what he felt wrapped up and buried deep for years. Spilling it now?

Just wondering if you're ever going to do anything about it.

It's complicated . . .

Hell. He was lecturing Abby about living life and letting go, and here he was, afraid to grab *on*.

The woman he wanted like he wanted his next breath was standing *right there* and he was afraid to even make a move.

She turned away as he stood there, still wrestling with the very thought of it, need burning in him and twisting him into tight, hungry knots. Damn it. *Damn it.* He needed to do this—

"It will take about an hour or so," Abby said.

I'm thinking longer—

"They're pretty busy."

"What?" Distracted, he dragged his eyes away from the curve of her ass and focused on what she was saying.

"The pizza place. They said it would be about an hour or so—asked if they should come around to the back and I told them yes."

"That's fine." He dragged a hand down his face. "Ah . . . I need to get back to work."

"I was thinking about going to grab some wine or something."

Good idea. Wait. "You can't." He turned around and headed back into the main area of the shop, found the consent forms he needed. Abby was behind him, although he hadn't heard her. When he turned around, she was just a foot away and the scent of her went straight to his head and Zach had to wonder just what in the hell he'd done to get this kind of torture thrown into his life.

"I can't go get wine?" A smile curved her lips as she tipped her head to look up at him.

"I can't do the tattoo if you do—I won't put one on anybody who has been drinking. Saves me trouble later on. And you need to read through the consent form and sign. Make it all nice and legal."

"Ahhh . . ." She took the paper and moved over to one of the seats, crossing her legs as she started to read. "I guess I should be totally clearheaded. Otherwise, I could end up having arms like yours."

"Nah. I might try to talk you into having *Forever Nate's* tattooed on your ass, but that's it." He gave her a strained smile and turned around. Distance. Serious distance was needed here so he could get back on track.

As he headed down the hall, she called out, "Yeah, sure. I'll do that when you have a heart with *Kate* somewhere on *you*."

Once he was in his office, he rubbed the heel of his hand over his chest.

What in the hell would she do if she knew he already *had* her written on his skin?

Not Kate, of course.

He hadn't fallen in love with Kate.

He loved Abby and always had.

He'd loved her when she ran away from California all those years ago . . . and he'd waited until she stopped running, so he could follow.

He'd loved her when she came to him and told him she was getting married . . . to a man who didn't deserve her.

And now she was laying out a plan to go and have a torrid affair. With who?

Curling one hand into a fist, he crossed back to his desk. "Why in the hell not me?"

Chapter Four

Wine *would* have been a good idea, Abby thought. Maybe he didn't want her drinking *before* he got started, but after? Yeah, it would have helped.

Stretched out on her belly, she closed her eyes and tried to think about *anything* but the pain.

"You okay?"

Zach's hands on her weren't helping her zone out, she decided. It was one hell of a distraction, but it *wasn't* helping her zone out.

Swallowing the knot in her throat, she croaked out, "I'm as good as I think I can expect to be."

"And how good is that?"

"Lousy."

He laughed a little. "Why don't you talk to me? We're halfway done," he said. "If you talk, you'll get distracted and it will be done before you know it."

"Okay." She scrunched her eyes tightly closed and tried to think of something to say. Her mind was blank. "I don't know what to talk about."

"You always have something to talk about," he teased,

his voice low and easy, and she knew even without looking at him that he was smiling.

"Not right now I don't." Well, she *could* think of a thing or two. But those weren't really things she could say. Were they? No. She'd thought this through. She wasn't going down that road with Zach.

"Okay. I'll help. What is this new life plan you've got laid out? Besides the tattoo?"

I plan on flipping my life upside down.

She bit her lip to keep from blurting that out. That would make him worry. She loved him dearly and she didn't need him worrying about her right now. "It's not a *life* plan exactly. It's just a *for now* plan," she said slowly. "Some things to keep me distracted until I figure out what I'm going to do with myself. There's the tattoo thing, which you're obviously helping with. I'm going to try to stop worrying so much. One of them, though . . . I plan on calling up Roger and telling him off."

He grunted. "Good plan." Something soft brushed against her lower back and she hissed a little.

Damn it, that hurt. It felt like something was slicing right through her skin.

Distraction. Talk, damn it. About anything.

"I don't get it," she said softly, some of the confusion and pain breaking free. "I mean . . . I thought he loved me. How could he love me and walk away like that? Over the life I *used* to have? That's what it's all about. I used to be an actress. I'm not anymore—I haven't been for *years* and I'm happy with that. How can he not see that? If he loved me, wouldn't he be able to see that I don't *want* to act anymore?"

Zach didn't answer.

Turning her head, she peered over her shoulder at him.

He had his head bowed, the gold-streaked strands falling down and hiding his features from her.

"Zach?"

He sighed. "Do you really want to hear what I have to say about this right now, sugar?"

"I always want to hear what you have to say."

"Okay." He used the cloth again on her back and then bent down, staring at her skin like there was nothing else in the world but her back and the design he was inking on her flesh. "He never loved you."

It was a strike, square to her heart.

She closed her eyes.

"If he loved you, he wouldn't treat you the way he did. When you walked into a room, it would have showed on his face . . . if he really loved you. Either he'd have been so busy staring at you because he just had to see you, or he would have been looking away so nobody *could* see it. Except he was going to marry you—you were his and he had every right to let the world see how he felt." Zach dabbed at her back again, still focused on the work.

She was almost glad of the pain now, because it was easier to think about how much it *hurt* than to think about what he had to say.

"But when you walked into a room, that fucking prick was too busy either messing with his damned gadgets or looking at everybody else to see what *they* thought about you. He was in love with the idea of having Kate the cutie on his arm—the son of a bitch just loved to talk about his fiancée, the *actress* . . . and don't tell me you never noticed. He might have loved the idea of being with *Kate* . . . but he never loved *you*."

He paused what he was doing and for a brief second, the world fell away as he looked up and met her eyes. "He never loved you, and the son of a bitch sure as hell didn't deserve you, sugar."

Her heart slammed against her ribs as his blue gaze held hers.

And then, as it started to feel like all the oxygen in the room had dwindled away, he turned his attention back to the task at hand.

It felt like he was flaying the flesh from her bones. And she decided that was just fine, because now she needed *that* distraction.

Was he right? she wondered.

She'd noticed, and tried to ignore, Roger's fascination with her old life, but she'd chalked it up to him just wanting to *know* about her. They were getting married . . . they *should* know about each other. But what if Zach was right?

What if Roger had never really loved her at all?

And that thought, as much as it infuriated her, also made her wonder one simple thing.

Had *she* loved him?

"Okay, here are the important things," Zach said as he studied the design. It was cute and sexy as hell. If he found out another guy was the one who got to press his lips to that dragonfly where it curved low over the flare of her left hip, he thought he just might go insane. "I'll send you home with some instructions on how to care for it, but you need to make sure you keep it clean. No scrubbing at it or anything—you need to be gentle when you wash it. I've got some ointment I'll send home with you and I'll go into detail about using that, too."

She was still staring at it over her shoulder in the mirror. Worrying her lower lip with her teeth and eyeing the dragonfly like she expected it to take flight or something.

"I need to get the bandage on," he said softly.

"What? Oh."

She continued to stand there and he reached up, pressed his hand between her shoulder blades. "Lean forward a little."

Hunger screamed, jerking on the leash inside him as he eased the waistband of her skirt just a little lower so he could get the bandage in place. Bent over the table like that, he could so easily imagine pulling the hem of the skirt up. Slipping his hand between her thighs. Would she sigh? Moan?

No. This was Abby and she'd freak the hell out and then she'd run away and he'd lose her—

A soft, shaky sigh caught his attention as he smoothed the bandage down. Keeping his head bowed, he checked the mirror from under his lashes and his knees almost buckled.

Fuck.

Abby was staring at their reflection and her face was flushed.

What. The. Hell.

Abruptly, he stepped back and moved away. If he didn't move away *immediately*, he was going to grab her and do things he should never do to his best friend. The woman he loved. That was the problem. He'd loved her for too long and he was misreading the signals and—

"Do you really think all that's true? About Roger?"

Hearing that shithead's name on her lips snapped his temper. He turned around and glared at her. "If I didn't think that was the case, Abs, I wouldn't have said it. He's an egotistical, arrogant piece of work and he never loved you. You deserved a hell of a lot better and I knew it all along. But he was what you wanted so who in the hell was I to say any different?"

"You're my best friend," she said quietly.

"Shit." He went to pass a hand over his face and stopped. He still had his gloves on. Stripping them off, he tossed them into the red trash can near the door and headed over to start cleaning up. "Yes. I am. You asked me what I thought and I told you. But I can't tell you what is in that fucker's head. You can always ask him when you call him to tell him off, although I doubt he'll tell you the truth. He doesn't even *see* the truth anyway."

"Have you ever been in love?"

In the middle of gathering up his supplies, he paused. Zach closed his eyes and started to mouth every single foul, nasty curse he could think of. He had four brothers. He could think of a *lot* of cusswords. Halfway through one that involved anatomical improbabilities and a goat, a hand touched his shoulder.

"Zach?"

Damn it, he couldn't do this. Moving away, he started grabbing his supplies at random. Dumping trash, slamming the tools here, there. Being fucking careless with them, but he couldn't look at her yet. If he did, she might see—

He went to dump the trash and turned around.

Abby was right there, dark brown eyes locked on his face, her shirt still knotted just under her breasts, leaving her belly bare.

"What is this?" she teased. "You make me play twenty questions all the time."

Edging around her, he focused on cleaning up. "I'm thirty-two years old, Abby. Yeah. I've been in love," he said, keeping his voice flat and his eyes on the task at hand. "It didn't work out."

"Why not?"

"She never seemed to notice that I was staring at her when she walked into the room." Eventually, he had to stop staring, because other people *did* notice . . . and then she started dating Roger, got engaged. She wasn't his and he spent night after endless night wondering about all the chances he might have had.

Was he going to let that happen again?

Had fate dropped one more chance into his lap?

From the corner of his eye, he saw Abby approaching and he tensed. She leaned in and he blamed it on insanity, the devil, or his own desperate desire, but something pushed him. Turning his head at the very last moment so that the kiss she'd meant to brush against his cheek hit his lips.

It was light, quick, and soft . . . and he felt her gasp. The taste of her went straight down to his dick, tightening every muscle in his body, sending his heart into a full-on gallop.

Lust and love tangled inside him and he fisted his hands on the metal tray in front of him to keep from reaching for her.

A second later, it was over and Abby backed away. Fast. So fast, she practically tripped over her feet.

He pretended not to notice as he went back to work.

"Um. Well. Whoever she is, she's got to be wrong in the head for not noticing you."

Two a.m. . . . and all's not well . . .

Abby lay on her right side, staring into the darkness and trying not to think. It wasn't working well because every time she closed her eyes, she could only think about Zach. And that bare whisper of a kiss.

She should be sleeping.

If not sleeping, she should be working on the books. Running your own business meant there was *always* something to keep you busy.

If not *that*, she could be writing out a nice little script for what she planned to tell Roger when she called him.

But what was she doing?

Thinking about Zach.

Her heart stuttered in her chest as one very, very vivid memory flashed through her mind. As he'd been slipping the bandage onto her hip, she'd glanced over. Something about the look on his face, taut and unyielding, had sent her pulse racing up into the near-dangerous zone. His other hand had rested higher on her back and she could recall the way his touch had felt.

And damned if she hadn't wanted to move back against him.

What would he have done?

"He would have thought you'd lost your mind."

Groaning, she snatched the phone.

Zach was her best friend. But he was a guy and there were some things she just couldn't discuss with a guy. Even when the guy was somebody you'd laughed with over bad porn back when you were teens.

For certain things, a girl just needed the ear of a girlfriend. For those things, she called Marin. Marin, another former child star, had thrived on the life and was currently one of Hollywood's darlings.

Punching in Marin's cell, she rolled onto her back and then yelped as her newly tattooed skin came in contact with the bed.

"Ah . . . Abby? Is that you?"

"Hey, Marin," she said, easing into a sitting position and groaning. "Yeah, it's me. I need . . ." she stopped and blew out a breath. Then she groaned as her eyes caught the clock. She'd totally forgotten how late it was. "I'm an idiot, calling this late."

"Well, I'm awake anyway. Just got in. Why are you calling?" She paused and then asked softly, "Still upset about Roger the Rat?"

"You and Zach need to stop," Abby muttered. "I'm going to start picturing him with a long tail and big teeth."

"And the problem with this is . . .? Seriously, baby, you need to quit worrying and hurting over him. I know that—"

"He's not why I'm calling." Zach's blue eyes flashed through her mind, and her skin, still hot even though it had been hours . . .

"Okay. So why *are* you calling at two in the morning?"

"Zach."

"Zach?"

"I . . ." She bit her lower lip. Because she felt better with something in her hands, she hit the light and grabbed her new journal. "I've got this new plan."

"Abby, you and your damn plans—"

"Would you just listen?" she snapped. "It's not a *life* plan thing. It's just to get me . . . rebooted or something. I need to quit freaking out and trying to plan things. I *know* that. So I made a new plan. I'm going to stop worrying so much about the future. That's the first thing. Second thing is to tell Roger off. I might do that tomorrow . . . or today, actually. Third up is to flip off the photographers next time I'm in LA. I already did the fourth one—get a tattoo."

"You got a tattoo? What is it? Did Zach do it?"

Abigale rolled her eyes. "Who else would I let do it? And yes. It's a dragonfly, on my left hip, before you interrupt again." She cleared her throat. "The last one . . . well. It's having a torrid affair."

"A torrid affair." Marin said it slowly, like she was rolling the words around on her tongue. "Just what do you mean by a *torrid* affair? Have you ever had one?"

"You know the answer to that."

"Exactly. For you, a torrid affair would be having sex with a guy you're attracted to . . . not somebody you were dating for months. Just how many lovers have you had, Abby?"

Abby made a face. "I've had two. And the first one was pretty damn good, too. It's not my fault he turned out to be a two-timing, scum-sucking son of a bitch."

"True. Actually, we might be able to count Jason as a torrid affair . . . he was just one that lasted for six months. Are you looking at a short-term thing or long-term thing?"

"I haven't planned that out." Abby started to pace the bedroom, tapping her journal against her thigh and trying to think about how to say this next part. She needed Marin to talk her down. But she needed Marin to understand she hadn't lost her mind or something. She was just having a minor breakdown. That was all. Understandable. "I just . . . I want somebody who'll make my heart stop, and then make it race all over again. I want somebody who'll make me *remember* every damn second we were together, and not just the moment we were in bed. I want something to remember, Marin."

Her friend laughed softly. "Damn, if you succeed, I'm going to be seriously envious, sweetie." Then she sighed and said, "So have you thought about *who* you want this to be with? After all, strangers aren't exactly safe, you know."

"I know. I . . ."

Her throat closed up.

"Abby?"

"I—"

Marin muttered something and then demanded, "You

said you were calling about Zach. Are you thinking about having an affair with *Zach*? *Our* Zach?"

She opened her mouth to say, "No. I want you to talk me out of it. It's a bad idea."

But what she heard herself saying was, "Yes."

Damn it, you moron! She smacked herself in the forehead and stormed over to her window, shoving open the curtains so she could stare out into the night. The desert and the mountains spread out in front of her, usually a sight that calmed her, but try as she might, she couldn't get anything to calm her tonight.

"It's a stupid idea, I know," she said quietly. "I know that. I just need you to talk me out of it."

"Why would I do that?" Marin yawned. "Sorry. Long day. Anyway. I think you should go for it. He's hot. He cares about you. And if you're attracted to him? Go for it."

She opened her mouth. Closed it. "You're not helping," she whispered quietly. "Damn it, he's my best friend. Things like this don't tend to end well and I *can't* lose him. You know what he means to me. You're supposed to talk me out of this. That's why I *called* you . . . so you could make this easier."

Marin laughed. "Hey, friends aren't supposed to be about making it *easier*. Besides, you didn't tell me this was one of those *tell me what I want to hear* discussions. I gotta go . . . love you!"

Marin stood there, arms crossed over her chest as she stared at the phone. It was late and she had to be out of the house by seven a.m. for an interview. But oddly, she wasn't at all tired.

Marin was one of the other kids from the *Kate + Nate* show, although *she* had been Kate the cutie's rival on the show. In real life, they'd liked each other. Quite a bit. Of course, Marin had been jealous as hell of Abigale for a long while, because while Zach had been eyeballing Abigale, Marin had been eyeballing him. She'd gotten over her infatuation. Zach never had, because his thing for Abigale went a hell of a lot deeper. It wasn't just infatuation, something Marin had figured out a long time ago. He was shit-faced in love with Abigale, but for some reason, he'd never made a move on her.

And if Abigale wasn't so damned set on planning her entire life down to the nth degree, then she might have figured out one crucial detail. The perfect guy had been waiting for her all along.

"And she thinks I'm going to tell her to back away from having an affair?"

Marin snorted as she turned away.

The only question in mind for *her* was whether or not to warn Zach.

Nah. She figured it would be more fun for both of them this way.

Chapter Five

Abigale looked up as a rather domineering and arrogant chef appeared in her line of vision. His name was Raul. At least that was the name he'd given her when she'd told him that she was going to help cover for her friend Grace. Grace was supposed to make the desserts at a bat mitzvah and she'd gotten sick—a bad stomach flu was going around and she'd asked Abigale to cover for her. They were friendly and when she could, she liked to help her friends.

Raul was not her friend.

And she'd bet her eyeteeth that Raul's Italian accent wasn't authentic. Especially since he kept dropping it when he was pissed off.

Glancing over at the prep for the canapés, she paused long enough to study them, then study the mini-tarts she'd been working on. "Am I being paid to help with the canapés?" she asked mildly.

He gave her a sharp-edged smile. "We believe in helping each other in this business, *bellezza*."

"Really?" She smiled back. "I'll keep that in mind when I ask for help opening a door later. You slammed it in my face when I was juggling six bags earlier." Then she shot a look at what he was working on. If he didn't get some help, he was going to ruin the food. She didn't like the asshole, but that wasn't the fault of the client.

It wasn't precisely their fault that the guy had an ego the size of California and that he was too stingy to hire out for extra help when he clearly needed it. Wiping her hands on a towel, she headed to the stove and judging by the look of things, she'd made it just in time.

What was he going to do, let it burn? she wondered.

Possibly. Some people would do that just to prove a point. Throw a tantrum.

"How are you doing these?" she called over her shoulder.

"My *sous*-chef can advise you," he said, his voice all but *reeking* with imperiousness.

Abigale decided then, in that very moment, that she wanted to smack him. Hard.

Instead, she gripped the skillet's long metal handle and rotated her wrist, smiling a little as the smell of onion, bacon, and spice filled the air. He might be an ass, but he knew his way around the kitchen.

"He likes to . . . ah . . ."

She glanced over at the boy next to her. Well, young adult male, she supposed, but he was so nervous, so jumpy, it was hard to call him an adult. When she looked at him, he couldn't meet her eyes, and when she smiled at him, he tucked his chin low and seemed to wilt while a blush stained his cheeks red.

"Just tell me how we're doing this," she said, smiling at him. "I can handle it. You just keep doing what needs to be done. Otherwise we get to listen to him bark for the rest of the day."

Abigale tried to elicit a smile from him.

But all he did was shoot a nervous look over his shoulder at his boss and then back at her, like he just might be sick.

Damn it.

She really wanted this day over with.

Sighing, she focused on the stove. This was why she liked running her own business. If she was putting up with the assholes, at least they were *paying* her. She was getting paid here, but not by the prick with the pots and pans over there.

Abigale smirked a little as she settled down to work.

"I just wanted to thank—"

The woman stopped in the doorway, staring at Abigale. Her daughter was the young lady of the night and having a very grand time, from the way it sounded, and the look of pleasure on the woman's face was almost worth the head-ache of working with *Raul*.

Almost.

"I . . ."

Abigale mentally sighed and reached for a rag to wipe her damp hands off.

"Madam, is everything . . ." Raul paused, pursing his lips as though he was searching for the words.

Abigale was pretty certain the woman's name was Anna Wendell. They hadn't had the chance to meet but she re-membered that Grace had kept referring to an Anna. And Anna was staring at her with a look that Abigale was pretty familiar with.

"Is it . . ." Anna licked her lips and laughed, the sound more than a little nervous. "Ah, this is going to sound ter-rible, but . . ."

Raul shot Abigale a dirty look and then stepped for-ward. "Madam, if she's caused a problem with the party, I'm terribly sorry. As you know, Grace was ill and we had . . . we had to settle."

Settle? Oh, she'd show *him* settling. After she punched him. The pompous windbag.

Anna gave him a horrified look and then shot a look at Abigale again. "Raul, don't be silly. Everything was wonderful. That's why I came back here—I was worried there would be problems with Grace getting sick. But . . ." She edged around him, coming closer to Abigale, but her steps were slow, almost hesitant, like she was still trying to decide if she wanted to say anything.

Abigale decided she wanted to get out of there. She couldn't leave *yet* but since the party was going well and her part was done, she would take a few minutes outside. Setting her shoulders, she put a smile on her face and stepped forward with her hand outstretched. "Hello, Mrs. Wendell. Abigale Applegate."

Anna's jaw dropped. "Oh . . . oh, my goodness." Instead of reaching out to shake her hand, she covered her mouth. "It *is* you!"

"Madam . . ."

Anna started to laugh, waving her hands a little as a smile stretched across her face. "Ms. Applegate . . . wow. Oh, my goodness. Wow. You won't believe this, I know and I bet you hear it all the time, but I'm one of your biggest fans. *Kate + Nate* was one of my most favorite shows ever . . . and when it went off the air, I thought I was just going to die."

The lady rushed over and as her arms came around her, Abigale hugged her back.

"It's such an honor to meet you!"

"The pleasure is mine," Abigale said softly and she meant it. One thing she had enjoyed about that life was meeting the people who'd enjoyed the show. That had been fun, something that made it worth it. Even now.

"Uh . . . who in the hell is Kate?"

Looking up, Abigale smiled and she couldn't help it as she met *Raul*'s gaze. "I was . . . once. Raul, what happened to your accent?"

Ten minutes later, she'd signed autographs and then managed to sneak her way outside. The warm evening air wrapped around her and she sighed as she made her way over to one of the benches that lined the outdoor gardens of the pavilion the Wendell family had rented.

Stretching out her legs, she flexed her calves and wished she could take off her shoes, but then she'd have to put them back on . . . *not* going to happen. Once those puppies came off, they were staying off.

"You're really a famous actress?"

At the sound of that young voice, she bit back a sigh and then sat up, smiling as she saw Kenzie Wendell standing over at the edge of the garden. "Well, hello." Peering past her, she glanced toward the corner where she could just barely see the faintest edge of the bright lights that spilled out from the event area in the back. "Shouldn't you be at the party?"

Kenzie shrugged. "I can always be at parties." She rolled her eyes a little and with the temerity of the young, she headed over to the bench where Abigale sat and plopped down beside her. "I'm having fun and stuff, and I *love* the presents, but I've been to like eight of these parties this year. I've never talked to anybody famous before."

Abigale laughed quietly. "I'm not famous anymore, really."

"Sure you are." Kenzie cocked her head and the dim lights glinted off the pretty little jeweled band in her hair. "You were on a TV show for like *forever.* My mom has them all on DVD. I even watched a few." She paused and then grinned, her nose wrinkling up as she added, "Nate was kind of cute. Were you two really . . . um . . ."

Abigale grinned over at her. "It was a TV show. Nothing you saw on it was real." Then she frowned. "Well, the guy who played Nate *was* cute."

"But you two weren't like boyfriend and girlfriend or anything?"

"We're friends." She smiled a little and glanced back at the teenager. "You want to hear the truth? We still are friends . . . we've been friends since the show was on. He's the best friend I've ever had."

"Wow. You've been friends for like . . . forever."

Abigale winced. "Well, really, it's like twentysomething years, but to a thirteen-year-old girl, I guess that seems like forever."

"Yeah." Kenzie was quiet for a minute and then she asked, "Is he still cute?"

Abigale's mouth went dry. *Cute.* Cute might have touched on what Zach had been all those years ago, but now? She thought of the dark, heady blue of his eyes. Thought of the way his hands had felt on her, and all he'd been doing was giving her a damned tattoo. And it had *hurt*, but she'd still loved the way his hands had felt. She was sick. So damned sick.

She thought about the way those tattoos twining around his arms had always gotten to her, and the way she could lean against him and just *know* things were going to be okay if he was there.

Something odd shifted in her heart as she realized that last thing wasn't anything new. Yeah, her serious interest in his tattoos wasn't a new thing, either, but Zach was a physical work of art. All long, lean muscles and those colorful tattoos that curved and colored and lined his skin only accentuated the utter perfection of his body.

It went deeper than that, though. So much deeper.

Zach . . . he'd always been there.

"Yeah," she whispered softly. "He's still cute."

"Kenzie!"

Kenzie groaned and shoved upright off the bench. "That's my aunt. She's going to insist on more pictures, I know." Then she grinned back at Abigale. "It was nice meeting you."

Abigale smiled back, but her mind was still on Zach.

A good four hours passed before she was done. Nearly one o'clock in the morning and the city was quiet, the night sky spread out around her like a blanket. The brilliance of the stars was so much more vivid than it'd ever been back in LA.

If she wasn't so damned tired, she wouldn't have minded going for a drive through the desert, just her and the night sky. But there was no way. She was tired, her body was sore, and her clothes smelled like she'd been cooking all day.

Which was true.

So instead, she drove home and brooded over the tasks on the list that she hadn't done.

Call Roger.

That was the most pressing thing, although she couldn't exactly explain why.

Unless it had something to do with the way his words kept haunting her. *You're not being true to yourself.*

Not being true to herself.

She *didn't* want Hollywood back.

Yeah, there were odd, random thoughts that would drift through her mind every now and then. But it was more like a pang of nostalgia for the few good times she remembered about that life. Not anything that she wanted to have again. Sort of like high school. Plenty of people thought fondly of those days, she knew, but most of them wouldn't go back if you *paid* them.

But something about what he'd said was really just getting to her and she couldn't figure out what it was. *You're not being true to yourself . . .*

Not being true to herself. Was she hiding from something she really wanted? It sure as hell wasn't that life. But if it wasn't the life, then what was it?

Yet again, Zach's face flashed through her mind and she found herself thinking back to her conversation with Kenzie Wendell. And the way her thoughts had shifted and taken their own path.

Zach had always been there.

She hadn't ever been one of the girls who'd had a mad crush on him.

He was just Zach to her, and always had been. Why was that suddenly changing?

And just what in *hell* was she going to do about it?

* * *

The last thing she should have been doing before she drifted to sleep was thinking about Zach.

Because the first thing she did once she slid into the dark, warm embrace of dreams was think about *him* . . . and there he was.

Steel Ink wasn't precisely the place she would have expected to find herself, but as she lay back in the chair, she decided she wouldn't complain. And she already knew she was dreaming. It was the only way to explain why she was in the chair wearing nothing but panties and a tank top, and why he was bent over her, wearing nothing but a pair of jeans. He wasn't doing anything sexual. At least it shouldn't *feel* that way, but as he transferred a design onto her skin, Abigale had to bite back the urge to moan.

Long, agile fingers stroked down her hip and although she didn't know why, when he peeled the paper away, he leaned in and pressed his lips to her hip bone. Her breath caught in her chest as she felt the glide of his hair across her skin. "Is . . . ah . . . is that part of the service?"

"No." He kissed a little higher, nudged her shirt out of the way. "This is a special service. Just for you."

Her laugh sounded breathless, even to her own ears. Then he caught the hem of her shirt and dragged it higher, exposing her breasts, and she didn't have the breath to laugh, to think . . . "And just what does this service entail?" she asked.

"Whatever you want." He curved a hand over her knee. At the same time he caught one nipple in his mouth, tugging it gently with his teeth as she arched up against him, her back leaving the cushioned softness of the bench behind her. "What do you want, Abs?"

The low, husky sound of his voice hit her square in the heart. And lower. Heat spread through her and because it was a dream, because it was safe, she caught his hand and guided it between her thighs. "I want you."

His mouth closed over hers. Shocking and hot, the kind

of kiss she hadn't had in far too long . . . and neither of the two men she'd been with had been able to make her feel like *this*. Like she was the very center of everything. Zach's hand cupped her core, but he did nothing else as he kissed her and the kiss was even more intimate, more erotic than the feel of his hand between her thighs. His tongue stroked along the curve of her lower lip, teasing her until she opened for him and then teasing a little more until she was about ready to scream. When she might have pulled away, he shifted, pulled her off the chair and onto his lap.

"No pulling back now," he muttered. "You wanted a torrid affair, I'll fucking give you one."

She tensed, caught off guard. Just a dream . . . only a dream, so yeah, he knew. But could she really?

"It's a dream," he whispered against her lips. "You do what you want."

"I want you."

Lifting her head, she stared into those familiar blue eyes, eyes she'd known for more than half of her life. So dark and hypnotic. So amazing. Lifting her hands, she cupped his face, her fingers pushing into the gold-streaked brown hair that fell to his shoulders. Holding him steady, she lowered her head to his, pressed her mouth to his. Against his lips, she murmured quietly, "I want you."

Between her thighs, through his jeans, her panties, she could feel him throbbing against her and it was enough to make her moan. "Then have me," he whispered. "Have—"

"Abs!"

Abigale jerked upright, her breath coming in harsh, ragged pants as she stared around. Confusion, heat, and hunger burned inside her. What in the world? The dream burned inside her brain like an afterimage, searing along the pathways of her mind and she groaned, flopping back on the bed and closing her eyes.

"Abby?"

Her eyes flew open and she shot back up, staring toward the door.

Two seconds later, Zach appeared in the door.

Then have me.

Those words, whispered against her mouth only seconds ago, echoed in her mind, and the dream, so vivid and bright, flashed through her memory as she stared at him.

He leaned against the doorway, arching a brow. "You're still in bed."

"Ah . . ." Glancing down, she stared at her rumpled sheets and blankets and then back up at him. "Ah, yes. Um. Late . . . late night."

She swallowed again and then looked back up at him.

"I can see." A faint grin curved his lips and he asked, "Were you up late formulating your response to Roger? Or carrying out some other nefarious step on your new life plan?"

She made a face at him even as blood crept up her neck to stain her cheeks red. Dreams didn't count as carrying out nefarious steps. "Neither, you jackass. I was covering a job for a friend who ended up with the stomach bug that's been going around."

"Grace?"

She arched a brow. "How did you know that?"

"She's about the only one you like well enough to take on a big job for at the last minute. Anyone else, you refer out to Midnight Delite."

Sighing, she shoved her tangled hair back from her face. "You know me too well."

"Hey, isn't that what friends are for?" He shoved off the wall and swung the bag he had in his hand. "I was going to make you breakfast, if you were interested."

"Breakfast, huh?" Eyeing the bag, she asked, "And just what are you making?"

"The only thing I can do that passes muster for the professional caterer." He winked. "Bacon and an omelet."

"Hmmm." Her belly rumbled. "Well, I guess that decides that." She went to climb out of the bed and that was when she remembered she'd been too damned tired to dig for clean pajamas last night. Wearing just a camisole and panties, she stood by the bed. Blood crawled up her neck, but she casually grabbed the robe from the foot of her bed and put it on. Hell, it wasn't like Zach hadn't seen her in less. Toward the end of their show, they'd had a few . . . mini-make-out sessions, including one where she'd been wearing just jeans and a bra. And hell, they went swimming together all the time in the summer.

Still . . .

Hell, he isn't going to notice, she told herself as she tied the robe around her waist. Keeping that in mind, she made herself smile as she shifted her attention back to him.

And the look on his face stole the air right out of her.

His face could have been carved from stone and his eyes burned. They burned so hot, it was a miracle the air around them didn't explode.

Shaken, caught off guard, she licked her lips as his gaze slowly moved up along her body, but before he met her eyes, he closed his eyes and in that moment, the strange tension in the air shattered. It fell apart and dissolved, like spun sugar in the rain. When he opened his eyes to look at her, it was as though it had never happened.

"So . . ." With his easy, cocky smile on his face, he met her gaze. "You want breakfast or should I just head home and eat it all myself?"

Chapter Six

His hands were shaking.

Once more, she'd done this to him.

Damn it, this was out of hand.

He'd dropped one of the eggs on the counter. He'd almost cut his finger off with the damned butcher knife and his hands were shaking as he went to flip the bacon.

Upstairs he could hear the pulse of the water and if he closed his eyes, he could just picture her standing under the spray. Water gliding over all those lush pale curves, her deep red hair hanging in wet ropes along her spine.

It wasn't a new fantasy. He didn't *have* new fantasies about Abby. He'd dreamed everything imaginable about her, but somehow, seeing her in that ridiculously thin, skimpy little top that she'd slept in and a pair of pale pink panties, it hit him square in the gut.

No. Actually it was lower and all he wanted to do was close the distance between them and go to his knees. Beg her to see what was right in front of her . . . *who* was right in front of her.

He wanted to press his lips to the soft swell of her belly. Along the lush curves of her hips. He wanted to palm those amazing round breasts in his hands and taste her . . . see just what color her nipples where. He'd caught a glimpse of the dark shadows through the top she'd been wearing, but what color were they? Pink? A soft, warm rose brown?

"Man, you've got to stop this or you'll end up crippling yourself."

He could still hear the water.

And it was so very, very easy to imagine himself climbing those stairs. Stripping his clothes away and joining her.

"Ow!" Hot grease splattered his hand and he jerked back as the small flame flared. Jerking his head back on track, he went to grab a small hand towel and caught the handle of the skillet.

"Fuck!"

With her back leaning against the warm, smooth walls of her shower, Abigale closed her eyes. Her breath came in harsh, broken little pants as the showerhead pulsed and warm water beat against her.

In her mind, she was back in that dream.

That heady, erotic dream.

Bringing herself to climax had become habit, but it had never been so painfully necessary until now and she was all but ready to cry. Her muscles tightened, locking up on her as she started to rock her hips, desperately empty inside.

The heat of the water pounding against her clit felt so damned good, but it wasn't enough . . .

"Zach . . ."

Focusing on his face, she imagined he was there. Coming to her through the cloud of steam and heat. Stepping between her thighs. Or maybe kneeling . . .

And just that thought did it. Pushed her right over the edge.

With a sob, she climaxed, biting her lip so the man downstairs wouldn't hear her as she cried out.

* * *

A few minutes later, a little embarrassed but feeling more relaxed, she tugged her robe back on and stood in front of the mirror drying her hair.

A muffled shout came from downstairs and she paused, then frowned.

Reaching for the doorknob, she cocked her head.

Then Zach's pained shout echoed through the house and she took off running.

Stumbling to a halt in the doorway of her bright, open kitchen, she stared. She didn't see any blood. There was a big butcher knife on the island, so no blood was a good sign. There was a skillet on the stove, smoking—too hot. Grimacing, she headed over to it and then saw the mess. The island had been blocking it.

Bacon and grease splattered all over the floor . . . and Zach was at the sink with the water running. Groaning, she turned off the stove and then edged around the mess.

"Let me see your hand."

He shot her a dark look. "I got it."

"Zach, let me see your hand right now, or I'm going to call your damned mother," she warned.

He curled his lip at her. "That's such teenaged shit, Abs."

"And it works." She reached for his forearm—everything looked fine there and he didn't seem to be trying to get it under the water, so she figured it was safe. "Come on, Zach. Let me look," she said, softer this time.

Leaning in, she sighed as she saw the leather bracelet he had on. "You're probably ruining that," she said quietly, gently unsnapping it. It was harder to make out anything on his wrist and lower forearm, thanks to the vibrant colors of his tattoos, but the back of his hand, spreading down across his fingers was a vibrant, angry red. "You burned it good."

"That's why I'm putting it under cold water," he said, his voice grouchy.

She shot a glance up at him, smiling a little. "Cranky."

"It *hurts*," he snapped.

"Yeah, I bet it does." She put the stopper in the sink and filled it up, getting the water as cold as it would go.

"I was going to ice it—"

"No. Ice is bad for burns. Can affect circulation." She guided his hand back into the water and held it there as the water started to fill up, slowly rising over his wrist and forearm. Once it was up a few inches over the burned areas, she shut it off. "There. You need to keep it in there for twenty minutes or so. We'll keep letting the water out as it warms up and adding in more cold."

"I need to finish the food," he muttered, staring down into the sink.

She rose onto her toes and kissed his cheek. "I'll do it. It's the thought that counts and all."

"I was supposed to be doing the breakfast *for* you . . . not having you cook for me. You always cook for me."

"I don't mind." She went to glance at him. Such a mistake. That dream, that torrid, wicked dream continued to dance through her mind and when their gazes locked, the heat in his dark blue eyes was enough to leave her feeling like *she* had been scalded. Only there was no pain.

Just burning, burning heat.

The breath whooshed down out of her lungs and for a moment, she could picture herself doing exactly what she'd done in that dream. Reaching up, framing his face with her hands, and holding him as she pressed her mouth to his.

Have a torrid affair with a hot guy.

Such a simple thing, it seemed.

And if this was anybody but her best friend . . .

Sucking in a breath, she eased away from him just as he opened his mouth. Nerves punched through her, hard and vicious, and she caught the bright edge of them dancing in her voice as she said, "So, what do you want in your omelet? Do you want to be able to taste anything afterward or do you just want it your normal level of spicy?"

*   *   *

The pain in his hand seemed to pale in comparison to the sudden, vicious ache in his dick. Zach brooded. Staring at the back of her head, he had to swallow twice and clear his throat before he could manage anything more than a rasp to answer. "Just do what you want," he said. "I'm not picky."

Then as she knelt down on the floor, the robe she'd pulled on riding high on her thighs, he had to swallow back a groan. "Abs, I'll clean that up. Why don't you go get dressed?" *Please? For the sake of my sanity?* "I didn't mean to drag you out of your shower."

When she glanced at him, he nodded toward the stove and said, "It's not like anything is going to burn."

"You need to keep soaking your hand and I'd rather get this cleaned up before it becomes a bigger mess." She shrugged and went back to the task at hand.

He went back to fighting the urge to stare at the creamy slope of her breast, which he could see all too easily from where he was standing. And *fuck . . .* now he knew the answer. Her nipples were a deep, dark rose. Feeling like a fucking Peeping Tom, he dragged his eyes away from her and focused back on his hand. "Sorry about the mess, Abs," he said.

"It's no big deal. I'm just glad you didn't do anything worse to your hand. Grease burns can be nasty."

Staring down at the red splotch spreading across his skin, he grimaced. This was going to be a bitch to deal with for a few days—he could only imagine how much fun it was going to be trying to work. And it served him right. Down here, mentally jacking off while she was in the shower, blissfully unaware of what was going on in his screwed-up head. Yeah, he was lucky it wasn't a lot worse.

He shot another glance over at her and wondered if maybe he just shouldn't scrap his entire plan. He'd come over here because he'd thought about trying to work up to telling her that he'd seen her journal. Or getting her to tell *him* what was in the journal.

Then what? he thought sourly. He'd done such a bang-up job so far this morning. Making a mess in her pretty little kitchen. Burning the fuck out of his hand. He ought to just—

"You look pissed."

Startled, he looked up as she moved to come stand next to him. "Huh?"

"You heard me." She smiled at him, her dimple flashing. She checked the water. "I'm going to let some of the water out and add in some more cold water real quick."

As she leaned in, the robe she wore gaped and he had another glimpse of smooth, soft breasts. *Stop it, Zach.*

He swallowed and doggedly stared out the back window at the rock garden and pond she had set up. There was a sitting area, too, with an outdoor fireplace. They'd spent many a night out there. Nights where he'd tormented himself and watched how firelight danced over that soft, ivory skin—

"How does it feel?"

Don't ask. Mentally, he swore and then looked down at his hand. It was still red. It still hurt. And he had a feeling it was going to blister, too. "It hurts like a bitch," he said honestly. "Ah, why don't you go get dressed? You can turn the bacon down, or off, for a few minutes. And I'll just stand here and not mess with anything since I seem to be screwing everything up today."

A faint blush crept up her cheeks, dusting her skin with a soft pink. "Yeah. Probably not a bad idea to grab some clothes. I'll be back in a few."

"Take your time." He flexed his hand and wiggled his fingers. "I'm at your mercy right now. If I try to cook with my head where it is, I'm going to burn the place down."

As it was, he was going to walk with a permanent limp or something if he couldn't get his thoughts on a safer track. Priority number one was seeing Abby in something other than that short, thin robe.

"It's going to blister," Abigale said, nibbling on her lip as she pulled Zach's hand out of the water. They'd soaked it a good thirty minutes while she finished up breakfast, but it was still red. His palm felt rough against hers and his fingers were long. She had to suppress a shiver at the memory of the feel of them on her skin as she studied the burn. *Help . . . you're supposed to be helping. Not lusting.*

Except she was still thinking about number five on her list. Right?

"Serves me right," Zach said, tugging his hand away. "I was distracted and that's never a good idea with hot grease splattering around, right? Come on. I'm hungry."

"Go sit at the breakfast nook. I'll bring the food."

"I can get the food. Why don't you get us something to drink?" He flexed his hand and added, "I suspect I should stay away from the coffeepot."

She laughed. "I don't think you're a hazard in the kitchen all of a sudden, Zach."

He grumbled something under his breath that she couldn't quite make out, but as he grabbed the plates, she didn't see the point in arguing with him. She already had one cup of coffee but she refilled his. He was going on his third cup.

"You have a bad night last night?" she asked as she put his coffee down.

He shot her a sidelong look and shrugged. "Didn't sleep well."

They lapsed into silence for a few minutes as they ate although Abigale had to force herself to do more than pick at the food. It was like chewing on sawdust. How in the hell was she going to be able to follow through on number five when lately all she could think about was Zach?

"You done anything else with this infamous new plan of yours?" he asked, bumping her with his shoulder.

In the process of slipping a bite of the omelet into her mouth, she froze. She lowered the fork to the plate and sat there as she chewed, stalled a minute by taking a sip of the juice she'd poured for them both. She should have made screwdrivers, damn it.

"So far, no," she said honestly. "There's just the . . ." She glanced over her shoulder at the hip closest to him and then shrugged. "That."

He grinned. "It's called a tattoo. How is it looking?"

"How would I know?" She made a face at him. "I've never had one and I can't exactly see it all that well. But I'm doing what you told me to do. So . . ."

"I'll take a look."

As he slid off the stool, her breath froze in her lungs. "Ah, is it really that big a deal?"

Long, warm fingers brushed against her skin, nudging her forward. "If it's not healing well, yeah. You want it looking good, don't you?"

Her breath hitched a little as he tugged the waistband of the wraparound skirt she wore out of the way, easing it lower. "It's looking fine," he said after a minute.

Face flaming, she focused on the plate in front of her, keeping her head bowed as he settled back on the stool. "So why haven't you done anything else? The Roger thing *really* needs to happen, by the way."

"Oh, I know." She tried to get rid of some of the tension trapped inside, but instead of subsiding, it was mounting. Her skin felt hot and her heart was racing. Faster and faster. Still, as she took another sip of her juice, she was damned proud to see that her hand was steady. "I was planning on doing it this week, but it's like everything known to man has gone wrong. A couple of my employees were sick so I was working shorthanded. Then I had to cover for Grace . . ."

She trailed off and shrugged. "It's been one thing after another. Endlessly."

A sly grin curled his lips as he looked at her. "You could call him now."

"You just want to hear me tell him off," she said, laughing a little. She'd always suspected Zach hadn't exactly loved the guy, but she hadn't realized just how deep his dislike had run. He'd kept it hidden pretty damn well, because she'd never *seen* it, and she should have.

"Maybe I do." He shrugged a little and shifted around on the stool, lifting one leg to brace his foot on her stool, while stretching his other out behind her. She could feel the heat of him, he was so close. She felt almost surrounded by him now. "How's the *not worrying* thing going?"

A faint smile curled her lips and she shot a look at him. Immediately, her heart flipped over a little in her chest and she had to remind herself just what she was supposed to be doing. Saying . . . he'd asked something . . . oh, yeah. She remembered now. "That's actually going a little easier. I'm not all keyed up to get to every single thing on the list right away, which is good. There are a *few* things I wanted to do right away, but I'm not letting it twist me up."

"Was Roger one of them?"

"Yeah." She reached for her juice but instead of drinking it, she just braced it between her hands and spun it back and forth, staring down into the glass. "I know what I want to say to him. I have it all jotted down . . ."

"Jotted down." He started to laugh. "Abby, did you go and make a damned script or something?"

She glared at him.

He just laughed harder.

She shot out a hand and poked him in the ribs. It was like jabbing a hand into a rock wall. "You jackass," she muttered as he kept on laughing. She shoved a hand against his shoulder and he caught her hand around the wrist. "It wasn't a *script*. I just . . . hell. I made notes."

"Notes . . ." He stroked his thumb over her wrist. "So you made notes. Why haven't you called him?"

She tugged on her wrist but he didn't let go. Sighing, she shrugged. "It just hasn't happened yet. You know . . . Never mind." She went to slide off the stool, but before she could, the hand on her wrist slid up to her arm.

"What?"

"Nothing."

His thumb stroked against the inside of her arm and the dark blue of his eyes bored into hers, like he could see clear into her soul. "That look on your face isn't nothing, Abs," Zach said, his voice a low, soft rumble. "Something's bothering you."

She swallowed and stared off past his shoulder. "It's Roger . . ."

The grip on her arm tightened for just a second and then he tugged her off the stool, into the vee of his legs. Her heart, already racing, jumped up into a gallop that just couldn't be healthy. That scent of his, all soap and male skin and the detergent he used on his clothes, shot straight to her head. Her mouth started to water and instead of looking up at him, she rested her head on his shoulder. "You can't keep letting that dickhead twist you up, Abby," he said, stroking a hand up her back to curve it over the back of her neck.

She wanted to whimper. Instead, she forced herself to talk. "It's not that. Not exactly." The last thing she wanted him thinking was that she was still all terribly upset over what had happened with Roger. Logically, she *should* be but she just wasn't. "It's what he said . . . about not being true to myself. I *know* I don't want that life back. He's out of his mind, and I know it. But I keep hearing him say that, *You're not being true to yourself*, and it's echoing in my mind. Now I'm wondering if maybe there's something else that is missing from my life that I just can't see. Does that make sense? Something that I *do* want, but I can't see it?"

He sighed. She felt the motion of it, felt his chest rise and fall against hers and she had to bite back a whimper. Then he pressed a kiss to her temple. "You've spent so much of your life trying to control everything you could, Abby. There are probably a lot of things you want that you can't see. Just . . . hell, just try not to worry. Let your life happen for a while." Then his voice took on a teasing slant as he added, "After all, she who shall not be named can't exactly come back into your life and take things over again, right?"

She laughed a little and lifted her head to look at him. "That's true," she murmured.

The breath caught in her lungs as their gazes locked.

Things that she wanted that she couldn't see . . . Right

now the problem was that she knew exactly *what* . . . no . . . she knew *who* she wanted. But it wasn't a good idea . . .

He reached up and tugged on her hair. "So what's the other thing you planned on doing, Abby?"

You.

The word almost jumped out of her. She had to fight to keep it locked inside and not just because it sounded trashier than hell. She wasn't exactly planning on *doing* a man. She'd planned to have an affair. A torrid affair. With a hot guy.

Yet the only guy she could even imagine doing this with right now was Zach.

"Ah . . ."

That familiar smile of his, a little devious, a little wicked, curled his lips as he wound one of her curls around his finger. "What is it, Abby? You weren't planning something really bad, were you? Going to rob a bank? Get a part-time job as a stripper?"

She snorted and eased back away from him, reminding herself that she needed to breathe. She needed to think. That was what she needed to do. "Sure, Zach. I'm going to become the Stripper Bank Robber. I'll wear a mask and a G-string and pasties."

"Can I be your getaway driver? I'd love to see this," he teased, his voice husky.

And the look in his eyes was . . .

Whoa. Her mouth went dry and again, her skin felt all hot and tight. She couldn't seem to suck in enough oxygen. "Well, you'll just have to picture it your dreams. Stripping and bank robbing weren't on the list."

"I dunno . . ." A wicked light glinted in his eyes and he leaned in closer. "You look awful guilty, sugar. Just what else is on the list?"

Get up. Walk away. You need to think—

That voice, the voice of reason, the voice of sense, the voice she'd listened to her entire adult life, seemed to shriek at her, blaring a warning loud and long as she stared at him.

Another voice, sly and seductive, whispered, *you said you'd stop worrying. You wanted to live . . .*

The dark brown of her eyes seemed to burn as she stared at him.

Zach was torn between just closing the distance between them and just calling this whole idea off. More than seventeen fucking years, damn it. That's how long he'd loved her and she'd never known.

But you've never told her.

Yeah, because she'd never seemed to—

Abby slid her off her stool.

Mentally, he sighed. Shoving a hand through his hair, he glanced away from her, tried to find something else to look at, focus on, think about. He'd been teasing her and pushing her as far as he figured he could go without saying outright, "I read the damn journal. If you have to have an affair, why not me?" But she wasn't exactly following and—

Her hand touched his shoulder.

Zach looked back her. His heart seemed to jump up into his throat as she closed the distance between them.

Everything in the world faded away as she pushed up onto her toes.

And then, as she leaned in and pressed her lips to his, Zach realized this was what it was like to have a dream actually come true. As her mouth parted under his, he was almost certain he was dying. Maybe he'd already died. Yeah. He'd been eating something and choked, died, and now he was in heaven.

Except he figured there was no way he would end up there.

So maybe Abby really was kissing him. Groaning, he reached for her and hauled her closer, pulling her to stand between his legs. With one arm wrapped around her waist, he slid his free hand up her back and tangled it in the crazy, soft curls of her hair. Soft as silk, just like he remembered.

And her mouth was sweet, every bit as sweet as he remembered, but there was no director, no crew, no brilliant stage lights shining down and this kiss wasn't choreographed or scripted.

Abby wasn't kissing him because she had to, wasn't kissing him because it was in some fucking script, and she wasn't going to pull away and make some stupid joke to break the tension.

Abby was kissing him, damn it.

It was *real*.

Real, and he was going to make the most of it.

Using his grip on her hair to tug her head back, he tasted and teased the curve of her lower lip and dipped inside her mouth to stroke her tongue with his own.

She whimpered and arched closer.

Closer, so that through the thin silk of the tank she'd pulled on, he could feel the soft weight of her breasts, the lush curves of her body and it wasn't enough. He wanted, no, he *needed* more, but . . .

Tearing his mouth away, he buried his face against her neck.

Her body vibrated against his.

"Abby . . ." he whispered, all too aware of how ragged his voice sounded. All too aware of the fact that his hands were probably shaking and the muscles in his body were bunched, tensed, ready to take.

But what in the hell was going on?

Her hands stroked up his arms, one curving around his neck while the other slid into his hair.

Her lips brushed against his cheek as she turned her head. "I could tell you one of the other steps, Zach, but you'd either think I was crazy or you'd worry about me."

Lifting his head, he stared at her with a narrow gaze. Her face was flushed and her eyes were a little glassy. But she didn't look away. Long seconds ticked by and then she tried to ease back from him.

No, damn it. She wasn't pulling back now.

Glancing around, he studied their surroundings and then he grabbed his stool with one hand, keeping his right arm banded around her waist. He managed to drag the damn thing a foot or two down the length of the breakfast nook to the bar and then he sat down.

Abby yelped as he lifted her up onto his lap and the skin on his burned hand screamed at him. He ignored both. Her skirt tangled around her legs and *that* was a bit of a hindrance, but he tugged and pulled until she was sitting astride him with the skirt tucked up around the sweet swell of her hips.

Rushing it, man. Pushing too far, a calm, rational voice said. But how the hell could he be rushing it? He'd loved her for most of his life and his problem was that he'd never made a move. Now *she* had and damn it, he wasn't letting her walk away just like that.

"The only thing that worries me about your life is the fact that you never really live it," he said, hooking his arm around her shoulders and staring at her.

Her face was flushed and her eyes were overbright. Her gaze bounced around like she couldn't look at him and she kept squirming around—considering her position, that made things *very* interesting. "Abby . . . be still, damn it."

She wiggled even more. "Put me down, Zach."

"Why?"

"Because . . ." She stopped and then lifted her eyes to stare at him. Her tongue came out to wet her lips and because he just couldn't stop himself, he pushed his hand into her hair, tangled it around his fingers, and took her mouth.

The way he'd always dreamed about.

It was a moment made for dreams, it seemed.

Every time he'd thought about doing this, he'd been certain he'd get any reaction other than this. Anything but her hunger. Anything but her meeting him ragged breath for ragged breath, hungry touch for hungry touch. Desperate kiss for desperate kiss.

A soft, startled gasp escaped her and he swallowed it down. Yet another dream came true as he felt her wiggle closer and wrap her legs around his hips and arch closer.

Abby . . . he had Abby on his lap and she had those lush, wonderful legs wrapped around him.

Fisting one hand in the tangle of her skirt, he dragged it higher, forcing the layers of material up out of the way until he could rest his palm on bare skin. The fabric brushed against the back of his burnt hand and pain slashed through him, but it faded in comparison to everything else.

Her arms wrapped around his neck as he slid his hand back behind her hips, nudging her closer. Closer . . .

Fuck . . . right there—

A broken moan escaped her as she tore her mouth away, her head falling forward to slump on his shoulder. Her nails bit into his shoulders, tension rocketing through her body as she started to rock against him and through her panties, through his jeans, he felt the heat of her.

Using his grip on her curls, he tugged her head back and pressed his lips to the hollow at the base of her neck. At the same time, he held her hips steady and started to move her, battling back the urge to come up off the damn stool and spread her out on the bar next to him.

No. Not the bar. Not enough room there.

The floor . . . nah. The table. Room there. Lots of it. He could undo the tie on her skirt, like he was unwrapping a present. Strip away her tank . . .

He settled for guiding her hips back and forth across the painfully hard ridge of his cock, listening to her broken gasps. When he heard her whisper his name, her voice a little dazed, he almost lost it. Damn near came in his jeans like a teenager.

Her hands came up, dipping into his hair as he used his chin to nudge the strap of her tank out of the way, nuzzling and nibbling his way down the smooth, pale flesh. The swell of her breasts was right there . . . so fucking close.

Maybe he could—

Her body tightened.

Her knees tightened around his hips and she arched, her body a lovely, sweet bow. "Zach . . . ?"

Turning his head, he caught the lobe of her ear between his teeth and bit down. "Come for me, damn it." Too many years spent wanting her and now, everything he wanted, everything he needed was right here. "Come for me, Abby . . ."

Those husky words sent her flying higher than she'd ever been.

Unable to breathe, unable to see, caught in the circle of his arms and the heat of his body, Abby experienced a climax that all but devastated her. The oxygen seemed to disappear from the world. And it took the light with it. For long, long minutes, she was blind, deaf to anything and everything.

And then, as rational thought started to intrude, she forced her eyes to open.

They were moving.

Or rather, *Zach* was.

The hot rush of blood leaped to her cheeks as those stupid rational thoughts started to intrude, but she couldn't very well spring away from him and get herself under control because he was carrying her.

"If you try to jump away from me, you're going to hurt us," Zach said quietly, pressing a kiss to her temple. "Walking up the stairs and having panic attacks aren't very good combinations."

Her tongue seemed to glue itself to the roof of her mouth, but she managed to get the words out. "Why . . ." Okay. She got *one* word out. Clearing her throat, she tried again. "Why are we going upstairs?"

"Because I want to sit down and hold you for a little while without you taking off and locking yourself in your room. I figured I'd just lock myself in there with you."

Her brain shut down.

Locked in her room.

With Zach.

That sounded so very appealing.

And it felt even better, she had to admit a few minutes later as he laid her down and tucked himself up behind her, one arm wrapped around her waist, his palm flat against her belly. The heat of him spread through her body, lulling her, calming her, seducing her.

Too perfect for words, she decided.

She could handle this, she thought. As long as she didn't think. As long as she didn't—

Watch out, her brain warned her. *You're starting to think.*

Desperately, she closed her eyes and tried to clear her mind. *Focus on him. Just him. He feels nice, right?*

Oh, yes. He felt better than nice. Better than anything she'd ever felt, really.

But what in the hell is going on? You were going to think things through and now—

Stop it. The calm, rational part of her mind got a little louder. But it just wasn't enough and before she even realized it, she blurted out, "What in the hell just happened?"

Zach's lips touched the back of her neck. "Well, I'm no expert, but I think you kissed me," he said, his voice teasing. "And I'm pretty sure we both enjoyed it. But maybe we should try again."

And then she found herself on her back, staring up into a pair of dark blue eyes that she knew very, very well. They'd always seemed to glint with mischief, or trouble . . . but she'd never realized just how much they glinted with *that* kind of trouble.

Not until now.

As his mouth came down on hers again, Abby barely had time to catch her breath. Then she was wondering why she'd even bothered. He stole the oxygen right out of her with his kiss. His tongue stroked along hers, moving into her mouth with an easy assurance that belied his words.

I'm no expert.

Oh, yes. Yes, he was.

She whimpered as he took the kiss deeper.

The hand on her belly caught the material of her skirt, dragging it upward and although panic crowded inside her head, there was nothing in her that could make herself pull away. Nothing that would make her say *stop*.

He'd do it. There was no doubt in her mind.

The problem was she didn't *want* him to stop.

As his fingers flirted with the waistband of her panties, Zach lifted his mouth from hers and whispered, his breath dancing over her swollen, sensitive lips, "Abby . . . ?"

She knew what he was asking. He was giving her a chance to call a halt to this. A halt to this crazy, insane . . . what was this thing?

Swallowing, she forced herself to open her eyes and stare at him. "What's going on, Zach?"

He sighed and instead of slipping his hand inside her panties, he smoothed a palm over her thigh. He lowered his head, resting it on her breasts. "That's the twenty-thousand-dollar question, I guess, isn't it?"

She felt the puff of air against her sensitive skin and groaned as her nipples responded, tightening as though he'd been nibbling on them instead of just talking to her. This was insane.

Completely insane.

She'd just had the climax of her life . . . with Zach. And both of them were still fully clothed. They hadn't had sex. They'd only barely been making out and she'd come harder than she could ever remember coming in her life.

Insane.

And all she wanted to do was strip herself naked, make him do the same so they could see just how far they could ride this insanity.

"We should stop." Her body shrieked at the very idea of it. So did just about every other part of her. Hell, even her mind wasn't getting on board with the idea of *stopping*. She closed her eyes. "Shouldn't we?"

He rubbed his cheek against her skin. "Is that what you want?"

No. Terror locked the word in her throat. Yes, she'd been the one to kiss him and yes, she wanted more, so much more. Lately, the things she seemed to want from Zach terrified her. But he was her best friend. There was nobody she loved more than him, nobody who meant more. He was . . . everything.

What if she lost that?

The weight of his head left her breast and she opened her eyes to find him watching her, with his measured, steady gaze. "Abs . . ." He stroked a hand along her cheek, cupped her face in his palm.

Licking her lips, she nudged him back. "Let me up a minute."

Something flashed through his eyes. It might have been disappointment, she thought. But she was afraid to think about it too long.

As he eased away, she shifted away from him and climbed off the bed to pace. "I'd say something like this is crazy. Except I kissed you so it's not like this came out of nowhere." She shoved her hair back from her face.

"Are you trying to tell me you wish you hadn't kissed me?"

She shot him a look and then wished she hadn't.

Wow.

How in the hell hadn't she noticed this before . . .

He sat with his back pressed against her headboard. The walls of her bedroom were pale green and the headboard was white. The boards were reclaimed wood and the overall feel of her room was a shabby chic look, feminine without being too fussy. Zach should have looked incredibly out of place on her bed, with his beat-up jeans and black t-shirt. But he didn't.

He looked like he belonged there. In her room. With her, with that faint smile on his face and that intimate, watchful look in his eyes. The vivid color of his tattoos wound around his arms and she found herself wanting to pull his shirt off and learn the detail of those tattoos in ways she'd never done before.

He was too beautiful for words.

Logically, she *knew* that. She'd appreciated the sheer beauty of him before. But *knowing* it and having it hit her like this were two very different things. Her belly, all hot and tight, twisted with need as she stood there staring at him and it took her a few more seconds to remember that he'd asked her something. A question. Oh, yeah.

"No," she said. She didn't regret kissing him at all. "I just . . ." She shook her head and shifted her gaze to somewhere other than him.

"Why did you kiss me?"

Blood rushed to her face and she turned away, focusing her attention on the sprawling window that stared out over the desert. At night, she could stare out at the spread of the sky and feel lost in the beauty of it. During the day, she could stare at the desert and find some peace in the chaos of her day.

But right now, it wasn't working.

Hearing a faint movement behind her, she turned around as he came to a stop just inches away. "No answer?" he murmured, reaching out to tug on a lock of her hair.

She jerked her chin up and fell back on the attitude that had gotten her through things when little else could. "Hey, it was a spur-of-the-moment thing. I could always ask *you* why you kissed me *back*," she shot off.

A hot grin appeared on his face and he dipped his head to whisper in her ear. "But I can give you an answer for that. Are you really sure you want to hear it?"

Abigale rolled her eyes and tried to back away from him. But he followed her. Step-by-step, until she stood with her back braced against the wall just by the window, the heat of the sun already warming her skin. "I probably already know what it is," she said, curling her lip at him. "You're a man, right?"

"Well . . . there is that." He closed his hands around her hips, holding her steady as he leaned against her. She felt the heat of him, the length of his cock like a brand against her belly and her breath caught in her lungs, lodged there as he started to rock, slow and steady.

Each movement sent flickers of heat flying through her, turning her brain into absolute mush.

"But there's the real reason." He rubbed his lips against hers. "You see . . . I've only been waiting for you to kiss me for a good long while now. I can't be held responsible for liking it when you finally do it."

As he took her mouth again, a hot wave of delight flooded her.

That skirt of hers was going to be the end of him, Zach decided as he gathered the flowing material back up in his hands, dragging it up over the length of her legs. Once he could palm the curve of her ass, he nipped her lower lip and then lifted his head and stared down at her. "I wanted you to kiss me. I wanted to kiss you . . . and I wanted to do this . . . feel you, just like this. And a hell of a lot more, Abby."

She blinked up at him, her eyes wide and dazed, fogged with heat, with surprise. Her tongue slid out to wet her lips and he followed the path it had taken with his eyes, ready to devour her, completely.

But he needed to slow this down.

She was already nervous as hell and he wasn't about to blow this.

"Do you want to know what else I've wanted to do?" he whispered, shifting until he could push one thigh between her legs.

Her lashes fluttered down and he watched her head fall back, exposing the elegant line of her neck. Sweeping his head down, he raked his teeth along the delicate curve and then muttered against her ear, "Do you want to know?"

Long seconds ticked away, broken only by the ragged sounds of their breathing. But then, finally, she said, "Yes."

Easing back, he caught her hands and guided them down until she was the one holding her skirt up. A bright pink blush settled on her cheeks but she held his gaze as he lifted his eyes to look at her. "This skirt is going to drive me out of my fucking mind," he said conversationally. "Just like *that* and you're naked, you know that?"

A grin danced around her lips. "Well, that's the thing about clothes. If you wear them, you're clothed. If not, you're naked."

"This skirt ain't much different." It covered everything, but it was just a dream, really. One tug and it would fall away. But he didn't want that. Not yet. Stepping back, he studied her, her skirt hiked up, baring the blush-colored fabric of her panties, the lush curve of her thighs and hips. Placing his hand on her belly, he continued to watch her as he eased his way down . . . down . . . down.

Her breath hitched in her chest, causing her breasts to rise and fall. He used one hand to nudge the straps of her tank down her shoulders. The pretty, lacy straps of her bra remained and he dipped his head, pressing his lips to the lace. "I want you naked, Abby."

"Zach . . ."

He heard the hesitancy in her voice and he murmured, "Shhh . . . not yet. Not yet."

He wasn't rushing this. No way in hell.

Besides, he had just slid his hand inside Abby's damned panties and he could feel the silky curls against his fingers and hot damn, he thought he just might come from that alone. "I've wanted this," he muttered against her skin. Leaning in closer, he braced his free arm on the wall over her head and listened to her ragged sigh as he circled his index finger over the tight little bud of her clitoris.

She cried out, the sound of it bouncing off the walls around him. "Like that?" he murmured, giving her another slow stroke. Then he moved in a quicker, firmer rhythm and felt her buck against him. "Or like that?"

"Zach . . . please!"

She was hot as the desert sun under his touch, but slick and wet as rain, and so perfect. He wanted to go to his knees before her, taste her, worship her, love her . . . instead, he stayed where he was, forgetting about the rest of the world as he stroked his fingers over her sweet, swollen flesh.

Her nails bit into his sides, her hips rocking forward, fast, hungry. "Damn it, Zach," she groaned.

"Do you want more?"

"Yes!"

"Push your panties down, then." He kept his free arm on the wall. He wasn't making love to her today, damn it. He'd finally gotten her to see him and this wasn't going to be a onetime thing.

But he couldn't listen to that hungry, desperate plea in her voice, either.

Her hands were shaking as she reached for the waistband of her panties, stretched tight around his hand. He held still as she pushed them down but then they caught around her knees and she swayed as she shimmied her way out of them. Feeling the soft, warm weight of her body as he braced himself against her was almost his undoing.

Almost.

He held on through will alone. Teeth gritted, eyes closed, he kept his face buried against her neck until he thought he could continue without losing what little control he maintained.

"Spread your legs, sugar."

He felt her weight shift and then he lifted his head, stared into her eyes. Soon, damn it, he told himself as he eased his finger down and started to circle her entrance. Soon he'd be preparing her to take *him* inside . . . not just his finger, but him. All of him.

And please, please . . . let her want to keep him. Forever.

Because he couldn't think about that and keep her from seeing more than he was ready to show her, he shoved it all aside and focused just on this. The slick, clenched feel of her sex as he pushed one finger inside. She tightened around him and the feel of it was sheer bliss, glory . . . perfection. He wanted more. Needed it, but he settled for burying his finger inside her and then slowly retreating. Then again . . . again . . . as she started to rock against him, he added a second finger and started to rotate his wrist, screwing them in and out of the sweet, slick well and listening as she cried out.

"That's it, sugar," he muttered, watching her face, watching as her eyes took on that dazed, lost look, watching as a flush spread up her neck, across her breasts. "Come again. I want to see it, I want to feel it . . ."

She gave him all of that and more. And when she sagged against him as it ended, she wrapped her arms around him and let him carry her back to the bed.

Chapter Seven

"You never answered me."

Abigale lay sprawled on her belly, her head on Zach's chest, and for once, her brain was a dazed, blissful blank. "Huh?"

She looked up to see him watching her. The smile on his face was one that made her heart flip over in her chest, for the oddest damn reasons. It wasn't that wicked grin, and it wasn't the mischievous one, either. She loved both of those, but this was a smile that was a little more rare from him and it was one that had always melted her heart.

It was almost the same smile she'd seen on his face when she saw him holding his baby nephew for the first time. A lot of pleasure, mixed with awe . . . but this was different, because he was looking at her, a grown woman and there was something possessive in his gaze, too. She couldn't quite define it, but having him look at her like that was doing bad, bad things to her.

"You didn't answer me," he said again, reaching up to brush her hair back.

She caught his hand to distract herself. Her brain had

just realigned with her body and she knew what he was talking about. And everything in her screamed . . . *Stall!* So she did. The brilliant red burn along the back of his hand had her wincing in sympathy. And sure enough, it was starting to blister in a few places. "We should be more careful."

Zach grunted and tugged his hand away. "It's fine. I've gotten worse helping my brother on his bike." Then he grimaced and wiggled his fingers. "Granted, it's usually not as big as this but still." He stretched his arm over his head and focused back on her face. "You're still avoiding the question."

"No." She wrinkled her nose and sat up, heaving out a sigh. "I'm actually trying to figure out the right answer. I . . . damn it, Zach, you went and got in the way of a good plan, you know that?"

"And how did I do that?"

She closed her eyes. There was no getting around this. She either had to come clean and explain about the journal or just screw the idea entirely. But he might be mad . . .

"Fuck it." She shoved up off the bed and walked over to the little secretary where she kept her journal. As of a few weeks ago, her pretty little leather-bound journal had picked up a partner, the paperback one titled *Wreck This Journal.* "By the way, just so you know ahead of time, this wouldn't have happened if you hadn't bought me this goofy journal. So keep that in mind if you get mad at me when I go to explain all of this."

She turned around to see him pushing up onto his elbow, gold-streaked brown hair falling around his face, blue eyes locked on her face, and that long, lean body showcased in jeans and a black t-shirt. Once more, she found her gaze drawn to the tattoos twining around his arms and she wanted to go to him, kneel down by him, and just spend hours learning his body.

"Be mad about what?" he asked, lifting a brow at her and drawing her attention back to the matter at hand.

A conversation.

They were having a conversation. Right?

Tapping the journal against her palm, she sighed. "My new plan."

"Why would I be mad about your new plan?"

It wasn't so easy to force the words out now. Wasn't so easy at all . . . a knot the size of baseball lodged in her throat and she could feel her breath coming in harsh little bursts as she stared at him. "I . . ." She stopped and licked her lips. "I—*shit.*"

She covered her eyes with one hand and tried to find the words. "Look, damn it, I wasn't planning on this. None of this. I just . . ." Lowering her hand, she stared at him. "I felt empty inside and I . . . I wanted to not feel empty. So these ideas . . . they kind of came to me. The tattoo. The thing with Roger."

Slowly, Zach pushed up into a sitting position, his eyes narrowing on her face. Drawing his knees upright, he braced his elbows on them and continued to watch her. "The photographers . . . not worrying. All of that sounds fine. What's to get mad about?"

"I also planned on having an affair."

A muscle jerked in his jaw and something dark moved through his eyes. But to her surprise, it wasn't anger that she got from him. "Abby, you're thirty years old . . . that's plenty old enough for an affair."

"Except I can't think about anybody else anymore," she snapped, glaring at him. "The past few weeks all I can think about is *you*. And I can't have a damned affair with *you*. You're my best friend. I love you and I can't—"

He rolled off the bed and the words lodged in her throat as he came prowling across the carpet toward her.

When he reached out and caught her arms in his hands, the book fell from numb hands to bounce onto the carpet. Abigale barely even noticed. "Why not?" he murmured, stroking his thumb along the skin of her arm.

Who in the hell would ever have believed such a simple

touch could be so amazing? But it was . . . it was like he was stroking her everywhere else, all at once. "Why not what?" she asked, dazed.

"Why not have an affair with me?" His hair fell around them as he lowered his head and caught her mouth. Right before he kissed her, he muttered, "I think I've made it pretty damn clear that I want you like hell."

"But . . ."

He stole the breath from her with a kiss. "But what?"

"We're friends, Zach."

"Yes." He eased her closer and the feel of him against her was nothing she could even describe. One hand slid around to press against her back, his fingers splayed wide and she shuddered at the feel of it.

"I . . ." She shook her head and said, "I don't want some friends with benefits thing with you. You're my best friend and I . . ." Her voice trailed off because she just didn't know what else to say.

"Friends with benefits . . ." He laughed, hooking his other arm around her neck. "Sugar . . . friends with benefits is too casual for the kind of friendship we have. The kind we've always had. But I still want you."

He boosted her up into his arms and reflexively, she wrapped her legs around him, groaning at the feel of him between her thighs.

Staring down at him as he carried her back over to the bed, she tried to let her brain catch up to everything that was happening, but it just didn't seem possible. He lay her down and bent over her, watching her with a stark, hungry look on his face as he started to drive his hips against hers.

Heat streaked through her and she gasped, reaching up and catching onto his arms, her fingers digging into the swell of muscle there. "Zach!"

He drove his hips against hers again and again and she was so damned wet, she could feel the fabric of her skirt sliding back and forth over her slick flesh. It was so damned erotic, it sent every last nerve ending aflame.

"Do you feel that, sugar?" he demanded, hunkering

down over her and catching her chin in his hand. "Nothing casual . . . not in what we have friendship-wise, and not what I want from you. You want to live? You want to have an affair? Do it with me, Abby. I'll make love to you and leave myself branded on your skin and when you're ready, if you want to walk, you can walk. But nothing will change our friendship or what I feel for you."

Her eyes were glassy as she stared up at him. Slowing down to a stop, Zach cradled her face in his hands and brushed his thumb over the curve of her lower lip. "Abby . . ."

"Zach." Her lids fluttered down and for a long moment, she lay there, her breath coming in hot little pants, her breasts heaving under his chest.

He had to fight back the urge to start kissing her all over again, strip away her clothing, and take everything that he had wanted for so long. Because he'd wanted this, needed this . . . needed *her*, though, he had to wait and he knew it. So he contented himself with staring down at her gently flushed face, the dark fan her lashes made against her cheeks, and the pretty bow of her mouth.

Finally, she lifted her lashes and looked up at him. "You're making this damned hard, you know."

"You're one to talk," he teased, nudging his hips against the soft heat between her thighs.

A blush lit up her face and she jabbed him in the side. "Stop it. I'm trying to be serious." Then she slid her hand up his side, along his neck to slide it into his hair. "And what happens if we do this and things get screwed up, Zach? You're the most important person in my life. I can't lose that."

"You're overthinking this . . . but to answer that . . . you're the most important person in my life, too, and you know it." He pressed his brow to hers. "We've handled everything else life has thrown at us and plenty of it wasn't fun. This could be damn fun. Sex doesn't have to screw things up. We just lay the rules out now . . . and we stick to them."

"Rules?" She wrinkled her nose at him and then nudged his chest. "Rules and an affair don't seem to go hand in hand very well."

Rolling off to the side, he watched as she sat up and shoved her hair back from her face. "Anybody who doesn't lay some sort of ground rules is asking for trouble." *I promise I'm not going to rush you. That's rule number one for me . . . not that I'm going to explain that just yet.* Then he reached over and caught a lock of her hair, winding the dark curl around his finger. "It's not like we're writing a guidebook for it or anything. Just laying things out so we understand things. If we do this, then we have a right to know what to expect from each other. I won't be seeing anybody else when we're together . . . I'd appreciate the same from you."

She slid him a look from under her lashes. "Well, seeing as how so many men are beating a path to my door, that's going to be hard . . . but that's a deal."

"So does that mean . . . yes?" His heart just about jumped into his throat and it was a damn good thing he was laying down because if he hadn't been, he might have found himself falling over his damned feet. Abby . . . shit. Abby was going to—his brain blanked out.

He was going to have an *affair* with her? Like hell. What he was going to do was make her fall in love with him, damn it.

But she hadn't answered . . . jerking his eyes up to her face, he found her watching him, that hesitant look in her eyes. Hesitant. Watchful. Like she didn't know what in the hell to think. *Think about* me. He wanted her to be as caught up in him as he was in her. That was what he wanted. What he needed.

Rubbing his thumb over the silk of her hair, he waited.

And then she leaned down, pressed her mouth to his. He held still, letting her take the lead, although it almost killed him when he felt the tip of her tongue teasing his lips. He opened for her, but still just waited . . . played the willing recipient and when she took the kiss deeper, he groaned and slid his hand up to cup the back of her head.

Just when he thought he was going to lose control, she broke the kiss and lifted her head, her gaze full of heat and smoke and wonder. "Yeah, Zach," she whispered. "I think it's a yes."

Then she bit her lip and laid a hand on his chest, stroked it down.

Chapter Eight

Abigale glared at her reflection.

Nothing worked right.

Zach wanted to take her out to dinner and damn it, even though she had a damned closetful of clothes, *nothing* worked.

The black jersey dress that was her fallback just seemed too hot and clingy.

The green silk was too dressy.

And—

"Damn it," she swore, spinning away from the mirror and tearing at the zipper of the dark blue sheath she'd just tried on. All of the colors were the right ones for her, but nothing seemed to suit her.

Part of the problem was *her*, though.

She was edgy and had been ever since he'd left her house without doing much more than kissing her again—*after* she'd told him, *Yes, I'll have an affair with you.*

Maybe not in so many words, but she'd agreed to have an affair with Zach. Her best friend. The person she turned to when everything in her world was falling apart.

And here she was. Falling apart. Falling for *him*, it seemed. And what was she *doing*?

Having an affair . . . with him. But they hadn't even had sex yet.

Yet. She wanted him so bad, so damn bad, she ached with it and they hadn't done anything more than some killer make out sessions. Her body was all tight and achy just thinking about it, her heart kept jumping into these odd little twitchy races that stole the breath out of her and if she didn't know better, she'd think she was having a heart attack.

No, she was just dying from want, but had Zach done anything?

After the make out session to end all make out sessions, had he done anything to follow through?

No.

Damn it.

Throwing the dress down, she moved into the closet and stared at her clothes. She had plenty of them. Nice stuff. Not designer stuff like she might have had if she'd stayed in LA but that didn't matter. It was still seriously gorgeous clothing and—

The ringing of the phone interrupted her train of thought.

Zach.

She rushed over to the phone but the racing of her heart did a slow, hard thud before everything faded to ashes as she saw the name on the caller ID. *Blanche Levine*.

Curling her lip, she turned away.

Mommy Dearest.

Storming back to the closest, she tried to focus on her clothes again, ignoring the ringing of the phone. She might have done just *fine* if her mother hadn't decided to leave a damned voice mail.

Hello, darling. It's Mommy. I heard about the wedding . . . I'm so sorry. You know that if I'd had any input—

Abigale curled her lip. "If you'd had any input, you would have sold me to the highest bidder when I was eighteen."

This Roger just doesn't seem like he was the right man for you. But I'm so sorry you were hurt.

"Yeah. I bet."

I keep trying to get in touch with you. Did that nasty Zach boy—

Spinning on her heel, she stormed over to the phone and snatched it up. "That nasty Zach boy treated me better than you *ever* did, Mother."

"Oh. You are there. Abigale, how are you?"

At some point in the past twenty years, her mother's Midwestern twang had changed to a soft, breathy little drawl that just didn't suit her. Abigale couldn't care less.

"I was doing so much better until *you* called. How in the hell do you keep getting my number? You have any idea how annoying it is to keep getting it changed only to have you track it down?"

A few seconds ticked by before Blanche bothered to answer. This time, she responded in a flat, level voice. "Perhaps if you didn't persist in treating me like a pariah, it wouldn't be needed. Abigale, I'm your mother, I have every right to expect to be treated with the respect that position deserves."

"Oh, really." Abigale smirked. "Mother . . . I'm your daughter. I had every right to expect to be treated with the kindness that position deserves. Instead, you stole my money, you let your boyfriend paw me, and you did every damn thing you could think of to get me to earn more money . . . for *you*. There was *nothing* left for me when I got away from you. *Nothing*."

"I put a great deal of time into your career," Blanche said, her voice cool. So calm and disconnected.

Sometimes, Abigale thought that was what hurt the most. Her mother's complete inability to see why this had hurt her so much. With a sad smile, she shook her head. "You don't get it, Mother. You never will. I'll be calling the phone company on Monday. Save us the headache between now and then . . . don't call again."

Then she cut the call off and tried to brush it aside. Her

mom, in the end, didn't matter, really. And for the most part, she even accepted that. But as she went to lay the phone back in the cradle, her hands were shaking. Trembling, like a leaf in a storm.

"Good-bye, Mom."

This time, she hoped she meant it.

A few minutes later, and a few mental kicks in the butt later, her iPhone chimed a reminder and she groaned, snatching it off her bureau to check the time. Twenty minutes. He was going to be here in twenty minutes and she hadn't even done her hair.

She was still torn between grieving for a relationship she knew she'd never have and kicking herself for even *caring*.

And she had twenty fricking minutes.

Storming into her closet, she stared at the dresses and in desperation, she grabbed a pink one off the hanger. Pink and her didn't always work. It was bullshit that redheads couldn't wear pink. *Some* redheads shouldn't, but she did okay with it, depending on the shade of pink and this one was her shade. The problem was the style of the dress.

Marin had bought it for her and although it fit like a dream, it was so full of subtle sexuality that Abby had never felt right wearing it. It was modest, but there was something about it.

Fingering the material, she sighed and then headed back out into the bedroom. "Once more into the breach." She had to change her bra. It had to be strapless to work with the dress and since she was wearing a different bra, she needed different panties, too. She could feel herself blushing as she found herself pulling out a pair of panties that had garter straps attached. It was sexier than anything she'd worn for Roger, sexier than anything she normally wore.

"That means it's perfect." She was having an affair. Right? That called for sexy. Making up her mind, she found a pair of silk stockings to wear with the rest of the clothing.

Ten minutes later, she found herself standing in front of the mirror, staring at her reflection and panicking.

The dress, just as she'd remembered, fit like a dream. It

looked almost whimsical, almost sweet with the pink material dotted with black polka dots. It was cut with a full circle skirt and nipped in at the waist.

The bust had a black lace overlay and it cupped and curved around her breasts like a lover. She wore a DD bra and the dress's bodice showcased her assets to perfection, she had to admit.

She looked hotter than hell. She knew enough about appearances that she could admit that. Although the makeup was wrong. She hurriedly washed it off and went for a more old-fashioned style, using neutral colors on her eyelids and a darker eyeliner than normal. She echoed the neutral color with her blush and went for bold, bold red on her lips.

There wasn't any time to deal with her hair. Just as she finished applying her lipstick, she heard the doorbell.

Frowning, she checked the time on her phone. Zach only knocked half the time. Why was he bothering now?

She opened the door with a smile.

And it fell immediately as she found herself staring at Roger.

Roger.

Today.

Of all the days. She had to deal with her mother *and* Roger?

What was life trying to do, just grind her into the dirt?

The scumbag stood there with a smile on his face, one that froze as he stared at her. His gaze dropped down to linger on her chest and then jerked back up as she crossed her arms.

"Abigale," he said, clearing his throat. He gave her that charming smile, one she remembered all too well.

Once it had made her sigh with happiness. Roger all but *oozed* normal, nice, controlled. But every once in a while, he'd flash her a certain smile that had just seemed to burn with dirty thoughts. Granted, he'd sucked on the follow-through.

Now she found herself staring at him and thinking, *that looks just a little too practiced*. She wanted to kick herself, too. If *anybody* should realize when somebody was a fake or not, it was somebody who had lived their life selling a lie.

Still staring at him, she arched a brow and waited.

His smile faded as the silence dropped between them, heavy and thick. "I . . . I guess you're not happy to see me," he said softly.

"Whatever gave you that idea?" She tapped her fingers against her arm and wondered where in the hell Zach was.

"Look, Abigale, if you'd give me a few minutes, I can explain. I just wanted what was best for us and I thought—"

The sound of a throaty, powerful engine interrupted him and he frowned, glancing behind him. The sight of the car pulling up in front of the house had him clamping his mouth shut. "You have plans with Zach."

Abigale smiled as Zach climbed out of the car, and then, to her bemusement, she felt her heart skip a few beats—ten at the most—at the site of him. Black shirt stretching across those lean muscles, covering all those lovely, lovely tattoos, but he looked so damned hot, it was almost okay. A pair of slate gray trousers and Italian leather shoes completed his outfit and she realized she felt the urge to fan herself. Zach rarely put on anything but a t-shirt and jeans and the sight of him now had her libido doing bad, bad things.

"Yes." Abigale stared at Zach as he came her way. "I absolutely have plans with Zach." *We're having an affair.*

Abruptly, she realized she didn't like the way that sounded, not even in her own mind. *Affair* sounded cheap. Easy. Disposable. Nothing she'd ever felt for Zach had been cheap, easy, or disposable. Especially not this.

Zach mounted the steps and Roger continued to stand where he was, keeping his body between them. "I take it another one of your brothers is getting married or something and you need a date?" he asked, his mouth pinching a little as he stared at the other man.

Zach lifted a brow and then looked over at Abigale. "What the hell is he doing here?"

She sighed and shrugged. "Beats me. He just rang the

bell and I assumed it was you, so I opened the door without looking." Wrinkling her nose, she added, "I won't make that mistake again anytime soon."

Zach grunted and then, ignoring Roger, he studied her, his gaze lingering first on her mouth and then traveling over her body until he'd reached her feet, clad in a pair of simple black Jimmy Choos. "You look wonderful," he murmured. "Are you ready?"

"Once I get rid of . . . Roger." Her skin hummed a little under that look and she hung on to that nice, pleasant buzz as she looked back at her ex-fiancé. "Roger, Zach and I have a date, so whatever you want, it will have to wait. You can call or e-mail, or whatever. But I'm busy."

She reached for the purse she'd left by the door and grabbed the key fob. She'd arm the system once she was outside. She shut the door, but because Roger hadn't moved, she was trapped uncomfortably close to him as she set the locks.

"Did you say you had a *date*?" he demanded.

Just behind him, she saw Zach standing there. Waiting. The look in his eyes was murderous and his face was set in stony lines, but he held himself still and she appreciated that. Very much. Taking a second to focus her thoughts, she shifted her gaze from Zach's face to Roger's. "Yes. I have a date. With Zach. And you're sort of standing in my way."

"What in the hell does that mean . . . a *date*?"

From the corner of her eye, she saw the look on Zach's face and she shook her head. *Don't*, she thought, hoping he'd understand. She had this under control. "It means just that. A date. We're going out."

"Since when did you two *date*?" Roger snapped.

She circled around him, her arm brushing against his since he wouldn't move out of the way. "Since today," she answered. "Although it's none of your business, really. After all, you can't marry me . . . I'm not being *true* to myself, remember?"

"Damn it, Abby, that's why I'm here." He caught her

arm before she got more than a foot away. "I wanted us to talk."

Staring into his beseeching eyes, she realized it. She'd never seen him before, not clearly. But she did now. This *nice, normal* guy that she'd tried to plan her life around had only been out for one thing.

He'd wanted to use her.

Just like her mother had.

Just like so many others had.

She waited for the pain to slam into her—it should *hurt*, damn it. But it didn't. All she felt was . . . resigned.

The man she'd planned to marry hadn't loved her. And now she realized she probably hadn't loved him, either. She'd just loved the *ideal* of it. Of him. Of them.

That wasn't enough.

"You want to talk," she said softly. "After three weeks, after you called off the wedding and I had to handle all of that mess on my own, you want to *talk*." She shook her head. "No. I don't want to talk to you. I'm done with you. I want to go out with Zach. I want to see a movie, or have dinner, or just go for a drive through the desert—I want to do something that doesn't involve thinking about you, looking at you. I want to be with him."

She glanced over at Zach and smiled a little. "He never expected me to be anything more than what I am, Roger. He was happy with me just being me. And I've finally realized the truth . . . *you* never were."

"I just wanted you to be *happy*. This life isn't you," Roger said. His fingers tightened on her arm.

Too tight now, almost painfully tight.

Looking down at his hand, she said quietly, "You need to let me go now, Roger. And you need to leave. Don't call me. Don't write. Don't come by. You obviously don't know *anything* about me because that *life* you think I want? It made me miserable."

Jerking her arm, she tried to break free.

"Abigale, please, I—"

"That's enough," Zach said, his voice calm and easy. The look in his eyes was anything but and Abigale knew him too well to mistake that calm, level tone for apathy.

Mentally, she swore and then looked up at Roger. He was still staring at her. Good. She moved in toward him, giving him a smile. He blinked, caught off guard. And the feel of him, so much closer now, left her cold. But . . . *yes*, she caught him by surprise and the grip he had on her arm loosened just enough so that when she jerked back, he wasn't able to keep hold.

"Okay, Zach . . ." She turned and gave him a bright smile. "Let's go."

He stroked a hand down her hair, along her shoulder. Then his fingers stroked her arm. The touch sent fire singing through her. And just *when* had that happened? When had Zach developed the ability to turn her blood to lava with one simple touch? she wondered.

"In a minute, Abs," he said quietly, his gaze locked on her arm.

She followed his look and she could have groaned.

She had sensitive skin. Always had. A bump into the wall would leave a bruise on her.

And now her arm bore a vivid red mark where Roger had been holding her arm. He hadn't been hurting her, not really. Yeah, his grip had gotten tight there for a second, but she'd handled it.

As he went to go around her, she caught his arm. "Zach . . . let it go."

He was still staring at Roger like he was trying to decide if he should cut him into two parts, three parts, or four.

"I'll be done in a minute," he said, flashing her that mean little grin, the same one he had on his face when he spoke with her mom. It spoke of bad, bad things, she knew. "You can wait in the car if you want to."

"No." She squeezed his arm. "Zach . . . he's not worth it."

Roger seemed to have been frozen into silence, watching Zach with an expression of macabre fascination and fear. The fear was smart, Abigale knew. Roger had absolutely no idea what Zach was capable of when it came to those he loved.

None.

Under her hand, the muscles in Zach's arm tensed and bunched and she could feel the tension radiating off him. Then he sighed and slanted a look at her. The gold-streaked brown of his hair fell into his eyes and she was tempted to reach up, push it back. But just then, she was afraid to move, afraid to do anything to distract him.

Slowly, he nodded, reaching out to brush his fingers across her arm. Then he looked back at Roger and said softly, "You don't want to touch her again, my friend. Not ever. And if you leave another mark on her, I'm going to turn you inside out. Your own mother won't be able to recognize you when I'm done." A smile curled his lips, one that was so deadly and so beautiful, Abigale felt her blood go cold. "Are we clear?"

Roger didn't say a word as he beat a retreat off her porch.

Seconds ticked away and finally, a heavy sigh escaped Zach.

He scrubbed his hands over his face and turned to look at her. "I want to hunt him down and beat the hell out of him. Just so you know."

"I know." She smiled at him and closed the distance between them as Roger laid rubber, backing out of her driveway. Wrapping her arms around his neck, she said, "Just consider it an exercise in patience. I had to have one all damn afternoon."

"Hmmm." He rubbed his cheek against hers and murmured, "And why is that?"

"A bunch of reasons." She could name about fifty-two dozen and they all started with Zach. But instead of listing those, she rested her head against his shoulder and said, "My damned mother called."

"Ah. She who shall not be named."

Abigale grimaced. "She called and instead of ignoring the call, I answered it." She breathed in his scent and felt a punch of heat spread through her. He was wearing cologne, she realized. Something subtle. Something faintly exotic and dark. It teased her senses and made her want to press her face against him and seek out the source of it.

His palm came up and rested low on her spine. "If it would make you feel better, I could go call her. Yell at her. Snarl or swear or do something worse. Would that help?"

A gurgle of laughter escaped her and she tipped her head back, staring at him. "No." She touched her hand to his cheek. "I think I'm okay. Mostly."

Dark eyes searched hers for a long, long moment before he nodded. "If you're sure. You really do look amazing, Abby. And I think I need to distract you."

"Distract me, huh?" She arched a brow at him. "And just how are you going to do that?"

"I've got my ways," he said easily. He stroked a hand down her back, up and down, slow, teasing strokes that felt like they'd drive her out of her mind if she wasn't careful. "I'm going to have a hard time doing anything but staring at you." Then he smoothed a hand down over the skirt, cupping her butt in his palm. "Are you wearing panties?"

She jolted in his hand. "Well . . . yeah."

"Go inside and take them off."

She blushed and jerked back, staring up at him. "What?"

"You heard me." He flashed a wicked grin at her. "You want a hot, wild affair, right? Why not go out to dinner without your panties on?"

"No." She pulled away from him, only to have him catch her elbow and pull her back against him.

"Oh, come on . . . it's a pair of underwear," he teased, nuzzling her neck. "And I can't tell you what it would do to me to think about you sitting across from me without any panties on . . . you can take the stockings off and . . ."

She pulled back and wrinkled her nose. "No. But you come inside and I'll show you something that might make it hard for you to think anyway."

*   *   *

Maybe he should be careful about the games he was going to play, Zach thought after Abby had shut the door behind her and disarmed the alarm. She shot him a nervous look. Nervous . . . and hot. There was both dismay and heat in her eyes, as though she wanted to bolt and plunge right into this.

Whatever this was.

Deciding to make it easy on her, he moved a few feet into the house and sprawled on the staircase. "So what were you going to show me?"

She fingered the material of the full skirt flaring around her legs. The material was pale pink, glowing against her skin like a rose. Zach smirked to himself as he thought it. She went and made him start thinking poetic thoughts like that, turned him into a knot with just a smile. He was a mess.

The heels of her shoes clicked on the floor as she came toward him and he found himself mesmerized by her legs. The skirt was modest, just an inch below her knees, but still, the heels and her legs . . .

"Ah . . . you know, if you don't show me soon," he said, dragging his eyes up to stare at her face. "I think you should have to take the panties off. Just on principle."

"That's a weird principle." She smiled at him, still fingering the skirt and watching him with that hot, almost fevered look in her eyes. "But I'm going to show you. Or better yet . . . you can see for yourself."

She caught a fistful of her skirt and dragged it up and Zach felt his heart all but stop.

That grin on her face danced into somewhere just shy of devilish. "I need some help, Zach," she said. "The skirt and the petticoat are a handful."

He blinked, a little dazed. "Petticoat . . . ?"

Then he looked down and saw the black sliplike thing under it. Petticoat. Yeah, he knew what that was. Peeking out from under the skirt, tangling around her legs. He swallowed the saliva pooling in his mouth and started to drag it up and then his heart really *did* stop.

Yeah, she was wearing stockings . . . and garters. And they . . . He closed his eyes and said hoarsely, "You're keeping the damn panties on. You need to tell me where in the hell you got them because I want to buy stock in the place." Tangling his hands in the layers of skirt and petticoat, he held all of it up to her waist and stared.

Black silk stretched over the round curve of her hips. He could see himself gripping those hips, holding her steady as he settled between her thighs and started to ride her. She'd cradle him just perfectly, all lush curves and sweet heat. Dark silk encased her thighs and those thighs . . . damn. A thing of beauty, he knew.

The straps of her garters ran down from her panties to hold up her stockings and he slid one finger under the strap lightly as he leaned in and pressed his mouth to her.

Abby gasped and braced her hand against his shoulder. "Zach . . ."

And before he let himself do anything else, he stood up.

Dinner was at an exclusive little spot overlooking the desert. The music was low, the conversations were muted, and Abigale found herself tucked into a little alcove with Zach where the waiters were silent and the food appeared almost like magic.

There had been a few times when she'd been wined and dined before, but never like this.

After the dinner plates had been cleared, Zach turned toward her, half curving his body around hers as he leaned in to murmur, "I keep thinking about what you've got on under that skirt and it's killing me."

Tipping her head back, she met his gaze. "Well, now you have an idea how I've felt ever since you left me high and dry."

The flash of his smile in the dim room had a fist closing around her heart. "So is this about punishment, sugar?"

"Maybe." She reached for her wineglass and took a sip. She was so parched, she could have downed the entire thing and still needed more. But her head was already spinning. Because of Zach. Getting tipsy on wine wouldn't be wise. Especially since she had every intention of getting him inside her house tonight. And doing more than showing him her panties.

A reckless thought occurred to her and she almost blurted it out. She didn't want to *show* him her panties. She wanted him *in* her panties . . . inside her. Muffling a groan, she took another deeper drink of the wine but it only made her feel even hotter.

Zach's hand curved over her thigh, resting just above her knee.

Turning her head, she stared at him under her lashes.

He watched her from under a hooded gaze and murmured, "Just what are you thinking right now, Abby? That look on your face is pure sin."

"I'm thinking about you." Biting her lip, she reached up and touched his cheek. "I'm having a hard time processing all of this, but it's like you're inside my head all the time. Ah . . . are you going to come home with me tonight?"

He turned his face into her hand and pressed a kiss to her palm. "I brought you on a date . . . I have to see you home, right?"

"That's not what I meant."

He leaned in and pressed a kiss to the nape of her neck. "I know. But there's no rush on this . . . no timetable."

Chapter Nine

"This is *insane*," Abigale muttered as she slumped in the shower.

One more burning hot dream.

One more trip to the shower just to get through the day without falling down in a quaking spasm. Those nifty showerheads were like the most amazing gift to womankind ever, she had to admit.

But after two more dates with Zach, and no sex, she was getting desperate. It had been a *week* since they'd decided to have an affair.

And she *hated* that word. Hated it. With a passion. But still, it was what it was and they hadn't slept together. She'd set out to have a sexual escapade, right? But there wasn't any sex going on and there wasn't much in the way of escapades, either, unless she counted the solo ones.

She was dying bit by bit from terminal horniness and she hadn't been successful at trying to coax him into staying the night or anything. Maybe she should just—

Her phone chimed.

Wrapping the towel around her breasts, she picked it up. And despite her frustration, she had to smile when she saw Zach's name on the screen.

What are you up to? his message read.

Just got done showering.

A smiley face appeared. *Are you naked?*

She rolled her eyes and glanced down at the towel. What the hell? *Well . . . you usually shower naked, right? At least, I know I do.*

There was a two-beat pause before his response. *That means yes, right?*

Yes. She laughed a little. *I'm naked. I just climbed out of the shower, I'm dripping wet, I'm cold, and I'm naked.*

Fffffuuuuccccckkkk, Abby.

Well, I've been trying to do that, but you're not cooperating. The second she sent it, she cringed. She couldn't believe she'd just done that. Damn it, Zach was turning her into a damned tramp. And she loved it. The more she thought about *him*, the more she thought about sex. Not just *any* sex, of course. It had to involve him. But she was thinking about it *all the damned time.*

What in the world was wrong with her?

Just how wet are you?

Her heart slammed against her ribs at the next question and although she usually wasn't much for self-pleasuring outside the damned shower, she found herself aching. Almost desperate for it. Her chest ached as she caught her breath.

Abby?

She licked her lips and responded back. *Up until a few minute ago, it wasn't that bad. Then you got to texting me and . . . I dunno. And like I said, it would be better if you were more cooperative.*

The screen glared at her, silent for so long she started to get even more nervous, her heart banging against her ribs and her palms slick with sweat. Then finally, another little message bubble popped up. *I'm plenty cooperative, sugar.*

I just don't see any reason to operate on whatever crazy timetable you've got going in your head. Now . . . tell me, how wet are you?

She groaned. *Zach . . .*

Go lay down on your bed.

Her breath hitched in her chest and she almost told him to stop. Almost.

But she didn't.

Instead, she tugged off her towel and hung it back up in the bathroom. What the hell . . .

Back in her room, she stretched out on the bed and lifted the phone. *You know, this would be easier if you were here.*

Yeah, but if I was there, I'd be inside you and I'm not ready for that yet. Are you on the bed?

Not ready? What in the hell did that mean?

Scowling, she tapped out the response. *I'm on the bed. And I think I'd rather you BE here.*

Touch yourself.

Her breath froze. Right there, in the middle of her chest, a black wall seemed to echo through her mind at that simple command. *Touch—*

Licking her lips, she shook her head, even though he wasn't there to see.

A second ticked by.

Another.

Another.

After nearly fifteen, a message popped up. *Are you listening?*

She groaned and responded, *No.*

Why not?

She could think of a bunch of legitimate reasons. But *none* of them seemed to really fit. Raggedly, she whispered into her iPhone, "Send Zach a message."

She slid a hand down her belly. "Yes . . . I'm touching myself."

And under her own touch, she was hot and wet.

Zach's message flared on her phone. *Are you wet?*

"Yes . . ."

Good. I'm going to make you hotter. Wetter . . . Speaking of which . . . you doing anything this weekend?

"Crazy timetable?" she muttered, whimpering a little as her fingers slicked over the swollen bud between her thighs, shuddering even as it just made her need ratchet even higher, swell tighter.

She didn't *have* a timetable. Granted, she'd figured once they'd decided to have an affair, they'd be doing it already. And *whoa*, was she ready to do it. With Zach. Even thinking about it turned all the female bits inside her body to hot, burning lava.

"No," she said, opting to use the voice-to-text. Seemed safer that way. "I'm not doing anything. Why?"

I made arrangements to have Keelie run the shop for the weekend. Come away with me?

A weekend away with Zach.

Oh, yes. She'd like that.

She licked her lips and replied. And already, her mind was burning. If he thought he'd keep her on pins and needles much longer, he was out of his mind.

He'd brought her to the mountains.

Abigale sighed as she climbed out of the car and stared at the little cabin in front of them. It was perched on the mountainside with a view of the mountains spread out around Flagstaff.

After the heat of Tucson, the cool air was a welcome change, but the skimpy tank top she had on wasn't much protection against the chill in the air. It was closing in on nine o'clock and at this elevation, it could go from mild to outright cold all too fast. Shivering a little, she wrapped her arms around herself as she moved off the path to stare around her.

The wind blew her hair into her face but before she could brush it back, Zach was there. He caught it and tucked it behind her ear. "You need a jacket," he murmured, sliding his arms around her waist.

"Hmmm. I don't know if I packed one." She glanced at him over her shoulder. "You didn't say we were going to the mountains."

"I've got one for you." He pressed his lips to her neck. "But then again, you might not need it. Once I get you inside . . ."

She rolled her eyes. "Uh-huh." She'd been living in a state of near-constant arousal for a week, and hovering just under that for the past few weeks. She didn't see him changing his tune just because he had her at some pretty little cabin in the mountains.

The wind kicked up and she shivered, despite the warmth of his embrace.

"Come on . . . let's get our stuff and head inside," he said. "We can look around later."

She glanced over toward the west, watching as the sun dipped closer and closer to the horizon. "It's going to be a gorgeous sunset, though."

A grin tugged at his lips. "Come on. You won't miss it."

A few minutes later, she understood. Huge windows dominated the back of the cabin, facing out to the west, leaving it impossible to miss the sunset. It was also impossible for her to miss the rather lush feast spread out on the table in front of those windows.

A tantalizing scent filled the air and her belly rumbled. "You sneak," she said, sliding him a look. "How did you set this up?"

"I have my ways." He took her bag from her and then caught her hand. "You hungry?"

The trick, Zach had figured out, was to keep her off balance. He knew Abby too well. If she got comfortable enough to think, she was going to try and work all of this into some nice, neat little place in her head and that wasn't going to happen. Not until he'd had time to make her fall in love with him.

She already loved him. And he knew that. Half the time,

that hurt more than anything, knowing she needed him, knowing she loved him. Just not the right way.

But now she wanted him . . . the attraction was there. If they had the friendship and they had the attraction, could he get her to fall for him?

He was betting everything he had on it, including his heart.

Right now, with the lights in the cabin off and nothing but the setting sun to illuminate the room as they ate, he just hoped he wasn't fucking this up. So far, nothing *seemed* terribly different. Except the way she'd watch him. They'd be talking the way they always did and then she'd get this look in her eyes, this hot look that just about drove him insane. Then there was this other look . . . this puzzled, bemused sort of expression, kind of amazed, kind of pleased. He couldn't decide which one he liked more, but he liked seeing them both.

Most of all, he just liked being able to be there with her without having to completely hide everything he felt. As she leaned back from the table with a satisfied sigh, he decided all the wrangling, hassling, and begging he'd done to get this thrown together at the last minute had been worth it. Very much worth it.

When she went to pick up her plate, he caught her hand. "Just leave them. Somebody's coming to take care of the dishes in about ten more minutes." He'd timed that perfectly, too.

"Come on." He stood up and held out a hand. On the way to the deck tucked against the side of the house, he grabbed a blanket. She hadn't put on a jacket and he didn't want to be in the house when anybody else was there. It would wreck things, he thought. And wasn't that stupid?

Still, it wasn't like he didn't have plans.

Waiting just by the door was a covered silver tray and he tucked the blanket into Abby's arms so he could grab it. Her brows arched as she studied the tray. "More surprises?"

"Yes."

"And what's in there?"

"Open the door for me and you'll see," he said.

A few minutes later, as they stretched out on one of the lounges, he put a glass of ice wine into her hand and handed her a plate. It held a variety of bits of fruit and a few cookies, all dipped in chocolate. Simple and basic, and if he knew Abby, that would suit her just fine.

Especially the wine. It was too sweet for him, but she loved ice wine with something bordering on obsession. He hadn't let her see the label and now he got to watch her sip it, watched her eyes widen as she took the first taste. "Oh . . ." Her lashes fluttered closed and a slow smile curved her lips. "That's yummy."

He pressed his lips to her shoulder and hummed in appreciation. "I agree."

She snorted and bumped her elbow against his belly. "I'm going to make a new rule to go along with this affair thing—no teasing. Until you're ready to follow through, you can't touch. You're killing me."

Zach chuckled. "That's not a good rule. Teasing is half the fun. Did we ever make all the rules?"

"I never wanted rules," she reminded him, pausing to take another sip. "*You* did. Which is crazy. I'm the rule girl. You're not."

"No, I'm definitely not a girl for rules," he agreed. He stroked a hand down her belly, glancing at his watch. His phone buzzed. He eased away and pulled it out, read the message. *Coming in for the cleanup—be there in a few.*

He responded and put the phone down.

Abby eyed the phone. "Who is that?"

"The elves who took care of the meal." He heard the motor a few seconds later and reached for one of the strawberries on the tray. "Here . . . try one. You love this stuff, right?"

She took a bite and he almost groaned as a bit of the juice clung to her lips. Leaning in, he licked it away.

She turned her head away. "You're breaking the new rule."

"I never agreed to the new rule." *Five minutes, damn it. It should take them five minutes to clean the fucking place up.*

He fed her the rest of the strawberry and reached for another one, eating that one himself as he listened to the noise coming from inside the cabin, just a few feet away. *Hurry the hell up.*

"Were there other rules, Abs?" he asked hoarsely as he fed her a piece of pineapple. Anything he needed to know while he was still capable of thinking?

She looked down, focusing on her glass. "What happens when this ends? How do we decide that, anyway?"

"We'll know." *If I have my way, it ends when my heart stops.* That seemed a good time limit. He took one of the cookies and broke it in half, feeding one half to her and popping the other piece into his mouth. He wasn't hungry, but if he didn't distract himself . . .

He'd been working up to this point all week, although the decision to go out of town had been a spur-of-the-moment thing. But now that it was here . . .

Fuck.

He lay his hand on her belly. "When it ends, if that's what happens, we're just back to us. Nothing is going to change, Abby."

"You seem so sure of that."

"Because that's how it will be." No matter what, even if she walked away, he wasn't going to lose his best friend. Even if she wouldn't be his lover, his woman always, she was still the most important person for him and he wouldn't give that up. "And that's a question . . . not a rule. Was there anything else?"

She shrugged a little and took a drink. "Not that I can think of."

His phone buzzed. Glancing down, he saw the message. *Gone, dude.*

That was all it said.

Taking the phone, he dumped it on the floor next to him.

"If that's it . . ." He caught her glass in his hand and put it down on the little table next to her, and took the tray of fruit and dessert. "There's something I need to do."

Then he put his hand back on her belly and took her mouth.

Abigale would have thought she'd be prepared for his kisses by now.

She would have thought she could handle them.

But this . . . this was different.

As he laid her down onto the chaise, it was like he was trying to consume her. Like he was trying to brand himself on her. And damn, was it working. Her mouth opened wide under his and she fought free of the blanket tangling around her shoulders. Once she had her hands free, she clutched at his shoulders, her fingers digging into his arms as she arched up against him.

His mouth left hers to press a stinging line of kisses down over the line of her throat and she shuddered. "Damn it, if you stop again, Zach, I'm going to hurt you."

"Not stopping, Abby." He caught the straps of her tank top.

Her brain stopped. It simply stopped and she couldn't process anything. He tugged her upright and she stared at him as he crouched over her, staring down at her with dark, stormy eyes. "Zach . . . ?"

He said nothing, but his hands jerked the straps of her tank down until they tangled around her arms, half trapping them against her sides. He did the same to her bra and then he dipped his head.

The cool air danced across her flesh, tightening her nipples and then there was his mouth. Oh . . . his mouth.

Hot and wicked, and oh, so knowing. It closed around one tight, swollen nipple and pleasure lanced through her. Too much pleasure for such a simple touch, she thought. It blistered her skin, blinded her, and left her gasping for air as he bit down lightly and tugged, tugged . . .

She clutched his head closer and arched against him, desperate for more.

And then, even as she tried to get closer, he was gone. Crying out, she opened her eyes but before she could get a word out, he had her in his arms, hauling her up off the lounge. "Inside," he muttered, his voice harsh, a far cry from the easy tone she was used to. A far cry from the teasing tones she'd heard each time she'd tried to take things further. "Grab the wine . . . we're going inside. Now."

Dazed, she looked around and spied the cobalt blue wine bottle on the table. She closed her hand around it and cradled it against her chest as he carried her across the deck. Once they were inside, he paused by the kitchen counter and said, "Put it down. You aren't going to be drunk on anything but me tonight."

Her skin seemed to burst into flames.

"I think I already am," she said, her voice shaking a little as he carried her through another door, into a room she hadn't seen before. And she didn't even see it then, not really. He hit the lights but all she saw was the huge bed and Zach as he laid her down and came over her, his hands tangling in her hair.

The impact of that kiss was enough to make her nerve endings implode, one by one. She heard them exploding, sizzling through her as she wrapped around him, desperate to get closer. His shirt was in the way and she shoved it up, needing to get at his skin.

He leaned back and tore it away but when he would have come back down over her, she braced her hands against his chest, keeping a few inches between them as she stared at his chest and shoulders. Her breath hitched a little as she smoothed one hand down over his pectoral, lingering over the bleeding heart design that had been inked there.

Ironically, it was just above where his heart was. A dagger pierced it and there was stylized, twisting scrollwork done around the blade and the heart. It should have looked ridiculously feminine, she thought, but like every other tattoo he had, it suited him. She shifted her attention to the tiger that crouched just across from the heart. It was so vivid, so detailed, she could almost imagine it coming to life, muscles bunching as it leaped from Zach's skin into reality.

"I've never told you this," she murmured, flicking him a look. "I've never told anybody . . . but I really love your tattoos, Zach."

He covered her hand with his and caught her wrist, dragging it away and pinning it over her head. He did the same with her other one and she caught her breath as she felt his bare chest against her own. "You can pet them and play with them all you fucking want," he promised as he caught her earlobe between his teeth and bit her lightly. "After."

She shuddered, her entire body going tight at the thought. *After.* He was serious. Finally. Lifting her foot, she stroked it down his calf, feeling the worn denim against her sole. "You're still wearing too many clothes."

"So are you."

He eased upward to crouch above her, reaching for the tie that held her wraparound skirt in place. "You wore this skirt again."

"You seemed to like it." She was about ready to order a dozen more, too.

"I like you in anything. I think I'm going to like you naked best, though." He freed the skirt, but didn't open it yet. Instead, he eased her upright and fought with the tangle that had become her clothing, easing her shirt and bra up and over her head, tossing them to the floor and guiding her back down. And still, he didn't remove her skirt.

She wanted to groan. Wanted to scream. And then she wanted to sigh as he caught her breasts in his hands and plumped them together, using his thumbs to tease her nipples.

"You told me your little secret, Abby," he said, lifting his head to stare into her eyes. "Now I'll tell you one of mine. I fucking love your tits."

Blood rushed to her face as she stared at him and her skin went hot, tight.

"Is that a problem?" he murmured.

She blinked, a shudder wracking through her body as he continued to stare at her, his gaze bold and unapologetic. "Ah . . . I . . . I don't think so."

"So you're not going to be pissed off at me if I tell you that I often have to kick myself in the ass because I'll find myself staring at these pretty tits and then have to remind myself we're supposed to be friends."

A whimper caught in her throat and before she could stop it, it squeezed out of her. "We . . ." She licked her lips and finished in a rush. "We are friends."

"Yes." He lowered his head and raked his teeth along the slope of her right breast. "We are . . . and as your friend, I shouldn't have to kick my own ass to keep from checking out your tits and wondering what it would feel like to do just this. But I did it. All the time. Is that a problem?"

It should be, she thought, dazed. It really should be. But all this knowledge did was make her hot. *Hotter*. It burned her so hot, she could barely breathe and even if this ended tomorrow and they were back to friends, she didn't know if she could regret knowing what he'd just shared with her.

"No." She somehow managed to answer as he continued to wait, watching her with wicked eyes, the blue burning with promises.

His thumbs stroked around the tips of her nipples and he dipped his head to catch one between his teeth and tugged. "Good."

Her head fell back as he did it again and each small pull arrowed straight down between her thighs. The pleasure was almost staggering, so intense, so huge. She went to cradle the back of his head, intent on pulling him closer but then he was gone, moving so suddenly, her brain couldn't even process it.

Years, damn it. Zach had been waiting for this for years, thinking about how he'd touch her, the ways that he'd seduce her, the ways he'd make love to her. And now that the moment was here, the only thing he could think about doing was just touching her. Learning that lush body with his hands and bringing her to climax so that he heard his name on her lips as she came.

The material of her skirt spread around her, still hiding her lower body from him, although it spilt just above her right knee, leaving her calves bared to his view. Her breasts, full and round and topped with deep rose–colored nipples, all but begged for his touch and he had to focus on the task at hand to keep from staring at her.

His hands felt too clumsy as he scrambled to deal with his jeans. The button seemed too damned big and if he wasn't mistaken, somebody had gone and glued the damned zipper shut. But finally, *finally*, he managed to get rid of the damn jeans, remembering just in time to pull out one of the rubbers he'd tucked into his back pocket before he'd left home.

He had more packed away, but for now . . .

Keeping it tucked in his hand, he went to kneel on the bed and stilled.

Abby was staring at him, her breath coming in harsh little pants that had her chest rising and falling in the most interesting way imaginable. A flush started low on her chest, spreading up her neck and higher, higher, suffusing her entire body a pale, gentle shade of pink. Her eyes locked blindly with his and her voice was a little shaky as she said, "Damn it, Zach. When did you get to be so beautiful?"

Something hot and satisfied moved through him as he crawled across the bed and leaned over her, dipping his head to catch her mouth. "Hey, they weren't trying to get me on the stupid *Bachelor* show for nothing," he teased. He had his share of arrogance, he knew. But nothing equaled the rush of pride he felt right now.

The look of want in her eyes was almost enough to lay him low.

It almost rivaled what he had inside for her. Almost.

Her tongue slid against his as he kissed her and her hands curled around his shoulders, tugging him down. But he resisted. He had plans, things he needed to do now that this was finally happening.

And one fantasy . . .

Pulling back from the temptation that was her kiss, he settled on his knees next to her hips and waited until the fog cleared from her eyes. "You know, the other day, when you were wearing this skirt," he muttered, stroking a hand down one of the panels. "I kept having this fantasy. Unwrapping you like a damned present. I get to unwrap you now. Unwrap . . . undo . . ."

"You've been undoing me for the past month." She curled her fingers into the material of the comforter beneath her.

"A month?" He slowly started to peel it away, staring into her dark brown eyes. "That's nothing. I've been waiting for this a lifetime."

A gasp caught in her throat, but he didn't keep watching her just then. He needed to remember he'd planned to proceed with caution and he seemed to be throwing *caution* out the window lately.

Smoothing the first panel out of the way, Zach stroked one hand down the curve of her hip and bent over her, pressing his lips to the point where her bone pressed against her flesh. A soft sigh escaped her and she stroked a hand over his hair. "Zach . . ."

He straightened back up and grinned at her. "I always did like to take my time with my presents."

She just stared at him, the brown of her eyes darkened to near black. As he reached for the other panel of her skirt, a breath shuddered out of her, almost a sob. Spreading the material out next to her, he kept his gaze on her face as he shifted around, moving her legs so that he had the room to kneel between them. The blush on her cheeks brightened and she caught her lower lip between her teeth, worrying it a little before letting it go.

He rested his hands on her hips, holding her gaze for a long, silent moment. And then, as her lashes drifted down, he let himself look.

So beautiful. The red banner of her hair spread out around her, one lock curling around her shoulder, the end of it curving around her nipple. The swell of her breasts, the fragile span of her ribs, the indent of her waist, and the curve of her hips. So female. And so his.

Finally his.

For now, at least. And he planned on branding himself on her so that she never thought about going to another man.

The tangle of curls between her thighs was a few shades darker than her hair and glinting with moisture. His mouth watered, but his hands were shaking and his muscles were locked, screaming at him. Need battered at him, chewed angry holes through his will, and he knew he wasn't going to take his time on this. Still watching her, he tore the rubber open and unrolled it down over his cock.

Her mouth parted a little and his cock jerked as her tongue slid out to wet her lips. He could see her doing just that, right before she went to her knees in front of him—*Stop it*, he told himself. Had to stop.

Coming down over her, he tangled one hand in her hair and tugged her head back, watching her face. "I wanted to take this slow, take our time, and make this last." He pressed his mouth to hers. "But I can't. You're the one who's undoing people, Abby, and I'm completely undone here. I'll make it slow, make it matter, make it special next time, I swear."

Her hand slid up his back, dipping into his hair as she pressed a soft kiss to his mouth. "Zach . . . it already matters . . . it's already special." She brought one leg up, pressing her knee against his hip and arching up.

He groaned as he felt the wet heat of her core brush against him. Reaching down, he held himself steady, started to press against her.

The soft, sweet flesh yielded around him, gloving around

him, so slick and so damned soft. So damned amazing. She whimpered and arched, twining her arms around him and crying out as he started to withdraw. The sheer dismay in her voice wrenched at his heart. And then as he sank back inside her, hearing that ragged cry of pleasure, savage satisfaction flooded him.

Her nails bit into his flesh, digging in and leaving hot little marks of pleasure as he started to move faster, shuddering at the slick, tight feel of her. Gripping him so tight, so smooth and sleek.

Brushing his lips against the curve of her cheek, he whispered her name.

Blindly, she turned her face toward his, seeking him and he met her, kiss for burning kiss as flesh slicked over flesh and their rhythm turned frantic.

Against his chest, he felt the soft pressure of her breasts, the fiery little points of her nipples. Her hands clutched at his shoulders and she rocked to meet each thrust.

"So fucking beautiful," he muttered against her lips. "So beautiful, Abs."

The tension in her body ramped up. Too much . . . too much . . . as he surged back inside her, it was like sinking his cock into a fist of silk—impossible and every bit as sweet. Then she cried out, a look of sheer bliss washing over her face.

As she started to come, he surged against her, harder, faster, forgetting about finesse, grace . . . forgetting everything but the fact that this was Abby.

The one woman he'd always wanted.

The one woman he'd thought he'd never have.

Chapter Ten

"Umph."

Abigale wanted to keep her face buried in the pillows, dead to the world.

But Zach apparently had other ideas. "Come on, beautiful. It's not even ten. You're not going to bed yet."

As he swept her up in his arms, she poked a finger into his ribs. "Why the hell not?" She turned her face into his neck and sighed.

"Because I plan on putting you into a hot tub, scrubbing you clean, and then fucking you all over again."

That sounded enticing. Abby opened one eye and peered up at him. From somewhere through the door off the right, she could hear water running. "Are you getting in the tub, too?"

"Yes."

She debated for a few seconds, but as tired as she was, she really couldn't see any downfalls to this idea. Other than being tired, but she could always sleep, she figured. "Okay."

* * *

The bath was amazing and she had to admit, she
felt all nice and loose as he helped her out nearly a half an
hour later. And if it wasn't for the burn of lust in her
belly . . . *Stop it*, she admonished herself. Reaching for a
towel, she tried to remind herself that she'd just had sex.
Just had him.

He caught the towel from her. "Let me," he murmured.

She stood quiescent as Zach stroked the towel over her,
drying her hair, her body. In front of the mirror, she could
see him behind her and she decided then and there that it
was painfully erotic to watch a man do this.

Her breath hitched a little as he passed the towel over
her breasts once more and then paused to drape it around
her.

"I want to check your tattoo," he murmured against her
ear.

She glanced over her shoulder at him, but he was already looking down at her hip. She moved forward a step
and braced one hand on the edge of the sink, turning her
head to see it better.

All she could see was a glimpse of black ink and skin.
It wasn't as swollen as it had been so that was good, she
figured.

"How does it look?" she asked as he trailed his fingers
along the slope of her hip.

"It looks good." His fingers flexed and he stroked another hand down over her hip. Before he could let go,
though, she reached back and caught his wrist.

"The night you gave me this, I saw you looking at me,"
she whispered. "We . . ." She stopped and cleared her
throat. "Were you thinking . . ."

He slid a hand up and tangled a fist in her hair, holding
her steady as he moved in. One leg came between hers,
nudging them farther apart. "I saw you looking at me, too."
He dipped his head and pressed his lips to her shoulder as

he cuddled his cock against her rump. "Yes . . . I was thinking about this. I can't look at you without wanting you, Abby. I've wanted you for too long."

The words slid over her like a caress and she wondered just how that was possible. Why hadn't she seen it? And then she couldn't think about anything except how much she wanted him. How much she needed him. One hand trailed up her back, then back down and she whimpered as he butted his hips against her once more. Whimpering low in her throat, she lifted her eyes and stared at him in the mirror.

Dark brown hair fell in his face, half shielding his gaze from her, but she saw the blue of his eyes glittering at her.

"Stay there."

He moved away from her and without his hands on her hips to steady her, without his strength there, she had a hard time staying upright. Locking her knees, she lowered her head and sucked in a desperate breath of air. Blood roared in her ears and her heart thudded so hard, it was a miracle it didn't leap out of her chest.

Although he didn't make a sound, she knew when he was back in the bathroom. Jerking her head up, she watched in the mirror as he came to stand behind her. She heard a foil packet rip and her knees started to go weak. Images of that day in his shop flashed through her mind and she sucked in another breath.

Moments later, she felt him nudging against her gate, hard and slick, separated by the thin shield of the latex condom he wore. She rather hated that barrier, needed to feel him, just him. But then he was pressing inside and she forgot about everything but the wonderful feel of him stretching her, and the gravelly sound of his groan as he buried himself inside her.

Hands spread low on her spine, Zach rocked against her, alternating his view between staring where they joined and looking up to watch Abby's face in the mirror.

The edge of hunger rode him hard, but it wasn't so brutal this time, wasn't so breath-stealing. He could take it just a little slower and he intended to draw it out, make it last as long as he could.

Although it already felt like a fist was gripping his balls, fire licking down his spine as she clenched tight around him and shuddered.

Her damp hair fell around her shoulders and back in crazy spirals and he reached up, catching a fistful of it as he moved closer. He drew her body upright, the depths of his thrusts slowing down so that he was barely rocking inside her now. And it was still incredible bliss.

Staring at her in the mirror, his arm banded around her waist, the colors of his tattooed arm vivid against her pale skin, he held her gaze in the mirror as he circled his hips against hers. "Look at us, Abby. See how we fit?"

She nodded slowly, reaching back up with her arm and twining it around his neck. It arched her breasts out and forced her hips down more firmly against him and a ragged, breathless snarl tore out of him as he continued to watch them.

Words rose inside his throat, words he had to fight back for now. Not yet. Not until he thought she might be ready. He couldn't have her running. But it was a ragged refrain in his head. *I love you . . . always you.*

"Zach . . ." Her voice, shaky and hoarse, danced through the air and the sweet glove of her sex tightened around him, the tension in her body ratcheting up until she was rocking back and forth against him almost frantically. He gritted his teeth and stroked his hand down her belly, sliding his fingers through the curls between her thighs.

The hard knot of her clit all but pulsed against his fingers and he pressed against her lightly, smiling as her cry bounced off the walls in the bathroom. "Fast?" He settled on the rhythm that had pushed her over the edge earlier. "Is that how you like it?"

But her eyes had already gone glassy and she didn't even seem to hear him.

She moved faster, working herself up and down, the movements short and shallow, but it didn't seem to matter.

He groaned as she started to come, vising down around him and coming with a cry that sounded like glory.

He wasn't far behind.

There were some mornings that were just made for lazing in bed, for that slow glide from sleep into wakefulness—and this was one of them. Stretching, Abigale rolled to her belly as her body tried to urge her brain back to sleep, back to dreams.

And wow. Had there been dreams.

Zach . . .

Zach—

She turned her head and cracked one eye open.

The view of the mountains greeted her. Mountains weren't an unfamiliar sight for her to wake up to, but these weren't the mountains she was used to. Staggering, soaring peaks and evergreens, the sky so blue it hurt to look at it . . . all in all, completely beautiful. And nothing like the beauty of the desert back home.

Flagstaff.

Swallowing, she sat up and stared out the window.

She was in Flagstaff. With Zach.

Glancing down, she found herself staring at her naked body and then she groaned, covering her face with her hands. She was naked. In Flagstaff. With Zach.

And that meant last night had really happened. *Really.* She'd slept with Zach. She'd . . . How did she describe last night? The word *sex* seemed inadequate. She felt like he'd turned her inside out, shattered her, and then completely remade her.

Need to calm down, she told herself. She needed to do it, and do it now before he walked in and saw her freaking out.

Slowly, she took a deep breath and when she did, she became aware of something . . . enticing. Bacon. Coffee.

And despite the nerves twisting through her, a smile tugged up the corners of her lips. He was making her breakfast. She hoped there wasn't a repeat of the last time.

Her belly rumbled demandingly and she got to her feet, looking around for something to put on. Her clothes had been in a tangled mess across the floor last night. She remembered leaving them that way on her way in here with Zach. Now they were tossed in a small wicker hamper over by the door. Shoving her hair back from her face, she moved over to the closet and tugged it open. Their bags were still sitting in there but at some point, Zach had unpacked a little. Industrious man. He had a sweatshirt hanging up and a few of her shirts. Her blouses were all short-sleeved and it was chilly in the cabin. She grabbed the sweatshirt.

Just as she pulled it on over her head, Zach appeared in the doorway with a tray. A wide grin flashed across his face as he said, "Oh, come on now . . . I made you breakfast in bed. The least you could do was stay naked for me."

"Breakfast in bed?" She glanced down at her naked feet on the gleaming hardwood floors and then back up at him. "I'm not in bed now."

"Smart-ass." He came farther into the room and settled the tray on the smooth, wide surface of the bedside table before he came and caught her in his arms. His mouth covered hers even as she tried to turn her head.

"I need to brush my teeth," she mumbled against his lips.

"And I need to kiss you." Which he did . . . thoroughly. By the time he had lifted his head, she was panting for breath and her legs were about ready to fold underneath her.

She curled her hands into the faded material of his t-shirt and rested her brow against his chest. Zach slid his arms around her, his head pressed against the curve of her neck. She could feel the warmth of his breath drifting over her skin and he had one hand stroking absently up and down her spine, like he just had to be touching her. Stroking, kissing, something.

It was driving her out of her mind with want for him.

"You're one hell of a wake-up call," she said softly.

"If you ever want to keep me on service permanently, let me know," he whispered. "I can tuck myself into your bed and I'll give you a personalized wake-up call whenever you want."

She shivered a little at the thought. Thinking about waking up to Zach was an oddly intriguing and terrifying thought.

"You ready for some coffee? Breakfast?" He kissed her neck once more and then lifted his head to look down at her, pushing her hair back from her face.

"In a minute." She eased away from him. "Bathroom."

She locked herself inside and even though it felt like her bladder was about to explode, even though she wanted to wash her face, brush her teeth, and just get out there and see him, she took a minute and leaned back against the door, eyes closed.

Zach.

What in the hell . . .

She'd wanted a torrid affair. No denying that.

She'd wanted something memorable, she thought. That was what she'd told Marin.

I want somebody who'll make my heart stop, and then make it race all over again. I want somebody who'll make me remember every damn second we were together, and not just the moment we were in bed. I want something to remember . . .

There was no way she'd be forgetting *any* of this.

The only problem was that she was starting to wonder if any other guy would *ever* live up to this. Her lips still buzzed, still burned from the heat of his kiss. Pressing the tips of her fingers to them, she realized she already knew the answer.

One week with Zach. That was all she'd had, really. One week. And they'd spent *one* night together and she already knew every guy after this was going to come up short.

Yet there was no way she could see herself regretting any of this.

Shoving away from the wall, she quickly used the restroom, washed her hands and face. Once she'd done that, she dug out her toothbrush and toothpaste, brushing her teeth. She lingered in front of the mirror, finger-combing her disheveled hair but there was only so much she could do without a shower.

And she wasn't leaving Zach out there with her breakfast too much longer. He was one hell of a guy, but he'd drink all the coffee and eat most of the bacon.

As she opened the door, she saw him laying back on the table, munching his way through a thick-sliced, crispy piece and she narrowed her eyes at him. "There better still be some for me."

He patted the bed next to him. "I made plenty." Then he winked at her. "But if you want it, you have to come join me so I can feed you."

She settled next to him, sitting up with her legs folded. Zach pushed up onto his elbow, his gaze zeroing down and locking on her lap. "That's a picture," he said gruffly. "Fuck breakfast . . . I think I want—"

As he went to sit up, she planted her hands into the middle of his chest and shoved him back. "*I* want breakfast." She eyed the tray for a second and then looked at him. "Are you feeding me, like you said, or is your brain already in your pants?"

"Men are like dinosaurs, sugar. We have two brains, completely independent of each other and capable of separate thought." He sighed and sat up, moving around until he could grab the tray.

"Dinosaurs . . ." She pursed her lips and shook her head. "I don't think dinosaurs have separate brains. That's earthworms, right?"

"Hey, there's the stegosaurus. Some scientists thought they had two brains." He shrugged and moved around until he had her settled up against him. "But that's not the point.

I can feed you and still carry on a conversation while my dick is yelling at me to pull that sweatshirt off of you and get you under me again. Which I plan to do very shortly."

Her breath hitched in her chest and she tried to remember how to breathe.

A slow grin lit his face as he held up a cup of coffee. It already had plenty of cream in it and she figured he'd added enough sugar to make him cringe—that one would be hers. "Coffee, Abby?" he asked, still smiling that hot, devilish little grin.

She licked her lips as she closed her hands around the mug, grateful to see that her fingers weren't shaking. *She* was shaking . . . all but quivering inside as she lifted the mug to her lips. Still, it didn't show in her hands, on her face, or her voice as she said easily, "Zach . . . if I'd known I'd get breakfast in bed, I think I would have gone after you ages ago."

"I'll do it every damn week if you keep me around."

Keep you . . . damn it. I'm starting to want just that.
"You better be careful. You just might tempt me." She took a sip of the coffee and it was perfect. She couldn't have made it any better if she'd done it herself. "You apparently know exactly how I like my coffee."

"I've only been watching you make it since you were sixteen years old," he said.

She frowned at the edge in his voice and glanced up. "Is everything okay?"

He flashed her a smile. "Couldn't be better." He reached for a piece of bacon and held it to her lips. "See? I can do it without making a mess or burning the hell out of my hand."

She nipped a bite of the end and picked up a piece to feed him. "Not bad, Zach. If you ever get tired of the tattoo biz, I could use a hand with my catering business."

"Nah." He laughed softly. "Breakfast is pretty much the beginning and end of my cooking skills."

The rest of the meal passed in companionable silence, although she was acutely aware of just how much he watched her.

Had he always watched her like that? she wondered.

She thought maybe he had.

But she really wasn't certain.

One thing she did know was that she rather liked how it felt when he watched her. Liked how it felt being with him . . . like this. It was deeper than what she was used to, but still the same on some basic level. She knew that this was the one person who understood her, knew all of her flaws, all of her foibles . . . and loved her anyway. That, in and of itself, was a wonder. But this just felt . . . *more*. It felt like . . . everything.

And the thought of that scared her more than a little. So she pushed it aside.

Chapter Eleven

I know how she likes her damn coffee, he thought sourly as he carried the tray into the kitchen.

Yeah, he knew how she liked her coffee.

He knew how she liked her tea, and he knew which kinds she drank, and at what time of the year.

He knew the kinds of wines she liked, the kinds she hated—anything that wasn't sweet enough to cause a cavity—and he kept her particular favorite on hand at his place even though he couldn't stand the stuff.

He knew what movies she loved, knew what movies she hated, and he knew what kind of books were likely to get thrown across the room and which ones were going to make her cry, and which ones would make her laugh.

Yes. He knew her.

Dumping the dishes in the sink, he rinsed everything off and loaded the dishwasher, taking those few minutes to try and get the frustration out. It should be a little easier right now, he thought. *Should* be. He finally had his chance, right? Granted, this wasn't exactly evolving because he'd been up front or anything . . .

One hand curled into a fist and he realized that was something he had to do. Something he needed to do before this moved too much further.

Now.

He'd go do it now.

He finished up and dried off his hands, mentally bracing himself as he headed into the shower.

Dread curdled in his gut, but if he didn't do this, he was going to risk fucking it up for good. And he couldn't risk that. No matter what.

. . . into the shower . . .

Abigale groaned at the random page she'd found in the journal. Take the damn thing into the shower? It would get ruined.

Except . . . well. That was the point, right?

Wrecking it.

She sighed and kicked her legs off the bed, glancing out the door into the main room. Zach was still out there, moving around in the kitchen. Something was bothering him, but she didn't know what. He'd told her he'd clean up and although she had wanted to argue, she hadn't pushed.

Not once she saw that glint echo in the back of his eyes. He tried to hide it, and she let him, because there was no point in pushing him when he retreated into one of his moods. Besides, she got damn tired of washing dishes.

She'd tugged the journal out of her bag, thinking she'd just jot a few things down, but then she'd remembered she was supposed to actually be *doing* these things and she'd told herself she'd do *one* thing today.

One thing.

"Take it into the damn shower." She headed into the bathroom. Hitting the lights, she laid the journal on the marble counter as she stripped her borrowed sweatshirt off. The bathroom was ridiculously lavish with a shower bigger than a queen-size bed. There was a long bench along two of the walls and before she could change her mind, she tossed the book onto one of them. That should do it, really. It would be in the shower with her. In there, where it wouldn't get *too* wet. She didn't have to get it soaked, right?

Just looking at it there made her uneasy so she turned her back to it and focused on getting the water going. She'd just leave it there. If it got wet, it got wet. It was *in* the shower, after all.

Once she had the water going, she was able to forget about it. A little. Standing with the hot water blasting down on her, she sighed, welcoming the pulsating blast of water coming at her from the multiple showerheads. That was just about perfect, she thought. Just about perfect.

Turning around, she angled her back under the main spray and opened her eyes.

A shriek escaped her as she caught sight of the shadow at the door.

"Damn it, Zach!"

He chuckled and slid the door open, eyeing her with a look that was rapidly becoming very familiar. "You're wet."

Shoving her hair back from her face, she glared at him. "I'm in the shower. You get wet in these things."

He reached for the hem of his shirt and pulled it off. "Is that a fact? I should try it out."

She might have had a response to that. If she could have thought. About anything, other than the fact that he had just peeled his shirt off and was now unzipping his jeans.

In a matter of seconds, he was inside the shower and as he came to her through the crisscrossing sprays, her heart jumped up into her throat. "Zach . . ."

She licked her lips and shifted around so that the water wasn't constantly running down into her eyes to blind her. That, unfortunately, or fortunately, maybe, had her with her back against the wall. He followed her and caught her around the waist. "You do get wet in these things." He hauled her close. "Imagine that."

"Very wet." She groaned as she felt the head of his cock nudging her against her belly. "We . . . well, I didn't exactly bring anything in here. I wasn't planning on water sports."

"I was." He flashed a packet at her and tore it open. "I heard the water come on and made a detour."

She tugged it away from him and tossed the wrapper onto the bench after she'd pulled the condom out. It missed and landed on the floor, but she didn't care.

As she started to unroll it, Zach's chest shuddered. His hands gripped her hips, fingers kneading her flesh restlessly. "Hurry up," he rasped, dipping his head to rake his teeth down her neck. "Fuck . . . hurry."

"Impatient." She smoothed the thin shield of latex down over him and before she could say another word, think another thought, even blink, Zach had her in his arms. He boosted her up and she caught her breath, staring into his eyes as he wedged the head of his cock against her sex and pressed.

"Now." He stared into her eyes, watching her like he sought to see down into her very soul. "Right now."

She nodded, sucking in a breath. It wasn't enough . . . she was still scrambling for oxygen, scrambling to think, to function as he slowly sank inside her.

"You have no idea." He stared down into her eyes. "No idea how bad I need this. Need you. I waited . . . I wanted . . ."

I waited . . .

Those words burned through her brain and she knew she needed to think that through. But she couldn't. Not when he pulled back and then surged forward, driving so completely inside her.

"Tell me you want this," he demanded. "Tell me you want *me*."

Dazed, she stared at him. He shot a hand into her hair and tangled his fingers in the curls, jerking her head back, forcing her to watch him. She whimpered as his mouth crushed against hers. Hard and desperate, that kiss ripped a response from her and she was all but sobbing when he lifted just enough to peer down into her eyes. "Tell me you want me, damn it."

"I want you," she said, and her voice trembled with the

force of that want. "I want you so much I can't breathe for it. I dream about you and I feel your touch on me even when you're not there."

Her eyes, nearly black, stared into his as she spoke and Zach tried to cling to the hope in those words.

It meant something.

Had to.

But just then, all he could do was give in to the madness that had ripped through him when he'd seen her in the shower. One more time, damn it. Before he explained, because if he lost her . . .

She arched against him, her wet hands sliding down his arms, then back up along his shoulders to tangle in his hair. She swiveled her hips and he moved back a little, changing their angle so that her shoulders rested against the wall and he could stare down, watch as he moved within her.

Her flesh was pale as cream, unmarred and smooth. And he loved the way his hands looked on her as he guided her hips, lifting her up as he pulled away, dragging her back down over his cock as he sank back in. "Mine." For that moment, at least. She was his.

Abby keened, a low, rough sound of female pleasure that had his balls drawing tight and his gut twisting in a blinding knot of need.

He pushed her harder. Faster. Giving in to the burning edge that had ridden him for so damned long.

As she clenched down around him and started to come, his own climax tore through him like a tornado, nearly undoing him.

He saw the journal on the long, narrow bench as he went to pull off the condom.

That journal.

That wonderful journal.

That stupid journal.

Part of him wanted to bronze it while another part of him wanted to rip it apart.

Except right now, it needed to be dried off.

After he'd dealt with the condom, he glanced over at Abby and said, "You like the journal so much you brought it into the shower with you?"

She was still leaning against the wall, her lips curved in a smile of pure, smug female satisfaction. It went straight to his dick and he wanted nothing more than to go back to her and do a repeat of the past five minutes. Except maybe make it last *longer* than five minutes. Hell. He touched her and lost all control.

But if he didn't do this now . . .

"Abby." He nodded to the journal again and said, "The journal is getting soaked."

She made a face at him and said, "It's supposed to. Have you *looked* at what's inside there? It's got a page that says *take this journal into the shower with you.* Or something like that. Okay? It's in the shower." A funny little grin curled her lips upward. "I was stressing about it pretty bad before you came in."

He moved to block her view of the journal, catching one of the showerheads and wetting his hair down. It wasn't because he was in any hurry to wash up. He just needed a way to distract himself. To not look at her while he thought this through. "Abby . . . ah. Actually, about the journal . . ."

She sighed. "I should probably get it out of here before it's ruined, shouldn't I?"

Swallowing the knot in his throat, he turned away and grabbed it. It was dripping wet as he nudged the door open and placed it on the floor. "It should be fine." His voice sounded like he'd swallowed a frog. Turning around, he looked at her.

She had her head cocked. "Are you okay?"

"Ah . . ." Scooping his damp hair back, he glanced around. Then he held out a hand as he settled on the bench near the jets. A fine mist wrapped around them, but it didn't soak them and that worked. He thought. "I need to tell you something. You're going to be mad at me. I . . ." He groaned as she hooked an arm around his neck. Slamming his head back against the marbled tile of the wall, he closed his eyes. "I told you, just a few minutes ago. It wasn't just . . . um. It wasn't just my dick talking when I said I've been waiting to touch you like this. That I wanted you for a while."

All my life—

"Zach . . . ?"

He opened his eyes and made himself meet her gaze. He figured it would be better to play it down a little. "You just . . . hell, Abby. You were engaged and all. What was I supposed to do?"

Her hand splayed over his cheek as she stared at him.

"Ah . . . this . . ." She closed her eyes and dropped her head down on his shoulder. "Well. Um. I'm sort of thrown here, but okay. I figured out the fact that you weren't exactly oblivious the second or third time you had your tongue down my throat."

He cupped a hand over the back of her neck. "No. Not oblivious. I just . . . Don't be mad at me. Abby, I saw what you had written in that damn journal. I knew you were planning to have an affair with somebody and I wanted it to be me."

She stiffened.

Her hand fell away from his cheek.

Pain ripped through him as she pulled away and stood up. A few seconds later, she left him alone in the shower and he sat in there, eyes closed.

Had he just fucked it up for good?

Please . . . no. Just. No.

"He wanted me. I was engaged. Shit."

It was only the fifteenth time she'd muttered that, or some variation over the past twenty minutes. Dressed in her woefully inadequate clothing, a blanket wrapped around her with her damp hair making her even more miserable, Abigale stood on the balcony, freezing her ass off and brooding. She could go inside, dry her hair, lock herself in the bedroom, but just then, she needed the space. So she stood out there, freezing and cranky and confused.

"Don't be mad, he says."

Swearing, she dropped down onto the chaise lounge and buried her head in her arms.

Don't be mad . . .

She wasn't *mad*, exactly.

She was . . . embarrassed. Sort of. She'd been so miserable and uncomfortable about the major lust-on she'd developed for her best friend, and he'd been doing the same thing for her. For . . . hell. A while. She'd been engaged for almost two years.

She was *uncomfortable*, but with herself. How hadn't she seen it?

And she was aggravated, yeah, because he'd been nosing in the journal, but she wasn't mad, really. That was just typical Zach. If she wanted him to leave something *alone*, she specifically had to *tell* him or keep it *away* from him.

The door opened and she lifted her head, shooting him a dark look.

He stood in the doorway, hands jammed in his pockets. His hair was still damp and while he'd tugged on a pair of jeans, he hadn't buttoned them and he hadn't bothered with a shirt, either. Lust and desire and all sorts of crazy needs hit her, so hard and fast that she just had to look away from him before she lost it.

Before she came up off the lounge and just jumped him.

"So are you done?"

His voice, hard and flat, was like a slap in the still air and she barely managed to keep from flinching. Shooting him a narrow look, she asked icily, "Am I done *what*?"

He averted his head, a muscle pulsing in his cheek.

Done.

What, did the jerk think she wasn't allowed to be irritated? She wasn't allowed to be confused or pissed? He thought she was out here having a sulk over *nothing*? Is that what he thought? Surging up off the lounge, she let the blanket fall as she stormed over to him. "Am I done *what*?" she demanded.

He turned his head and stared at her, but still didn't answer.

She curled her hand into a fist and thumped it on his chest. "You think I don't have a right to be aggravated, Zach? You think I'm out here sulking and I'm just supposed to stop at a certain—"

His hands came around her waist and he spun her around. The rough brick of the wall scratched against her spine as he backed her up. "Damn it. *Me*," he snarled down into her face. "Are you done with *me*? Is this it? Did I fuck it up? I'm sorry, damn it. I shouldn't have been messing with your stuff and if I'd thought I was going to see something like that . . ." He stopped and looked down, a ragged breath escaping him. "I'm sorry, okay? I'm sorry. I just . . . shit. Maybe I should have come clean or something, but I just had to watch you spend three fucking years with that prick Roger and if I had to see with you somebody else . . ."

Oh.

Light dawned as she stared at his bowed head.

I've been waiting . . . I wanted you . . .

It wasn't exactly a shining, beautiful declaration of love, but she hadn't been expecting that. Zach wasn't in love with her. She knew that. He'd already told her that he'd been in love and it hadn't worked out.

"No, Zach. I'm not done."

He jerked up his head, staring at her with that intent, focused gaze. It went right to the very heart of her and made her ache. Hell. Whoever that woman was, she was an absolute moron. If Zach had been looking at *her* like that . . . ?

"Abby?"

She reached up and touched his cheek. "I'm not done. I'm irritated as hell over you messing with my stuff, but I'm not done. I'm irritated, and I'm confused . . . but this isn't anywhere close to done for me."

Chapter Twelve

"I hear you and Abby went out of town for the week-end."

Zach really shouldn't have answered the damn phone without looking at the caller ID. He never did when he was in the shop, but damn it, he should have. Grimacing, he shoved a hand out of his hair and tried not to think about the fact that his brother Zane already knew how he felt about Abby.

It wasn't like he had to *explain* anything here now, right?

Zane knew. The twins, Trey and Travis knew. Even his obnoxious and annoying little brother Sebastian knew.

Mom knew. Dad knew.

Everybody in the family knew.

The question was . . .

"Who in the hell told you about that?"

Even over the phone, he could hear the sly amusement in Zane's voice as his older brother said, "Oh, I have my ways."

Zach curled his lips. "You probably came over here sniffing around Keelie's skirts again. Did she plant that combat boot in your face again?"

"At least I got the balls to make a move on the woman

I'm interested in and didn't sit around mooning over her like a pussy for twenty years," Zane pointed out.

Sighing, Zach rubbed the back of his neck and tried to focus on the sketch in front of him. He had a young widow coming in here later that week who wanted a tattoo. Her husband had been killed in Afghanistan and Zach wanted to make sure he had the design right.

He'd been doing fine up until his brother called, too. Had his focus on the job, had the right sort of vision in mind, and everything. "Listen, man, I don't know about you, but I actually work during the day. You might sit around jacking off all day and staring at naked models on your screen, but I need to get some designs done so if you didn't call for a reason—"

"I did." Zane's voice lost some of the amusement. "I guess that answers that. I was hoping you'd finally worked up the courage and did something, but you wouldn't be so fucking uptight if you'd gotten laid."

The pencil he'd been using snapped. "Shut the fuck up, Zane," he warned.

"Look, man, I just thought—"

"I don't care what you just thought. If I just needed to get fucked, I could get that from plenty of places." He shoved back from the desk and started to pace.

"Damn it, that's not what I'm getting at. Would you . . ." Zane trailed off into a long series of muttered cursing. Then abruptly, he said, "Look. I wasn't meaning anything by it and definitely not that. I'd be the first one in line if I thought some asshole was chasing after her like she was just a piece of meat. You know I love Abby. She's like a kid sister to me and that's the last thing I'd be thinking about. I just . . . look. Sooner or later, you're going to have to make a move or she'll end up hooked up with another loser like Roger. Is that what you want?"

Zach stared at the wall that held some of the work he'd done, but he wasn't seeing any of the pictures, any of the designs he'd done on his own.

He was seeing Abby. The way she'd looked as they

stayed out on the deck Saturday night, watching the sun set over the mountains. Neither of them had been wearing a damn thing, just laying on the lounge with a blanket pulled over them. He was certain it had been the most perfect moment of his entire life.

"Let me worry about my love life, Zane," he said gruffly.

"That's the fucking problem. You don't *have* one. You just—"

He hung up on Zane and lowered his head to stare at the worn toes of his boots, trying to think, trying to figure out why he hadn't just told him. Out of all of his brothers, he was closest to Zane and if he could tell any of them, it should have been Zane.

But just then, he couldn't imagine telling anybody.

And he knew why.

Once he told people, it would become real.

And when it became real, it would be too easy to break . . . to see it end, to see it fall apart.

She hadn't walked away once he'd owned up to what he'd done. That was the worst thing he could imagine happening . . . *at the time*. But there was something far worse and he had to face it.

Abby was already planning for it to end and if he couldn't get her to fall in love with him, it *would* end.

Absently, he reached up and ran his thumb over his heart, wondering if she'd noticed it at all. Nah. If she had, she would have said something.

"Zach?"

Lifting his head, he saw Keelie standing in the doorway. The look on her face was nervous and he sighed, turning away and heading back to his desk. He just didn't have time for this today. Dumping the phone back in the cradle, he said, "I'm busy, Keelie. I've got several custom designs I still need to get done and I'm sure my asshole brother will be calling my other brothers so I'll have more fun conversations for later on."

Bent over the sketch, he tried to block her out, but she didn't seem to take the hint.

"I'm sorry," she said.

Sighing, he leaned back and met her gaze. She had un-usual eyes, one pale gold, almost the shade of whiskey. The other was pale, pale blue . . . almost ice blue. She'd forgone the heavier makeup she often wore and her face looked almost naked. Frowning a little, he sighed and asked, "Are you okay?"

She shrugged and edged a few feet into his office, turn-ing to stare at the design board. "I shouldn't have said any-thing to Zane when he came by. I knew he'd give you a hassle. Dunno why I didn't think about that."

"Don't worry about it." The last thing he needed was Keelie feeling all guilty because his brother was acting . . . well. Like himself. No reason for her to feel guilty that Zane was just Zane. When he put his mind to it, Zane could charm a fucking cobra and while Keelie seemed as mean as a damned snake sometimes, she wasn't. Not really. It was a problem that Zane seemed to have developed a thing for her and Zach figured he needed to step in and make his brother back off.

He smiled a little. He could do it this weekend. They were all getting together for the twins' birthday and he could pick a fight with the jerk . . . the mood he was in, it would be fun. He should feel bad, he figured, thinking about picking a fight with one of his brothers at a family get-together, but . . . well. It was going to happen sooner or later anyway and he figured his mom and dad were used to it.

"Look, Keelie, Zane is just being Zane," he finally said. "Don't worry about it."

She shrugged a little and toyed with the sleeve of the formfitting black shirt she wore. "He wanted me to come to the thing at your folks' place up in San Diego."

Zach blinked. *What?*

Zane didn't invite women to family things. Period. *Ever.*

She turned around and glared at him. "Don't worry. I'm not going. I know I'm not going to fit in or anything so—"

"Keelie . . . shut up."

She sneered at him. "Bite me, Barnes."

He might have fired something back at her if she hadn't looked so damned sad under the anger he thought he saw. What the hell . . . ? Swearing under his breath, he stood up and came around his desk. "Keelie, I don't know what this shit is about fitting in with my family, but you need to drop it, okay? If Zane invited you and you want to come, then come."

She glared at him. "Yeah, like your folks will just love having me there. I've heard you all talking about your family things, Zach. And you're probably asking Abby . . . I'll *really* fit in well with that crowd."

"Abby and my family aren't a *crowd*." Screw this. Turning around, he said over his shoulder, "If you're that much of a coward, Keelie, then fine. Be a coward. But the problem is *you*. It's not my family. Not a damn one of them has ever given you a reason to think you wouldn't be welcome around them so don't act otherwise."

"Screw you, Zach," she snapped.

He ignored her and settled down to work.

He didn't need this.

Not at all.

Asking Abby . . .

As Keelie stormed out of his office, he shifted his attention to one of the few pictures he had on his desk. All but one were of his family, his mom and dad holding their one and only grandchild . . . his brother Trey and his wife Cara. She'd died only a day after their baby had been born, something that had left all of them reeling from the shock. A picture of their son, an imp in kid's clothing if such a thing existed.

The only other picture was of him and Abby and it had been taken by Zane. Zane, when he wasn't standing behind a bar and charming women out of their panties, liked to hide behind a camera. He could make it in a big way with photography if he'd ever put his mind to it. He had a way of pulling emotions out of people, but he also had a thing about not really investing in anything. Zach didn't know why, didn't care.

But his brother had a gift and the proof of it was right in front of him, in the image of him with Abby, this picture that had captured every damned thing he felt for Abby and put it out there for all the world to see.

Of course, Abby never seemed to see it.

Reaching for the picture, he thought about the upcoming weekend. She'd be there.

Abby always handled the catering for anything his mom put together and it didn't matter that she had to either fly or drive out there. He'd once told her that she didn't have to keep doing it, and she'd looked at him like he'd grown another head.

She'd be there, handling all the food, talking to his brothers, flirting with his dad, and joking with his mom about whether or not she'd ever get any more grandkids. He stroked his finger down the frame, staring at Abby's laughing face.

She was watching him with a smile in the picture, her arms thrown around him and her eyes glowing. It had been taken last summer . . . his mom had decided to surprise Abby with a birthday party and she'd roped Zach and the rest of them into helping with it.

Near the end, Abby had come up to him to thank him and he'd brushed it off. It hadn't been his idea, so why thank him?

And she'd hugged him.

It had been so hard, not to kiss her. When she lifted that smiling face to his and he looked down into her dark brown eyes, lost in them . . .

Abby hadn't seemed to notice, but he had. Everybody around them had. An odd, tense silence had fallen. Not awkward. But like everybody had been waiting. Then she'd just brushed her lips against his cheek and gave him a tight squeeze before she pulled away and headed back over to that fuckhead, Roger.

A week later, this picture had been waiting on the desk for him, along with a note from Zane.

You need to quit waiting, man.

Yeah. He had to quit waiting.

So what did he do? Ask her if she felt like making this weekend at his family's a date sort of thing?

"I can't exactly do a date sort of thing," Abigale said. Nerves jangled inside her belly and if she wasn't making the batch of cookies for an event that evening, she would have been tempted to just start eating some of the dough to calm those nerves.

A date . . . They couldn't do a date, not around his family. Denise would get the worst idea. Not that it would be bad, Denise thinking about her and Zach—

What? Her mind skittered to a halt as she realized just *what* she was thinking. There was no *way* she could go around Zach's mom and dad and let them think they were *dating.* As much as she loved to tease Denise and Ron about their unending quest to see their boys settled down, she knew what would happen if she showed up there as Zach's date.

Denise would get that look in her eyes.

That hopeful, starry-eyed look.

And then when it ended . . . It was a thought that made an ache settle right square in her heart. *When it ended . . .*

Strong, warm arms folded around her. "What are you thinking so hard about, sugar?"

Abigale tried not to let herself react as he rubbed his lips over her neck but it was damned hard. They'd been having their . . . *torrid affair* for less than two weeks. They'd spent the week together and had sex more times than she could— well, that was wrong. Seven times over the weekend. They'd had sex *seven glorious times* over the weekend. Less than two weeks and one weekend together and her body was already responding to him like she'd been made to do just that.

"I'm thinking I need to get the cookies done so I can

start prepping for everything else . . . this is something I'm doing for a friend and I've got a lot of work to get done," she hedged.

"Why do you try to lie to me?" He nuzzled her neck. "You never were any good at it. You can pull it off with everybody else, but you can't ever lie to me worth a damn and we both know it."

She sniffed and slammed the bowl down on the counter with a *thunk*. Wiggling around in the circle of his arms, she glared up at him. "I can, too. And I'll have you know I *do* have a lot of work to get done."

A grin tugged up the corner of his mouth and he said, "The hell you can."

He reached behind her and she smacked his hand. "Damn it, Zach. That's for a PTO thing tonight. You can't have any."

"A PTO thing?" His brows came together over his eyes. "Somebody is paying you to cater a PTO thing? Parents are supposed to bake the cookies and cakes and pies themselves."

She sighed. "It's some kind of meeting with the school board. The lady who contacted me is a friend and she told me, and I quote . . . *'I want them in a good mood and if I don't provide the desserts, they'll be coming for my blood.'* So I'm doing the desserts. We worked out a trade, though. Her husband handles my landscaping and I need some more work done so she said she'd talk him into cutting me a deal if I'd help her out."

"Pushover." He dipped his head and nipped her lower lip. "Now . . . what were you thinking about? It sure as hell wasn't cookies. You can do cookies and just about everything else blindfolded." Then he flexed his hand and grimaced. "Although I don't recommend it. Kitchen accidents are hazardous to your health."

She squirmed and tried to wiggle away from him but he just leaned his hips against hers.

Oh . . . her lids dropped and a sigh shuddered out of her. That just felt so very right. Like almost nothing else ever had. "You did hear the part about me having a lot of work to do, right?" she asked. She pretended not to hear the way her breath hitched in her throat.

"Yes . . . and if you want to get to it, you should answer." He slid a hand down her hip and toyed with the hem of the skirt she wore. "Otherwise, I'm going to think of something else to distract myself with. Hey . . . I know."

She jabbed him in the ribs. "You're such a juvenile."

"Hmmm . . ." He cupped his hands over her hips and rocked against her. "And you're so female. So do I start looking for distractions?"

From under her lashes, she stared at him and then sighed. "Zach . . . you know how your mom is. If we go there on a date sort of thing, as you call it, she's going to get her hopes all worked up. And when this thing ends . . ."

He stroked a hand up her side, along her collarbone, and up her neck until he could rest his fingertip on her lips. "Why are you in such a rush to talk about everything ending, Abby? We just got started."

"Ah . . ." She had an answer for that.

Really.

But even as she tried to figure out what it was, his mouth replaced his finger and she couldn't possibly think when Zach Barnes was kissing her.

His arms hooked over her shoulders, his body caging her in, the kiss should have been greedy and demanding . . . and she could have met that, could have handled that. Hell, a quickie in the kitchen sounded like it would go hand in hand with a torrid affair, right?

Although she should really move it out of there while she worked . . .

But it wasn't a greedy, demanding kiss.

His lips, light as an angel's touch, brushed over hers and even when she opened for him, he didn't take it deeper. Instead, he skimmed his lips up along her cheekbone to brush along her temple, then he rubbed his cheek against hers. "You thinking to call it quits already, Abs?"

"Call . . ." She had to force the word out through a tight

throat. It had just been a kiss. Just a simple kiss. "Call it . . ."

Her brain processed what he'd said and it was like somebody had sucked the air out of the room, the light out of the world. "Call it quits?"

Jerking her head back, she stared at up at him. Was he——

He skimmed a hand through her hair and said softly, "I was barely getting warmed up and it seems like you're already planning my good-bye party."

"No, I'm not." Okay . . . he'd been talking about something else. She wasn't exactly sure what, but there you go. That was Zach for you. "What in the hell are you talking about?"

"I ask you for a date and you're over there talking about things ending and my mom being heartbroken." He slid his hands down her arms and caught hers, twining their fingers together. "I'm kind of happy with how things are going, but it seems like you're already looking at the finish line. Is that what you're doing?"

The finish line . . .

Blowing out a sigh, she shifted her attention to a point past his shoulder. The silvery reflection of her refrigerator was nowhere as appealing to look at as he was, but when she looked at him, her brain had developed this annoying habit of just not functioning the right way. "Well . . . I'm not exactly looking at a finish line, but we never really did set out for this to be . . . be . . ." The word lodged in her throat. Shit. Shit, she couldn't say that to Zach. They were having an affair. It was amazing, and wonderful, and she loved it, but that was all it was. *That's not all you want anymore, though . . .*

"A relationship," he finished.

Jerking her gaze back to his, she swallowed. Damn it, that knot was choking her now. Hesitantly, she nodded. "It was just supposed to be . . ."

The dark fan of his lashes swept down, shielding his eyes from her as he blew out a sigh. He dipped his head and pressed his brow to hers while one hand came around her waist, tangling in the gauzy material of the shirt she'd pulled on over a camisole-styled tank that morning. "You planned on a torrid affair, Abby. That doesn't mean it can't be something more."

Her heart jumped into her throat and a hope she hadn't even realized she'd been harboring started to rise inside her, growing so fast, so strong . . .

Zach's lids lifted and she found herself caught in the intense blue of his eyes. "If you want more . . . if I want more, who says we can't have more?"

"Is that what you want?"

Something flashed in his eyes. There, then gone.

That look, whatever it was, left her head reeling, spinning . . .

Sucking in a breath, she almost couldn't hear his words over the roar of blood in her ears. Almost. "Abby . . . you have no idea just how much more I want from you."

Chapter Thirteen

"So . . . you're here with Zach . . ."

Pulling the lasagna out of the oven, Abigale braced her-self for the next inquisition. She recognized the low, smooth sound of Sebastian's voice without even turning around and she already knew how to handle this one.

Over the past few hours, she'd handled the curious ques-tions from the twins, seen the odd gleam in Ron's eyes, and almost went head-to-head with Keelie, although she really didn't know why Keelie despised her so much.

The easiest person, by far, had been Denise and *that* had been a shock. Denise, Zach's mom, was the one person Abigale had been sort of dreading to face over this and she hated that, because she *adored* Denise. Because she adored Denise, because she knew and loved the woman, she knew what Denise wanted most was to see her kids all happy.

Denise didn't necessarily equate *happy* with *married*, but more than a few late-night conversations had cemented one certainty in Abigale's head.

Denise suspected her second-oldest son was lonely.

Not crying-in-his-beer lonely, Denise had told her once. But he was looking for something.

Abigale hadn't ever seen it, and that bothered her because she was his best friend, but Denise had told her that there were some things a mom just knew. Maybe so. It wasn't like Abigale had the best mom to really judge things by.

But Denise had been easy.

Sebastian was the other person she'd been dreading having to face over this. *Might as well get it over with*, she told herself as she reached for a towel and turned around to look at him.

They were alone in the kitchen, although that wouldn't last long, she knew.

Denise had been bustling in and out of the kitchen for most of the afternoon and in a few minutes, Abigale knew she'd be pulled out there to enjoy the party as well. Pretty little Chinese lanterns strung throughout the back swayed in the breeze and people were laughing, calling out to each other. All in all, everybody seemed to be having a good time, even Trey, although every now and then, he'd get a far-off look in his eyes and Abigale knew he was thinking about his wife. Cara had only been twenty-three when she died. Too young, Abigale thought. Far too young.

Blowing out a breath, she surveyed everything around her. She was pretty much done. It was a buffet-style meal and she wasn't feeding an army. A party for thirty people was easy for her. Somebody else was handling the cake and everything so she was almost at the point that she could take a few minutes, but she'd rather take those minutes with Zach. Playing twenty questions with Sebastian wasn't her idea of fun.

It was going to happen, though.

"I'm often at places with Zach," she pointed out, giving Sebastian an easy smile. They were friends . . . usually, and got along well enough, when Zach wasn't in the picture.

But the two of them lived very much in two different worlds.

"You probably don't remember a lot of it, but Zach and I have often been in the very same place for more than twenty years." She winked at him and added, "There were even a few times when I was there while *you* were there . . . in diapers."

Sebastian was twenty-two and the youngest of the crew. He was also the prettiest, prettier even than Zach, and it seemed he was determined to chase after the career Zach had walked away from. He still lived in LA and he was doing pretty well lately . . . a few small parts on a TV show and there was talk that his character was going to become a regular next season.

He looked up to his older brother with something that was near adulation, she knew. Zach could do no wrong. He was almost fiercely protective of him. But Sebastian had tunnel vision. He was almost *certain* that Zach's main issue in life was that he just hadn't found the right venue back into Hollywood.

Sometimes she wondered if Sebastian and Roger had been drinking the same Kool-Aid.

"So I hear your show is going well," she said, shifting his focus from Zach to his other love in life.

Or trying to.

She failed.

He shrugged and said, "It's going well. But you know how it goes." Shrewd eyes, just a shade darker than Zach's, studied her face. "You know, if Zach ever decides to come back, my agent is there to help him . . . and I know you're done with it. How are you going to feel if he does it?"

Instead of pointing out that Zach had said *a hundred times* that he didn't want to go back, she reached for the knife and started slicing up the last loaf of bread. "Zach's life is his own, Seb. I can't control it." She shot him a look and then went back to the chore in front of her, hoping he'd take the point. *See . . . look at me, I'm busy, busy, busy.*

He laughed a little. "Yeah, that's what you think."

The undercurrent in his voice got to her, rubbing her so very, very wrong. Carefully, she put the knife down. Because she didn't want to get pissed off here, and pissed off at Sebastian, she took a minute to reach for her wine. It was more to give herself a minute to think through anything she might say, to puzzle through just *what* that might mean. But she had no stunning revelations in the thirty seconds it took to drink the yummy ratafia that Zach always managed to keep on hand for her. It came from a winery in Albuquerque and she was tempted to toss the entire glass back and then pour another.

But she doubted it would do a damn thing to lessen her irritation.

So instead, she lowered the glass back down and lifted her gaze to study Sebastian. "Okay. So you think I can control Zach's life. Exactly how do I do that?"

"You got him to move away from LA." Sebastian's eyes narrowed on her face and although his voice never once raised, she heard the resentment there.

And it was strong. Damn it, where in the hell had *that* come from?

"*I* got him to move?" she asked, pushing away from the counter. "Exactly how did I do that? We've been seeing each other for exactly two weeks. He moved to Tucson years ago."

The door opened, but neither of them paid it much attention.

"He's spent more than half of his life doing exactly what *you* wanted him to do, Abby," Sebastian said, his voice icy, full of disgust. "Are you ever going to—"

"Sebastian."

He cut a look over his shoulder at Zane. "Back off," he snapped. "This is between me and Abby."

"There shouldn't be a damn thing between you and Abby," Zane said.

Abigale glanced over at Zane and the look on his face was one of apology, but she ignored it, looking back at Sebastian. "Am I ever going to what?" she demanded.

"Sebastian, if you don't shut the fuck up," Zane warned. "I'm going to—"

Whipping her head around, Abigale glared at Zane. He'd been like the big brother she never had, teasing her, protecting her, needling her. And right now, he was pissing her off.

"Zane, *you* shut the fuck up, or I'm going to punch you," she said.

She was vaguely aware the door had opened again, vaguely aware that more people had trickled into the kitchen, but she didn't give a damn. Sebastian was still glaring at her, although when he shot the people around them a look, a muscle pulsed in his jaw.

"We'll discuss it some other time," he said quietly.

"Oh, the hell we will." Crossing her arms over her chest, she glared at him. "You started this here. We finish this here. I want to know just how in the hell I'm controlling Zach. I want to know how I'm stopping him from chasing after a life back in California . . . even though he *sure as hell doesn't want it*."

"How would you know?" Sebastian snapped. He shoved a hand through his hair and advanced on her, bending down to snarl in her face. "You don't know *shit* about what he wants, because the one thing he does want? You've never even—"

His eyes shot over her shoulder and Abigale watched as he slowly straightened. His jaw clenched and that pretty face of his went hard as stone. "Zach."

A hand came up and curled over Abigale's shoulder. Abruptly, the rush of anger cleared from her head and she felt a little sick as she looked around. Almost the entire family had gathered in there. Not just Denise and Ron. Not just Zach's brothers and their dates. But cousins, kids, friends. Nearly thirty people had managed to squeeze their way inside the brightly lit kitchen and they were now watching the entire thing.

Pressing a hand to her belly, she blew out a breath and then shifted her attention over to Denise and the twins. The hell if she apologized to Sebastian, the jackass. But Denise, the twins . . . it was their day. "Denise, guys, I am so sorry," she whispered.

Denise's eyes snapped and burned, but she smiled at her. "Abby, I don't think you're the one who needs to apologize."

Sebastian's eyes narrowed as he slid his mother a look.

Then he looked back at Abigale and like he was chewing off ragged bits of rusty metal, he bit out, "Sorry."

Without looking at anybody else, he turned to go.

Zach, until that moment, hadn't said a word. But then, after a gentle squeeze on her shoulder, he eased around her. "Sebastian, kid . . . you and me need to have a word."

Abigale groaned. She knew that tone.

Passing a hand over her face, she said, "Zach, just let it go."

But it was like he didn't even hear her, and before she could try to go after him, Zane barred her way. "Leave the two of them alone," he advised.

"They don't need to be fighting at the twins' party—there are kids here. They don't want to fight around the kids."

A grin split his face. Thick brown hair tumbled into his eyes as he caught her in a hug and pulled her close. "Oh, now come on, Abby. Since when have we ever managed to have a single party or even a cookout without one of us getting mad about something?"

She scowled and wiggled away from him. "Just because you *always* do it doesn't mean you have to *keep* doing it." Shoving her hair back from her face, she looked around and figured she could take another break, since nothing was in the oven, and all the food was outside except the next round of bread. "Look, I'm—"

Most of the family had started to trickle out, but Denise was still there and Abigale felt the blood start to crawl up her neck under the weight of that gentle, watchful gaze. "I'm just going to talk to Zach," she finished lamely.

A shout came from somewhere off in the depths of the house.

"Abby."

As she untied her apron, she put a lot more focus on the task than she knew she really needed to. "I'll just be a few minutes, Denise. I—"

"You're so stubborn." Denise slid an arm around her shoulders. Then she hugged her. "Leave the boys alone. They'll work it out. Sebastian has words he has to say. He's wrong. He needs to figure that out. And Zach probably has a few words of his own, and after that scene? He's more than entitled." She reached up and brushed Abigale's hair back. It was such a gentle, familiar, *loving* gesture, it left an ache in Abigale's throat. "Leave them be for now, okay, sweetie?"

Another shout rose, this one followed by a string of curses.

Denise winced. "If they were a few years younger, I'd have to dig out the bar of soap over that one."

Abigale closed her eyes. "I knew this was going to turn out bad."

"Oh, hush." The older woman kissed Abigale on the cheek and then stepped back. "Come on. Let's get the bread out there and eat so we can dig in to the cake. I tried that new lady you recommended and it looks divine."

Zach pressed a knee into Sebastian's back. If the idiot kid didn't stop jerking around, he was going to get really mad and hurt him. Just then, he was trying to remember that Sebastian *was* still pretty damn young, and like the typical youngest sibling, he was spoiled as hell. He was also headstrong, thought he could do no wrong, and thought he knew everything.

Zach was tempted to disabuse him of all that in a painful way, but he figured it wouldn't help things if he broke his baby brother's nose when the jackass was supposed to be back at work in a few days. "Kid, if you don't stop it, that pretty face you're so proud of isn't going to be so fucking pretty. I'm going to do some rearranging and you'll have a lot of fun explaining *that* to the agent you're always trying to ram down my throat."

Sebastian grunted and tried once more to dislodge Zach and when he couldn't, he swore. "Look, man. The reason you're so pissed is because you know I'm *right*. I'm fucking *right*."

He slammed Sebastian's head against the floor. "The reason I'm so pissed is because you're interfering . . . right when I finally get things where I want them and you're trying to fuck it up for me." Anger blistered through him and he knew he had to move before he did something he regretted.

Swearing, he surged up off Sebastian and stormed across the room. Distance. Needed to get some distance. Because the longer he thought about what he'd just walked in on, the madder he got.

Hearing Sebastian get to his feet, he spun around and glared at him. "What the hell, Seb? You want to tell me why in the *hell* you're trying to fuck my life up?"

"This isn't your fucking life!" Sebastian glared right back. "You sit in a damned hole-in-the-wall and play with needles and ink and act like that makes you happy while you wait for that woman to notice you're alive. If she hasn't done it yet, when is she going to?"

It was a punch in the gut and a blow to his pride and damn it, Zach knew there was truth to it. Had he been waiting a long-ass time for Abby to finally *see* him? Damn straight. Were there days when he thought it was just never going to happen? Hell, yes.

And he'd been willing to deal with that, willing to live with it, because he couldn't see himself anyplace else. Where she was, that was where *he* had to be.

Things had changed and damn it, he was going to make the most of it. And what the hell was Sebastian doing, trying to screw it up for him?

Gut in a knot, he glared at his younger brother. "And just what in the hell do *you* think I ought to do?" he demanded. "Go back to a life where the only women interested in me were interested because of *what* I was? *Who* I was? They didn't give a damn about me. And here's another problem, Seb . . . *I don't want that life.* It suits you, but I grew out of it. It's not *me* anymore."

"And sitting around waiting for *her* is?"

"I'm not exactly waiting right now!" Spinning around, he slammed his fist into a wall. For about five seconds, that helped. A lot. But then, as the adrenaline faded and pain bloomed in his hand, he had to bite back a groan. *Smooth, Zach. Real smooth.* That had been the hand he'd burned and the healing skin was no longer *healing*. The scabs across his knuckles split open and as he stared at the blood, he muttered, "Now that just tops it off."

Sighing, he headed over to the bar and grabbed one of the towels from under it.

"She just got dumped by her fiancé," Sebastian said, his voice flat. "Do you really think you're going to have a chance building anything there?"

"Seb," Zach said softly, taking his time as he wrapped the towel around his hand. "You don't even have a clue what I *want* out of my life, you know. Not a damned clue. You think because you're happy with where you're heading, that life is going to suit me, too."

Sliding his brother a look, Zach shook his head. "You're wrong. You're so very wrong."

A muscle pulsed in Sebastian's jaw and finally, he looked away. "Maybe you don't want that anymore, but I'm not wrong about Abby. She's never going to see what you feel, Zach. I . . . I don't want you to get hurt."

There were a thousand things he could have said. Probably a million. But he didn't want words between him and his brother that couldn't be taken back. So instead, he just chose the few words that *had* to be said. "You need to keep out of what's going on between me and her," he warned, still focusing on the towel. "It doesn't concern you."

"You're my fucking brother," Sebastian snapped. "How am I *not* supposed to be concerned with shit that affects you?"

"You're my fucking brother." Zach laughed a little. "And you're acting out of concern for shit that affects me? Oh, that's rich, Seb. Because what you just pulled had a pretty damned big effect. She makes me happy, damn it. You're trying to fuck it up and she makes me happy."

He found her in the backyard.

She wore another one of those dresses that just drove him nuts and all afternoon, he'd been watching her in the kitchen and having insane fantasies about that lovely, pale green dress and the pretty white apron.

Just then, she had the skirt hiked up to her knees and she was sitting with her feet in the water while she watched some of his cousins playing in the pool with his nephew, Clayton.

Lowering himself down onto the edge, he took a minute to pull off his socks and boots, rolling his jeans up to the knees and sliding his legs into the water. Abby didn't look his way.

"Are you mad at me?" he asked quietly.

A sad sigh escaped her and she reached over, caught his hand. "Why would I be?"

"You don't like it when I fight with my brothers."

He watched as she ducked her head. She'd pulled all of her hair into a thick, complicated twist but a few wayward curls were starting to escape, trailing down her neck, curling around her ears. He wanted to catch one of them and wind it around his finger, but just then, he hesitated to touch her.

"Right now, I'd almost like to fight with one of your brothers." Then she nodded at his hand. "Did you hit Seb?"

He glanced at his hand. He'd taken a minute to go into the bathroom and actually bandage it, then he'd cut a wide berth around his mom, hoping she wouldn't notice. He wasn't counting on it. Moms noticed *everything*.

Wiggling his fingers, he shrugged and said, "Nah. I hit the wall. It's almost as hard as Seb's head, and it wouldn't cause problems when he heads back to work. If I busted his pretty face, it would cause a headache and a half and it's not worth it just because he's an ass. At least not yet."

He stroked his thumb down the back of her hand, looking across the pool. Sebastian had finally come out of the house and their mom was heading for him. The kid had the look on his face of a deer caught in the headlights of a car bearing down on it, at oh . . . two hundred miles an hour.

Zach could pound him into the ground and Sebastian would fight right back.

Put their mother in the mix and the two of them felt like they were back in middle school.

"I can still go punch him if you want," he offered, watching as Sebastian tried to get lost in a crowd of the cousins. *They aren't going to protect you, kid.* Nobody got in their mom's way when she was on the warpath.

"Yeah, sure you will." Abby snorted. "I see what you're looking at. Denise's after him now. You want me to believe you'd go punch him now when she's about to get a piece of him?"

He ran his tongue across his teeth. "Sure." She was bluffing. Abby wasn't that mad.

She let go of his hand. "Have at it, slugger."

Aw, hell.

Panic shot through him. Now what in the hell did he do? Slowly, he pulled his feet out of the water, his mind working rather furiously as he tried to figure a way out of it. But he'd said he'd do it, and damn it if Sebastian didn't deserve it and—

Abby caught his wrist, laughing a little. "Damn it, Zach. The look on your face is just about priceless. Enough. You don't have to go risk your mom's wrath on my account."

He was only a little relieved. Okay. A lot. Zach would slay just about any dragon for her.

But his mom wasn't a dragon. His mom was . . . hell.

Blowing out a breath, he tried to put on a brave face. He

could still act, right? "I can go do it," he lied through his teeth. "It's not like he doesn't deserve it."

"Oh, he deserves it, all right," she agreed. "Stupid ass." Then she blew out a breath and shrugged. "But being a stupid kid and having you punch him in the face and cause problems on set isn't worth it. Besides, then people would start wondering how it happened and we don't know everybody here. It would get out and that would just lead to a hassle there. For all we know, they'd start speculating on *why* you punched him in the face."

"According to the media, I'm on everything from drugs to human blood." He shrugged and shifted in closer, bracing one hand on the ground behind her. Dipping his head, he pressed his lips to her shoulder. "What's it matter if I punch him in the head?"

She shrugged and smoothed out a crease in her skirt. "What was he rambling on about, anyway? He's acting like I dragged you out of California or something." Her eyes cut his way, lingering for a second, before she went back to toying with the full material of her skirt. "I'm pretty sure I didn't kidnap you and lock you in the trunk of my car when I headed out here."

"Don't worry about it," he said, dancing around the edge of the subject. *Don't ask . . . don't ask . . .* He couldn't very well tell her that the very second she'd told him she was leaving California and had found a place in Tucson, he'd started looking for a place there as well. That wasn't going to help matters any, was it?

"Look, Sebastian is just being . . . Sebastian. You know how he is. He gets an idea in his head and it's like he can't see anything else. It warps everything he does, everything he sees."

She opened her mouth, but this time, before the words could escape, he leaned in and kissed whatever questions she had away.

Sooner or later, he thought. He'd explain it all sooner or later.

Just not yet. This was all too new and he needed to give her time first. If he knew a damn thing about Abby, it was how she reacted and if he told her that he'd been in love with her for well . . . forever? Yeah. That was the kind of news that was best delivered after she'd had some time to get used to things. Used to having him in her life like this, as something more than just her friend.

Questions.

Damn it, Abigale had been planning to ask him a question . . . or five.

But as his hand caught her face, all thoughts of questions, all thoughts of Sebastian and everybody else seemed to fade away.

Only *one* thought seemed to exist for her now.

Only one *thing*.

Zach.

That was it.

Groaning, she opened for him as he twisted and leaned into her body, his warmth wrapping around her. The noise of the party, the high-pitched giggles of the children, the low hum of music, everything faded away . . . nothing but Zach existed.

His hand curled into the wide lapel of the button-up dress she wore, his thumb stroking back and forth over her skin, slow and steady. A simple touch. Almost innocent, but not quite. And she was melting inside. Melting and burning and shaking.

Finally, he eased back, but he didn't pull away. Instead, he stayed that way, his brow pressed to hers, his eyes lingering on hers. "Abby, I . . ."

"C'mon! It's time for me to eat Daddy's cake!"

The moment shattered, but it was broken with laughter as they pulled back, grinning at each other for a minute before they looked over at Clayton, Trey's son.

"Is that what it's time for, pal?" Zach asked, reaching

over and catching Clayton's ear. He tugged on it lightly and ruffled the boy's hair.

"Yeah!" Clayton practically bounced on his heels as he looked around. "Meemee told me that I could eat it as soon as I got *all* of you ready so I gotta find everybody else!"

The four-year-old took off with the single-minded intensity of the young. Sighing, she looked back at Zach and reached up, cupping his cheek in her hand. "You ready for some cake?"

He kissed her palm. "I'm ready for what I was just having." Then he pulled his feet out of the pool and stood up. "But cake will work for now. The sooner we finish up the birthday stuff, the sooner we can go."

Chapter Fourteen

He's spent more than half of his life doing exactly what you wanted him to do, Abby.

Brooding, Abigale stared out the window over the bay.

Usually when they came up to San Diego for one of the family things, they stayed with Zach's folks. There was even a room that Denise had set aside for Abigale. Abigale wouldn't go so far as to say it was *her* room, but whenever she was here, that was the room she stayed in.

But Zach had told her he had reserved a room for them at a hotel and she had been just fine with that.

It had been . . . odd . . . all night.

Even after Sebastian had left, not long after the presents were opened, things had felt off. She suspected it was her, but still, she couldn't brush off that odd, uneasy feeling.

Zane had kept his distance and Denise had chattered about everything under the sun. Nobody else had said a single thing about her being there with Zach. But everybody had watched them.

It was almost like they were seeing things she wasn't.

He's spent more than half of his life doing exactly what you wanted him to do, Abby.

A warm pair of arms came around her waist and she closed her eyes, sinking back against the warmth of Zach's body. Part of her wanted to turn to him, curl her arms around him, and just get lost in him so she didn't have to think.

But her mind just wasn't going to shut up right now.

"What was Sebastian talking about, Zach?" she asked. She'd tried to get the answer out of him earlier but he'd brushed it off. She wasn't about to let him do it this time.

She felt his chest rise and fall against her back, felt the warmth of his breath stirring her hair. One hand smoothed down and curved over her hip. "Abby, Seb doesn't even know what he's talking about half the time. How should I know?" he murmured. He rubbed his lips over her neck and that felt so good, sending small little shivers down her spine. "Right now, he's so fixed on the idea of dragging me back here, I don't think he can see straight, much less think straight. I wouldn't be surprised if he'd heard some of those stupid *Bachelor* rumors and thought maybe he'd see if he couldn't work it from his end."

"So you have no idea what he meant when he said I made you leave California."

His hands curled around her waist. "Abigale . . . I'm pretty damn certain you were in Tucson for months before I saw the ad for the shop. You aren't the one who told me to buy it. You aren't the one who put the idea in my head of opening my own place."

Some of the tension eased out of her and she managed to breathe a little easier.

"Is that what's been bothering you?" he asked.

Licking her lips, she shrugged. "Some. Although I couldn't figure out what the hell he was ranting about. I . . ."

Zach turned her around.

In the dim light of the room, her dark eyes were almost black. As he reached up and slid his hands into her hair, he said softly, "I'm in a hotel room, alone with a beautiful woman. You know the last thing I really want to talk about is my baby brother and his hard head, right?"

He dislodged the pins in her hair and watched as the curls went tumbling down her back. Then, as she opened her mouth, probably to keep talking about the disaster that had happened earlier, he cradled her skull in his hands and rubbed his thumbs along her scalp.

Her lids dropped down. "That feels good."

"I've been wanting to take your hair down all damned day." He eased his way around to the base of her skull, worked there for a minute, and then nudged her back against the wall. She went, smiling a little at him as he reached for the wide black belt that nipped her dress in at the waist.

"Zach . . . are you trying to distract me?"

"No. I *am* distracting you," he said, shooting her a look. "I don't see why we have to keep talking about Sebastian. He thinks he knows what my life should be about and I think he needs to go pull his head out of his ass. There's nothing else to keep talking about."

"Hmm." She reached up and curled her hands around his wrists. "So he's got his head up his ass. And that's it?"

"Yes." Leaning in, crowding her body against the wall, he took her mouth, quick and hard. "Now . . . can we stop talking? It's been like three days since I had you naked."

She smiled against his lips. "Wow. Three whole days? However did you stand it?"

"By fantasizing about what I'd do with you once I had you naked in a hotel room." He twisted his hands out of her grip and reached for the buttons that held her dress closed. It was a cute little retro piece, a soft pale green that made her skin glow. It was pretty, sexy in a subtle, quiet way and all damned day, he'd thought about either unbuttoning all those buttons and fucking her while she still wore it, or maybe turning her around and bending her over . . . maybe both. The blood drained out of his head as he pondered the possibilities. By the time he'd eased the fourth button free, his fingers were shaking. A bra peeked through the vee of her dress now and he leaned in, pressed his mouth to the pale flesh, licked the outer curve of one breast.

He managed to free all of the buttons, but he wasn't quite done, he realized. Pale, gauzy white material still separated him from her and he stroked one hand down it, feeling the firm length of her thigh underneath it before he slid her a look. "I'm thinking about taking you while you're still wearing your dress, you know."

"What . . ." Her voice cracked a little and she stopped, clearing her throat. "What's stopping you?"

Besides the fact that he felt like he was about to come just looking at her? Not a whole lot. Crouching down in front of her, he slid his hands under the skirts of her dress and petticoat, catching her panties with his fingertips and dragging them down. She went to step out of the heels she was still wearing and he shook his head. "No," he whispered. "Those stay on, too."

She blushed, her face flaming red and he laughed a little, stroking one finger down her foot. "You've looked so beautiful, so elegant, and so sweetly sexy all damned day. Now I get to muss you up and I'm going to enjoy it," he said.

"And I have to wear the heels?"

"Well. No." He went to catch her calf. "Take them off if you really want to."

"No." She closed her eyes and shook her head. "I'm fine."

Then she laughed a little and the sound wrapped around him, settling inside his heart and warming every dark, cold place. "You know, I've never once had sex while I'm wearing so many clothes, never once—"

The rest of her words were a muffled shriek against his mouth.

He just couldn't think about that. Tangling his hand in her hair, he used his free arm to boost her up. "Don't," he muttered. "I can't . . . just don't."

He had to live with watching her fall in love with another man, although he knew she hadn't loved Roger. The other guy before Roger, though? The jerk in college? Yeah, she'd loved him, and he'd hurt her. Zach had to stand by and

watch it; had to watch her laugh with other guys, be happy
with them while he bled and died silently inside. But he
couldn't listen to this.

He carried her over to the long, low gleam of the dining
room table set up on the other side of the door. The hotel
was one of the nicer ones and he'd thought they could order
breakfast in, eat, and just enjoy the view over the bay.

Now, though, the only thought in his mind was the table
was there. And it was close. Kicking the nearest chair out
of the way, he sat her on the edge and bent over her, bearing
down on her until she lay with her back flat against the surface. She whimpered against his mouth, her hands fisting
his shirt while her knees came up and gripped his hips.

He tore his mouth away and lifted up, catching her legs
and spreading them wide. His name was a strangled cry on
her lips as he dipped his head and pressed his mouth to the
hot, sweet core of her. Her hands tangled in his hair and she
went to arch herself closer, but before she could, he caught
her behind the knees, shoved.

"Be still," he growled against her. Open . . . he wanted
her open for him. Open and vulnerable, just like he was for
her.

Stabbing at her with his tongue, he worked her closer
and closer, felt her climax moving in on her. Knew it was
close when her body started to tighten, clench with every
touch, every stroke of his tongue. Knew it was close . . . and
he stopped. Surging upright, he tore at the fly of his jeans
while she gasped for breath and lay there staring at him.

She sat up, reaching for him and he let her, shuddering
as she sank her teeth into his lower lip, as he felt the press
of her breasts against his chest, the scratchy material of her
petticoat caught between them. Abruptly, her kiss eased
and she lifted a hand and cupped his cheek. "Zach . . ."

The look in her eyes was almost his undoing. He could
have gone to his knees before her and everything he'd felt
inside for far too long was boiling inside him, threatening
to spill out.

Swearing, he tore back and pulled her off the table, spinning her around and urging her forward. She made a startled sound and he dipped his head, pressing a kiss to her nape.

"Shhh . . . shhh," he murmured as he guided her forward. "Bend over for me, Abby. Just . . ."

She glanced at him over her shoulder, her eyes dark and unreadable. So dark. But then, as a sigh shuddered out of her, she bent forward, bracing her hands on the table. He urged her lower, until she was flat against the surface and he slid his hands under the tangle of skirt and petticoat, pushing it up to her waist. Then he swore, long and low, at the sight of her ass, the sleek, wet core of her, exposed to his sight.

On her hip, he could see the elegant lines of his tattoo and he dipped his head, kissed the soft skin just next to it before he straightened and moved in, tucking the head of his cock against her gate. Soft, wet heat greeted him, closed around him and then, eyes closed, he surged forward—

"*Fuck*," he snarled, slamming a hand onto the table by her head.

Abby moaned and rotated her hips back, clenching down around him.

"Abby . . . don't. Be still." Sweating, shaking, he braced his hands on her hips. "Rubber. I need . . ."

"Zach." Her lashes lifted and she turned her head a little, watching him through her lashes.

And despite his best intentions, even as he pulled put, he found himself surging back in. Silk. She was slick, wet, smooth silk and she felt so damned good. "I need to stop," he panted. "I don't . . . I didn't put a rubber on."

"I'm on the pill." She licked her lips, blood rushing up to stain her cheeks red. "And . . ."

He froze, bent over her. "Abby . . ."

"I had a physical done a couple weeks ago," she whispered. "When I . . . well. I had one done. It had been a few months since Roger and I were . . . *oh!*"

He shuddered and swore as he drove back inside her. "Don't say his name when I'm inside you, Abby. Just don't."

"It's been a while," she said, glaring at him. "And I'm good. You don't need . . ."

He knew what she was saying. And it shouldn't matter. Smart adults didn't do this.

But when it came to Abby, Zach wasn't a smart adult. Bracing one elbow on the table, he rotated his hips against her again, felt her clench around him and he groaned.

"Do I stop?" he demanded.

"No." She held his gaze and when he pulled out, eased back in, she clamped down on him like she never wanted him to leave.

That worked just fine for him.

But not like this . . . not now.

Straightening, he pulled out and listened to her ragged groan, the soft sound of disappointment. But then, as he turned her over, her eyes widened. He reached for the hem of his shirt and dragged it off before pulling her hips to the very edge of the table. Her legs hung off the edge as he tucked the head of his cock against her gate. "Like this. Watching each other . . ."

Her gaze caught his, held his as he slid his arms under her knees, holding her open . . . vulnerable . . . as he surged deep inside, the soft, slick tissues of her pussy yielded to him and she cried out his name.

Naked and smooth, tight and hot, she closed around him. Perfect.

So damned perfect . . .

I love you, he thought, staring down at her.

And he had to fight to keep those words trapped inside. Lifting one of her legs, he pressed a kiss to her calf, stroked his palm along her smooth skin. Her eyes, dark and wide, locked on his face and he hated the dim light, wished he'd turned it on so he could see her, see all of her, the way the lacy, flouncy material of that insanely female petticoat tangled around her waist as he rode her, wished he could see the way her skin was so pretty and pale against his own.

"Fuck, Abby," he muttered, and his own voice shook.

But she didn't seem to notice as she twisted and arched under him, a soft, desperate little moan escaping her.

"Zach," she whimpered.

And he knew. He heard it and the need in her voice just hit him in the heart, in the gut. Releasing his hold on her knee, he slid his hand along her inner thigh and sought out the hard little knot of nerves just above her entrance. Slowing down the rhythm of his strokes, even when all he wanted was to *take take take*, he stroked her clitoris and felt the answering tension in her body.

A harsh, breathless scream echoed through the room as she clenched down, milking him as she started to come. Hard and fast . . . and so fucking sweet.

Once he knew she was falling, he let himself follow. Always . . .

In the darkness of the room, Abby lay sprawled with her head on his chest and he toyed with her hair as he stared out the window.

"Are you mad at Seb?" she asked drowsily.

Closing his eyes, he bit back the instinctive answer. *That* answer wasn't complimentary, but he knew if he let her know just how pissed he was, she'd want to know why.

"Other than irritated about him having his head up his ass?" he said, keeping his voice easy. "Nah."

Guilt tugged at him for lying to her and he knew he shouldn't. *Well, I'm not. Not exactly. He does have his head up his ass, and that's why I'm pissed. I'm just not clarifying what I'm pissed about.*

It was splitting hairs and he knew it, but this just wasn't a talk they could have yet.

This was too new.

As she stroked her nail along the line of the tattoo over his chest, he rolled his head over to look at her. "You ever call the dickhead?"

She wrinkled her nose. "No. It just doesn't seem as important now."

Zach blinked. "But it's in your journal."

"Yes. The very *weird* journal." She moved closer to the dagger where it pierced the heart. "I think if it's a *very weird journal* that means I'm allowed to modify the rules as I see fit."

"But you don't *modify* rules." He shifted in bed and tumbled her onto her back, pausing a moment to appreciate the shift in positions as her thighs parted to accommodate him. Then, before he could get distracted, he settled his elbows on the bed next to her head and peered down at her face. "You get locked on one certain thing and you have to see it through. *Tattoo*, check. *Affair*, check. *Stop worrying . . .*" He paused and stroked a thumb down her cheek. "How is that part going?"

A grin curved her lips and she shrugged a little. "Zach, lately, you've got my head spinning around so much, I don't have *time* to worry about anything. And I'll have you know, I still plan to flip off the next photographer who snaps a picture of me. *Then* when they plaster *that* picture of me in the next gossip rag, they can talk about how I'm fat *and* angry."

"You're not fat," he snapped. He shoved back on his knees and settled between her thighs, staring at her, the long, lush curves of her thighs, her breasts, the gentle curve of her belly. "You're so beautiful, you make my teeth hurt."

She blushed a little. Then she shrugged. "I'm not saying *I* think it. Although compared to what they want in Hollywood these days . . . baby, I'm an absolute cow. Which is probably yet another reason I'm glad I never plan to go back there." She eased upright and settled on her knees in front of him.

The dark silk of her hair spilled down to curl around her breasts. "Seb's so certain you miss it, although he never questions my choice to leave it. It's funny, if you think about it. We both got into it at the same time, did it for the same length of time . . . and it ended at the same time for us." She eased closer, wrapping her arms around his neck and studying him. "If it's no big deal for me to walk away, why not you?"

Cupping her ass in his hands, he shrugged. "Hell if I know. Sometimes, I think he sees himself as the way I was when it ended for me. Maybe he thinks if I'm done with it, that's what he faces. But I left because I wanted to. He doesn't want to. I don't know what his deal is." Then he rubbed his lips against hers. "And, Abby, if you keep talking about other guys while I'm sitting here buck-ass naked with you, it just might hurt my ego."

"Your ego, huh?" She laughed a little and reached between them, closing her hand around his cock, stroking up, then down. "This ego?"

"Yeah." He flashed her a grin. "Matter of fact, I think you might have already hurt it. Maybe you should kiss it and make it better."

"Hmmm." She squirmed backward and eased downward.

And Zach shuddered as her mouth closed around him.

Breakfast was a lovely, luxurious affair at the table where they watched the bay and Zach kept whispering in her ear about how he'd never see another dining room table with thinking about what they'd done on this one.

Consequently, she spent most of the meal red-faced and was so turned on, she jumped him in the shower when they were supposed to be getting ready to check out.

Which meant they were late for their lunch date with Marin.

Marin waved at them from her table with a glint in her eye and a wide grin. "You two, if I'd known you were going to be late, I wouldn't have gotten up so early to head down here."

Abigale rolled her eyes as she slid into the seat next to Marin. "Oh, be quiet. Like you sat here . . . what? Fifteen minutes?"

Marin laughed. "Actually, it was five. I was a few minutes late myself." She slid Zach a look and smiled. "You're looking nice and . . . relaxed there, Zach."

"I had a nice breakfast," he said blandly.

Under the table, he rested a hand on Abigale's knee and

she could feel the blush settling on her skin. But she didn't knock his hand off, either. Instead, she covered it with her own. When he turned his hand around and laced their fingers, something in her heart tripped a little. Sighed . . .

Marin rested an elbow on the table and studied her. "Abigale Applegate, I have to tell you this. I don't think I've ever seen that look on your face."

"Ahhh . . ."

"Lay off, Marin," Zach said easily, slumping in the seat. He pinned her with a flat, direct stare and while his tone was level, the look in his eyes was anything but.

The little round table only sat three people, tucked into a secluded little alcove where they had some privacy. Abigale flushed a little as he lifted their hands out and pressed a kiss to the back of hers and then eased in closer, resting an arm on the back of her chair.

Marin chuckled. "Laying off, although, damn, it's going to be hard when you can't seem to keep your hands off of her."

Zach smirked a little as he reached for his water. "You're just jealous."

"No. I got over your cute ass years ago, Barnes. I can't help but think it's going to be fun to watch this." Marin sipped from a glass of wine and gestured to the bottle in the middle of the table. "Would you like a glass?"

"Watch what?" Abigale asked, squirming a little. Then she shot the wine bottle a dark look and shook her head. "Absolutely no. I hate your taste in wine. That stuff tastes like shit."

Marin chuckled. "That cab costs about seventy-five dollars a bottle, you know."

"Then it's pricey shit. Although I've seen you spend that much on just a *glass* of wine. So maybe it's mediocre shit, depending on your point of view." She reached for the wine list and sighed as she skimmed through it. Typical. The only kind of wines she could typically stomach at most restaurants were the ones they'd serve for dessert and it was too early. "I'll just stick with coffee for now."

"Hmm. Needing the caffeine boost and it's only eleven." Marin's grin widened. "Didn't sleep much?"

With a baleful glare, Abigale reached for the menu and resigned herself to an . . . interesting meal. Marin had gotten it in her head to mess with her and that was exactly what her friend was going to do.

"You tramp, you went and did it."

Tucked inside the bathroom, Abigale sighed and leaned in closer to the mirror as she pretended to check her makeup. She'd barely put any on and she wasn't overly concerned with how it looked anyway, but it was a way to keep from just glaring at Marin. A way to keep from fanning a hand in front of her face when she thought about how she'd . . . gone and did it.

With Zach. Wow.

Feeling the weight of Marin's watchful eyes, she looked up. She pasted a patently false smile on her face and said, "Went and did what?"

"You're having an affair with Zach."

Affair . . .

Frowning, she pushed away from the mirror and turned to look at Marin. "We're seeing each other, yeah."

Marin's blonde brows arched over her eyes. Her eyes were pale blue and they matched the fragile silk tank top she wore. And just then, those eyes were sharp with questions and so very watchful.

"Seeing each other," Marin said slowly. "For some reason, I get the impression that's different from *having a torrid affair.*"

Abigale leaned her hips against the long marble counter and stared down at the floor while she tried to figure out the right way to answer. Oddly enough, she didn't find the answer on the rose-streaked black tile or the red polish she'd slicked on her toenails, and she certainly didn't find the answer in the peep-toe black Jimmy Choos she'd chosen to wear with her dress that day.

"Abby."

Swallowing the knot in her throat, she looked up at her friend. There weren't any answers in Marin's gaze, either, but she did find more questions. A lot of them. Swallowing the knot in her throat, she asked, "Yeah?"

"*Is* there a difference?" Marin asked.

"I . . ." She licked her lips and shrugged. "Yeah. There's a difference. I just don't know what it is yet."

"Okay . . . well, let's try this. When you planned to have a torrid affair, just how did you see it ending?"

Abigale rubbed her fingers against her temple. Now *that* question she could answer easily enough. "I imagined a guy, a hot guy, that I'd have a few hot and easy flings with, and then it would be over. No fuss, no muss, and no regrets when it ended. I'd have a wonderful memory, something I could look back on and smile about, but I wouldn't regret that it had ended."

"That sounds like a good description of a torrid affair," Marin mused. She settled into place beside Abigale. She went to say something, but the door opened. As a lovely, sleek little blonde came bustling in, Marin and Abigale lapsed into a light, easy conversation that touched on anything and everything except the things that mattered.

Once they were alone again, Marin bumped her shoulder against Abigale's. "So how are you imagining things with Zach?"

"That's not so easy to answer." She pressed a hand to her belly. Shoving away from the counter, she started to pace. Damn it, they didn't have time for this. They'd already been in here five minutes. "You know . . . I was thinking about what I was looking for, back when I was having to deal with cancelling the wedding plans. Started thinking about what I *needed*. Did I need a guy to make me happy? I mean, I wanted kids, but did I need a guy? Not *technically* . . . I just wanted one. But I realized, even then, I'd been settling. I really wanted somebody who'd make me laugh. Make me think. Who'd be there for me for always . . ."

"That's Zach," Marin said quietly. "That's always been him."

Abigale lifted her head to stare at her friend. "I know. I even thought that very same thing. But Zach was a friend. Just a friend. That's all he'd ever been. My friend. Now . . . hell, it's like he touches me and my brain shuts down. And that's wonderful. Lately, when he's around, I can't think about anything *but* him and it's not just because the sex is so amazing."

"Is it amazing?"

Abigale stopped in her tracks and just stared at Marin. Her heart skipped a little around in her chest and then banged a few hard beats against her ribs while her lungs worked to accommodate the sudden lack of oxygen. "Ahhh . . ."

A wicked grin lit her friend's face. "Okay. I just had to know. I used to . . . well. You know. Hell, the guy is hot. But I'm over it. Really."

"You better be," she muttered, reaching up to toy with a loose lock of hair. "But it's *not* just the sex. He's—" Her belly jumped again and she pressed a hand to it, swearing as the butterflies there threatened to take flight. "He's my best friend, Marin. I mean, the two of you are . . . but . . ."

"Zach's always been there, Abby. I know that. We've established that, right? I know what the two of you mean to each other. It's cool. Besides . . ." She wagged her brows. "No matter how close the two of you are, there are certain things you just need a girl for. Like this. So . . . but *what*?"

"Things are changing lately. He's my best friend, and I'm scared because I can't lose that, but this thing . . . it's getting huge. I think about him all the time, and I want him more than I want to breathe and I . . ." She slumped against the counter again, staring at the floor. "I'm scared. What if it falls apart and I lose *everything*? Not just this, but my friend, too?"

"Now I just don't see that happening. The two of you have too much between you. You talk about how he's the one who makes you think, makes you laugh . . . how he's the one who is there for you. That's a real thing between you and it won't disappear, Abby." Hooking an arm around her neck, Marin hugged her tight. "You're falling for your best friend, Abs. That's all it is. And to be honest, I think that's pretty amazing. You're supposed to be friends with the man in your life . . . and you two already are."

"But what if it doesn't last?" Abigale asked, her heart slamming against her ribs as Marin put everything into words. So plainly stated. *You're falling for your best friend.*

Falling . . . yes. Hell, she'd already *fallen*, if she was completely honest with herself. She'd fallen hard.

"What if it does?" Marin returned.

Abigale groaned. She covered her face with her hands and then, because she had to say it out loud, she whispered, "And what if I do fall for him, *really* fall for him . . . and he doesn't feel the same way?"

Oh, sweetie. Marin squeezed Abigale's shoulders and tried to decide on the best course of action.

You blind woman . . . he's been in love with you for years didn't seem to be the right thing to say.

Why don't you take it as it comes was the exact *wrong* thing to say to somebody like Abigale because Abigale *planned* things. *Controlled* things.

"Well, I can't speak for Zach," she finally said, carefully testing each word in her head before she spoke. "But I'd say the fact that the two of you are already involved, that he's obviously attracted to you, and the fact that you two have so much already between you . . . hell, Abby, it's more than some people have."

She squeezed her shoulders again and then, as the door opened, she pressed a kiss to Abigale's cheek and said, "We need to get out there before he decides we made a break for it or something."

Chapter Fifteen

"You realize this would be a lot easier if you just told her you are in love with her."

Zach glared at the phone. It wasn't particularly effective since Marin couldn't see him and it didn't make him feel any better, but he couldn't keep himself from glaring, either. He almost flipped the damn thing off but figured that was a waste of time.

It was almost midnight, he was alone in the shop, and the last thing he needed was to be scolded by Marin.

Especially after he'd already heard a variation of the same from his mom.

Especially after he'd dealt with Keelie's cranky ass all week.

Especially after he hadn't managed so much as five minutes alone with Abigale since they'd gotten back from San Diego.

"I don't need advice on how to handle my love life, Marin," he said sourly when the glare didn't magically disconnect the phone call. It should work, he thought. If life was fair, it would have worked and then when she called back, he just wouldn't answer.

"The hell you don't." Marin sighed. "Zach, listen . . . have you given her any inkling that you want something more out of this than sex?"

He flushed and rubbed the back of his neck. He was *not* discussing his sex life with Marin, either. She was like the sister he never had. "You realize we've only been going out a few weeks, right?"

"Long enough for you to start banging her," Marin pointed out.

His hand clenched so hard around the pencil, it was a wonder it didn't snap. The way he was going, he was going to have to buy stock in a damned office supply company.

"Marin . . . if you're trying to piss me off, you're doing a damn good job. I'm not *banging* Abby."

A few seconds passed and then Marin sighed. "Zach, would you lighten up? It's not like I think you're fucking her and writing her name on the boy's locker room door, okay? I know what she means to you. What I'm trying to get at is this . . . she's falling for you. Hard. But she doesn't know how serious this is for you. And she needs to."

"Fuck." Shoving back from the desk, he got up and started to pace. "And then what, Marin? When I tell her that I've loved her forever and that freaks her out, then what do I do?"

His heart lodged in his throat as she pointed out, "Zach . . . sweetie . . . what are you going to do when she *doesn't* freak out?"

"Marin . . ." He groaned and dragged a hand down his face as he fought with each answer. Did he *want* to tell her? *Yes.* But he didn't want to scare her off and he didn't want to—

The buzzer rang.

Scowling, he said, "Marin, somebody's at the back. I need to go."

It was more than an hour past closing time so there were just a few possibilities. He thought maybe it could be Abigale, although she usually went to the front. The back of the shop faced out over an empty lot and he didn't like any of his employees to be out there alone.

He checked through the judas hole and didn't see any-body.

But the buzzer rang again.

Tension crawled along the back of his neck, making the hairs stand on edge. Bracing a hand on the wall by the door, he glanced at the alarm panel. It was active and engaged. He'd had his place broken into a few times. It would prob-ably happen again—

A fist pounded against the door.

"Yeah?" Zach called out.

As somebody flung himself against the door, Zach hit the panic button on the alarm panel and dodged off to the side.

The call came in just before one in the morning.

Damn late for calling, but Abby smiled when she saw Zach's number. She was exhausted after spending most of the day dealing with a bridezilla who practically *defined* the *zilla* part.

The one good thing was that the bride's daddy was rich and Abby had no problem making them pay through the nose for the headache they were giving her.

The bad news . . . she was almost too tired to talk to Zach.

But tired or not, she needed to hear his voice.

"Hey, gorgeous," she said, smiling a little as she padded into the bathroom. She eyed the tub and thought about run-ning a bath and soaking for a while. It would keep her awake while she talked—

"Hey . . . ah." His voice was raw, heavy with exhaustion as he asked, "Can you come to the hospital?"

She froze and the cloud of exhaustion cleared from her head. "Hospital?"

"Yeah." He paused for a second and then in a rush, said,

"I'm fine, okay? But somebody busted into the shop while I was there and I got . . . well, I'm here and I . . . Look, I need somebody to take me home. Can you?"

Her heart dropped down to somewhere in the range of her soles when she saw him. Zach lay half propped up in the bed and the bright fluorescent lights were unapologetic as they highlighted every damned bruise, every damned wound. And there were a number of them.

"Zach . . ."

His lashes lifted, and slowly he turned his face toward her. "Hey, Abs," he said, his voice thick and rusty. He had a cut on his mouth. That beautiful mouth was busted up, she thought, and her heart tripped up and stopped as she eased a little closer.

"Damn it, Zach, what happened?"

"I got the crap pounded out of me by a couple of punks looking for some quick cash." Then he grinned a little. "I pounded the crap out of them, too. One of them got away, but the other one is down the hall. Broken leg."

"You broke his leg?" She gaped at him.

"Well, me and one of the chairs in the break room. I'm not entirely sure how it happened, but I tackled him. He went down, and his leg snapped." His lids flickered a little. "Ugly sound, you know. Hearing a bone break."

"What room is he in?" she asked. "I'll go break another bone so I can hear."

"Bloodthirsty . . ."

He yawned and sat up, blinking a little as he looked around. Then he focused on her. "Abby?"

Frowning, she moved to the side of the bed and laid her hand on his cheek. "Zach, baby . . . are you okay?"

He slid an arm around her waist and smiled at her. It was a slightly loopy smile, she decided. No. Very loopy. "They gave you something for the pain, didn't they?" Zach couldn't take anything much stronger than Benadryl without it hitting him like a fifth of whiskey.

He pressed his face against her belly and nodded. "Ribs hurt. Nothing's broke, but it hurts."

Smiling a little, she brushed his hair back from his face. "Well, I guess that explains why I'm here."

He hooked his arm around her waist and held her tighter. "You're here 'cause I need you," he muttered, rubbing his lips over her and even through her t-shirt, she felt that teasing caress. "I want to get the fuck out of here."

She didn't really hear much of anything else he said.

You're here 'cause I need you.

Bending over him, she closed her eyes and wondered just how much. How much did he need her . . . and was it because he needed the damn ride? Because they were friends?

Or was it more?

She really, really hoped it was more.

He woke in pain.

Pain *every* fucking where. His lip throbbed, his hands throbbed, every muscle in his body ached, and when he went to roll to a sitting position, his ribs screamed at him.

Fortunately, Abby wasn't in there, so he didn't have to worry about the fact that he might have almost whimpered a little as he made his way over to her bathroom. Bright morning light shone through the frosted glass window and he had an unrestricted view of his battered face.

Left eye was black and blue, with the bruising spreading down over his cheek.

Mouth was busted. Tats covered much of his chest but they ended just below his pecs and he could see the vivid bursts of bruises forming there. The jerks had whaled on him hard and the one time they'd managed to get him down, they'd kicked the hell out of him, too. He'd kicked the legs out from under one of them and used that brief second to get back to his feet and that was when he'd lunged for the other one.

Not more than a couple of minutes had passed before the

cops arrived to check out the alarm he'd sounded, but one of them had taken off.

Whether or not they found that guy would depend on if the punk they'd arrested last night decided to talk. Regardless, Zach had every damn intention of pressing charges. This was the third time somebody had decided to break into his place and he'd been in there last night.

His gut twisted a little as he thought about everything that could have gone wrong.

Javi or Keelie could have been in there.

Abby could have been there with him.

"Stop it, man." He turned away from his battered reflection. That *what if* game was a bad, bad thing to get started. Blanking his mind, he hooked his thumbs in the gray boxer briefs he wore and went to shove them down, but even that had him almost doubled over as his ribs screamed at him.

"Need some help?"

He shot Abby a dark look as she came into the bathroom. She wore a pale green chemise with skinny straps that just barely skimmed her hips and her dark red curls were still tousled. He wanted to bury his face against her neck and just stay there. For about forever.

Instead, he looked away. "I can handle the damn shower."

"Cranky."

He glared at her. "A couple of assholes broke into my shop, I get the shit beaten out of me, and there's not an inch of me that doesn't hurt. Yeah, I'm cranky." Then, as she arched a brow at him, he groaned and looked away. "Sorry. Just . . . I need a shower and I'll find some Motrin and . . ."

She sauntered inside, moved around him to open the cabinet just beyond his shoulder. She pulled out a bottle and popped the cap. She shook out four and held her hand out. "The doctor ordered that dosage so here . . . you've also got some narcotics downstairs."

"No, thanks," he muttered, swiping the orange pills out of her hand. "That stuff makes me loopy."

"Hmmm. Trust me, I'm well aware." She filled the lit-

tle glass from the side of the sink with water and held it out
to him.

Once he'd taken the pills, she stood in front of him, eyeing him critically for a long, long moment. Then she moved
in and slid her hands down his ribs, carefully, her palms
ghosting over his flesh.

"Abby, I . . ."

"Shhh . . ." She slid her hands inside his boxers and
tugged them down. His cock swelled in response and when
she brushed the back of her hand against him, he groaned.
"I don't know if I'm up to this, sugar."

"Oh, really?" She grinned at him and closed her hand
around his cock, stroked up, then down. "You feel pretty up
to me. But . . . don't worry. I think we should take it easy
for now."

He almost whimpered just then, because as sore as he
was, when she went down to her knees in front of him,
every damned thing in him responded.

A faint smile tugged her lips and she shot him a look.
"See? You're more than up for what I've got planned," she
murmured, leaning and placing a hot, openmouthed kiss to
the head of his cock.

He caught her hair in his fist when she lingered and slid
her mouth down, then back. "You . . ." He closed his eyes
and rested his hips against the counter of the sink. "I think
I can only handle about five or ten minutes of this in my
condition."

She rolled her eyes up to meet his, and the wicked glint
in her eyes just might have sent him to his knees. He didn't
think he could get back up if he went to the floor, though.
Swearing, he braced one hand against the cool marble of
the counter and fisted his free hand in her hair, tangling the
crazy curls around his fist and shuddering as she sucked
him deeper, taking him so far back he felt the head of his
cock bump against the back of her throat.

She did it again and again, and for a few minutes, Zach
forgot about the aches in his body, forgot about anything

and everything but the slick glide of her mouth over his cock and the silk of her hair fisted in his hand.

Her fingers stroked up over his thigh and he hissed out a breath as she closed her fingers around the sac of his balls, gripped him tight.

Her teeth scraped over the sensitive underside of his cock and then, as she took him back inside, so fucking deep, she hummed a little, and he thought the top of his head was going to come off as he started to come. He rocked forward to meet her, muttering and panting under his breath as he reached out with his other hand to hold her steady.

She moved with him, her mouth hot, sweet, and wet. It was pure, sheer bliss and for those few minutes, the pain he felt faded away and all that mattered was her. Her, and that amazing mouth, her tongue curling over the head of his cock before sucking him deeper, harder. Her fingers, tormenting him as she gripped his balls.

As pleasure streaked through him, building higher and higher, he cupped her head in his hands and surged forward, holding rigid, legs locked as the climax tore through him. All the way through.

Abigale licked her lips and wiped the back of her hand over her mouth as she stood up, kicking his boxers out of the way. "You know . . . all I'd really planned on doing was helping you get out of your boxers," she teased. "I figured you'd have trouble moving much with your ribs and all."

He gave her a heavy-lidded look and cupped her face in his hand, stroking a thumb over her lower lip.

"You a little less cranky now?" she asked, sliding her arms around his waist.

He caught her around the waist and she went, easing her body against his, careful not to press against him as he tucked his chin against her shoulder. "I don't know." He kissed her neck and then asked, "If I say no, will you do it again?"

She laughed a little. "No. But if you're nice, I might

climb into the shower with you. You don't look like you can wash your hair without hurting."

He jabbed her in the ribs. "I'll have you know I can wash my hair just fine, Abs."

"Yeah, yeah. I'm sure you can and you'll hurt and suffer for it." She leaned back and brushed his hair back from his face. "Let me help, Zach."

Dark blue eyes met hers and he groaned, dropped his head to rest his brow on hers. "You help just by existing, Abby. But you're killing my ego here."

She snorted. "Your ego is just fine. Besides, you got jumped by two thugs and you kicked ass."

"The chair helped. The idiot tripped and the chair helped break his fall." Then he stroked a finger down her back. "I guess I wouldn't mind seeing you all wet and naked. Might get me in a better frame of mind for when I call my folks and tell them what happened."

"Hmm. And you better get that done before they find out some other way."

"I'm coming out there."

Zach winced and said, "Now, Mom . . . you don't need to do that."

"You had to go to the hospital, you're hurt, and I'm coming *out* there," she said, her voice flat. "You live alone and you need somebody there to help you."

"I . . . ah . . ." He flashed Abby a look and without batting an eyelash, threw her to the wolves. "Well, I got somebody. Abby is staying with me."

There was a pause. One of those heavy, lingering pauses that seemed to carry the weight of the world. Abby stood in front of him, her hands propped on her hips and her brows arched as she studied him. He mouthed out, *Sorry.*

She started to tap her foot.

"Abby . . ."

"Yeah, Mom." He started to shrug and then swore as it sent pain crashing through him.

Through the roar of blood in his ears, he only barely heard his mom's voice and since he was struggling to catch his breath, he went ahead and listened and turned the phone over to Abby.

A few seconds went by before he could focus past the pain to hear the conversation.

"Yeah, Denise . . . I'm here with him. Honestly, other than being battered, I think he's fine." She watched him with a questioning stare and he grimaced, pressed a hand to his side as he made his way over to the kitchen counter. The amber bottle of pain meds beckoned and he blew out a breath, deciding to go ahead and just get it over with. One pill. He'd take it, pass out, and hopefully when he woke up, the worst of it would be done.

As he opened the bottle, he heard Abby's heels clicking on the floor and by the time he had a pill in his hand, she'd slid a Coke in front of him. He gave her a tired grin in thanks and popped the evil little pill in his mouth, washing it down.

"Uh-huh," Abby said, still talking to his mom. "Hmmm . . . yeah. I can handle him, I swear. I've been doing it a long time. I promise I'll call if he gets to be too much of an ass."

A few seconds later, the phone was back in his hand and he caught Abby's waist, tucking her up against him before she could pull away. "So can you sleep tonight, trusting I'll be okay?" he asked.

"No," Denise replied. "You smart-ass. Because I'm going to try and figure out what in the hell drove you to open that shop where you did. I'm going to worry about what would have happened if you weren't used to fighting two idiot kids at once—we should thank your brothers for that crash course they've been giving you all this time— and I'm going to worry about every other thing that could have gone wrong."

"Hey, in the end, things could have been worse," he said. "I'm here and I'm fine."

"Yes. You're here. You're fine. And you're with Abby . . ." There was a smile in her voice, one that he heard loud and clear, but he wasn't going to unravel that mess just then. "So. I'll stop worrying some. Now. Have you taken the pain medicine?"

"I just did. I got a few minutes before I start getting completely stupid with it."

"Okay. Get off the phone then. And Zach? Make sure you're not being . . . stupid about other things."

The phone disconnected and he sighed, putting it on the counter and hoping Abby hadn't been paying that much attention. *Stupid about other things.* Yeah, Mom. Real subtle, that hint.

"So. Just how completely loopy do you get with the pain meds?" Abby asked, brushing his hair back.

He grimaced and shot her a look. "I took something last night. Did you notice any . . . ah . . ."

"Oh. Yes." She grinned. "There were a few moments. And I've seen you on pain meds before. It's just been a while. I was wondering if it had gotten any better."

"Shit, no. If anything, it's just gotten worse."

"You want to tell me *why*?"

Zach folded his arms over his chest and stared at a point somewhere over Abby's shoulder. "Look, are you going to give me a ride in or not? If you're not, I'll call Keelie or one of the others. Hell, I can call a cab if it's that much trouble."

"Trouble . . ." Her eyes narrowed on his face as she drawled the word out and he suspected that probably hadn't been the ideal way to try and move this conversation forward, but fuck. All he needed to do was go to the shop for a little while.

Clenching his jaw, he counted to five silently. "I spent all day laying around yesterday. I took it easy. Now I'm getting back to work."

"You can't even move without hurting."

"I'm aware of that fact, thanks." He went to shove a hand through his hair and had a dismal reminder of that *fact*, one that left him biting back a curse as his ribs shrieked at him.

"Gee, Zach . . . did that feel good?"

He glared at her. "Can we go or am I calling somebody else?"

"Are you *trying* be an ass?" she demanded, propping her hands on her hips. She tapped her nails against her skin and part of him was thinking about the way she'd raked those pretty nails across his belly as they'd woke up. That was a thought that just made him *more* irritated because when he'd tried to pull her on top of him, she'd given him a nice little kiss on the cheek and then rolled out of bed.

She had him twisted up, damn it. She'd always had him like this, but it was worse now and he couldn't even tell her how much worse it was. The bad thing was that if she really pushed it, he'd probably go ahead and do whatever in the hell she asked him, just because he didn't want to see her unhappy and *fuck*, but he couldn't do that. Couldn't live that way and he knew it.

"I need to go in," he said, keeping his voice flat because if he started to yell, they'd end up fighting and he didn't want to fight with her. "I need to get an idea of what damage was done and figure out what to do about insurance and all. Keelie never thinks about it. I want my guys to see I'm okay and if by chance it's some thug from the neighborhood, they are damn well going to know that this bullshit doesn't mean I don't go to work."

"You're right," Abby said mockingly. "And resting through the damn weekend, giving your body a couple days to recover really proves what a macho piece of work you are."

Shifting his eyes to hers, he just stared.

Their gazes locked and after a minute, she looked away and groaned. Zach closed his eyes and rubbed his hand over the back of his neck.

Did he *have* to go in?

Hell, probably not. But he needed to.

It was what *he* needed to do and couldn't she—

He didn't let himself finish that thought because the answer was going to hurt too much. Things were changing, he thought. He hoped. And maybe someday she'd understand what Steel Ink meant to him. Why he had to go. But not yet, he thought sourly as he turned away and pulled out his phone. It wasn't quite ten. Keelie was probably heading in and she had to get there to open but he could probably get Javier to pick him up. "I'll call Javi," he said brusquely. "He only lives about twenty minutes or so from here. I—"

Abby's hand closed around his and she plucked the phone away with the other. "No."

"Abby, I—" Whatever he planned on saying was cut off as she reached up and pressed her fingers lightly to his mouth.

"No," she said again, her voice quiet. "Look, I'm sorry. I . . . damn it, Zach, I don't *get* why you can't let yourself take another day when just looking at you hurts me, but if it's that important for you to go in, I'll damn well be the one to take you."

Then she lowered her hand and leaned in, kissed him gently, avoiding the cut on the right side of his mouth. "I'll take you in. You either call me or figure out a way home. And I'll bring you dinner tonight and when you're sore and bitching about how you shouldn't have bothered going in, I get to point at you and say *ha, ha, I told you so.*"

"Is that how it works?" he asked, ignoring the way his voice went kind of raspy on him as he wrapped his hand around her ponytail and tugged her head back.

"Yeah. And you *will* say it."

"I can't believe he came in," Javi muttered, watching as Zach limped around the break room, surveying the damage.

"Me, neither," Abigale said.

Keelie snorted and glared at them both. "Javi, you should know better. I'm surprised he didn't stumble in here *yesterday*, although I know it was late when he finally got out of the ER. Zach all but bleeds this place." Then she gave Abigale a look of mocking condescension. "Although I'm not surprised the glamour girl doesn't know any better."

Javi chose that minute to beat a retreat, disappearing down the hallway. Abigale couldn't say she was sorry. Folding her arms over her chest, she shot Zach a look, but he was preoccupied and the music Keelie had blaring from her office was loud enough to offer at least the illusion of a private conversation. Narrowing her eyes, she studied Keelie and debated. Did she go for subtle?

Keelie met her gaze with a bold, almost hostile glare and Abigale decided subtlety would be pointless.

Fine. Screw subtle.

"Keelie, you want to tell me what in the hell your problem is with me?"

Keelie shrugged, her narrow shoulders moving restlessly under the fishnet top she wore over a skintight tank top. Flowers and scrolled tattoos wrapped around her biceps and danced along her collarbone. Beautifully done, elegant . . . almost soft, Abigale thought sometimes.

Ironic, because Abigale didn't think there was anything soft about Keelie.

But then again, anytime Keelie was around *her*, it seemed like the woman was pissed off.

"Who says I have a problem with you?" Keelie asked.

"Pretty much every word out of your mouth, every look you give me, and the general *why don't you kiss my ass, bitch* attitude you seem to have with me," Abigale said, shrugging. "Look, maybe that's just you, but I don't see you calling everybody you meet glamour girl. I'd think maybe you had a problem with people from the entertainment industry, but I saw you talking to Sebastian and you didn't treat him like something you'd scrape off your shoe, and you work with Zach just fine. Which leads me to think it's just me."

"I don't care what *industry* you worked in," Keelie snapped. She gave Abigale a dismissive glare and added, "If you think being an actress makes you *special*, you're dead wrong."

"I agree. It doesn't make me special. It was a job and it's not one I miss. So . . . if it's not that, what is it?"

It was quick. Very quick, but Abigale saw it. That flicker of a glance toward Zach. Swallowing, she waited as Keelie gave another one of those jerky, dismissive shrugs. "It's nothing."

"You have a thing for him," Abigale said when the other woman went to turn away.

Keelie stiffened.

Slowly, she lifted her head and Abigale could see her staring at Zach. And the man was still oblivious, squatting on the floor and eyeing the damage to the door. It was clear somebody had attempted to clean things up yesterday, but the door would have to be replaced. He had a look of resignation on his face as he shoved a hand through his hair. Even with his face battered and the bruising from his eye spilling down over his cheek, he looked beautiful. Too beautiful. Hell, just then, he looked a little *more* beautiful . . . like a fallen angel ready to go on the warpath.

A second later, Keelie turned back around and her mismatched eyes met Abigale's. "A *thing* for him? You think *that* touches it?" Her voice was low and angry. She paused, her mouth working as though she was looking for something else she needed to say. Finally, she just shook her head. "You don't know *what* I feel. But that's not a surprise. You don't even know how *he* feels about shit, half the time. You're so fucking clueless, and that makes you pathetic. You're supposed to be his best friend, but you jerk him around like a puppet. No wonder Sebastian was so pissed off at you."

The venom in Keelie's voice was like a slap in the face and the fury in her eyes was almost palpable. Keelie opened her mouth to say something else, but then she snapped her jaws together and shook her head. "You know what? Fuck this."

She turned on her heel and stormed away, while Abigale stood there and tried to figure out what in the world had just happened.

Just what in the world . . .

Chapter Sixteen

"You going to tell me what had you so upset earlier?"

Zach put the empty plate on the coffee table as Abby stood up.

It was late, almost nine and it had been a long, tense hour. Hell, it had been a long, tense day and not just because the two of them had almost had their first fight as . . . whatever the hell they were.

"What?" She gave him a distracted glance and then shrugged. "Oh, nothing. Here, let me . . ."

He caught her wrist before she could take the plate. "Leave it for a few minutes."

She resisted at first but as he continued to tug on her wrist, she sighed and placed her plate with his and went to sit down next to him. He caught her hips and tumbled her onto his lap, shifting her so she didn't bump against his ribs.

"Zach, damn it," she said, trying to pull away. "You need to be careful. Did you forget about your ribs?"

"I was." He combed a hand through her hair and leaned in, pressing his brow to hers. "Besides, they're *my* ribs. If I do something stupid, it's my own fault. Now . . . what's bothering you?"

She squirmed again. "Nothing."

"Liar."

She slid him a look out of the corner of her eye and then just shrugged. "I . . ." She stopped and sighed, leaning in to rest her head on his shoulder.

Closing his eyes, he curled an arm around her. How many nights . . .

"We've done this a lot," she murmured in an eerie echo of his thoughts. "Just this, you know that?"

Opening his eyes, he glanced down at her and saw that she was looking up at him. And unless he was mistaken, there was a look in her eyes that held both satisfaction and sadness.

"Yeah. I know." Brushing her hair back, he leaned in and touched his brow to hers. "Abby . . . what's wrong? I know you too well to buy the *nothing* bit."

"Do you know me?"

Alarm stirred inside him. "Yeah, sugar. I know you. Hell, how could I not? We're best friends." Tracing his finger down her neck, determined to make sure she hadn't forgotten, he added, "And more . . . now. I'm pretty damned pleased with that *more* bit, let me tell you."

She curled a hand around his wrist and some of the tension knotting his gut eased a little as she added quietly, "So am I." Then she shifted her gaze away from him. "I do think you know me. Better than anybody else. But . . ." She cleared her throat and paused, her mouth opening, then closing like she was trying to find the words. "Lately, I'm wondering . . . hell. *I* wasn't but then people keep saying . . ."

People.

His mind shot back to earlier in the day. He'd seen Keelie standing there, seen her storm down the hall and the woman had been in a mood all damn day. But Keelie was a brat and a half most of the time anyway. Now, though? Not to mention the conversation he'd interrupted between Abby and Sebastian.

Stroking his thumb over her skin, he said quietly, "People keep saying what, Abby?"

Pink crept up her cheeks and she shook her head, leaned back in against him. "This is stupid, Zach. Hell, you've had the worst couple of days and I'm sitting here griping." Once more she tucked her head against his chest and seconds ticked by, but he knew her too well to trust that it was done. The odd tension in her body, the way her hand fisted his shirt, knotting the fabric up, then smoothing it out, over and over. Yeah. She wasn't done, not by a long shot.

"Sebastian and Keelie are both mouthing off about how I don't know you," she finally said. "Are . . . are they right? Do I know you?"

He was going to kick his little brother's ass. Screw being considerate and not messing up his brother's pretty face. If the idiot wanted to make sure he wasn't messed up for his job, maybe he shouldn't have been messing with Zach's woman.

His hand tightened on her waist as those words rolled through him. *My woman* . . . damn. He'd only been waiting half his life to be able to say that. Think that.

And . . . she'd never known.

Do I know you?

The sadness, the uncertainty in her voice ripped at him. Yeah, there were things she didn't know, but those were things he'd kept from her. Things he hadn't let her see. That was his issue, not hers. And fuck Sebastian, fuck Keelie, for putting that pain in her eyes.

Shifting around on the couch, he tumbled her down onto her back, ignoring the screaming pain that went through him as he did it. He didn't care how much it hurt just then, because he needed to touch her, needed to hold her, and he needed to see her and have her see him. Tucking her body under his, he pressed his face against her neck as he waited for the pain to fade a little before he spoke.

"How old was I when I decided I should start smoking?" he whispered against her neck.

She skimmed a hand up his back and sighed. "You were

fifteen. And I laughed my ass off when you got sick on set and puked your guts up because you were trying to finish the damn cigarette with that cute extra you were trying to impress."

He'd been trying to make Abby jealous, but that was beside the point. It hadn't worked and that was because the feelings just hadn't been there on her side.

"Yeah. And Mom thought I had the flu . . . right up until she smelled the smoke on my clothes. I had her convinced somebody else had been smoking around me but then you went and tattled on me." He lifted his head and brushed her hair back from her face. "You remember how long I went without speaking to you?"

She laid a hand on his cheek. "A week. It was one of the longest weeks of my life."

"Mine, too." He rubbed his cheek against her palm and then dipped his head so he could kiss her mouth. That mouth, damn it. He'd only been waiting years to kiss her. "Although I *did* manage to get most of the scenes done in one take that week."

She made a face at him. "Yeah, one week out of how many years? I *always* nailed things in one take."

"You didn't that week." He stroked a thumb down her cheek.

"You probably had fun watching me screw up." She pushed a hand through his hair. "I couldn't help it. You were mad at me and I was miserable. I couldn't concentrate."

"I didn't have fun watching you screw up." Turning his face, he pressed a kiss to her wrist. "I missed talking to you, teasing you while we went through our lines. And I kept trying to think about how I could fix things."

She stared up at him, her eyes solemn, dark . . . and still sad.

"When did I first start talking about opening a place of my own?"

"After your first tattoo. Zach . . . I know I *know* stuff about you, but lots of people know stuff." Then she averted her face and sighed. "Damn it, I sound like an idiot. Look, forget I said anything—"

"Have I ever cried during a movie?"

She blinked and then started to laugh. "Okay, now Zach . . . that's bad. You cry every damn time you watch *Old Yeller.*"

"I don't." He pressed a kiss to her collarbone. "I wouldn't dare let myself do that if my brothers were around. Or anybody else, really. With you . . . it's different."

She snorted and rolled her eyes. "Geez, thanks."

He skimmed his lips along the delicate line of her collarbone, along her neck, up until he reached her ear. Then he caught her earlobe in between his teeth. "What's one place I've always wanted to go, and haven't been?"

She lapsed into silence and when he lifted up, she stared at him. A slow, faint smile tugged at her lips. "Alaska. We were watching *Into the Wild.* Both decided we had to go."

"You were going there. The honeymoon." The word was like acid on his tongue even though the wedding wasn't happening. "Now it's off. Maybe one day we can try for it together."

"I'd love that." Then she bit her lip and caught his shirt in her hands. "Who was she, Zach?"

Distracted, he rubbed his lips over hers. That thing she did, when she was just a little nervous, biting her lip like that . . . she didn't do it often, just around him really. It drove him nuts, though, and made him want to do all sorts of crazy things. Like bite her. In the same spot she was biting. Then he'd . . .

"Zach."

Her hand tangled in his hair and tugged a little just when he was getting ready to do just that.

Blinking, he focused on her face. "What?"

"I was asking you a question." Then she muttered, "I can see where *your* mind is."

He grinned at her and then swore as the cut in his lip split. "Shit." He shifted his weight to his elbow and pressed

the back of his hand to his mouth. A spot of blood appeared
and he sighed. "I really want to beat on those punks even
harder sometimes."

Her eyes glinted. "Can I take a swing or two?" Her
fingers were gentle as she touched his cheek. "I'm still having some bad moments here. But you didn't answer my
question."

"What was it?" he asked, catching her finger between
his teeth and biting gently.

"Who was she?"

It would have been easier if he could pretend he didn't
know what she was talking about. He took his time, though,
formulating his answer, debating on whether or not *to* answer. Levering his weight off of her, he headed to the bar
that separated his kitchen from the living room. "Why are
you asking?" *Stall*. That was the way to go.

"Because I want to know. I want to know who she was,
how much she mattered. I want to know what happened and
if you still love her."

Reaching for a bottle of whiskey, he splashed some into
a glass and tried to figure *which* of those questions he could
answer without lying. "Sometimes, sugar, people come into
your life and they mean everything," he said slowly, staring
down into the amber liquid.

He heard the soft pad of her footsteps on the floor and
looked up to see her crossing over to him. "So she means a
lot to you," she whispered, her eyes dark.

A voice in the back of his mind insisted, *Just tell her*.

But, hell, what if she wasn't ready for this? They'd just
gotten together and things were going *good*, damn it. He
knew she felt something. *Finally*. What if he told her and it
scared her and she took off running from him?

She reached out and touched a finger to the glass. "You
know, if you're going to take any of the pain medicine, you
can't drink that."

"This works better than pain medicine," he said absently. "And I don't make an ass of myself."

Sighing, he tossed half of it back and let it burn its way

down his throat before he lowered the glass and then focused on Abby. The sadness was back in her eyes and he had to get it out, had to do something.

Catching her hand in his, he studied her face. He knew that face so well: every expression, every line of it, every curve, the way a smile would show in her eyes even if it didn't show anywhere else. And the same for pain. The same for sadness. Right now, there was sadness.

"People come and go all the time. But there's only been one woman who came and stayed and mattered . . . it's you," he said quietly. It wasn't *exactly* what he wanted to say, but he wasn't entirely ready to say that, just yet.

She flicked him a look. "That's not what I was asking, Zach. I know I'm important to you. I just—"

He came out from behind the bar and tugged her toward him, hard. She landed against him with enough force to make his bruised ribs scream but he didn't care. Cradling the back of her head in his hand, he lowered his mouth to hers. "Important . . . Abby. *Important* describes what I have to do by April 14. *Important* describes getting my license renewed, my bills paid, payroll . . . Abby. You're not important. You're everything."

Her breath froze in her lungs and for a moment, she was even convinced her heart had stopped. As Zach lowered his mouth to hers, she was afraid to even move. She felt the rough edge of the wound on his mouth and for fear of hurting him, she didn't even kiss him back, but the gentleness of that kiss just about stole the strength out of her.

He pulled back and reached up. He was still holding her gaze as he freed the top button of the simple black blouse she'd worn for work today. Unable to look away, she just watched him as he stripped her blouse away, then her bra, letting them fall to the floor.

Her skirt and panties followed and then he caught her hands, guided them to his shirt. "Zach, are you . . ."

"I'm fine," he muttered. "Hell, I was fine this morning

when you gave me a little peck on the cheek like I was a schoolboy or something. It's not like I've never had a few bruises or anything."

A few bruises, she thought weakly as she drew his shirt up. Ribs bruised, his eye swollen, knuckles ragged and torn, not to mention his mouth. But any argument she might have had faded away as he helped her pull his shirt away, throwing it to the ground.

The muscles in his chest and arms flexed and her mouth went dry at the sight. Then fury and concern, a fascinating mix, twisted through her as she stared at the dizzying array of colors that had bloomed across his torso.

She leaned in and pressed her lips to his ribs, traced a path along his flesh until she'd gone from one side to the other.

"I think there's some bruising down lower," Zach teased, cupping his hand over her head.

She laughed, blushing a little as she straightened. Placing her hands flat against his chest, she tried to stop thinking about the bruises and focused just on him. Under her hand, she saw the edge of the dagger piercing the heart. The scrollwork around it was stylized, some of it all but lost in the color, and the dim light made it even harder to see, but she still took her time, tracing the line of the dagger down to where the blade pierced the heart. Leaning in, she pressed her lips to it and reached for the snap of his jeans.

"Bruising down here, huh?" She dragged the zipper down and grinned as she felt him jump against her fingers. Laughing a little, she said, "Well, I can tell you're definitely up for this."

"I'd have to be dead not to be up for you."

She shoved the jeans down his hips and he nudged her back to finish the job but when she went to move back in, he caught her around the waist and spun them around, backing her up until she found herself against his dining room table. The long, solid length of mahogany felt cool against her naked butt as he lifted her up and set her on the edge.

"Lay down," he said, staring down into her face.

Licking her lips, she eased herself backward, first to her elbows, then going flat, watching his face.

His eyes remained locked on hers for a long, long moment, but instead of touching her, he moved away.

Abigale frowned, watching his naked back as he disappeared around a corner.

When he came back in, he had a long wooden box under his arm. Eyeing it nervously, Abigale went to push up on her elbow. "Ah . . . what's that? If this is your way of telling me that you've got some kinky sex secrets . . ."

He laughed a little. "Oh, there might be a few kinky fantasies, but anything you don't want to do can remain a fantasy as long as I've got you in my bed." He put the box on the table and opened it. She blinked at what she saw inside.

Paint.

Cocking a brow, she said, "I dunno . . . being into finger painting and sex might be called kinky."

He snorted and put his hand on the middle of her chest, nudging her back down. "Do you trust me?" he asked, leaning over her and staring down at her.

Golden brown hair fell into his face, and against the stark bruising and swelling around his left eye, his blue eyes looked even more blue, even more compelling. Licking her lips, she caught his face in her hands and tugged him down. "Like I never trusted anybody else."

"Then close your eyes and let me do something . . ." He quirked a grin at her. "Call it a kinky sex thing if it makes you happy."

Nerves fluttered in her belly, but she hadn't lied about trusting him.

Slowly, she pulled her hands from his hair and lowered them to her sides. Then, after one last look at him, she closed her eyes.

The familiar scent of rubbing alcohol filled the air and she wrinkled her nose. "That's not exactly a comforting smell, Zach."

He laughed and swiped something down her breasts, along each curve, her nipples. She hissed as she felt the flesh pucker and draw tight. He continued down and as whatever it was dried out, he swapped it out for another. As the alcohol dried on her skin, she said, "If I feel another tattoo needle, I'm going to beat you. I wanted *one* tattoo. Just one."

"Relax," he said easily. "Not like I can do anything permanent here anyway. And you know I wouldn't do that to you."

She pursed her lips and tried to relax.

Then she felt him swabbing her skin again, followed by the press of something that felt an awful lot like paper. He'd done something like that when he'd done her tattoo back at his office. "Zach—"

"Shhh. Give me a second to do this first thing and I'll grab you a drink."

"Who said I wanted a drink?"

"Does that mean you *don't*?"

She stuck her tongue out. That resulted in him crushing his mouth to hers and she groaned, reaching for him, but he was pulling away before she had a chance.

Frustrated, she went to put a hand behind her head and he caught her wrist. "Can't do that. You'll mess up the lines. I'll get you a pillow."

She heard him moving away and she went to push up.

"No peeking, Abby."

Groaning, she stayed flat and kept her eyes closed. "You know, when you stripped me naked and spread me out on the table, I thought we were going to get down and dirty and have sex."

"Oh, we'll get to that," he promised and his voice was a husky murmur just inches away.

Opening her eyes, she found him bent over her. He grinned down at her and said, "You're peeking."

"Just at you."

"You always did cheat at things." He kissed her temple and said, "Eyes closed and lift up."

"I do not cheat," she muttered, easing up. He helped her and when she settled back, there was a narrow, but fluffy pillow under her shoulders, neck, and head.

"That better?"

"Yeah."

"Want a drink?"

She thought it through and then decided against it. She wrinkled her nose and stuck her tongue out in his direction. "No. Because I can't figure out how I'd drink it and lay down with my eyes closed without it dribbling down my chin. That's a sexy picture, I tell you."

"You're naked and spread out in front of me. There's no way this can't be sexy," Zach said, pausing to trail the tip of his finger down her middle. "But if you change your mind, let me know."

Adjusting a little, she tried to be patient. She figured it lasted maybe thirty seconds before talking again. "How long will this take?"

"As long as it takes. And I'm having fun, too."

She shivered as he stroked his fingers down her side. A few more minutes passed and she figured he'd repeated whatever he was doing with the paper things maybe four or five times over, in a line that spread over from her left breast down to her right hip. Finally, though, he seemed to be done. "Is that it?"

"Not even close," he said. And if she wasn't mistaken, his voice was hoarse. Hoarse and ragged.

"Zach?"

"No talking, Abby."

This time, when she lapsed into silence, it was strained . . . but not for the same reason. Something wet stroked across her skin and she hissed out a breath.

"Cold?"

She nodded, a knot swelling in her throat. "A little. Tickles." She cracked a smile and said, "And let me guess . . . you're going to tell me to be patient, because you're not done, right?"

"Not done. But I can grab you a blanket or something."

She shivered again as she felt something stroke around her nipple. "No . . ." A tug of arousal centered down low in her belly, sharp and strong, so sharp. So insistent. "I'm fine."

"You're so fucking beautiful . . . you got any idea how long I've thought about doing something like this with you?"

As the ache in her chest threatened to expand, she tried to tease him. "Zach, if you wanted to do finger painting, all you had to do was ask."

"Ha, ha." Abruptly, she felt something hot . . . his mouth. Closing around her right nipple, sucking, tugging, his teeth working it for a second before he pressed it against the roof of his mouth and suckled deep.

She moaned his name and yet again, when she went to reach for him, he pulled back and nudged her hands down to the table.

"On to the next one," he said, his voice a little ragged but cheerful.

Abigale whimpered.

The lotus blossoms spread out along her torso in a delicate rainbow of color. He was just about done and most of the ink had dried. As he finished the one just above her right hip, he bent down and blew on the ink to help it dry quicker. Had to be dry because his hands were shaking and in about five more seconds, he knew he was going to just lose it if he didn't get his cock inside her.

"Are . . ." Her voice broke a little. "Are you done?"

He tossed the brush down and capped the inks. He ought to clean everything, tuck it all up nice and neat, but he didn't care. If he had to buy new supplies, he had to buy new supplies.

"Yeah," he said raggedly, straightening up and staring down at the temporary tattoo he painted across her skin. It was a vivid rainbow across her pale torso and he was absolutely certain it was the most beautiful thing he'd ever had the pleasure to create. "I'm done."

A nervous smile curled her lips and she asked, "Can I look?"

He shot her a look and then eyed the tattoo, feeling a little nervous himself. He never felt nervous about his work. Especially something as temporary as this. He had the kit on hand for parties and stuff, or for when he had a friend who wanted a tattoo but wasn't sure. Nothing like seeing how you'd look with ink for the rest of your life to help you decide if you wanted it or not.

But Abby wasn't just anybody and she sure as hell wasn't just a friend.

"Yeah." He went to pass a hand over the back of his mouth and then stopped, remembering the cut just in time. "Come on, we'll go to the bathroom so you can see it all. But no peeking yet."

With her eyes closed and her hand in his, Zach guided her to the bathroom. He hit the lights, revealing the sprawling, custom-designed bathroom with its glass-enclosed shower and the tub almost big enough to swim in, all of it done in colors of copper, rust, and gold.

Resting his hands on her shoulders, he guided her to the double sinks and swallowed the knot in his throat. "Okay . . . just remember, it's temporary. It will wash off . . ."

Her eyes opened.

And her jaw dropped.

Her fingers shook a little as she lifted her hand and a look of wonder crossed her face as she trailed them over the blossom that covered her left breast. A sucker punch of lust struck him right in the gut and he swore, gripping her hips and spinning her around. "Fuck, Abby," he snarled, lifting her up and pushing her legs open.

"Zach, I'm still . . ." Then she gasped as he pushed up against her and surged inside. "Oh . . ."

"Look later," he rasped as she closed around him, so soft

and wet, every bit as aroused as he was. Slamming one hand against the mirror beyond her shoulder, he stared down at her. The rainbow of color danced over her skin, rippling with each breath she took and he shuddered.

"I need you . . . damn it, I need you so much." *I love you . . .* those words danced on his tongue and he managed just barely to keep them restrained.

She braced her hands on the copper-colored marble of the counter, staring up at him with wide, dazed eyes, her hair falling down around her back in a tumble and the sheer, erotic beauty of her was like a fist to the gut. In the middle of the red and gold of his bathroom, her hair a deep, fiery banner, her skin as pale as ivory, and the delicate rainbow hues of the lotus blossoms stretching across her skin, he knew he was staring at the most amazing sight he'd ever seen.

His muscles shook and need gripped him, turned him into stone as he fought the urge to take, to savage.

"So fucking beautiful." He stroked a hand up her thigh, over her hip. He danced his fingertips over the lines of the paint he'd swirled along her flesh before he captured her curls in his hand and tugged her closer.

Dipping his head, he took her mouth and this time, he didn't care about the fact that the cut on his mouth split, didn't care about the pain.

"Zach," Abby whispered. "Your mouth . . ."

"I don't give a damn." Then he pulled back a little, stared down at her. "Do you?"

She twined an arm around his neck and tugged him closer. "No."

As Zach covered her mouth with his again, Abigale was almost certain she'd just die from the pleasure of it.

Where had this been . . . all of her life? Where had *he* been? Except he'd been right here . . . and this hadn't ever happened.

She tried to tug him closer, but he kept the distance between them. "No . . . I want to see that on you . . . again."

For a second, she didn't know what he meant and then she felt his fingers tracing along her belly, her hip, back up over the lines of her breast and the look on his face was like nothing she'd ever experienced. It was a memory she'd carry forever. The way he looked at her . . . the way he watched her. She looked down, watched as he traced his way across the blossoms crossing her chest. Even as he swiveled his hips and drove his cock inside her, his touch was gentle, so damned gentle.

Involuntarily, she clamped down around him, twisting against him. She felt him swell, felt him stiffen and then he groaned, reaching for her thighs and hooking his elbows under her knees, drawing her close . . . opening her. She sucked in a breath as it forced her weight up back, until she was balancing on her hips and her hands as he surged inside her, so deep, so full. The ridge of his cock throbbed and swelled, stroking over sensitive, delicate tissues and she cried out at the sheer, utter bliss of it.

"Abby . . ."

Forcing her eyes open, she sought out his gaze.

And he was staring at her. Like he saw nothing else. Nobody else.

Dazed, she surged, desperate to get closer. He moved faster, closer . . . still taking care not to press his body to hers, but she felt surrounded by him. *Not close enough*—

With a breathless cry, she sobbed out his name and exploded, coming with a desperate sob.

And he wasn't far behind.

Chapter Seventeen

He took the next day off. There was only so much he could get done with the repairs and shit on a Sunday anyway. Abby wasn't around—she had a wedding to cater and he was so sore, so damned sore, it hurt to move. Why in the hell was today even worse than the past two days? Unless of course it was because he was pushing it so hard, and that was entirely possible. Not that he'd mention it to Abby because she'd *absolutely* say *I told you so*.

All in all, it was a wise, wise decision, because he spent most of that day in more agony than he cared to think about. Between hot baths, a couple of narcotic-induced naps, and a lot of cussing and swearing, he made it through.

But he wasn't happy about it.

One thing that distracted him was thinking about the conversation he planned to have with Keelie that night. He wasn't going in to work. He wasn't going in to do a damned thing except talk to her.

It was a conversation that was past due, he figured.

Sebastian was nosing around in his business. Granted, brothers did that, but still, enough was enough.

Keelie, she was like a kid sister to him and had been since they'd met six or seven years ago. But again . . . *enough was enough.*

Sundays were their shortest business day and he waited until five thirty before he headed over. Javi would be hanging around until Keelie left, because they weren't doing this shit anymore. Nobody was going to be in the shop alone from here on out, not even him. Zach was seriously thinking about moving, although that wasn't ideal for business. He couldn't risk one of his employees getting hurt, either. Up until the other day, nobody had ever been around during the break-ins, but this . . . yeah. He needed to reconsider.

It was just after six when he pulled into his spot behind Steel Ink. Javi's bike was there and so was Keelie's Jeep. He let himself in the back and checked out the front of the shop. A quick look in Javi's work space told him that he was finishing up. Keelie was in the process of explaining the aftercare . . . perfect timing.

They had time for their little chat and then he could get back home and be there when Abby got in, whenever the hell that was. He continued to stare at the back of Keelie's head until she realized he was there. When she turned her head to look at him, he lifted a brow and jerked his head toward his office. She nodded and he turned around, satisfied she'd gotten the message.

He did a detour by the break room, eyeing the quick fix somebody had done on the door. Probably Javi. It was enough to let the door close, keep it locked so they could keep the system armed, but that was it.

Sighing, he opened the fridge and pulled out a bottle of water. He half expected to see it was running low since he hadn't been able to make the supply run he usually did on Saturdays, but everything was in there, freshly stocked. He twisted the top off the bottle and turned around to find Keelie standing in the doorway.

"I picked up what we needed before I came in today," she said, rocking back on her heels and tucking her hands into her pockets. "I didn't figure we'd see you until tomorrow. You don't need to be here, you know."

"Yeah, I do." He edged around her and moved down the hall. "Let's go to my office."

He didn't bother to look back and see if she was there. He knew she was.

He listened as the door shut behind them and made his way over to his desk, pausing at the site of the manila folder sitting there. "What's this?"

"The insurance forms." She jerked a shoulder in a shrug as she flopped in the leather chair tucked up close to his desk. "I called our agent, asked her to come by and do whatever she had to do so we could get things rolling."

He quirked a brow at her. "Damn, Keelie. I didn't know you even had any clue about what we'd have to do."

"I'm not an idiot, Zach," she snapped. "Just because I prefer *not* to handle the business end of things doesn't mean I *can't*."

"You never showed much interest in it, that's all I meant." He flipped through the forms and grimaced. "What am I doing, just signing?"

"Yes. She's coming back out tomorrow."

He nodded shortly and then settled in his chair, raking his hair back as he tried to figure the best way to approach this. Subtle and Keelie didn't have a passing acquaintance, but he knew if he just jumped on her, she'd get pissed and wouldn't hear a damn thing he had to say.

And Keelie needed to hear this . . . needed to hear it very, very clearly.

It had been a wonderful wedding, a small affair that had pulled her out of bed before the crack of dawn, but now it was done. As her crew went about cleaning up, she sought out her assistant Paul and asked, "Can you handle the rest?"

"Sure." His brows arched over his eyes and he leaned a hip against the counter, studying her curiously. "Everything okay? You never cut out early."

"Yeah." She fidgeted with the tie on her apron for a second and then finally just shrugged. "My . . ." *Say it, you twit. It's not that hard.* "My boyfriend had somebody break into his shop the other day. He was there when it happened and he's fine, but I just . . . well, I want to be there."

"Your boyfriend," Paul said slowly, shaking his head. "What is this? You just broke off your engagement a few weeks ago and now there's a boyfriend?"

"It's been more than a month," she said. Then she shrugged. "Yeah, there's a boyfriend." She licked her lips and then tugged off the apron, wadding it up into a ball. Tossing it into the bin where the dirty linens were collected, she looked back at Paul and said softly, "I'm seeing Zach."

To her shock, he didn't blink at her like she'd sprouted another head and he didn't go, *Zach who?*

Instead, a wide grin split his face and he started to laugh.

She stood there for about fifteen seconds, shuffling her feet and then she lightly punched him in the arm. "Damn it, knock it off. What's so funny?"

"Oh, nothing," he said, shaking his head and looking back at her, that grin still dancing in his eyes. "I was just wondering *when* that would happen."

Squirming, she turned away from him. "What do you mean by that?"

"Oh, come on, Abigale. The guy's only been crazy about you for years. Shit, I kept expecting him to blow a gasket every time I saw you with Roger, but . . ."

Abigale frowned. "What do you mean by that?"

He shrugged. "Just that. I mean, I've been working with you almost since the beginning, right? When he first moved here, the way he looked at you and all, I thought there was already something there, but then . . . well. Anyway, I figured out it wasn't a two-way thing. But hell, anybody with eyes can see it," he said, reaching for a rag to dry his hands off. He studied her face for a minute and then added softly, "I'm just kind of shocked it took *you* so long to figure it out."

Surprise had her going still and for a minute, she just couldn't move.

When he first moved here . . .

The way he looked at you . . .

Slowly, she shook her head. "Zach hasn't been . . ." She stopped and cleared her throat. "Zach hasn't been waiting all this . . ."

I've only been waiting for you to kiss me for a good long while now . . .

I've been waiting for this for a lifetime.

"Son of a bitch." She turned around and braced her hands on the counter.

"Abigale?"

Slowly, she turned around to look at him. "I . . ." Licking her lips, she shook her head and asked, "Are you serious? I mean . . . really, are you serious?"

Paul blinked, shaking his head as he looked at her. "What, you didn't know? Hell, Abby. It's like . . ." He paused like he just didn't know what to say. One hand lifted like he thought that might make it easier to pull the words out of the air. "I remember the way I'd see him watching you. There was this party once. At your place. I was standing there talking to him, asking him about a tattoo I wanted to get and all of a sudden, he just stops talking to me. He's staring over my shoulder and I look back, thinking maybe that gorgeous friend of yours . . ." He grimaced and added, "Not that you aren't beautiful, but I thought maybe it was Marin Del Marco or something. But you were standing at the door, and he just stared at you. It's like when you're there, nobody else exists."

She never seemed to notice that I was staring at her when she walked into the room.

Zach had said those words to her. Just over a month ago when she'd asked if he'd been in love before.

Oh, shit.

Other bits and pieces seemed to connect inside her head.

"Hey, Abby . . . are you okay?"

Jerking her head up, she met Paul's gaze and nodded.

"I'm fine. I . . . um. If you're sure you can handle this, I'm heading out."

She didn't even bother to wait for an answer, just grabbed her keys and hit the door.

She never seemed to notice that I was staring at her when she walked into the room.

Those words echoed in her mind every step of the way as she ran for her car.

Zach . . . ?

Was that even possible? she wondered. But her brain already had the answer for that. Yes. It was possible. It had been there, she realized, for a very long time. And she hadn't seen it.

The real question was just how did she *feel* about it?

But the answer to *that* question wasn't so hard.

A warm, lovely sensation bloomed through her and she pulled out of the lot so fast, she practically left rubber on the pavement.

She could hear that voice of his, so low and familiar, soft as velvet and sinful as Death by Chocolate, as he murmured, *When you walked into a room, it would have showed on his face . . . if he really loved you.*

It would have showed on his face . . . And it did show. It just showed on the face of a man she hadn't bothered to look at for far too long. Zach. The man who'd always been there.

Her throat was tight as she thought back over the past few weeks. Zach's face. He could be talking to somebody, *anybody*, and he'd know when she was there. He'd look up at her, and that smile would come across his face.

Something warm and easy, but . . . more than that.

It made her heart ache more than once, and there was something in his eyes, too: possessive, hungry, proud, and wondering. It might have been too much, but when she looked at him now, she felt the same way.

She never seemed to notice that I was staring . . .

"Me." She slowed down at a red light. Had he really been talking about *her*?

But then she thought back to last night. Just last night. She pressed the heel of her hand to the tattoo he'd painted across her torso and thought back. He'd never really given her a straight answer, she realized.

She went to turn right, but abruptly realized she didn't want to go to the shop wearing her work clothes, smelling like she'd just spent the entire day cooking. Hell, the mule-headed man ought to be home but she knew he wouldn't be.

Groaning, she checked the time. He'd be there for another couple of hours. She could go home, but that would take most of those hours and she couldn't wait.

His place, though, that was close.

She usually kept an extra outfit for work, and a pair of jeans and a t-shirt there, although that wasn't exactly ideal. She'd make do.

On the drive, she replayed the conversation from last night through her head.

Sometimes, sugar, people come into your life and they mean everything.

So she means a lot to you.

People come and go all the time. But there's only been one woman who came and stayed and mattered . . . it's you.

That's not what I was asking, Zach. I know I'm important to you. I just—

Important . . . Abby. Important describes what I have to do by April 14. Important describes getting my license renewed, my bills paid, payroll . . . Abby. You're not important. You're everything.

Everything . . .

Yeah. The way he made her feel when he looked at her, when he touched her. She could believe that.

The drive to his condo took far too long, at least in her opinion. The clock said it was only fifteen minutes but what did the clock know?

Five minutes after she'd parked the car, she was letting herself inside. She reset the alarm and she tore into his bedroom, dumping her spare clothes on the bed as she stripped out of her dirty ones. With her fingers working the buttons of her shirt, she headed to his closet. Maybe she'd borrow a shirt . . .

Yeah.

There was a green silk one that she thought would work just fine.

He spent most of his time in t-shirts and boots, but he knew his way around nicer pieces of clothing. And he could rock a suit like nobody's business. She stroked a hand down the sleeve of a steel gray jacket and thought about seeing him in that . . . maybe soon, she thought. Maybe soon.

But for now, she was going to have to get her butt ready and go corner him in his office. And if he thought he could put her off *this* time, he was out of his skull.

"Keelie, you and I need to talk about something, and you're going to listen very carefully to what I have to say," he said softly, picking up a pencil and starting to sketch out a design absently. Better to do that than look at her, because he wanted to keep his temper. Keep his cool.

"Look, if you're going to rip me a new one because I took care of things after the break-in, then you can just kiss my ass. You had enough going on and I wanted to help," she said. He glanced up as she surged out of the chair and started to pace, her hands shoved deep in her pockets, her strides long and angry. "Besides, I *own* half the place, remember? I have just as much right as you do."

"You're right." He shook his head. "I'm not denying that. I appreciate you stepping up there a lot."

He dropped the pencil and stood up, moving around to cut her off as she started another circuit across the room. "But this isn't about the shop. It's not about the break-in. It's about something else entirely."

She lifted a brow and then turned away, sauntered over to his desk, and leaned back against it, arms crossed over her chest. "Okay. I'm all ears."

"You better be."

Her eyes widened just a fraction before she shot him a smirk.

Nervous, kid? Good. He hooked his thumbs in his belt loops as he continued to watch her for a minute, trying to figure out just how he'd made her mad enough at him that she'd decided it would be okay to fuck with his life. Hell, if she didn't know what Abby meant to him it would be one thing, but she did.

But he couldn't quite figure it out. He couldn't.

"Why, Keelie?" he asked softly. "Can you just tell me why?"

Her brows arched over her mismatched eyes. "Ah . . . tell you why *what*?"

"Why are you trying to get in between me and Abby? It doesn't concern you so why are you trying to mess with it?"

Her lids flickered and then she sneered. "Hell, what is that glamour girl telling you? I didn't do *shit* to her, Zach. Not a *damn* thing. So whatever she said—"

"I love her," he said softly. "My entire life, I've only loved *one* woman. I didn't have crushes on any of the girls we worked with. I didn't go chasing after anybody when I tried to make it for a while after the show ended. I didn't fall for anybody in college. I dated some but it was more because I wanted to try and forget about her, even though I knew it wouldn't work. She's *it* for me, Keelie. You understand that? I *love* her. More than I'm ever going to be able to love *anybody*. And now I finally have the chance I've been waiting my whole life for . . . and you and Sebastian are fucking things up. The two of you are making her doubt what we have going. Why in the hell are you doing that?"

She snapped her mouth shut with a click.

Shoving past him, she started to pace. "Look, man, I didn't *do* anything. I don't like her, but why in the hell should I? She doesn't see what's staring her right in the face. She can't appreciate you and she's hurt you a hundred times and she doesn't even see it." She sent him a seething look over her shoulder and demanded, "Why *should* I like her?"

"You don't *have* to like her," Zach pointed out. "But damn it, are we friends or not? Because I always thought we were. If we are, why would you try to mess this up for *me*?"

"I wasn't trying to!" She stopped and turned around, glaring at him. "She just . . . shit. She asked me what my problem was and I . . . just. Hell, she can't *see* it, damn you. And it hurts you and I can't stand it. How can she *not* see it?"

"Because I didn't let her." He crossed his arms over his chest and shook his head. "And that's not a good enough reason."

"She didn't *see* it because she didn't want to," Keelie muttered. "She doesn't deserve you, Zach. You need somebody who'll see what you have to offer, who'll appreciate you and everything you are."

Her voice softened as she crossed the floor to stand in front of him.

Alarm started to flare in his head as she murmured, "Love like that really can't be hidden, Zach. Don't you feel it when somebody loves you?"

She stopped just in front of him and that alarm screeched louder. "Keelie, look, this has nothing do with whether or not Abby saw anything before now. She's seeing it now and this doesn't even involve you. *This* is about the fact that you are causing me problems and when you hurt her, you hurt me. Why the hell do you want to do that?"

"Hurting you is the last thing I want to do," Keelie said. She reached out and caught his arm.

And that alarm in his head just screamed louder.

"When you look at me, do you see *anything* more than a friend looking back at you?" she asked and her voice was soft. Full of things he'd never heard before.

And damn it all to hell, as he stared into her eyes, he realized he hadn't been the only one hiding things.

"Keelie, the only thing I see in you is a friend," he said, shaking his head.

She slid her hand higher. "Just a friend, Zach? Is that all we can ever be?"

He caught her arm and nudged her hand down. "That's all we *are*."

"Because you've never given us a chance for something more. Maybe it's time you did."

And then she leaned in. Right as she touched her lips to his, the door opened.

Abigale smoothed a hand down the green silk shirt she wore and took a deep breath.

It was quiet in Zach's office. Very quiet.

The shop wasn't very busy and if she hadn't seen his car, she might have wondered if he was there.

With her heart knocking against her ribs, she went to push the door open.

And then, her heart stopped knocking against anything as it turned to ashes. All those ashes drifted away on the wind as she stared at the scene before her. If the scene had been written by some of the best in the biz, they couldn't have done it any more perfectly.

A gritty urban scene, she thought absently. The rugged, street-smart male with his face all battered from his latest battle. His hands curled around the woman's wrists as he stared down at her face. The woman, dressed in skintight black pants and a white tank under a fishnet top, stared up at him and the emotion on her face was as sharp as a blade. Even the lights around them seemed to be chosen to play it all up to perfection as Keelie leaned in and pressed her mouth to Zach's.

For that one brief moment, time froze.

And then it shattered, just like her heart.

Zach was the first one to notice, his head swinging around her way and those wicked, warm blue eyes locked on her face. That intensity that Abby had been so convinced was there just for her was in his eyes, all right. But a second ago, he'd been staring at Keelie with a hell of a lot of focus, too.

"Abby," he said, his voice rough.

She just stared at him for a moment and then she shot Keelie a dark look. To her surprise, the woman didn't meet her glare with a cocky smile, and she didn't glare back.

Instead, to her surprise, Keelie lowered her head and stared at her feet.

Abby opened her mouth to say something. Anything. But the pain ripping through her just wouldn't let her speak.

All she wanted to do was cry.

But screw that.

Grabbing the doorknob, she jerked the door shut with a slam and then she took off, running down the hallway.

She was almost at the door when she heard Zach roaring out her name.

But she didn't slow down.

Chapter Eighteen

For one brief moment, Zach wondered if maybe he'd taken one of those damned pain pills and just forgotten about it, because that might explain why in the hell everything had just started to trip out on him.

But the pain pills had always made things just glide and float, even if they did fuck his head up.

They didn't turn the world into a nightmare and that's what this was, he thought, jerking back from Keelie and staring at her like he didn't even know her. *What the hell—*

And then he realized they weren't alone.

Swinging his head around, he thought, *Not Abby, not Abby, not Abby . . .*

But he already knew who it was.

It was Abby, standing there, staring at him like he had just jerked her heart out of her chest and smashed it to the ground. And he imagined that just might be how she felt. He knew the feeling pretty damned well, but any time he'd ever seen her kissing that fuckhead boyfriend of hers, Abby hadn't ever belonged to Zach. He couldn't call it a betrayal.

This, though . . .

"Abby . . ."

She just stared at him for a long moment and then, without saying anything, she jerked the door closed.

"What the hell . . ."

"Zach . . ."

He shot Keelie a narrow look and then took off running out the hall after Abby. But she was running away again.

And this time, she was running from him.

"Abby!"

She shoved through the door before he could catch up to her and he watched as she bolted down the sidewalk. "Damn it," he snarled, shoving the door open. But she was inside her car. And then, seconds later, she was tearing off into the traffic on 4th Avenue.

Stunned, sick inside, Zach stared down the street after her. He'd wasted valuable seconds trying to chase after her, instead of going around to get his car from the back. There was no way he could catch her now.

He'd just have to talk to her at home.

Skimming a hand back over his hair, he nodded to himself. "Yeah. At home."

Shoving back inside, he ignored the wide-eyed looks coming from the patrons, he ignored Javi's concerned comment, and he ignored Keelie, who was standing in the hallway, a nervous look on her face.

In his office, he grabbed his keys and turned back around.

Keelie was in the doorway.

"You need to move," he said quietly.

"Look, let me call her or something," she said, misery on her face.

"You need to move," he said again.

"Damn it, Zach!" She stared at him, tears glinting in her eyes.

Part of him wanted to feel bad for her, but he just couldn't care that much right then. "Stop," he said quietly. "I don't want the *poor Keelie* routine. I don't give a flying fuck that you didn't know she was there—it doesn't *matter*.

You know I'm dating her and you know I'm serious about her. Serious . . ." he trailed off, shaking his head.

Abruptly, he started to laugh, although there wasn't anything at all humorous about this. Not a damn thing was funny. But just then, he felt like if he didn't laugh, he just might lose it.

"Serious," he said again. "Yeah. I'm serious about her."

Saying he was *serious* about Abby was kind of like calling Arizona *hot* in the dead of summer. Slanting a dark look at Keelie, he said softly, "I love her, damn it. She's my world. What the *fuck* possessed you to pull something like that?"

"What possessed me?" she asked, staring at him. Then she sighed and shook her head. "The same thing that possesses you to chase after the same woman for seventeen years. I love you."

I love you.

Those words didn't want to come together in his head. Oh, he *knew* what they meant, but coming from Keelie? Swearing, he shoved the heels of his hands against his eye sockets. "What the hell . . ."

"Yeah. What the hell. That pretty much describes all of this pretty damn well, Zach."

He lowered his hands to stare at her but she wasn't looking at him. She started to pace, her long legs scissoring as she stalked across his office, her head bent, eyes on the floor. "You wanted to know why and there you go. And now, maybe I get it. Because you're looking at me like I'm crazy. I've loved *you* for years. And you didn't know, did you?"

"No. Look . . ." He blew out a breath, trying to think past the haze of anger. But he just couldn't. Not then. "I'm sorry, Keelie. I can't talk about this right now, but it . . . it wouldn't ever work and you know it. Even if she walks away from me and never speaks to me again, I'll never . . . well. You're a friend, but that's it."

"I always thought . . ." She licked her lips and shook her head. "Part of me thought you knew and just pretended otherwise because you didn't want to embarrass me. Okay. I guess maybe sometimes people don't know." She flicked him another look and moved out of the doorway. "I'm sorry, Zach."

"I'm not the one who just had my heart ripped out," he said quietly.

He headed down the hallway, his mind already intent on finding Abby, on what he would say to her, on what he *could* say.

It didn't matter that he hadn't been kissing Keelie, that he hadn't been putting the moves on her or anything.

What mattered was that Abby had been hurt and he had to fix it.

Behind him, Keelie moved to stare after him. As he disappeared through the door, she rubbed the heel of her hand over her chest and sighed.

"No," she said, even though she was talking to thin air. He wasn't the one who had just had his heart ripped out. She had to agree there. That pleasure belonged to Abby . . . and herself.

But in the end, her heart was a problem of her own making. Something she'd have to deal with.

She hadn't been very fair to Abby, she decided. She had to find a way to fix that.

But figuring out *how* to do that was going to be hard.

"You haven't talked to Abby, have you?"

"Give me a minute, Zach."

Marin's assistant Leo put the phone on speaker, but judging by the sound of Zach's voice, she might have to rethink that decision. Facedown on the massage table, she glanced at Leo and said, "I need some privacy, Leo." She wasn't too concerned about the masseuse, Rosa. Rosa was paid to be discreet and uber-professional.

Leo could be as well, when it suited him. That was one of the reasons she kept him around. He let things slip and it was usually the *right* kind of things, things that helped with publicity and the like, but her friendship with Zach and Abby wasn't fodder for that particular mill. Leo didn't always get that, and she wasn't going to take that chance. Not with her two closest friends.

Once the door closed, she blocked out the brutally strong fingers that were trying to separate her muscles from her spine and said, "The last I talked to Abby was a few days ago. Everything okay, Zach?"

"No. When she calls you, tell her . . ." He stopped, sighed.

Something about the way his voice sounded set off a warning inside and even though he didn't say anything for a long, long moment, dread curdled inside Marin.

"Zach?"

"Never mind," he said, his voice flat now, emotionless. "But when you talk to her, see if you can find out where she is."

"Ahh . . ." She lifted a hand and Rosa stopped, huffing out a sigh of frustration. Fine. Let her be frustrated. Marin lifted up onto her elbows. "What do you mean, find out where she is?"

"We had a fight. She's gone. She isn't at home, she won't answer her phone, and I haven't seen her in hours. Just see if she'll tell you. I need to see her, okay?"

The misery she heard lying just under the flat tone of his voice made her heart hurt. *No. Not this,* she thought dismally. Things had finally clicked for them. Those two belonged together. That was something she had always known. What— *No. Just stop. It's a fight. Fights are normal. Couples have those sorts of things, right?*

"Zach, why don't you tell me what's going on?"

In response, she got a long stream of colorful cusswords that might have made her blush, except she'd already heard those variations and others from Zach or his brothers over the years.

"That's very inventive, sweetheart, but that's not a response," she interrupted.

"Shit." He muttered something else and then abruptly said, "I got to go. Let me know if you hear from her."

As the phone disconnected, she groaned and dropped her head down. Immediately, Rosa's nimble hands went back to work on her spine. "Wait, Rosa . . . I need to make a call."

"The massage isn't going to help with the tension if you don't let me do my job."

Yeah, well, she wasn't going to relax when she was worrying about her friends, either.

Speeding down the highway, ignoring the thick, dark blanket of the sky overhead, Abigale propped her left elbow on the door and rested her head on her hand, swallowing the knot in her throat.

She'd thought . . .

Stop thinking, she thought darkly.

Thinking *hurt*. When she *thought*, she remembered what she had just seen. She'd gone to Zach's *thinking* she'd figured out something amazing. Gone there thinking that maybe, just maybe, that *thing* she'd been looking for her entire life was already hers.

Have you ever been in love?

The expression on his face when he looked at her, then the careful way he *hadn't* looked at her when he answered that question.

I'm thirty-two years old, Abby. Yeah. I've been in love. It didn't work out.

Her heart ached and she tried to cut off that tide of memories.

She never seemed to notice that I was staring at her when she walked into the room.

Emotion swelled inside her throat and it was a miracle her eyes stayed dry. No matter *what* she did, she seemed to recall a hundred, a thousand times when he'd been staring at her when she walked into the room. When he'd look up at her, that slow smile would light his face. It was like he'd been waiting just for her and until he saw her, he couldn't really smile. Not *that* way. It was the kind of smile that said . . . *the day's complete now.*

And something *about* that smile *made* her day complete. It had been like that for a long, long time, too. She just hadn't fully understood it.

She'd been falling for her best friend, all right.

Falling . . . already fallen. Flat-out in love with him. She'd gone to tell him. Confront him and demand he tell her how *he* felt, although she thought she already knew.

Yet if he was in love with her, then *what in the hell* had she seen when she walked into the office back at Steel Ink?

And damn it, that hurt. Thinking about it hurt so much, she wanted to pull off the side of the road and just curl up into a ball. She didn't want to think about crying, though. If she started to cry, she'd never stop and she knew it. So the answer, really, was to just *stop thinking*.

The phone rang and she had to sniffle, had to grip the steering wheel in an iron grip just to keep from snatching it up and answering it. "Rebel Yell." Zach's ringtone. She ought to reprogram it to something like "Your Cheating Heart."

"Fuck!"

Focusing on the road, she realized she was almost at the state line. She'd been driving for hours and New Mexico loomed up ahead of her.

She had absolutely *no* idea where she was going. Sighing, she grabbed her phone. Holding the button down, she waited for the beep and then said, "Find a hotel close to me." She was *not* going back home. There was no way she could even think about it and never mind the fact that it was almost eleven p.m.

If she went home, she'd find Zach waiting there. She knew that. And she wasn't ready to talk to him yet.

She had to wait until she was up to talking to him without wanting to punch him. Kick him in the balls.

Rip Keelie's two-toned hair out. Actually, *that* idea held a lot of merit and she wasn't completely brushing that aside.

But she needed to pull over, get some sleep, and reevaluate. Look at things again in the morning. She didn't know. The only thing she *did* know was that she wasn't ready to go back and talk to Zach.

With something to distract her, the next few minutes passed with a little more ease. The nearest town with any decent hotel offerings was Lordsburg, New Mexico.

Sighing, she flicked another glance at the phone and grimaced. A Hampton Inn. She brought it up on her GPS and rubbed at her tired eyes.

Okay, she was going to Lordsburg. She could check into the hotel, collapse on a bed. Maybe find a liquor store and have a drink or two and rage about what she'd seen.

Try to *understand* what she'd seen . . .

The phone rang again.

"What the . . ."

As the strains of "I Will Remember You" by Sarah McLachlan filled the air, she was torn between disgust and fury. There was absolutely no justice in life. On the night when she really just wanted to be left alone to wallow in her rage and misery, Roger decided he was going to call.

She almost ignored it, but then she remembered. With almost savage glee, she thought about goal number two on her list. It involved Roger. Up until a few hours ago, she hadn't been too concerned about it, but just then, the idea of venting some of that fury inside her sounded really, really good.

"Item number two . . . Tell Roger off."

Snatching up the phone, she took the call and flipped it over to speaker before dropping it back down in the cup holder.

"What in the hell do you want?" she demanded as she checked the rearview mirror. Shooting over into the fast lane, she edged around a semi and checked the upcoming exits. She had about another twenty minutes before she'd be at the hotel.

Twenty minutes, then she could collapse and cry. In between now and then, she had the welcome distraction of giving her ex an earful.

"Hello, Abigale."

"I asked you what you wanted," she said flatly. "I didn't ask for conversation."

"I wanted to make sure you were okay," Roger said, his voice cool and detached. Modulated, even.

She wondered then if she had ever really talked to anybody who could be described as speaking in *modulated* tones. She was pretty certain she hadn't.

"I'm so delighted you're concerned about me," she said, sounding like a bitch and not giving a damn.

"Zach Barnes called . . . he . . . well." Roger paused, and when he spoke again, his voice wasn't quite so *modulated*. "He called and asked if I'd heard from you. I'm not sure why he'd think you'd call me, but it had me concerned."

"I can't tell you how much I'm touched by your concern." Something twisted inside her heart even as she sneered a little at Roger's *concern*. Zach had called *Roger*? She must really have Zach worried if he was calling a shit like Roger. "Oh, I'm just peachy, Rog. Was there something else?"

Seconds ticked away and then he said, "Rog?"

"I'm sorry. Roger. Was there something else, *Roger*?"

"Abigale, are you certain you're well?"

"Why wouldn't I be?" *I mean, other than the fact that I figured out that I'm in love with my best friend. Then I figured out that he's in love with me . . . or at least I thought he was. Then I see him kissing that bitch, Keelie? Oh, yeah. I'm just fine.*

A near-hysterical laugh rose in her throat, but she swallowed it back down.

"You don't sound like yourself," he said, his voice taking on a note of caution.

"Don't I? I think I sound just like myself, especially when I'm pissed off. But what do you know?" She tapped her fingers on the door, keeping an eye on the speed because the angrier she got, the faster she wanted to drive. "You seem to think you know me when you don't know jack shit."

"Abigale, there's hardly any cause to be rude," he said. "I was just concerned. I'll call back when you're—"

"Don't bother . . . you know what? I'm actually rather glad you called, because I've been meaning to call *you*. I kept getting distracted but there are things I need to say to you and those things need to be said. You're a fucking moron, *Rog*," she said, smiling at how good it felt to *say* that. It felt *damn* good, she realized. *Very* damn good. "You don't know anything about the life you *think* I want . . . a life where I'm up before dawn, where I'd have to starve myself to fit somebody else's ideal, a life where I'm constantly being judged, where I can't leave the house without makeup unless I want everybody to think I'm having a personal crisis—"

"Abigale—"

"Shut *up*," she snarled. "You think that's the life I miss? How about the two years I had to spend hours getting my hair dyed because it started getting darker and my mom didn't approve? I hated it but it didn't matter. Because I didn't suit my *part* and I had to *change* to fit it. You think I *miss* that? Trying out for every two-bit part that doesn't suit me just so I can get my name back out there? I know . . . maybe I should have taken that offer to act in a plus-size porno or I can start doing the *Dancing with the Stars* thing even though I'm just as likely to break an ankle as anything else."

"You're a serious actress, Abigale. That's where your heart is. I know you have doubts, but I—"

"I'm not done," she said quietly. She shot another glance at the mirror, checked her speed, and saw that she was edging up on nearly ninety. Letting up on the gas, she sucked in a deep, steadying breath. "I hated that life. I couldn't get away from it fast enough but you are determined to push me back into it. What in the hell do you know about where my heart lies?"

He didn't answer right away, but finally, he asked, "Isn't

there anything about it that you miss, darling? Wasn't there *anything* about it that made you happy?"

"Don't call me darling. You gave up that right."

"You're avoiding the question. That proves I'm not wrong about this," he said, triumph coloring his words. "If you'd just stop being so worried, you could go back to it. I'll be there. I'll—"

"*You* will be there? First, you're so wrong about this, it's sad. And second? *You* are no longer part of my life. Even if for some bizarre reason I *did* go back to that life? My life no longer involves you. As for your question . . ." She didn't have to think about it. "There's nothing I *miss* about it. The things that didn't piss me off I can have whenever I want them or need them. As to what made me happy . . ."

A face flashed through her mind and pain wracked her as she thought about him. Zach. Yeah. He made her happy. He'd *always* made her happy.

"Zach," she whispered.

"Abigale, I can't hear you."

She licked her lips and cleared her throat before she tried again. "You probably don't want to, *darling*," she said mockingly. "But you asked if anything about that life made me happy and the answer is yes. It's Zach. So . . . there you go. And I don't have to go back to Hollywood to have him."

She never seemed to notice that I was staring at her when she walked into the room.

"Zach . . ." Anger edged into his voice. "You actually think *he* can make you happy?"

"He already does." Ice crept through her as she thought about what had happened over the past few hours. But even *aside* from that, Zach had always made her happy.

"You're not serious about this," Roger said, his voice cool. "You need somebody at your side who will *support* you. That's all I ever wanted to do."

"Support?" She snorted. "I think you just wanted to be along for the ride if I ever *did* go back to Hollywood. You wanted it for yourself . . . not me."

He waited just a second too long to respond. "That's

insane, Abigale. We were together because we were a good fit. And I just wanted—"

"I don't care. Whatever *you* wanted wasn't what was right for me. Now, I think I've said everything to you that I needed to say. I don't think you need to call me anymore," she said softly. Without waiting for a response, she disconnected the phone.

Then she focused on the road.

There. She'd accomplished the second goal. She still needed to flip off a photographer but once that was done, she'd have done everything on her new *plan*.

The torrid affair . . .

Her throat ached, even thinking about it.

"Not now." She rubbed her temple. She needed to get off the road, get to the hotel.

Screw the liquor store.

She needed a clear head because she had serious, hard thinking to do.

"You haven't seen Abby, have you?"

"Huh?"

Zach shoved a hand through his hair and glared at the clock. It was nearly midnight. Zane lived in Albuquerque. She'd just driven away from his shop in a fury a few hours ago. No. It wasn't likely that Zane had seen her, but neither had anybody else and he was worried.

Hell, he was so desperate, he'd even called Roger. If he could talk to that asshole, then there was no reason he couldn't call his brother and wake him up at midnight . . . although . . .

"Hey, why in the hell are you in bed at midnight? You're a fucking bartender."

Zane grunted. "Night off and I'm tired. What's this about Abby? No, I haven't seen her unless she just up and relocated."

Pinching the bridge of his nose, Zach tipped his head back. "I meant have you talked to her. She just . . . hell. I saw her a few hours ago, but . . . we kind of had a fight. I can't get her to talk to me and I'm worried."

"Ah . . . shit." Zane's voice was low and groggy and a few moments of silence stretched out, as well as a mumbled curse, followed by a grunt. "Fuck. No, I haven't talked to her. What's going on? What are you two fighting about?"

With his heart twisting, Zach said, "I don't want to get into it."

"Can't believe you two are fighting already," Zane said, his sigh coming across the phone loud and clear, and grating on Zach's nerves.

"Oh, fuck off." He started to hang up.

"Hell, Zach. Ease up," Zane said. "Look . . . hell. Okay. I just— I can listen if you need to talk. I'm definitely the best bet if you gotta vent, you know that. Unless you want to give Seb a ring."

"I'd like to wring his fucking neck." Blowing out a sigh, Zach leaned against the car and continued to stare up at Abby's dark, quiet house. He wouldn't be able to loiter much longer. If he hung around here indefinitely, somebody was likely to call the cops and wouldn't *that* just cap his night off nicely? He'd thought about going inside, but he didn't think that was the right way to handle it. Of course, waiting in her driveway like a stalker wasn't exactly ideal, either, he thought.

"Did you know that . . ." Blood crept up his neck. He could feel it, the red crawl of it, leaving his flesh stinging hot. "Ah. Well."

"Just get it out, kid," Zane said, his voice a little clearer now. "I'm having one of those moments where I'm wondering why in the hell I stopped smoking."

"Because Mom was going to kick your ass if you didn't after Dad had that cancer scare." He closed his eyes and blew out a breath. "Keelie kissed me."

Silence dropped like a ten-ton weight, crashing down heavy and destructive, smashing everything into oblivion.

He could hear the call and chirp of the night creatures

but nothing else. It was like Zane had even forgotten to breathe.

And then finally, in a low, rough voice, the other man said, "What?"

Something sick moved inside him as he remembered something. Zane chased after hundreds of women, it seemed. Chased them, but it didn't really matter if he caught them. With Keelie, though . . . with Keelie, it was different.

Now as that sickness spread, he could have kicked his own ass. "Look, I need to—"

"Say that again, Zach," Zane said quietly. "Just say it again."

"She kissed me. I'm sorry . . . I think I . . . you got a thing for her, don't you?"

"It doesn't matter," Zane said softly. "What's going on with Abby?"

"She walked in. I was pulling away and . . . *shit*." He shoved away from the car and started to pace, fighting to hold the words inside him. He needed to talk, but he couldn't hurt his brother, either.

"Zach. Just talk okay?" Zane said tiredly. "Maybe I . . . fuck. Screw maybe. Yeah, I thought maybe there was something with Keelie, but I guess it's not ever going to work out so it doesn't matter. You and Abby, though . . . that's a different story. What's going on there, Zach?"

"She walked in," Zach said again, an ache spreading through him as he remembered the look on her face. "I was pulling away and I swear, Zane, there isn't *anything* between me and Keelie. I was pulling away, but I know that's not how it looked and—"

"You don't need to explain it to me," his brother said. "Look, you're so gone over Abby, there's no room left inside you for another woman. I *know* that. Anybody with a functioning brain stem should be able to see that, if they bothered to look. Abby excluded because she doesn't see it. That's because you always worked *damned* hard not to let her. But you're not as careful with the rest of the world as you are with her. You don't hide it and you never hid it from Keelie . . . so why in the hell did she kiss you?"

"She said . . ." He groaned and shoved a hand through his hair, staring down the road like that might make her car magically appear. It didn't work. It hadn't worked for the past few hours, but he wasn't giving up hope. If he just kept watching, if he just kept waiting, if he just kept hoping, that car of hers would show up.

"Keelie . . ." He blew out a ragged breath and then made himself continue. "She's got this fucked-up idea that she's in love with me. It's not real. It can't be. But—"

"Don't speak for her, Zach." Zane sounded even more tired now. Tired. Resigned. "She's a big girl and I'm pretty sure she knows her feelings better than anybody else does. And again, this isn't about Keelie . . . or me. I appreciate the concern, but it's not about that. This is about you and Abby, okay? Let's keep it about you and Abby. Have you talked to her?"

"No. She won't answer the damn phone. It's almost midnight and she's not home and . . ." He trailed off as his imagination started to supply him with all sorts of nasty scenarios.

"Well, it's not surprising that she hasn't called. She's pissed off. She saw you in a liplock with another girl."

"I wasn't kissing her, damn it!" he snarled.

"No. *She* was kissing you . . . and that will count for something, once Abby isn't so angry, when she gets past the hurt, but for now? She's hurt. Okay? She needs to get past that. Once she does, it will be okay."

Zach drove the heel of his hand against his eye socket. "Okay. Shit. It will be okay. Zane, what in the hell does that mean?"

A few seconds ticked by and then Zane said, "It means it will be okay. Look, I'll call her. Hopefully she can at least let me know she's fine. You'll feel better and maybe you can get some sleep and figure out where to go from here."

"Yeah. Okay." He continued to stare down the street, hoping against hope. Waiting. And watching. The car still didn't appear and the street stayed dark and the night stayed quiet. "Will you tell her . . ."

"No." Zane's voice was flat and firm. "Whatever you have to say to her, it needs to come from you. Look, I don't know what's happening with the two of you, but I saw how she was looking at you at the party. There's something growing there and Abby isn't an idiot. Let her cool down and then you talk to her, okay?"

Chapter Nineteen

The bed was a brick.

A bouncy brick.

And the newly married couple in the room next to hers was putting *their* bouncy brick to good use. Despite the pillow over her head, she could still hear the squeals and the grunts.

Her phone started to ring. Nickelback's "Photograph." Zane. Okay, if there was anyone *other* than Zach that she'd just like to avoid talking to? Zane was it.

She groaned and hugged the pillow harder as she tried to block out any and all noise. A few seconds later, the phone stopped ringing. But the banging, the squealing, and groaning continued.

After another five minutes, it eased up and she huffed out a sigh, pulling off the pillow and dropping it down on the bed. She reached for her phone and glared at it. Zach was now getting his *brothers* to start pestering her?

She'd ignored the numerous texts while she thought everything through and now Zane was calling her?

The little green bubble popped up on her screen. From Zane.

"Calling me *and* texting me," she muttered. "Wonderful."

Z's worried. If you're too pissed to talk to him, that's fine. But spare us both the headache and just let me know you're okay.

She continued to glare at the message for another thirty seconds.

Before she decided whether to turn the phone off, another message came through.

He just wants to know you're okay, Abby. He's pacing out in front of your house and he'll stay there until he knows or the cops show up to drag him away. Come on. Please?

She groaned and tapped out a message. And it had *nothing* to do with the fact that she didn't like to think about him pacing in front of her house when she was a good two hours away. *I'm fine. Tell the jerk I'll come home when I'm done being pissed.*

Zane's response was almost immediate. *Will do. But he'll probably show up at your work in a day or two.*

She stuck her tongue out at the phone. Fat lot of good it would do. She'd cut back on her workload for the next few months because she'd expected to be busy planning for *her* wedding. *Yeah, well, he'll be wasting his time. I'm not needed in until Wednesday.*

Then, with a sigh, she flopped back on the bouncy brick bed and stared up at the ceiling. It was finally quiet. She could think. She'd been walking into Zach's office.

Keelie had been rising up on her toes. Zach had his hands on her wrists. Had he bent down? Her heart wrenched a little as she thought about somebody else having that mouth on theirs—

"Stop it."

No. Zach hadn't bent down. He'd just been standing there. Just standing.

And Keelie had been up on her toes.

So maybe Keelie had been the one kissing him. Bits and

pieces of the puzzle started to line up as she thought it
through. Keelie didn't like her. She didn't think Keelie had
ever really liked her. And she already knew that the other
woman had a thing for Zach.

And Zach . . . her throat knotted up as she thought back.
Zach, always there. Always watching her. The look on his
face when she told him she was getting married.

He'd watched her, so closely.

His voice had skipped a little when he asked her if she
was sure that was what she wanted.

Then it had been steady as the sun when he told her if
she was happy, then he'd be happy for her.

Zach . . . always there.

I'm thirty-two years old. I've been in love.

Absently, she reached up and brushed her fingers across
the brightly colored blossoms he'd painted across her skin.

Who was she, Zach?

*People come and go all the time. But there's only been
one woman who came and stayed and mattered . . . it's
you . . .*

You're not important . . . you're everything.

She'd asked him. Point-*blank*, she'd asked him who he'd
been in love with.

And he could have told her.

But maybe he *had* told her, she thought. *You're everything.*

Sighing, she rolled onto her belly and buried her face in
the pillow, trying to slow her racing thoughts.

Yeah.

She'd asked him. He could have said it, could have just
told her outright. *I love you.* But the question was this . . .
if she'd asked and he'd told her the truth, was she really
ready to hear the answer? *Really* ready?

Up until a few hours ago, she just wasn't sure.

And if the answer wasn't *her*?

She still didn't know if she could handle it.

"Maybe that's the answer you need to figure out then,"
she told herself quietly.

Yeah.

That was what she needed to do.

Her mind started to calm and she sighed a little as some of the tension started to ease from her body. Okay. Plan made. It wasn't written down, but she had a plan in mind and she always functioned better with a plan. Now, maybe she could sleep. After she got some sleep, she'd be able to figure out where to go from here.

She thought.

She hoped.

Her lids drooped down—

Squeak, squeak, squeak—

Swearing, she groaned and pulled the pillow back over her head.

The early morning shoot had been one of the best Zane had in a long while, but sadly, it hadn't been outside. It kind of sucked that he had to get up before dawn to do an indoor photo shoot, but he was trying to get a little more serious about this job. So when the better-paying ones came his way, he tried to take them.

Still, it would have been a great day to spend outside. Maybe up in the mountains. Out of everything he loved about Albuquerque, he loved the mountains the most.

He loved the desert. He loved Old Towne. He loved how the place was a mix of old and new. And he loved the fact that he was far enough away from the rest of his family that they didn't just show up at the drop of a hat, but close enough that he could get to them with a short flight pretty much whenever he wanted to see them. He wasn't quite as financially solvent as a couple of his famous brothers were, but he did okay.

But he loved the mountains the most.

With the sun burning high in the sky, he stared at the stark, jagged peaks of the Sandia Mountains and decided he needed to get up early again, and soon. Not because he was getting paid to lock himself in a room with his camera, either. Just head up into the mountains with his gear and see what he could see.

He had a new Nikon and he was still getting used to it. Nothing like a day spent up in the mountains to do that.

With a cup of coffee in hand and his gaze locked on those distant mountains, he told himself he wasn't going to think about the phone call last night. Or Keelie. Or any of it. He'd been telling himself that same lie ever since he rolled out of bed after one miserable, sleepless night. He'd actually had some success for a little while . . . the entire four hours he'd spent on the job. And once he was done, his brain promptly went right back down that road.

To Abby.

To Zach.

To Keelie.

What in the hell had she been thinking, kissing Zach? She *knew* how that guy felt about Abby and . . .

And it didn't matter what he'd said to Zach. Jealousy twisted through him and nothing he did or said was going to make that burn of envy go away. Something about Keelie had always gotten to him and it shouldn't have. She was eight years younger than he was, full of anger and mistrust and attitude. The very last thing he needed to do was think about anything involving her. Especially when it was pretty damn clear that he'd been on target about the suspicions he'd had regarding her feelings for Zach.

"This is a clusterfuck," he decided as he lifted his coffee to his lips. That was just about the only way to describe it. He wanted Keelie. She wanted Zach. Zach wanted Abby and he finally had a chance at making that happen, and then Keelie throws a wrench in the works . . . the one thing that wasn't entirely clear was just what Abby wanted, but Zane had seen how Abby looked at Zach. There was something there. What he needed to do was just keep clear of it. What Keelie should do was just steer clear of it, too.

Let Abby and Zach untangle it and work things out.

It wasn't a bad plan.

They could untangle it and he'd stand there and drink his coffee and study the mountains.

Except the doorbell rang. He ignored it. He wasn't expecting anybody for a shoot and if it was a delivery, they could leave it on the porch. He had a nice brood going so he'd just stay right where he was and—

It rang again. Again. Again. Like somebody was leaning on it.

"Son of a bitch." Slamming the coffee down on a table by the window, he pulled off his glasses and rubbed at his eyes as he stormed down the hallway. It was cluttered with his camera equipment, boxes that he kept meaning to tear down and other stuff he meant to deal with and never got around to.

What did it matter, anyway?

He was a bachelor at thirty-five and considering the fact that the one woman he'd found himself interested in recently had just tried to put the moves on his little brother, it didn't look like things were going to change anytime soon.

As the doorbell rang again, he shouted, "This better be damn fucking im . . ."

He jerked open the door and the words died as he saw Abby standing there.

She glared at him, her chin angled up like she was spoiling for a fight.

And knowing Abigale Applegate, she probably was.

"Ah . . . hey, Abby."

She drilled a finger into his chest. "Don't you *hey, Abby* me."

"Um." He blinked and rubbed a hand over his chest. Was she trying to poke a hole in him? "Okay. What would you rather me say? Get the hell out? Demand a toll? Or should I call Zach and tell him you got lost on the way to Grandma's house?"

"Ha, ha. And I wonder why you're a photographer. Maybe you should write instead of Trey." She folded her arms over her chest and glared at him. "I need to talk to you. Can I come in or not?"

He stepped aside and as she passed by, he scraped his nails over his jaw and tried to figure out just how in the hell he'd gotten pulled into Zach's mess. Because that's what was happening.

Hadn't he just decided it was better off for him to *not* be involved in this?

Hell.

The one text from Zane had come after midnight.

Abby is fine. She'll come home when she's not ready to spit nails. But she's okay.

That wasn't reassuring, but at least Zach knew she was okay.

He also knew—thanks to his mad skills of observation—that she wasn't home.

He prowled through the house, looking for some clue as to where she was, but said clue didn't seem to exist. She hadn't come home since last night. He knew *that* because he fiddled around with her alarm system and saw that it hadn't been disarmed since she'd left yesterday.

That wasn't exactly reassuring.

Where was she?

Why hadn't she come home?

Why wouldn't she talk to him?

Slumping on the bottom step of the staircase, he braced his elbows on his knees and glared at the door.

And another question . . . would she forgive him?

"This isn't helping."

Shoving away from the staircase, he headed for the door. Brooding and prowling around her house wasn't going to make the situation any better, either, so he needed to get the hell out.

The only thing, really, for him to do was head on in to work.

His lip curled at the very thought of it.

Seriously, facing Keelie was just going to put the cherry on top of a couple of lousy days.

* * *

Keelie knew she'd seen him looking more tired, but she wasn't sure when.

Her gut was already in a tangle but when he came inside and stopped when he saw her, all those tight little knots jerked even tighter and she thought she just might be sick.

A muscle jerked in his jaw as she stared at him but he didn't so much as acknowledge her. The ache that had taken up permanent residence in her heart expanded until she thought she just might choke on it.

What did I do? she thought miserably.

As he stalked past her, she thought about just retreating to her little hole and staying there. She could work, could just get lost in her work and then go home. Keep at it until things got better.

But then she realized she couldn't work hard enough to undo this ugly little knot of misery.

She'd hurt him. She'd hurt Abby and she felt bad about that, too. But she'd hurt Zach and he'd never been anything but wonderful to her. He'd given her a chance when nobody else would, he'd been kind to her when others treated her like shit, and he'd stood up for her when she didn't even know how to stand up for herself.

And then what did she do?

She fucked up.

Any of the rationalizations she might try to offer were empty, too. So what if maybe she might want to think she just wanted him to know. She had plenty of time to *tell* him. She didn't have to do it right after things finally started to work for him and Abby.

She'd done that because she was a selfish bitch and she needed to make it right.

How she was supposed to do that she didn't know, but the first step had to be apologizing.

With her heart beating a dull, heavy tattoo against her ribs, she shoved her hands into her pockets and headed down the hall. He'd come in late which was weird for him, but he probably wanted to avoid being around her. That kind of sucked, she realized. She'd messed up a friendship. How could she do that . . .

The door was shut.

She almost turned away. But she had to do this. Being a coward wasn't going to fix this.

She took a deep breath and opened the door.

"Get out," Zach said quietly from behind his desk.

He didn't even bother to lift his head.

"I just need to say this and I will," Keelie said quietly.

"I don't want to hear it." He flicked her a dark look. "Get out."

"*I* need to say it. If you can't accept it, that's fine and I don't blame you. But I'm sorry. It was a shitty thing to do, both to you and Abby and I'm sorry." A thousand excuses and rationalizations bubbled up in her throat, but she kept them locked up. It didn't *matter*, none of it. She'd hurt him, she'd hurt Abby, and she needed to make it all right. "When I see Abby, I'm going to apologize to her as well."

Without saying another word, she turned on her heel and walked away.

Zach watched her narrow back disappear around the corner and then he sighed, rubbing his temple.

The misery in her eyes might have made him feel a little bad, but he was running a bit thin on everything but worry and frustration and desperation. Maybe once he found Abby and got her to talk to him, he could find it in him to care about something else, but until then . . . ?

He just didn't know.

Of course, it would be *nice* if he could just get her to talk to him.

Snagging his phone, he tapped out another message to her. Probably the twentieth. Maybe the thirtieth. He had lost track. And though he was beyond desperate, he tried damn hard not to let that or the frustration show in his words.

Just wondering when you'll come home so you can kick my ass and we can talk.

Things weren't how they looked, Abs. I swear.

Come home . . . please.

He gripped the phone and waited.

Seconds ticked by and not a message arrived.

After about two minutes, he gave up and tossed it back down.

He needed to get to work.

His schedule had him down to get started on the layout for a sleeve somebody wanted done. They had brought him a design that looked like a knockoff of a design inked on a pretty popular wrestler-turned-actor and *that* garbage wasn't happening in his place.

He had a few ideas that hopefully would work, but if they didn't, the man would just have to get his ink done elsewhere.

Hopefully, it would work.

Zach needed the distraction.

Chapter Twenty

Abby stood in front of the window, wearing a shirt that Zane was almost positive his mom had bought for Zach.

Her red hair was pulled up into a ponytail and her eyes had shadows under them.

She looked beautiful and tired and pissed and sad.

As he dropped down on the couch, he snagged his camera and turned it on. He had the first picture snapped before she realized what he was doing. By the time she turned to face him, he'd snapped a second, and the third one had her flipping him off.

He grinned at her as he lowered the Nikon to his lap. "I should sell that last one to the tabloids."

"Oh, bite me."

"What's going on, Abby?"

She flicked him a look. "It's not like you don't have a clue. You've already talked to Zach. That's why you were bugging me at midnight last night, because he was hassling you."

"Hey . . . I was *bugging* you because I was a little worried myself," Zane pointed out. Putting the camera down, he came off the couch and moved to stand next to her. Catching her hair in his hand, he tugged on it gently and then slid an arm around her waist, hugging her. "Yeah, I talked to him, but he didn't exactly explain what was going on. I know you're pissed off at him, otherwise you wouldn't have driven six hours to glare at me. Now why don't you tell me why you're mad?"

She wiggled away from him and started to pace, her gaze locked on the floor. "I'm not mad . . ." Then she snorted. "Screw that. I *am* mad, but that's not exactly why I drove here. I could handle the mad part in Tucson."

"Okay . . ." He suspected he needed more coffee for this. Circling around, he waited until she made another circuit and then he caught her arm. "Maybe we should have this discussion in the kitchen."

She slid him a sidelong look. "I'm not hungry."

"Me, neither." Then he smiled. "But I want coffee. I'm not tracking this conversation and I'm hoping the caffeine will help."

She muttered, "I'm thinking alcohol might."

"Well, I've got that, too."

She settled herself down at the island, one foot hooked on the rung of her chair as he poured himself a cup of coffee. He needed to brew another pot the way he was going. But instead of worrying about that now, he turned around and stared at Abby from across the kitchen. "Okay. I'm getting caffeinated. Spill."

He took a sip and waited.

"Is Zach in love with me?"

He choked and sprayed coffee all over the floor. Slamming the cup down on the counter, he pounded a fist on his chest while his eyes watered. Strong coffee, windpipe, shock: bad mix. Once the burning stopped, he snagged a paper towel from the counter and wiped it across his face. "Abby . . . shit. Don't you think that's a question you should ask *him*?"

"Hmm. Let me rephrase . . . has he been in love with me for . . ." Her voice trailed off.

Lowering the towel, he looked at her through his lashes and tried to figure out how in the hell to answer that. He knelt down and wiped up the coffee he'd almost choked on while a hundred different delaying tactics rolled through his head.

"Abby, why aren't you talking to Zach about this?" he asked softly.

"I've tried."

He flicked a glance at her.

She was staring at nothing while one hand rubbed at something under her shirt. Over and over. "He . . ." She stopped and bit her lip, like she was thinking something through. After a second, she looked back at him. "I had this plan, you know."

"Abby, you always have plans." He crooked a grin at her and shrugged. "That's nothing new."

"This was." She reached into the bag she dumped on the counter and pulled out a ragged, rather tattered book. And then, before he could even stand up, she threw it at him. "Hey, look . . . I did another thing from the book!"

He barely caught it. "Watch it," he said, looking down at it for a second without really seeing it. The he stopped and looked at it again. He'd seen this in bookstores before. "*Wreck This Journal*?"

"Yeah." She shrugged. "Zach bought it. I'm . . . well, I'm not writing in it much. I think I'm doing too much journaling and worrying, not enough living. But I had a plan. It's on one of the early pages."

Cocking a brow, he waited.

"Go head." She squirmed a little on her seat and took up a rapt interest in the surface of his island.

Curious, he flipped it open, grinning a little as he saw the first set of instructions. "Must have killed you to crack the spine."

"Zach did that one," she said softly.

"Ahhh . . ." He kept flipping until he came to a page where he saw the handwriting. He had to assume it was hers. Too elegant and neat to be Zach's, that much was certain.

Wreck this life: My new plan

1. *Stop worrying so much about the future*

2. *Call Roger and tell him off*

3. *Flip off the next photographer you see*

4. *Get a tattoo*

5. *Have a torrid affair with a hot guy*

Something twisted inside him as he came to the last step. *A torrid affair* . . . Was that what she was doing with Zach? "Abby, if you're just using Zach, you need to stop. He—"

"Zane . . . be quiet," she said, and there was steel in her voice.

Closing the book, he tossed it onto the nearest countertop and then he hooked his thumbs in his pockets, staring at her until she slowly lifted his head. "Be quiet?" he echoed. "That's my brother, Abigale. My brother, and I love him. Okay? I love—"

"Stop it," she said, sliding off the stool and coming around the island to glare at him.

Abby wasn't a small woman. She was nearly five nine and almost all of her was leg, it seemed. But Zane was still a good four inches taller than her. She held her ground as he advanced on her. "Look, damn it, you're not being fair to him if all you're doing is trying to make yourself feel better after that fucker dumped you," he snapped.

"I asked you a question," she said, her voice low and hard.

"Fuck the damn question." Zane caught her arm and glared down at her. "I know Roger treated you like hell. I get that and I understand if you need to . . . hell. I don't know *what* you're trying to do, but whatever it is, it shouldn't involve hurting Zach."

Her eyes glinted with rage as she glared right back.

"Just when have you *ever* known me to intentionally hurt him?"

"Intentionally? Not once. But over the past seventeen years, you've done it a lot. If you're just fucking with him, you need to pull back and now," he said, feeling a little sick inside as he stared at her. Damn it, this was going to kill Zach. It was just going to kill—

"Seventeen years." She shook her head.

"What?"

"Is that how long?"

He pinched the bridge of his nose and then turned away. "Abby, I think you should just leave, okay? I need to get some stuff done." *Call Zach. Call . . . hell. Maybe call Mom. I don't know.* "And I can't do it with you here. So can you—"

"Answer me!" she shouted.

His temper snapped and he spun around, glaring at the woman he'd known most of his life. "Answer you?" he asked. "You want me to fucking answer you?"

"That's why I'm here. I just want a straight answer." She jerked her chin up at him, attitude and disdain written all over her face. "How long, huh? Just how long has he been in love with me?"

"Forever!"

The word hung between them for an endless moment before he turned away. Slamming his hands down on the counter, he stared at the glass-plated cabinet in front of him, wishing he could yank those words back. "Shit. *Shit.* Damn it, Abby, this is something you need to be talking about with him. Not me."

Silence greeted him.

Looking back over his shoulder, he saw her leaning against the counter, a lost look on her face as she stared off at nothing.

"Abby," he tried again. "You need to go home. You need to talk to Zach."

She flicked him a glance. The expression in her eyes was so raw it was hard to even *look* at her. "I tried."

"You tried to talk about this with him?"

A soft sigh escaped her and he watched as her reflection turned and moved away.

Slowly, he eased around, watching as she moved back to the island and settled back on the stool. "Yeah." She hooked her hands over her neck, staring at nothing. "I did the tattoo thing first . . . we were talking. I said something about Roger . . . I dunno, but something like how could he do that to me if he'd really loved me. And Zach's response? He said that Roger never did love me. So simple. So easy. So . . . so *Zach.*" She paused and took a breath. "Anyway, a few minutes later, I asked him if he'd ever been in love. He said he had. But it hadn't worked, the woman hadn't ever noticed."

Now she lifted her head and stared at Zane. "It was me, wasn't it?"

"It's always been you for Zach." Blowing out a breath, he stared up at the ceiling. "He is going to pound on me if he knows I'm discussing this."

"Then maybe he should have answered me when I tried to talk to him about it the other day. I asked him again . . . and he just talked around it."

"He thinks you're going to run scared," Zane said gently. "You live your life by plans—you've done that ever since you were a kid. Your crazy mom, everything she put you through. Zach . . . well, he never fit into your plans. He doesn't want to scare you, especially not when he's finally got you to see that he *can* fit into your life . . . like this."

Her eyes swung to his.

"Can he?"

Abby closed her eyes and rested her head in her hands. "I never saw any of this coming, Zane. But I can't go a day without thinking about him anymore. Not an hour. Seems like it's a struggle to even go a minute."

"Is that a yes?"

Abby lifted her head. And although she didn't say a word, he saw the answer in her eyes.

*   *   *

Zane looked like he was going to puke as he finished setting up his equipment. "You realize he's going to kill me, right?"

"Oh, shut up." Abigale was nervous enough herself. She was also freezing. Which didn't make sense, because the lights in his studio were *hot*. Of course, she was only wearing the green silk shirt. That would explain why she was freezing. That, and nerves.

"We can do this another day," Zane said, his voice abrupt, edgy with his own rush of nerves.

"No. We're doing it now." She shot him a dark look. "If you can't handle it, I can hit the road and see if I can find another photographer back home."

He gave her a pained look. "And like *that* is going to make it any better. At least Zach knows I'm not going to be staring at you and thinking . . ." He went red and focused on the backdrop he'd planned to use. "Can you explain why it has to be *today*?"

"You'll see." The blossoms Zach had painted across her skin were already fading. If she waited more than a day or two, they wouldn't show as well for photographs and she needed to give him . . . something. Something that showed him what she felt. And nobody could catch a moment on camera the way Zane did.

Trying to distract herself, she stood in front of the counter where he'd spread out some of the photographs he'd taken. Most of them looked like they'd come from the barbecue, she realized. She saw herself, bent over the stove. Something about the way he'd caught her on film made her think of a time gone by. Of course, the old-fashioned sort of dress really added to that, as did the apron she'd put on.

There was another one of the twins playing with little Clayton, then one of just the twins. Travis had his arm slung around Trey's neck and if Abigale knew them, they'd been talking about Trey's wife. Her death had left such a hole in the family.

There was one of Sebastian, alone, staring up at the sky. Lost in the stars, the way he often seemed to be.

A close-up of Zach. She touched his face, stroked a finger down the line of his jaw. "I like this one," she murmured.

"Take it."

Glancing up, she saw Zane moving closer.

Pulling it from the pile, she smiled a little. "Sure you don't mind?" Slyly, she added, "You could always sell it to the tabloids."

He laughed a little. "Nah. If I'm going to sell a picture of my famous brother to the tabloids, I'll go for the one with more skin showing." He plucked another from the stack and said, "But Zach would kill me. And you know I wouldn't do that. Here . . . you might like that one, too."

It was another one of Zach, his upper torso and face, although he'd been staring at something off to the side.

It had been right after they'd finished playing a game of baseball and Zach had taken his shirt off.

She stroked her finger down the tattoo over his heart. She went to put them both down. But for some reason, something caught her eye just then. Maybe it was the lights . . . maybe it was the way Zane had framed the shot. Maybe she had just really *looked* for the first time.

She'd noticed the lines and whorls around the dagger before. Really, she had. But she'd never really *looked*. Seriously, how easily could she *stare* at Zach's chest? More often than not, he'd been wearing a shirt . . . at least up until lately. As much as she loved his tattoos, it wasn't like she could just blatantly stare.

But she was blatantly staring now.

And the lines and whirls around that blade settled into place, forming a very distinct image.

An *A*.

It was stylized, decorated, and worked to be part of the tattoo so it didn't jump out and *scream* anything. But there it was. The letter *A*.

"Zane . . ."

She swallowed as she stroked the tip of her finger over that letter and then looked up at him.

He was watching her calmly. "It's been there all the time, Abby. You just never saw it."

Sucking in a ragged breath, she turned away.

Tears clogged her throat, but she couldn't start to cry. Not right now.

A hand touched her shoulder. "Are you okay?"

"I'm fine," she said quietly. "Come on. Let's get this done. I need to go have a talk with this man of mine."

Chapter Twenty-one

The absolute last thing Abigale thought she could handle was that voice.

She didn't know how her mother had tracked her cell phone number down this time. She didn't know, and honestly, she didn't care. All she knew was that the name glaring at her from the display was one she knew too well.

Blanche Levine.

Her mother. Working on her fourth marriage now.

And still trying to drag Abigale back into her life.

Sighing, she took the call because it was either that or . . . run.

He's afraid you'll run.

Zach was right about one thing. She ran away from things, too often. Too easily. It had to stop. With everything. Including this.

Just before the call would have ended, she hit the button and pushed it so that it rolled over to speaker. "Hello, Mother," she said, keeping her gaze focused on the road in front of her. She still had a few hours before she'd reach her destination. Spending any of that time on the phone with

Blanche wasn't ideal, but getting it over with now was better than delaying it, she guessed.

There was a very brief pause but Abigale realized she'd surprised the other woman. "Abigale. Darling . . ."

"Stop it with the *darling*, mother. I'm not your *darling* anything. What do you want?"

"Can't I call just to speak with you? I miss you, you know. It's been such a long time since we've seen each other."

Not long enough. But instead of saying that, Abigale just shot the phone a glare before focusing back on the road. "It has been a while, hasn't it? Let me think . . . twelve years, if I remember right. That's when the judge ruled against you in court."

"Yes, well. Water under the bridge, of course. Listen, I was hoping that you and I could—"

"No." Abigale gripped the steering wheel.

"Darling, I haven't even managed to say the words yet . . ." Blanche laughed and the sound was just as grating, just as fake and empty as it had been back when she'd been a child.

"It doesn't matter. Unless you're calling to apologize for breaking my father's heart, for destroying him . . . unless you're calling to apologize for the misery that you made of my life, unless you're calling to tell me that you're sorry for the disaster that was my childhood, you and I *can't* do anything." She swallowed the scream trying to rise up inside her.

Her mother heaved out a terrible, put-upon sigh. "Abigale, I know your father's suicide was hard on you. It was hard on me, too, but—"

"Hard." She laughed. "Yeah. It was hard. I mean, it wasn't exactly *fun* for me, either, when the two of us walked in on you and that little swinging party you had going on. But I've dealt with that, because *you* don't matter to me that much anymore. My father did. And you destroyed him. You humiliated him and he left me."

"He killed himself," Blanche said, her voice flat and empty. "*I* didn't force that on him."

"No. You didn't. That was completely on him and maybe one day, I'll stop being angry at him. But I'm done with you. I'm not angry at you, but you're not welcome in my life, either. Now . . . please stop calling me."

She disconnected the phone in the middle of whatever her mother was saying. Whatever it was, it didn't matter. Abigale braced herself, waited for the pain she knew would follow. But it wasn't there.

She just felt . . . numb.

Her mother, at some point in the past few years, had ceased to matter.

Another ring belted through the air and she flinched.

"Rebel Yell."

Damn it.

Zach.

She *still* wasn't ready to talk to him yet.

She had a date, anyway.

One more thing to do before she went and confronted him.

She hit the button to ignore the call and punched in Marin's number. As Marin came on the line, she asked, "Are you going to be able to make it or not?"

"Oh, hey, Abby! So nice to talk to you, too . . . yes, the flight was wonderful, and my goodness, it's hot here in Arizona. No, I don't mind a bit—"

"Ha, ha," Abigale said, cutting into Marin's chatter. "Hi, Marin. How are you, how was the flight, and of course it's hot. It's *always* hot around here. Are you going to make it?"

"I already said I'm here. So . . . have you figured out what you're doing?"

Abigale rubbed the heel of her hand over her heart. "Yeah. I've got an idea. We just need to know where to go."

"Leave that to me."

Pinching the bridge of his nose, Zach listened as Marin droned on. After about another sixty seconds, he'd had about all he could take.

"Marin . . . this isn't helping. What I *need* is to know where in the hell she is."

Two days, damn it. He hadn't seen or heard from Abby in two days.

It was killing him.

"I don't know what to tell you, Zach," Marin said, sighing. "Look, just give her some time. She'll calm down."

"Time." He closed his eyes but two seconds later, he forced his heavy lids back open and stared outside over the twinkling lights of the city. "Give her time, you say. I've given her plenty of time, Marin. I waited seventeen years. I was patient. I hoped. I waited. And then she sees *one* bad thing and she takes off. Now she won't talk to me. How much more time am I supposed to give her?"

"She just walked in while you were kissing another woman," Marin pointed out.

"*I* wasn't kissing anybody!" he snapped. "Keelie kissed me and I stopped her the second I figured out what in the hell she was doing. *I* didn't plan it and I sure as hell wasn't on board with it."

"Zach . . . I'm sorry and I get that. But you need to see it from her side. How would *you* feel if *you* walked in and some guy had his lips all over *her*?"

He snorted. "I've walked in and seen that a hundred times." And he knew how he'd feel. It hurt. Like acid in a wound.

"But you never had a right to call her yours before now. It's different. It's a different matter entirely. She just needs to some time to cool down."

"If she'd give me five damn seconds, I could tell her there's nothing to cool down about," he grumbled. Spinning away from the window, he started to pace. "And damn it, I need to know she's okay. She's not coming home. She's not been to work. It's like she disappeared."

"You realize she's a big girl, right?"

Groaning, he dropped down on the coach. "So that means I can't worry? Is that what you're saying? I'm not allowed to worry?"

"Worry all you want. But I can tell you that she's fine. Okay?"

His gut tugged at him. Lowering the phone, he glared at it and then lifted it back to his ear. "Worry all I want . . . damn it, Marin. Is she in LA? Put her on the phone, damn it."

"She's not in LA." Marin laughed and the sound was easy, light . . . and completely full of bullshit. He *knew* it. "Zach, sweetheart, you need to calm down a little. Chill out. Hell, go hook up with one of your brothers and have a drink or something."

"None of my brothers *live* here," he snapped. "Put her on the phone and don't lie to me. She's in LA with you, I know you too well."

"She's not in LA with me, Zach." Marin stared across the room, eyeing Abigale narrowly as a thin Asian man with his hair dyed blond and done up in spikes bent over Abigale's bared chest. She was tempted to take a picture and send it to Zach. But that would be a bad idea. It would piss him off and he'd figure out that Abigale *was* with her. No, she hadn't lied. They weren't in LA. They were in Phoenix.

Marin felt more than a little guilty when she'd talked Abigale into meeting her. Not so she could tell her friend that . . . *yeah . . . I knew*. But . . . hell. Abigale said she had to figure out how to deal with this, and she had a plan, but she needed to make it better.

So . . . voilà.

They met at the airport and Marin had left her assistant scrambling to cover a few things. It wasn't anything major and it wasn't like she couldn't take a few days off. And even if it was major, even if she had to walk out on something very major, her friend needed her.

She wanted to go a little closer and look at the tattoo, but she knew Zach would pick up on the familiar sounds so she kept her distance. "Look, sweetie, she'll be home when she's home. If she's out blowing off steam . . . ? Then maybe it's because she needs to."

"Blowing off steam?" Zach muttered. "You realize this

is *Abby* we're talking about. Her idea of blowing off steam is to lock herself in her kitchen and cook up a couple dozen ancho-chocolate-chili cupcakes."

"Hmmm. Maybe she felt a change of pace was in order and she decided to lock herself in a tattoo parlor and get a tattoo of your name on her ass or something," Marin said, smirking a little as Abigale flipped her head around and glared at her.

Shut up! Abigale mouthed.

Marin smiled angelically.

"Marin . . . tell Abby to get her cute ass on the phone, or I'm going to call the damned paparazzi out on your butt," Zach growled.

"Oh, man. You're *really* pissed off." She lowered the phone and glanced at it, thinking back over the past few hours. She hadn't tweeted or posted anything to Facebook so there weren't any of those stupid geotags and she'd never done that stupid Foursquare shit. And her assistant didn't know *exactly* where she was. "Zach, one second, okay?" She muted the phone and looked up. "How much longer until we're done?"

"Forty minutes."

"If it's possible to hurry it up without *messing* it up? Please do it." Marin smiled at him and watched as a dull red flush crept up his neck. Hopefully it wouldn't be necessary. But no point in taking chances. After she unmuted the phone, she lifted it back up to her ear. "Okay, sorry about that, Zach. Personal thing. Where were we?"

"We were at the point where you get Abby on the *fucking* phone!" he snarled.

"Oh." She pursed her lips and studied her manicure. "I don't remember that scene. I'll tell you what. I'll call her again and let her know you're still looking for her. Zach . . . stop worrying so much. That's her specialty, right? That and ancho-chocolate-chili cupcakes . . ."

She disconnected before he could say another word. Blowing out a breath, she put the phone away. Lifting her gaze, she focused on Abigale's face. "Honey . . . I don't know whether to pity you or be envious. That man is all but desperate to find you."

Abigale closed her eyes.

"What are you going to do when you see him?"

"I'll think about that then."

Marin lifted a brow. "Maybe you should start thinking about it *now*," she suggested. "Before he actually tracks you down."

Abigale popped one eye open and focused on Marin's face. "What?"

"He's threatening to unleash paparazzi hell on my ass, sweetheart. He's determined to find you and he'll do it if you wait too long." She tugged the phone out of her pocket as it started to ring again. It was her assistant Leo. She'd told him not to call unless it was urgent. "And he's probably already on the move."

It was mostly an empty threat.

Mostly.

Because Zach knew one thing, almost as well as he knew his own name. Marin was with Abby.

Marin didn't give a damn if he set the beasts from Hollywood hell loose on her ass. But Abby would. So it was a *mostly* empty threat. He'd hold it in reserve in case he didn't track her down soon, but damn it, he was getting desperate—

The doorbell rang.

Hope was a funny thing.

It could burn inside him and turn everything inside him into electricity and even though he knew, he *knew*, that Abby was with Marin, he all but ran for the door.

He was less than a foot away when something was shoved under it.

The renovated loft where he lived was old. It was a wonderful place and he loved it, but it was old. Big open areas, huge windows . . . old doors. And whoever had just shoved that envelope under his door had absolutely no problem doing it.

He stared at the envelope for a split second and then lunged for the door.

The grate was already going down on the old freight elevator and he didn't make it in time to stop it.

Swearing, he debated between chasing it down or going back to his place. He opted to go back, because he'd glimpsed something. It had been a guy. All he'd seen were the shoulders, but it sure as hell hadn't been Abby.

Okay.

In the end, that was what mattered.

Back in the main room of his loft, he knelt down and scooped up the flat white envelope. It was the kind that Zane would send pictures in.

Zane . . . Narrowing his eyes, he jogged over to the window and stared down at the parking lot. He didn't see his brother's car. All he saw was somebody moving damn fast down the sidewalk, head bent, shoulders hunched, and a baseball cap tugged over his hair. And he was already too far away for Zach to get a good look at the guy.

Running his tongue over his teeth, he tore the mailer open.

And then he damn near choked.

Abby . . .

Minutes ticked away as he stared at the pictures.

It was Abby. Ten portraits in all. Some in color, others in black and white. Some were close-ups, some were full-body shots. Some of them had that soft focus thing going on while others were so clear and sharp, he almost believed he could reach out and touch her.

Stroke the soft shoulder bared by the green silk shirt she wore. A shirt that looked pretty damn familiar.

That was the first picture.

The second was her profile as she stared at the camera.

In the third one, she was looking away. She looked . . . ethereal. The black-and-white image had a soft, almost blurred look to it and she looked like something just not of this world.

The fourth one showed her fingers working down the buttons . . . another black and white, with the shadow and light playing across her skin. It almost made his heart stop, just from how beautiful and raw the image was.

And then blood started to pulse in his head as he realized something.

Zane had taken these.

He knew his brother's work. Nobody could take a picture quite the way Zane could.

His hands were shaking as he turned to the next one. Her left breast was bared, revealing the lotus blossom he'd painted on her skin. Abby was staring at the camera through her hair and there was a faint blush on her cheeks . . . and the glint in her eyes almost laid him low.

Abby . . .

That look.

Swearing, he laid them down for a minute and stormed over to the bar. He needed a drink. Needed to think—

He made it two feet before he was back over there, staring at the picture again. He had to find her. Had to see her. The sadness in her eyes. The pain . . . and unless he was mistaken, there was something else.

His hands were shaking as he flipped to the next one. She wasn't looking at the camera this time. Her shirt was open completely, but hanging so that all he could see was a bare strip of flesh.

In the seventh, she had let the shirt fall back to catch in the crook of her elbows. The shot was beautiful. It was erotic. And he was pretty damned certain this was as aroused as he'd ever been without actually having her *there*, with him. But if he didn't find her soon, he thought he might start to just whimper like a baby.

The eighth one had her head hanging low with the shirt dangling from her fingers, while her other hand covered her face and she was half hidden from the camera. Another black-and-white.

The ninth one was another close-up, but of her back, with her looking over her shoulder, all those wild, crazy curls spilling down her back.

He had a feeling the tenth one might just make him either die from a heart attack or come in his jeans like a teenaged boy. He didn't know. Passing a hand over his face, he sucked in a breath and tried to reach for some modicum of control. It didn't seem to want to come and he didn't know if he could keep it together.

And it didn't matter.

He had to see that picture.

Then he was going to get Zane on the damned phone and rip his head off, even if he had to reach through the phone lines to do it.

That decision made, he flipped to the photo, eyes closed. Once he thought had himself ready, he opened his eyes . . .

And just stared.

It wasn't the erotically beautiful image he had been expecting.

Zane had a way of capturing emotions with his camera. It was his gift. Something he'd been able to do even from the time he'd been a kid.

And the image he'd captured on film was the image of a woman in love.

She was sitting down, still wearing the shirt, with one knee drawn up. The look on her face was . . . her eyes stared into the camera lens, and although Zach *knew* she wasn't looking at him, he felt like she was. He felt like she was finally seeing him clear down to his soul.

And she was just fine with what she saw. Fine with it, hell. She wanted it. Needed it.

He blinked hard and then looked back at the picture again, trying to make sure he wasn't seeing something that wasn't there.

But it was.

He was almost certain he was seeing the same damn thing in her eyes that he felt every damn time he looked at her. Every damn time he thought of her.

Swallowing the knot in his throat, he gathered up the pictures and then laid them carefully on the coffee table. When he pulled out his phone to call Zach, he tried to figure out what to say, how to convince him to talk. The words weren't coming, though.

Damn it.

He'd just have to fly blind on this.

The phone didn't even make it through one ring before Zane answered.

"Don't kill me, Zach," Zane said. "She wanted the damn pictures and it wasn't like I could let somebody else do what she was wanting."

Zach pressed the heel of his hand against his eye. He could handle, barely, the thought of Zane seeing Abby naked. She was like a little sister to him and Zach knew that. He could handle it . . . *barely*. As long as he didn't think about it. "Just tell me where in the hell she is," he said quietly. "I need to talk to her."

Zane was quiet a minute. "You're not calling me to rip my head off?"

"No. But I'd rather not think about it. The photo fairy took those as far as I'm concerned. A female photo fairy."

"Okay. She's a talented fairy, though, right?"

"Very. They are amazing. Now where in the hell is Abby?"

Zane blew out a breath. "I don't know. But before you rip my head off, she had a message. She left here yesterday and I haven't seen her since, but I did talk to her. She said she'd find you today. So . . . make yourself findable."

As Marin cut through the Phoenix traffic, Abigale pulled out the battered journal and flipped through it. She needed to do more of the stuff in it, she decided. *Hang it in a public place* . . . she smiled a little and decided she'd find a way to string it up at Steel Ink and have people draw in it there.

She flipped to another page and almost winced at what she saw there.

Spill coffee . . .

Eyeing the cold coffee in the console, she caught her lip between her teeth and reached for it.

"What are you—*Abigale*!"

She snatched up a napkin from their fast-food lunch and dabbed at the coffee trickling down the pages. "I'm following instructions," she said softly.

"You've lost your mind!" Marin shot her a look. "You just spilled coffee on a book."

"The book told me to," Abigale said soberly. Then she flipped it around and displayed the messy result. "Look."

Marin kept her gaze locked on the highway. "That book has got to be the craziest thing on God's green earth. What in the world are you doing with it?"

"It's the journal Zach gave me," she said softly. "I made myself a new plan with it, you know. *Stop worrying so much . . . flip off photographers . . .*"

"And have a torrid affair." Marin pursed her lips. "All of this happened because of the damn book."

"All of this happened because it's supposed to." Abigale gingerly turned the pages, studying more of the instructions. She still needed to mail it to herself, and all sorts of crazy shit. She'd been so focused on the plan, and then on Zach, that she hadn't been paying as much attention to the rest of it. "It happened because Zach's been the one all along. And I never saw it."

"You just weren't ready to, sweetheart. And he never let you see it on his end." Marin reached over and caught her hand, squeezed gently. "It's happening now. Take it and grab it and don't let go."

A fist seized her heart and Abigale closed her eyes. "I don't plan on it. I just . . . hell. What if I'm reading this wrong? What if you all are off base?"

"We're not." Marin chuckled. "Trust me. We're not."

Abigale blew out a breath. "Man, I hope not." She plucked her shirt from her chest and eyed the new tattoo on her chest. It was covered by the dressing, angry and red and not at all the sexy little surprise she'd hoped to present him with, but he'd get the sentiment, she knew.

"He has an *A* on his chest," she whispered.

"I know." Marin glanced over her. "We've only had a hundred get-togethers a year, Abby. I see him without his shirt all the time. I asked him once what he was going to say when you finally noticed."

Abigale arched a brow, waited.

"He told me that you never did notice all that much about him, so it wasn't an issue."

Abigale winced. "That's not . . . completely true." She'd noticed plenty about Zach. When she let herself look. She just hadn't always let herself look. And now she couldn't *not* look. "Marin, this is insane."

"No. It's completely sane, and it's completely right. What's insane is that it took you this long to notice. Any idea what you're going to say to him?"

Abigale focused on the clock. "No. And the way traffic is going, I've got a while to figure it out."

Time enough. Too long. Not long enough. Closing her eyes, she started to try to puzzle her way through everything that had to be said between them.

Chapter Twenty-two

Make yourself findable.

That was what Zane had said.

Zach had spent half the day at home, but Abby hadn't shown up.

It was Tuesday. Tuesdays were a workday.

So maybe he should do the smart thing and get his ass to the office.

Of course, the *last* thing he wanted to do was *work*.

Still, he stomped through the back door of Steel Ink, up to the front, and watched as the employees scattered. All but Javi. Javi looked at him with a sidelong glance. "You look pissed."

Zach didn't respond to that. There wasn't any point. "Has Abby called?"

"Nope." He shrugged and said, "But if she does, I'll make sure you get the call, boss. Promise."

Zach grunted. As he turned around, he saw Keelie standing in the doorway to the hall. She held his gaze and he wanted to just push around her, but she had her tall, skinny frame planted there and unless he physically moved her, she wasn't going to budge. He could tell that from the look in her eyes.

"What?" he bit off.

"Have you been able to talk to her?"

Baring his teeth at her in a mockery of a smile, he replied, "No. She's avoided my calls and me ever since Sunday. Happy?"

"No." Keelie looked away and took a deep breath. "I've tried to call her a few times, but she's not answering the phone. Is she okay? Has anybody talked to her?"

He debated on whether or not he should just avoid answering that to make her feel bad. Part of him wanted to make her feel bad, part of him figured she deserved it. But the bigger part of him felt guilty for thinking that way. He didn't need to feel *more* guilty on top of everything else. When he could *think* without being pissed, worried, scared, he figured maybe Keelie hadn't really meant any harm and maybe they could get past this. Maybe.

"Oh, she's talking to *people*," he said, shoving his hands in his pockets and staring at her lowered head. "She's just not talking to *me*. She's talking to Marin. She's talking to Zane. But she won't talk to *me*."

"Zane . . ." Her lashes flickered.

Okay. Now he was ready to get mad at her again, all because of that look in her eyes. He didn't want his brother feeling gutted the way he did. "Yeah. Zane. Do me a favor, Keelie. Leave him alone."

"Leave him alone?" Something flashed in her gaze.

"He's got a thing for you." Zach crossed his arms over his chest. "Now he's hurting. He'll get over it, but since you don't give a fuck about him, don't keep acting like there might be something there when there's not."

Keelie opened her mouth, then closed it, shaking her head like she wasn't following the conversation. "What . . . you . . . damn it, Zach, I don't know what in the hell you're getting at here, but Zane and I are friends. I'm allowed to be *friends* with him."

"Yeah." He shook his head. "Friends. That's why he

sounded like I'd sucker punched him when I told him what happened. He's interested in you. You don't feel the same and that's fine. Look . . ." He blew out a breath and said, "I'm not ready to talk to you yet, but I might be. Later. Just don't mess around with my brother, okay?"

She gaped at him and, unwilling to stand there any longer, he nudged her aside and headed to his office. He couldn't remember if he had any appointments scheduled that day or not. He didn't want to *be* there. He needed to be out looking for Abby, but Zane had said she'd find him.

So he had to be *findable*.

The only place he ever was on Tuesdays was at his shop.

So he'd stay at his shop.

Until it was time to go. Shit. *Then* what did he do? Go home? Go to her place?

Swearing, he pushed through the door and slammed it shut. He headed for the desk but he hadn't been there any more than a minute before he found himself remembering that day. Forty-eight fucking hours ago. How could life go straight to hell in forty-eight hours?

Groaning, he closed his hands around his skull and tried to shove those thoughts out of his head. Tried and failed. Rubbing the heel of his hand over his chest, he bent over his desk and decided he'd deal with work. Work would keep him occupied for a little.

"His car is here."

Swiping her hands down the sides of the slim-fitting skirt of her dress, Abigale nodded.

"You need to breathe a little before you puke, honey." Marin poked her in the shoulder. "You look almost as rough as you used to before a press conference with she-who-shall-not-be-named."

"Blanche." She slid Marin a glance and said, "It's Blanche. I mean . . . I know you all know it and I know we were kids when we started that name, but it's past time we stopped. She's not the boogeyman." She grimaced and said,

"She's not Voldemort. She's just a shallow, selfish woman who never cared about anybody but herself. She called earlier, you know."

Marin laid a hand on her arm. Abigale smiled over at her. "It's fine. That . . . well. It needed to be done. Ages ago. I told her not to call again. I don't know if she'll listen, but it's done."

"And when she calls back?" Marin asked doubtfully.

"Then I decide then. But I'm done ignoring or hiding from her." She blew out a breath and stared at the shop.

Marin squeezed her hand. "Are you going to go in the back?"

She nodded.

And just sat there.

"Well." Marin drew the word out slowly, studying the back of the building with pensive eyes. "I could be wrong here, but I *think* the best approach would be actually getting out of the car."

"I'm scared."

Marin reached over and caught her hand. "I can tell." Then she turned her head and pinned Abigale with a level stare. "But this is the absolute last thing you need to be scared of. I know you don't know what's waiting for you inside there, honey, but I do. It's somebody who's loved you for your entire life . . . now go get him."

Bills paid.

That ate up an hour.

Supplies ordered.

That ate up another hour.

He sketched out a couple of designs for a client who lived over at the army base. That took up forty-two minutes. The client was still debating out in the shop. Zach wished he'd make up his mind, because if he wanted the work, doing the tattoo would take up the next couple of hours and then he could go home.

But now, with his mind empty and his hands free, he

found himself bent over his sketchbook and the image taking place wasn't anything he could ever put on anybody.

It was Abby.

The way she'd been in that last portrait. Her gaze locked on him, eyes dark and full of love. Need. Like she was staring into the very soul of him.

The curve of her lip. The line of her jaw.

Her hair, the way it glinted in the light . . . even though it was just a pencil sketch, he could see the dark, rich auburn and his hands itched to feel the softness of it again.

The door opened and he kept his gaze on the portrait. "Did the guy decide on which design he wanted?"

"I don't know. I didn't ask."

Dropping the pencil, he lifted his head.

Abby stood in the door, her head cocked to the side, arms folded over her chest. It was a dangerous pose, because in that dress, her breasts looked like . . . whoa. Yeah. He thought that summed it up pretty much.

As a matter of fact, the entire package was just *whoa*. She was wearing one of those pinup girl–styled dresses again: a formfitting black sheath that fit her form oh so nicely, all the way down to her knees. Against the black, her skin glowed like ivory and he was about ready to fall down and worship her.

She had on a pair of red heels . . . fuck. Red heels. Had he ever seen her in a pair of red heels?

He didn't know, but now it was his life's ambition to see her in *just* those heels . . . and nothing else. Assuming she wasn't going to kick his ass to the curb. If she tried, his life's ambition was going to be getting her to forgive him. It didn't matter that he hadn't wanted Keelie to kiss him. It had happened and . . .

Focus, Zach. He dragged a hand over his face and swallowed the knot in his throat. "Abby."

And his voice cracked.

This was going to go just *fantastic*. Clearing his throat, he pushed back from the desk, although he thought it might be wise to keep his distance for a minute, especially judging by the glint in her eyes.

"Ah . . . I've been trying to call," he said softly, eyeing her nervously as she came inside. He dodged a look at her hands. No sharp objects. No wooden bats. That was good . . . right? Very few people understood just how hot her temper burned. Zach was one of them and he respected that temper of hers.

Abby lifted a brow. "Yes," she murmured. "About fifty times. I noticed." A smirk curved her lips and he swallowed back a groan as he realized she wasn't just wearing a pair of red *fuck me* shoes. She'd slicked that pretty mouth of hers down with the same shade of red.

Abby rarely wore makeup anymore, but she'd gone all out tonight, it seemed. He wasn't quite certain he understood the reasoning. Jamming his hands into his pockets, he stared at her for a minute, trying to read the look on her face but he couldn't.

The glint in her eyes had him confused.

She looked pissed. Very pissed. But then he thought about the pictures . . . shit, if it wasn't for the fact that he'd just painted that tattoo on her, he'd almost think she'd done those *before* the mess with Keelie.

But that wasn't the case. He knew it.

"Saturday night wasn't what it looked like," he said, forcing the words out in a rush. "Keelie was the one behind that and I was pulling away even as she did it. I know it didn't look like that but I don't have any feelings for Keelie. I—"

He stopped, clamping those words shut behind his teeth just in time. Abby arched a brow, that smirking little smile on her lips. She turned away and sauntered over to the door and despite his best intentions, his gaze zoomed down to lock on her ass. That dress . . . damn it, it ought to be illegal when the woman had a body like Abby's.

The door clicked shut and he jerked his head up just in time to see her lock it.

"You what?" Abby said quietly, turning around to face him.

He stared at her.

She leaned back against the door and waited.

"I just wanted you to know that it wasn't what it looked like. I swear."

"Oh . . . I believe you." She waited a beat and then pushed off the door, swaying her way across the floor to him. Each click of her heels seemed to make his heart race even harder and he was almost certain the damn thing was going to leap right out of his chest by the time she reached him. She laid a hand against his chest and murmured, "I believe you . . . about Keelie. But Zach, there's something you're not being honest about and I think it's time we just get this out in the open."

A storm fired in his eyes.

Abigale watched it play out as her heart raced and her hands went all damp and sweaty again. Fear and terror, frustration and desire, they all tangled inside her and beneath it all was a love that all but stole her breath away.

All this time, Zach had been right here.

And part of her realized she'd *known*. Some part of her had *known*. But she hadn't wanted to look at that because it scared her. If it fell apart, if it didn't last, so many *ifs* . . . if she lost Zach . . .

He was her everything and losing him would rip the soul out of her.

But she couldn't hide from this anymore. She couldn't, and she didn't want to.

As he continued to stare at her, she fisted her hand in his shirt, thought about the tattoo she'd seen so many times before, but had never really *noticed*. Thought about the tattoo she had on her chest—the one that still itched and hurt, healing already under the dressing she wore.

"Anything to say, Zach?" she whispered, looking up into his eyes.

His lashes flickered and for a second, she thought he was going to make this easy, but all he did was reach up and cup her cheek. "I'm not really sure what you're talking about, Abby." He stroked his thumb over her lower lip.

She sighed, swaying closer so she could rest her head against his chest.

Okay, then.

It's somebody who's loved you your entire life . . .

Breathing in the sexy, warm scent that was Zach, she steadied herself again. She had to go through with this, because she had to know. That was all there was to it. Mentally squaring her shoulders, she lifted her head and stared up at him.

He wasn't wearing a t-shirt for once. It was a black button-down, the tails hanging out, the sleeves rolled up. Holding his gaze, she reached for the buttons and watched his eyes as she slid the first button free.

The blue of his eyes darkened to near black and his chest rose on a harsh, unsteady breath as she moved onto the second button. "Abby . . ."

"Did you get anything from Zane today?" she asked softly.

His lids drooped and the look on his face was almost as seductive as a kiss, as intimate as if he'd stripped her bare. "Yes." He reached up and pushed a hand into her hair, but when he tried to tug her head back for a kiss, she turned away so that his lips glanced off her cheek.

"I went to Albuquerque," she said quietly. She'd reached the final button and now she slid her hands up, pushing the shirt back and off his shoulders as she went.

He sighed and released his grip from her hair, rolling his shoulders back, letting her push the shirt off. "I figured as much. Abby, why are we talking about this? Don't you want to yell at me about Saturday?"

Smiling a little, she leaned and pressed her lips to the heart branded on his skin, just above *his* heart. "Oh, we'll get to that, although I can't really blame Keelie for having a thing for you. She touches you again, then that woman and I are going to have a problem. But that's not my main concern right now," she murmured.

As Abby reached up and traced the tip of her finger over the heart tattoo, blood roared in his ears. So loud, so fucking loud, he almost didn't hear the warning firing in his brain. And it was a damn loud warning.

She tipped her head back and once more, her dark brown eyes glinted with challenge. "You think maybe there's something you need to tell me, Zach?" she whispered, her voice husky and raw.

He reached for her, curved his arm around her waist as he dragged her against him. His legs felt too new, awkward beneath him even though he'd been walking on them for more than thirty years now. Stumbling back, he settled his weight against the edge of his desk and studied her face.

She didn't give him much chance to think anything through, though. A few seconds passed and then she lowered her gaze back to the tattoo on his chest. She didn't touch the heart, though. Or the dagger. Her fingers sought out the *A* that he'd designed to hide in plain sight. The lines and curves of it were part of the design and if you *looked* at it, the right way, you'd see it. But if you weren't looking, it was easy to miss.

Kind of like the way things were with him and Abby. She'd never seen it . . . because she hadn't looked.

But so many others had seen it. He hadn't been as able to hide it from them.

Swallowing the knot in his throat, he opened his mouth to try and force the words out as she trailed the tip of her nail along the *A*. "You've had this tattoo for a decade, Zach," she murmured. "Ten years."

She flicked a glance at him. "Walking around with a scarlet *A* on your chest for a long time there, pal. Somehow I don't think it stands for *adulterer*," she drawled.

He caught her wrist in one hand, twisted it back behind

her as he searched her face. He saw something in her eyes, damn it. He knew he did. Under that glint of anger, yeah, he saw something. He thought he also saw uncertainty and nerves, but it was more than that.

The pictures, damn it.

"You know what it stands for," he rasped, stroking his hand up her back and tangling it in her hair.

"Do I?"

He opened his mouth, closed it, tried to figure out just what he was supposed to say here. Damn it. This . . . damn it. He'd tried to picture this moment, but it hadn't come because she'd *sprung* the damn thing on him. He'd planned it out. Practiced it. Had a nice, pretty little set of lines all laid out.

And he was standing here empty. With nothing.

Nothing . . .

Staring into her dark eyes, he pressed his brow to hers. "Abby . . . hell, I . . ." The words had been trapped inside him so long, trying to force them out *now*, when he knew it was actually time to *let* them out, was almost painful. He cleared his throat and then lifted his head, watching her face. Where to start? Hell. How did he tell her that he'd loved her forever?

Maybe by just doing that.

Sliding his hand down her neck, he rested it there. Instead of looking into her eyes as he spoke, he watched as he stroked his thumb along the smooth line of her collarbone. "You remember that day that jackass boyfriend of your mom's tried to hurt you?" he asked softly.

She went tense. It wasn't a moment she liked to think about, he knew. But this talk, it had to start there. He'd started hiding it then. If he was going to come clean, he had to start at the beginning.

"Yeah." She reached up, gripping his wrist. "Zach, we need to talk about—"

"We are." He dipped his head and buried his face against her neck, remembering that day. It was something that was still all too vivid for him. Way too vivid and he'd cut it out of his memory forever if he could. "I'd gone over there for a reason. I . . ."

He stopped and sucked in a desperate breath.

Abby stroked a hand up his back and then eased away, putting a few inches between them. Her hand touched his cheek and when she guided his face to hers, he couldn't look away.

He'd hidden it long enough. Too damn long. "I was going over there to see if you'd go out with me," he said gruffly. "Like a date. A real one. And then I walk in and . . ."

She stared at him. Her gaze blank, like she wasn't following anything he'd said. Needing to get some distance before he did something stupid, like pounce on her or just fall to his knees and beg, he nudged her back and moved away, starting to pace. "I'd been crazy about you almost from the get-go. Mom and Dad thought it was sweet at first. Then they got worried. Then they adjusted. My brothers gave me shit about it. Dad would sometimes tell me that it would go away if I'd just look for somebody else." He stopped pacing and slid her a look. "There *is* nobody else. There can't be. Not for me."

Abby wasn't looking at him. Her shoulders were rising and falling just a little too fast, like she was having trouble breathing.

"You never noticed. Never seemed to see me, but I thought maybe if you'd just go out with me, give me a chance, I could *get* you to notice me. So I worked up the courage, spent all damn week psyching myself up for it. And that fucker was there, trying to hurt you." He stopped and stared at the design wall in front of him, but he wasn't seeing the pictures. He saw that day, everything playing out as it had a thousand times in his nightmares. "I could have killed him. I wanted to do it and I swear, sometimes, I think if I hadn't heard you crying, I might have done it."

Hearing the ragged sound of her breathing, he turned back around and stared at her averted face. "And if I said I was sorry about that, I'd be lying."

She finally looked at him. Her eyes were bright and hot, but dry. Thank God. If she'd been crying, he didn't know if he could keep talking. "The only thing I'm sorry about is that you got into so much trouble over it, Zach."

"I'm not sorry over any of it," he snarled. Crossing the distance between them, he caught her face between his hands. Even now, he still saw the fear. She'd been so pale, so scared, fighting against that thick-necked son of a bitch, trapped between him and a table, struggling to get away. And all he'd had was a damned skateboard. Swallowing the bile rising up in his throat, he waited until the fury passed and then he shifted his gaze away from her again. "I was just going to wait a few weeks. Just a few weeks. But when I went back over to talk to you again, you told me that you were glad that I was just me . . . just your friend. Not like any of the jerks out there and you felt safe with me. Safe . . ."

"Zach . . ?"

He shook his head. "So I wanted to stay that way. Safe. Not a jerk. Just your friend. For a little while longer, so you could feel safe." He smoothed a hand down her back and because she was there, because he wanted to touch her while she wasn't pulling away, he tugged her against him and when she let him do that, he dipped his head, pressed his lips to her neck. "I waited too long, though, and you had me shoved back into that corner as friend. Your dad died. You took off running. In college, you hooked up with that asshole. Then you finally settled down here . . ."

He stopped, fisting a hand in the back of her dress as he fought for the words.

Settled down here . . .

The light clicked on in Abigale's head. Sebastian . . . what he'd said.

You got him to move away from LA.

"You left LA for me."

He lifted his head, gold-streaked hair tumbling into his

eyes. "I'd leave heaven and earth behind for you. You were the only thing that ever mattered to me."

Her heart thudded against her ribs as the hand on her neck slid up to cradle her face. The way he touched her . . . the way he looked at her. All this time. Yes, he'd made her feel safe all those years ago. Zach had always been her haven. Her sanctuary. He was her everything, but she'd never seen that until recently. Never let *him* see it, either.

Swallowing the knot in her throat, she closed a hand around his wrist and asked raggedly, "And acting? Everything else you left behind? How much of that was because of me, too?"

"I left it behind because that wasn't my life," he said gently. Dark blue eyes watched her. "You know that. I never once regretted walking away. It doesn't suit me anymore. It doesn't fit me. I found the life I wanted. And the woman I've always wanted is standing right in front of me."

Her breathing hitched. "And why didn't you tell me?" she demanded. "Damn it, I *asked* you . . . just a few days ago. Hell, I asked you a *month* ago and you didn't say anything about . . ."

"About the fact that I've been in love with you since we were kids?" A wry grin tugged the corner of his mouth up. "Come on, Abs. A month ago, you'd just had that asshole fiancé of yours all but kick you in the face. If I'd said . . . *hey, Abby . . . I know I'm not Roger, but I've loved you forever. Will you give me a go?*"

She glared at him even as her heart skittered around her chest like it was trying to take flight. *I've loved you forever* . . . "And what about the other day, damn it?" She slammed her fist against his chest. "I . . . I was trying to work up the courage to tell you that I . . ."

She snapped her mouth shut as the words tried to break free.

It was hard, she realized. Harder than she'd expected.

Fire burned in his eyes and hard, strong hands closed around her hips. The room whirled around them and seconds later, she found herself seated on the hard, unyielding surface of his desk. "Tell me what?" he rasped.

She leaned back, sucking in a breath as she tried to calm the racing of her heart. But all Zach did was brace his hands on the desk and lean in over her, crowding in around her until he was all she could see. All she could feel. And all she was ever going to want, she realized. Everything.

His gaze rapt on her face, he rested a hand on her thigh as she remained silent. "Tell me what, Abby?"

"I . . ."

He stroked his hand higher, a small, almost sad smile curving his lips. "It's not as easy as you think, is it?" The tight material of her skirt caught around his wrist and he stopped.

Almost desperate for air, she watched his face. "That's why I didn't say it then," he murmured as he stroked his thumb over the sensitive flesh of her inner thigh. "It's something I held trapped inside me for seventeen years, Abby. Seventeen long years and letting it out was almost impossible. Even though there were times the words wanted out so bad, they all but choked me."

"Are you going to say it now?"

"Maybe . . ." He bent his head, pressing his lips to hers. "I guess maybe it's time. Past time even."

Her heart stuttered and slowed to a stop as he kissed her, soft and slow. It was almost like the first time they'd kissed. Not that breathtaking free fall like that first kiss, but still. It was like everything else in the world just stopped. Nothing mattered but the touch of his lips on hers, light, easy . . . and sweet. Her heart ached inside her chest, swelling until she could barely breathe around it and then he lifted his head and stared down at her. "Abby," he murmured, lifting a hand to curve around her neck. "I love you."

A sob slipped free and she wrapped her arms around his waist.

One of his hands cupped the back of her neck and cuddled her in close. As he bent around her, he whispered,

"I've loved you so long, I can't remember what it's like to *not* love you. And I'll go to my grave loving you. You're my everything."

"Zach . . ."

Blindly, she sought out his mouth and when he met hers, she almost cried, it felt so good.

All this time.

He'd been here . . . all this time.

Desperate for him, she reached behind for the zipper of her dress, but he caught her hands, eased them back down. "Zach, please . . ." she whimpered against his lips.

"Shhh . . ." He eased the zipper down.

Splaying a hand wide over his chest, she stared at the tattoo of the heart, at the dagger before shifting her attention to the *A*. Leaning in, she pressed her mouth to it and she would have done more, but he eased her off the desk and reached for the hem of her skirt, dragging it upward. "Damn it, Abby, what did you do, paint this on?" he muttered, his voice a ragged growl in her ear.

"Just about." She could hardly breathe, she thought, sagging back against the desk and bracing her hands on it as he tossed the dress on the chair nearby.

And then . . . nothing.

She sucked in a breath, feeling the heat of his gaze. Lifting her head, she found him staring at her.

More pointedly, at the bandage on her chest. "What . . . ?" Something fired in his eyes. That storm again.

She cleared her throat and reached for the edge of the dressing. It had been long enough, if she remembered right. But when she went to peel it back, Zach was already doing it. "You had me written on your skin all this time . . . I decided I was going to do the same."

His lashes lay low over his eyes.

"I didn't want you doing this one. I . . ." She swallowed and went to touch it, but he caught her hand, guiding it back down. Nervous, she babbled on. "I needed it on me when I came to see you. You've been here, right in front of me, all along. And part of me *knew*, damn it. I *knew*, but I didn't *let*

myself see it. You didn't let it show, but I didn't let myself
see and now I'm—"

His mouth crushed against hers.

The words died in her throat and anything, everything
else she might have died in her throat under the impact of
that kiss. If the last one had been soft, sweet, and gentle, this
was the opposite. Stealing the very breath out of her and
burning her from the inside out. His hand tangled in her
hair as he wrestled them away from the desk. She stumbled
and fell against him and he caught her, twisting them so
that when they went down, it was into the fat leather chair
dominating the corner between his desk and file cabinet.

He used it for when he was having nervous clients that
he needed to talk down.

He figured it had just about enough room for what he
needed to do with Abby.

She had a pretty little heart tattoo on her right breast. It
was delicate and sweet, with the word *Zach* etched inside
it. There wasn't any color and that was just fine. It had his
name in it . . . she'd written him on her skin, just the way
he'd done with her all those years ago.

Tearing his mouth away from hers, he urged her up so
that she was sitting astride him. "Unzip me," he demanded,
staring into her eyes.

She swallowed and then eased away.

He caught her hips, reluctant to let her go.

A smile curved her lips. "Zach . . . I need to move a little. This works better if I'm not sitting right on top of you."

He groaned and let go. Resting his hands on the armrest
of the chair, he busied himself staring at the tattoo. That
pretty little heart . . . then he hissed as he felt the back of
her hand brush against his cock. She took her time and
when she finally had his fly open, he was digging his fingers into the leather just to keep from reaching for her.

Abigale traced her fingers over the thick ridge of his
cock and smiled as it leaped against her touch. Gray cotton

covered him and she smiled at him as she hooked her fingers in the waistband of his shorts, dragging them down with a wicked glint in her eyes.

Dragging them down *slowly* . . .

Swearing, he shoved them down and reached for her, hauling her into his lap and crushing her laughing mouth to his. He guided her legs down on either side of his hips.

"What's your hurry?"

"Seventeen years worth of hunger." He tucked the head of his cock against her entrance and stared up at her as he drove straight home.

Her back arched and she bit her lip to stifle a ragged cry.

He wanted to hear her moan, wanted to hear each broken sigh as he fucked her. Instead, he rocked against her a second time, a third time, as he stroked his hand up her middle and circled the tattoo on her breast with his finger. He didn't touch it . . . the new ink needed time to heal before anybody else went messing with it but damn it, he wanted to press his mouth to that mark.

"I love you," he rasped, reaching up to tangle his hand in her hair and tug her down. "Damn it, do you hear me? I love you."

She pressed her mouth to his, her elbows braced against his chest. "I hear you." She whispered it against his lips, her gaze locked with his. "I hear you, Zach . . . I see you. And I love you. I want you . . . more than I want my next breath."

Love and desire ripped through him, so desperate and raw and wild, he didn't know if he could stand it. Twisting his hips, he drove deep inside her, hard, fast. She gasped and when he saw her mouth falling open, he caught her lips with his, swallowing the scream down.

Later, he thought dimly. Later, he'd take her home. To her place. To his. It didn't matter. Someplace where they were alone and he could make her sigh, make her moan, as he made love to her all night. While he told her that he loved her as often as he wanted.

For now, he focused on working her body into a burning frenzy, which wasn't hard. She was so hot, burning against him and whimpering into his mouth, her fingers digging into his skin while she swiveled her hips against his, hard and fast.

Faster . . .

Faster . . .

She broke over him with a ragged, breathless scream and when she tore her mouth away to breathe, he buried his face against her neck and let go.

The climax ripped through him, almost painful in its intensity.

And for once, the ache in his heart wasn't so raw and empty.

He held her as she shuddered and gasped for air. And he felt complete.

Chapter Twenty-three

Glumly, Abigale stared at the door as Zach zipped her dress back up. "What are the odds that nobody heard us?" she asked.

He was silent long enough that she paused to look back over her shoulder at him.

Strong, warm arms came around her waist and tugged her back against him. He'd already pulled his shirt back on and buttoned it, shoved a hand through his hair. He looked just fine, she'd noticed. And she'd seen a glimpse of herself in the mirror he kept on hand for clients. She looked . . . well. She looked like a woman who'd just spent the past few minutes having sex in a chair.

Her dress was wrinkled, her hair was tangled around her shoulders, and her lipstick—supposedly kiss-proof—wasn't all it was cracked up to be. He skimmed a hand down her arm and rubbed his cheek against hers before he answered honestly, "Slim to none."

As the hot rush of blood leaped to her cheeks, she groaned and dropped her head back onto his shoulder. "Damn."

"We could stay in here until after closing time," he offered, pressing a hand to her belly. "I can think of a good way to pass the time."

She slanted a dark look at him. "This place just got broken into not that long ago. A few days, remember?"

"Yeah. I still got the bumps and bruises to show for it." He sighed and eased away. "And you're right. I'm not keeping you here after the shop closes up. So we go out now. Face the music."

Groaning, she held out her hand.

He caught it in his and then, abruptly, swooped down and stole a kiss. "I bet you didn't see this coming when you were writing in that new journal, did you?"

"No." She laughed a little and then looked around, spying her bag. She caught the strap in her hand and hefted it up on her shoulder. She slid a hand into the side pocket, pulling the silly little green journal out. "I had a plan to wreck my life. And then you go around and totally remake it."

He hugged her against him and then, before they could get distracted, they left the office.

Abigale was still blushing as they moved through the main part of the shop. It was empty, save for Javi. He slid them a wicked grin. "Hey, Abby. Zach." His black brows arched over dark eyes, but he didn't say anything else.

"Javi." Zach glanced around. "Where is everybody else at?"

"We wrapped up the last customer forty-five minutes ago." Javi slid Abigale a look and added, "When Abby came in, I decided to flip the sign to 'closed.' Keelie is . . ." He frowned and glanced around.

"Right here."

Abigale and Zach turned.

Keelie stood in the hallway, head bowed as she tugged a pair of earbuds out. The music was still blaring from them and she took a second to turn the volume down before she looked up. Her mismatched eyes glanced at Zach but her gaze met Abigale's and held it. "Abby," Keelie said quietly.

Lifting an eyebrow, Abigale waited.

"I need to apologize to you."

A few seconds passed before Keelie blew out a slow, steady breath. "I'm sorry . . . and not just because you walked in while I was kissing Zach. And that's what it was. It was a shitty thing to do, but it was all on my part. He'd never . . ."

When Keelie trailed off, Abigale glanced over at Zach. He was staring at his friend with an unreadable face. *What the hell?* Abigale wondered. Looking back at Keelie, she said, "I know. It was shitty, he'd never, and it's done. We're cool."

"Just like that?" Keelie crossed her arms over her chest and stared at her, defiance written all over her face.

"Just like that." Shaking her head, Abigale said, "I don't know why you're so hostile to me, unless it really is all about him, but I just don't care that much. He loves me . . . and I figure you know that. I love him. There's no reason for me to get worked up over something that meant nothing to him."

Keelie flinched. "Ouch. You know how to twist the knife." Then, with a short, stiff nod, she turned and headed back down the hall. "It's over, it was shitty . . . we're cool. I can live with that, I guess. I'm gone for the night."

As she strode down the hall, Zach and Abby looked at each other.

Javi called out, "Wait a second, kid. I'm walking you to the car, remember?"

"Home?" Zach murmured, after Javi had slipped out the back with Keelie.

She went to answer: *hell, yes*.

But the weight of the book in her hand reminded her. "Just a minute." She glanced around, her gaze lingering on the counter. "You got any string?"

He blinked at her. "String?"

"Yeah." She waggled the book at him. "I finished the plan. Well, everything except the photographers, and hey, I *did* flip off your brother, so maybe that counts. Now I need to do the rest of the stuff in here."

"And you need string . . . ?"

She sighed and opened it to the page where it read:

Hang the journal in a public place.

Tapping on that page, she said, "I need to hang it up. Ask people to draw in it."

He skimmed it over and then flipped it to the very front where her plan was. "And when they see this?"

"Welllll . . ." She was blushing as she answered, "It's not like they know who it belongs to. Let them guess."

He sighed and then pushed it back into her hands.

While he was gone, she scrounged in her purse for a pen. Tugging it out, she added in a sixth item.

He came just as she was tucking the pen up.

"You sure you want to leave it lying around here for a day?" he asked, eyeing her skeptically.

"Zach . . . you worry too much. Besides, who is going to take it? Javi?"

Javi had just come back into the main room and he looked at them, puzzled. Eyeing the twine, he jerked up his hands. "Hey, I'm not into . . . ah . . . what are you talking about?"

Abigale flashed the journal at him and he leaned in, studied it. "Nope. I don't do journals."

"It will be fine," she said, looking back at Zach.

"Okay." He pushed a hand through his hair and then reached for it, using the twine he'd dug up and looping it around it, tying it so that the twine kept it open on just that page. Then he rigged it so that it was hanging just off the counter. "We'll watch it for a few hours tomorrow and then take it down, cool?"

"Sounds good." Licking her lips, she pulled out a pen and then shoved it into Javi's hands. "Hey, why don't you draw on the page?"

He shrugged and flipped it open, found the page and doodled for a minute. When he was done, there was a samurai

slashing his sword through the air. "Nice," Zach murmured.
"Hey, it was in a public place. We can take it home now."

"Relax. There's nothing in there I've got a problem with
people seeing." She flipped to the front and glanced down
as though she was reading it for the first time.

Zach glanced down and then back up at her.

Javi turned to leave. "I'm heading out, guys. Locking up,
right, Zach?"

"Ah . . ." He cleared his throat, his gaze falling away
from her face back to the journal. "Yeah. Yeah, Javi, I got
it. Thanks."

"Zach . . . ?"

He stared at the journal, ran his finger over the sixth line
she'd added to her plan.

"What's this?" he whispered, his voice rough.

"It's the next step in the plan . . . the one that matters the
most, I think."

He caught her in his arms and hauled her against him.

They didn't make it home for a while.

Wreck this life: My new plan

1. *Stop worrying so much about the future*

2. *Call Roger and tell him off*

3. *Flip off the next photographer you see*

4. *Get a tattoo*

5. *Have a torrid affair with a hot guy*

6. *Ask that hot guy if he'd maybe like to marry
   me . . . up in Alaska*

Turn the page for a preview
of Shiloh Walker's

THE PROTECTED

*Coming in September 2013
from Berkley Sensation!*

"You want me *where*?"

Vaughnne MacMeans stared at the man in front of her and decided she really wished she'd taken more time off.

Granted, she'd already taken three months of personal time. Then two weeks medical leave after the case to end all cases went to hell in Orlando, Florida. Maybe she should have made it three weeks. Her head was still so *not* in a good place after that last job.

She could handle another week off, she thought. Another week. Two weeks. Three weeks. Three months. Three years.

Because Taylor Jones just *had* to be shitting her.

"Orlando," he said again.

"No." She crossed her arms over her chest and glared at him. She didn't ever want to see that miserable, forsaken, hellhole of a city again. Just thinking about it was enough to give her nightmares. Thinking about what had happened in that dark, squalid miserable building . . . shit, sometimes she woke still feeling the despair of the women around her. She wasn't even empathic and it had gotten to her.

Of course, a person didn't have to be empathic to feel *those* vibes. That much misery was enough to screw with the head of any psychic, even if it was just to leave that cloying, dark layer of despair. She'd been caught in the middle of it and even though they'd shut that operation down, it wasn't enough.

They'd shut down *one* ring. Just one.

Who knows how many more were out there?

"Jones, I don't know if I can handle going back into that kind of work again," she said reluctantly. "Not after—"

"It's not connected to that. It's not about Daylin, at all."

Pain gripped her heart at the sound of that name. The wounds were still fresh and the pain was just as hot, just as vivid as it had been months ago. Was it ever going to fade?

Shooting him a narrow look, she took a deep breath and shifted her attention to the wall behind him. "I don't want to go back there, Taylor," she said quietly. It hurt to even *think* about it. It hurt to think about that place, to think about those women. To think about any of it. Most of all, it hurt to think about her sister. The girl she'd failed . . .

"As I said, it's not about the last case."

She shoved away from her desk and started to pace. An echo of a headache danced in the back of her mind, letting her know that it might not have been a bad idea to take a little more time to recover. Psychics were prone to odd, undetectable injuries sometimes and she'd wrenched the hell out of something, although it wasn't anything a doctor could diagnose.

Overuse of their abilities could definitely do damage and these headaches were murder.

Still, she had bills to pay, an empty refrigerator, and sitting at home had been driving her insane.

SAC—Special Agent in Charge—Taylor Jones leaned back in his seat and pinned her with a direct stare. If one was to try and find paper documentation of their unit, they'd be hard-pressed to do it. A lot of the agents knew vaguely of Jones and his odd team, and there were rumors, but if one tried to look up the FBI team of psychics, they weren't going to have a lot of luck. Technically, they didn't really exist.

Vaughnne still wasn't sure just how Jones managed it, but he did.

Just then, he was watching her, his blue eyes cool and unreadable, his face expressionless. That blank look didn't mean anything. He could be madder than hell, he could be amused. Hell, he could have a scorching case of herpes and she wouldn't be able to tell from looking at his face—she'd seen him facing down drug runners, child rapists, and psychopaths with a taste for human flesh with that exact same expression.

Inscrutable bastard.

"It's got nothing to do with that last case," he said again. "It's in Orlando, yes, but it's an easy job, mostly monitoring. It's practically nothing more than babysitting. You can handle a babysitting job, Agent MacMeans."

Sure she could. The problem was it was in *Orlando*.

Clenching her jaw, she stared at him. Babysitting. She wanted to tell him to shove it up his ass.

"Is there a reason why you can't do this job?" he asked, watching her the way he might study a suspect before he went in to tear them apart in an interrogation.

Shit.

She was screwed.

She could either take the damn assignment. Or resign. He hadn't said that, and she knew he wouldn't force that on her, but she also knew she couldn't avoid one particular area of the country, either. They were spread too thin as it was and she wasn't much for playing the chickenshit.

Either she could work and do her damn job, or she would quit and let him make room on the team for somebody who *could* do the job. He danced on a razor's edge to keep their unit going, anyway.

She'd worked too damn hard to get where she was just to walk away.

She wasn't a quitter, damn it. Besides, it wasn't like her particular skill set was in high demand out there, and she rather liked being able to *use* her abilities to do something worthwhile. Somehow she doubted any local law enforcement agency was likely to welcome a telepath into their midst. *Sure. Welcome aboard, and instead of using the police radio, just screech out into our minds like a psycho banshee, MacMeans. Look forward to working with you!*

Since she needed to work to live, she had to suck it up, put on her big-girl panties, and deal with this. Moving back to her desk, she sat down and crossed her legs. Absently, she started to swing her foot, one high-heeled shoe hanging off her toes. She was tempted to take it off and pummel Jones across the side of the head with it.

Orlando . . . so many nightmares. So many bad dreams. And the bitter knowledge that she hadn't been able to save the one person who'd always mattered to her.

"You know avoiding it won't make it any easier."

Jerking her attention back to Jones, she stared at him. "This isn't supposed to be easy," she said quietly. "But what in the hell would you know about it?"

For a second, though, as she stared at him, she thought she saw something in the cool depths of his eyes.

Then he looked down and it was gone.

"Just tell me about the job, Jones. Just who am I supposed to be babysitting?"

Gus Hernandez pulled the battered, beat-up truck into the driveway of the little house he was renting. It was falling apart and instead of paying five hundred a month as the landlady had originally requested, he paid three hundred . . . and did repairs. He was good with his hands and always had been. What he didn't know how to do, he was able to learn and he'd fixed the place up quite a bit over the past few months.

So far, he'd managed to tear up the rotting boards of the porch and replace those. He'd repainted three of the rooms. He still needed the fix the deck in back and it was an ongoing struggle to keep the yard free of weeds. If he had the money, he'd reseed it, but he didn't. Most of the work he did was either with scrap he found cheap at his other jobs or clearance stuff at the local hardware or home improvement stores.

He still needed to get more work done around the little place, although what he wanted to do was go inside the dark, quiet house and just sit. For a few minutes, with a cold beer and do . . . *nothing*. He didn't want to think, he didn't want to talk. He wanted to do *nothing*. It was a luxury he hadn't been able to indulge in for a good, long while, though, and tonight would be no different.

Although it was a bright, sunny day, he felt like he had a cloud hanging over him.

Always.

Pulling the truck into Park, he stared at the old place, studied it, made sure everything looked the way it had this morning when he'd left. He hadn't had a single phone call. Not one. So that was good.

It had taken more charm than he generally cared to exert these days, but he'd managed to convince the lady living across the street to give him a call if she saw anything, and that woman? Old Mrs. Werner was *nosy*. If anybody had been snooping around, more than likely she'd notice something.

It didn't let him breathe any easier, though.

He didn't think he'd ever breathe easy again.

Please . . . you must do this for me . . .

Blocking the echo of a woman's voice out of his head, he pushed the door open. Before he climbed out, though, he reached below the seat and took out the one thing he never went anywhere without.

The butt of the Sig Sauer P250 fit solidly in his hand. Slipping the safety off, he looked toward the passenger seat. A solemn pair of eyes looked back at him. "Come on."

The boy sighed and slid out of the car. "Do we have to do this every day?"

He'd asked the same question yesterday. He'd asked it the day before. He'd keep asking it, Gus knew. It would only get worse, because the boy wasn't exactly a child anymore, and that rebelliousness that always crept out during those years between child and adult was getting ever closer.

Still, there were things in life that didn't care that Alex wanted some freedom. Things that didn't care that the boy just wanted to live a normal life.

Gus's job was to make sure the boy *lived*. Period. Staring into a pair of eyes eerily like his own, he said quietly, "Alex."

That was all he said. Alex's lids drooped and his skinny shoulders slumped, but he climbed out of the truck, plodding around to stand next to Gus and stare up at the old house.

Alex grumbled under his breath. Gus ignored him as he looked around, eyes never resting in one place. Before he shut the door, he grabbed a bag from the back and slung it over his left shoulder and then pulled out his denim jacket, draped it over his arm and hand to hide the Sig Sauer.

"Are you listening to me?"

"Nope."

"There's *nobody* here," Alex said, his voice sullen, bordering on rude. He mumbled something else and Gus stopped, looked back at him. The anger in the boy was getting worse, flaring closer to the surface today than it ever had.

"We've talked about this, Alex," he said quietly. "You want to be angry with me, you got a right. But remember what we talked about."

Gus didn't blame him. The kid had every right to be pissed. Gus wasn't a twelve-year-old kid who'd had his entire life uprooted and *he* was pissed.

"This is so fucking stupid," Alex snapped.

Stopping in his tracks, Gus turned around and stared at Alex. "Watch your mouth," he said quietly. "Your mother raised you better than that."

Alex sneered. "Yeah, she raised me better but she's dead—"

The boy's voice cracked. And as the anger faded away

into agony, Gus reached out, hooked his hand over Alex's neck. "Yeah. She's dead. But she wanted you safe. And you'll be safe, Alex. Now come on . . ."

You must promise me . . .

A hard, shuddering breath escaped Alex but then he pulled away, looking at Gus with glittering eyes. The tears he wouldn't shed still shone in his eyes until he blinked them away. "I told you, there's nobody here."

"Yeah. I heard you. We're checking anyway."

Twenty minutes later, while Alex oversaw the dinner of macaroni and hot dogs, Gus stood at the sink, trying unsuccessfully to scrub the engine grease from his hands. He'd worked eight hours at the construction site, then picked up a hundred bucks helping one of the guys from the site do some work on his car. He was filthy, he was tired, and he was hot. He wanted to plunge his head under the cool stream of water coming from the faucet, but he just kept scrubbing at the grease on his hands.

The phone rang just when he'd decided to give up. Hurriedly rinsing his hands, he grabbed it, spying Elsie Werner's number. The sweet, incorrigibly nosy lady from across the street. "Hello, Elsie . . . need me to come clean out the pipes again?"

"Well, now that you mention it, the one in the bathroom is running rather slow," she said.

Gus would swear she clogged them up just so he could come over so she could ogle his ass. He'd had plenty of women ogling his ass in his lifetime. It wasn't a new experience. But to his knowledge, most of them weren't old enough to be his great-grandmother.

Still, the lady was kind. She'd made more than a few meals for him and Alex once she figured out neither of them could do anything more complicated than pizza, burgers and fries, or macaroni and cheese or hot dogs. If she had her way, she would have taught them both to cook.

But Gus was intent on keeping his distance. Very intent. Letting a sweet old lady teach him or the kid how to cook wasn't the way to keep a cool distance. It wouldn't help ei-

ther him or the kid, and, in the long run, it could harm her.
He had enough blood on his hands.

"I'll come by later tonight," he said. "Although I don't
know if I can fix it tonight. I may need to go to the store for
the drain cleaner."

"Well, that can wait. I wasn't calling about that, Gus. We
have a new neighbor moving in . . . did you see?"

The skin on the back of his neck prickled.

Lifting his head, he looked to the front of the house. "A
neighbor, huh?"

"Yes. A pretty girl. I was thinking about inviting her for
dinner . . . maybe you and the boy can join us?"

He relaxed only a tiny bit. They were less likely to send
a woman after him. But still, he had to see her. Would have
to let Alex see her—*shit*. And it had to be done tonight.

"I don't think dinner will work, Elsie," he said. "I'm
pretty worn out at the end of the day and I'm lousy company. But I'll be sure to introduce myself when I see her."

"Well . . . now is a good time." He could almost hear the
smile in her voice. "She's out front unloading boxes, Gus.
Alone. I'd go help her, but . . ."

The wheedling in her voice was anything but subtle.

If anybody would recognize trouble, it would be the boy.
There wouldn't be immediate danger, either. Nobody would
want to risk the kid being hurt. They'd try to take Alex alive
and Alex would know from a mile away if there was any
sort of threat. A fact that, sadly, Gus knew from experience.

He hated it, but he already knew the best course of action. It wasn't a good defense, but a good offense. They had
problems looking for them and if they'd found them, it was
best to know now, so they could leave.

Alex looked up at him, his eyes solemn.

"It's okay," the boy said softly.

"We need to make sure."

The boy's hand shook as he stirred the mac and cheese.
But then he nodded.

* * *

It should be a damn crime to look that good.

Vaughnne almost swallowed her tongue when she caught her first good look at her target. Well, one of them.

Wow.

Her libido, dormant for the past couple of years, suddenly rumbled to life and as she stared at the man coming across the street, she couldn't help but think . . . *Come to mama, pretty boy . . . pretty, pretty, pretty boy . . .*

According to the information Jones had given her, he was going by the name Gus Hernandez.

It wasn't his real name, though. She'd almost bet her life on it.

Leaning back on the porch, she braced her hands on the concrete behind her and pretended to be absorbed in the study of her flip-flops. One thing about this job . . . she could work in flip-flops and shorts. Much better than the skirts and heels, or slacks and heels, she generally wore when she was in D.C. Not that she spent a lot of time in the office, but she wasn't exactly running at full speed just yet and she knew it.

Office work would be her mainstay for the next few weeks if she wasn't doing the babysitting job. Until she could focus her gift for longer than five minutes without a splitting headache, she was useless in the field.

This, though, this was doable. She didn't need to actively use her telepathy to use her instincts and that was a lot easier on the gray matter. And even though she hated Orlando, the uniform here was a lot better.

So she'd just enjoy the uniform, and enjoy the view . . . and pretend she was somewhere else.

The view was fine. Damn fine. Excellent shoulders. Long, loose-hipped gait. Behind her sunglasses, she studied him, black hair tucked under a battered hat, a pair of cheap sunglasses that shielded his gaze from her. He wore a threadbare t-shirt and jeans so worn, they were practically white at the seams. Damn, he wore those jeans well, too.

Because the view was making her throat go dry, she reached for the bottle of Mike's Hard Lemonade at her side and took a long drag off of it as she shifted her attention to other things. Like the backpack he was carrying. Like the boy.

Her other target.

Two males and both of them were too damned pretty. Family, they had to be, although Jones's information on them was sketchy.

The boy was already every bit as pretty as the guy walking next to him, although he couldn't be more than twelve or thirteen. He'd break hearts when he was grown, she suspected. His name was Alex, and he had the angriest, saddest eyes she'd seen on a kid in a long, long while. They were a pale, misty sort of gray—set against his dusky skin, those eyes packed even more of a punch.

Yeah. He was going to break hearts, she thought. And she had a feeling he'd be breaking hers before this job was done. Babysit. What in the hell was going on here?

That gaze of his was a punch right to her heart. One that might shatter it, because while she couldn't read emotions worth shit, she knew what fear looked like. The boy was ripe with it. He had so much fear inside, it hurt to look at him. So much cynicism, she figured she probably would have looked idealistic in comparison.

And even without lowering her shields, she felt the wide-open power of his mind.

Damn.

That kid was practically a lighthouse on the shore in the middle of a raging storm.

All it would take was the wrong person looking for him . . .

A babysitter. Hell, what he needed was a bodyguard and a teacher. She might be able to handle the bodyguard job as long as there was nothing major going on, but she wasn't equipped to teach a kid like that.

Mr. Gus Hernandez pushed his battered cap back and gave her a sleepy smile. "Hi there," he said.

Okay. If the boy's eyes ripped at her, the man's eyes were going to put her on her knees, but for all the wrong reasons.

Wow. If she'd thought the kid's eyes packed a punch . . . hell.

This guy's gaze was enough to put her out for the count. The color of the mists that hovered over the river in the morning, that was what his eyes made her think of, a surreal shade of gray and so unbelievably beautiful, shocking pale against the warmth of his olive-colored skin. But it wasn't just the unnatural beauty of those eyes . . . the kid had that.

The man, though, he had a look in his eyes that made her throat go dry.

Sleepy and sexy, like he'd just tumbled out of bed but he'd be more than happy to tumble right back in. Since he was looking at her, the idea was probably supposed to be that he was going to tumble into bed with her, but she knew better.

That look was practiced. Way too practiced and she knew it. Still, it was a good look, and she might as well enjoy it. His smile, too. She was a little disturbed to realize that smile of his was making her feel all warm and tingly down in parts that were *not* supposed to be an issue, considering she was on a job.

He knew what effect he had, too. She could tell. It wasn't arrogance or anything, but he knew. Hmmm. A player? *That* was a harder puzzle, but she'd figure it out.

He was playing at something, but what was it? That was the question, indeed.

Taking another sip from her bottle, she tipped it at him. "Hey back."

The boy shot her a look from under his lashes and lowered his head. As he shoved his hands into his pockets, she felt it. A ripple of his gift, rolling across her.

She didn't react.

He was young and unless he'd encountered a lot of psychics, it was unlikely he'd recognize one if she wasn't using her ability. Which she didn't plan to do. Keeping her own thoughts tucked back behind a blank shield, she projected an air of boredom, exhaustion, and because he probably was used to it, she thought a few rather female thoughts about the overall hotness of the long, sexy piece of work standing across from her.

The kid blushed and darted a look at the long, sexy piece of work before he mumbled, ". . . help you move stuff?"

Vaughnne reached up and rubbed her ear. "I'm sorry?"

"I think my kid is saying we wanted to see if you needed help."

Those tingling parts started tingling again and she leaned forward, arms crossed over her chest, at the smile he shot her way. He glanced over at the boy. "Right, Alex?"

The kid lifted his head and for a long, long moment, all he did was stare at her.

Seconds ticked away and Vaughnne would have sworn she heard her heart beating, could have sworn she felt *their* hearts beating as the boy took her measure. And somehow, she suspected if that kid didn't like what he saw, there were going to be problems.

She was prepared for that.

Very prepared, although not quite in the way anybody would think.

But finally, the boy gave her a nervous smile and ducked his head again and that odd, tight tension faded away. "Yeah. You . . ." He licked his lips and looked over at the man who claimed to be his father before darting her a look. "You got lots of stuff and no help. We don't mind."

Don't mind, huh?

Yeah. She was sure they didn't. They didn't mind so much and if that kid had so much as whispered one bad word about her, she had a feeling she would have had to unload on the two of them just to keep the sexy piece of work from doing . . . whatever he had planned.

Uncurling from the bench, she let her bottle swing from her left hand as she sauntered off. "Sure. I wouldn't mind a hand, I reckon." She laid it on thick with the drawl and kept her smile wide and friendly. "My name's Vaughnne."

They'd decided it would be best to keep things close to

the truth with this one, and as the boy flicked her another glance, she felt that odd ripple again. Yeah. Good call. He smiled again and then glanced over at the man with him. "Alex," the boy said.

It was weird, the vibe between them, but she'd already figured it out. The kid's gift . . . the gift inside him, it was so strong, he almost glowed with it. Considering there was some sort of danger chasing them, it seemed the man had made the hard, but wise, choice to use the kid's instincts.

And there was something after them. Only reason why that kid would be so afraid, she figured. Not an easy choice to make. But death, danger . . . plenty of other things were far less pleasant and a lot less easy.

"Nice to meet you, Alex," she said, still keeping her thoughts tucked behind that surface shield of nice, normal thoughts. He held out his hand and once more, that power . . . as their skin touched, she shielded down as tight as she could.

His hand fell away and he looked over at the man, another smile.

Signals. She didn't know what they were communicating with those signals, but they were doing it.

"Gus." The man nodded and gave her another one of those lazy smiles as he adjusted his cap. "So, how much more have you got to move in, Vaughnne?"

She heaved out a sigh. "Too damn much."

He'd known beautiful women.

He'd known women so beautiful, they made the eye all but hurt to look at them, and the woman standing in front of him wasn't one of them.

But there was . . . something about her and Gus realized he couldn't look away from her.

A fine sheen of perspiration gleamed along the warm brown of her skin and unlike a lot of the women he'd known, it didn't seem to faze her. Her nose was sprinkled with a few freckles, shades darker than that warm brown, and her eyes, liquid gold, held his with a frank, unblinking stare as she nodded toward the moving van.

"Vaughnne," he murmured absently, turning the name over as he studied her.

Alex had read her. They had a system; it worked. He hated it, hated having to rely on the kid like that, but Gus wasn't going to risk the boy's safety when he had a tool that was just undeniable, either.

Alex didn't offer his name to anybody that set his internal warning signal off and he'd not only offered her his name, he'd let her touch him. Alex let very few people touch him.

So she had to be safe enough. Maybe that was why he felt his heartbeat kick up a few notches. It had been . . .

Please. You must do this for me.

As the voice roused from the depths of his memory, he shoved everything else to the back of his mind. It didn't matter if *she* was safe. Alex wasn't.